THE GOLEM
of PARIS

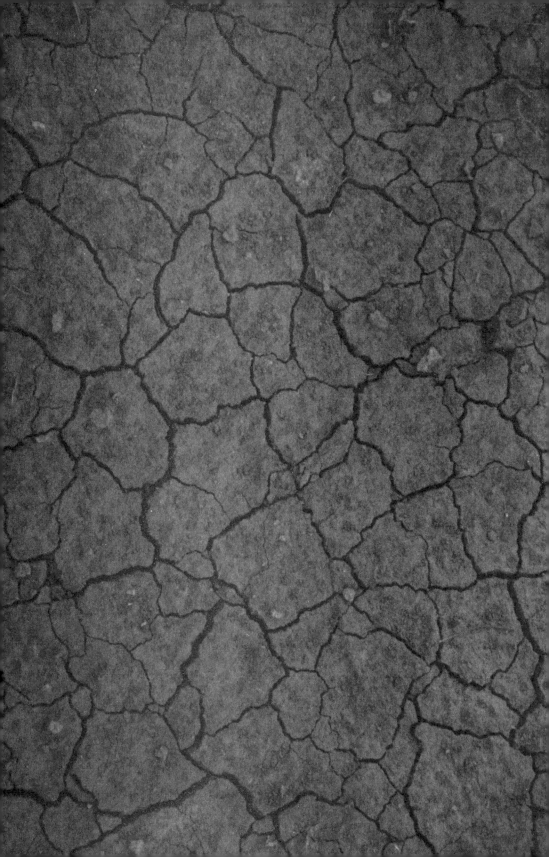

THE GOLEM
of PARIS

JONATHAN KELLERMAN and
JESSE KELLERMAN

G. P. PUTNAM'S SONS
NEW YORK

G. P. PUTNAM'S SONS
Publishers Since 1838
An imprint of Penguin Random House LLC
375 Hudson Street
New York, New York 10014

Library of Congress Cataloging-in-Publication Data

Kellerman, Jonathan.
The golem of Paris / Jonathan Kellerman and Jesse Kellerman.
p.   cm.
ISBN 978-0-399-17173-4
1. Golem—Fiction.   2. Murder—Investigation—Fiction.   I. Kellerman, Jesse.   II. Title.
PS3561.E3865G655   2015   2015025078
813'.54—dc23

Printed in the United States of America
1   3   5   7   9   10   8   6   4   2

Book design by Gretchen Achilles

To Faye and Gavri

THE GOLEM
of PARIS

CHAPTER ONE

BOHNICE PSYCHIATRIC HOSPITAL

PRAGUE, CZECHOSLOVAK SOCIALIST REPUBLIC

DECEMBER 17, 1982

The patient will wake up."

The Russian's voice is soft and careful, handling the words in Czech like an unfamiliar weapon.

She has taught herself deafness. How else to sleep in this deranged place, its nights clotted with moans and prayers to a God that does not exist, cannot exist, for the State has declared him dead.

The State is correct.

Proof of God's death is all around her.

Senseless, trying to hide. She cowers just the same as the Russian kneels to unlock her cage, his greatcoat opening like a pair of dark wings. The cell door stands ajar, admitting a sickly fan of light from the grease-smeared bulb that smolders in the corridor.

"The patient will stand, please."

She will be punished. Her cellmates want none of it. Fat Irena pretends to snore, blowing white balloons. Olga's fingers are knotted in the hollow of her belly.

The fourth bed is empty.

"Little bird," the Russian says. "Do not make me ask again."

She swings her feet to the freezing concrete, finds her paper slippers.

They step into the low, broad passageway known as *Bulvár šílenci.* Lunatics' Boulevard.

While the Russian finds the correct key, she assumes the mandatory posture, kneeling with forehead to the linoleum. Along the corridor, a feverish racket is stirring. The other inmates have heard jangling. They want to know. Who is leaving? Why?

"The patient may stand."

She rises, using the wall for support.

He leads her down the Boulevard, past the staff room, where orderlies doze in armchairs under heavy doses of self-prescribed sedatives. Past physicians' offices, exam rooms, Hydrotherapy and Electroshock and rooms unmarked except for numbers. Rooms that cannot be labeled truthfully.

The women's ward ends at two consecutive locked doors, gray paint peeling to reveal steel the same color.

Where is he taking her?

Syringes crunch beneath his boot-heels in the dank stairwell, the temperature dropping with every step. Upon reaching the ground floor, the Russian pauses to remove his greatcoat and drape it over her shoulders. The hem puddles. He places his *ushanka* on her head, ties the flaps under her chin.

"I would give you my shoes," he says, tugging off his gloves, "but I must drive."

He pauses, frowns at her. "Are you all right, little bird? You look unwell."

Bare fingers brush her cheek. The sudden warmth causes the cold to constrict around her viciously, and she recoils, shivering.

He withdraws his hand. "Forgive me."

He looks almost remorseful, twisting the thick black ring on his index finger. "Do not be afraid. You are leaving this place." He offers the gloves. "Please."

She steps out of the paper slippers and pulls the gloves on over her numb feet. They cover her to the ankles.

He laughs. "Like a chimpanzee."

She smiles obligingly.

They step out into the frigid courtyard.

The guard manning the hospital gate wears a Socialist Union of Youth pin on his lapel. The Russian returns his salute and says that the patient Marie Lasková has been remanded into his custody.

A riffle of paperwork, a signature, a second exchange of salutes.

And like that, she is cured, no longer a menace to society, but a healthy, sane, productive citizen of the republic.

The guard unlocks the gate and shoves it wide.

"Ladies first," the Russian says.

It's there, three steps away: freedom. Yet she does not move, gazing back across the courtyard, a brown scalloped mass. The snow of St. Catherine's Day, well on its way to Christmas mud. A single locust tree stands denuded, its branches pruned back to thwart escapees, the trunk wrapped in barbed wire for good measure.

The Russian watches her patiently. He seems to understand what she is doing before she understands it herself.

She is counting.

The rows of windows, chiseled through concrete.

The ravaged faces beyond. The afflicted bodies. The hunger and the thirst, the cold and the heat and the squalor. The names.

She is counting them all, inscribing them in the ledger of her mind.

She must bear witness.

"Come, little bird. We should not keep him waiting. I left the car running."

She asks who *he* is.

The Russian raises his eyebrows, as though the answer should be self-evident.

"Your son."

SHE TURNS THE CORNER, moving fast as she can in her gloved feet.

I'm coming, Danek.

But the car draws her up short: a Tatra 603, squat, matte black, tailpipe stuttering exhaust, identical to the car that brought her in for interrogation so many lifetimes ago.

Who knows? It may be the very one.

They came to her door one afternoon, a pair of men with cement eyes.

Inspector Hrubý requests that you accompany us.

So polite! You couldn't possibly say no.

She didn't worry. She didn't even bother to send Daniel next door, confident she'd be home in time to cook dinner. And what a dinner it would be: she had half a package of lasagna noodles. Not the gray Russian kind that boiled for hours without dissolving, but authentic, a little Italian flag on the box. Daniel was delirious with anticipation. When she went to the kitchen for her coat, he was eating them straight out of the box, crunching brittle planks between his teeth and giggling. She smacked his hand and stuck the box up on a high shelf, telling him she'd be back soon and not to be a pig.

Downstairs, she got into the Tatra and spoke the name of her contact. She knew what to expect. For the sake of appearances, they would take her to the StB headquarters on Bartolomějská Street.

Confirmation would require a phone call. They would let her go without apology or explanation, and she would board the tram back to her apartment. As they pulled into traffic, she sat back, preoccupied foremost with how to make a decent filling for the pasta without butter, cheese, oil, or tomatoes.

Now she sees the car, maybe the same car, and her bowels clench. It's a hoax, another ingenious ploy to grind down her will and pulverize her spirit.

The tinted back window drops in jerks.

"Matka."

The voice is impossible. The face, too. She left a laughing six-year-old and has returned to a sober little judge. Lank brown hair tumbles down his forehead. He is not smiling. He looks as though he has never smiled in his life.

"Why are you waiting," he says.

Why, indeed. Cheeks streaming, she waddles forth, climbs into the backseat.

And immediately he shrinks from her, pressing into the opposite door, his nose scrunched. She must stink. She takes his face in her hands and smothers it in kisses. Still he won't look at her, his eyes bent toward the ceiling. She says his name; kisses him, again and again, until he forcibly pulls away, and she falls back, her throat salty and raw.

The Russian gets behind the wheel. He tries to shift into gear and stalls out.

"Garbage," he mutters. Of all his cold-weather clothing, he has chosen to retain his scarf, and he pinches the fringe annoyedly, struggling to restart the motor. "You people don't know the first thing about making cars."

She says Daniel's name again, softly.

He sits with his body twisted away from her, glaring at the fists in his lap.

"Mercedes-Benz," the Russian says. "Now that is a car."

I thought I would be back for dinner, Danek. I thought we would eat lasagna.

It's too painful to look at the back of her son's head, so she wipes her wet face, tells her heart to hold its tongue. The Russian manages to get the engine going and the Tatra plods along through Prague 8, toward Holešovice.

She supposes she'll know their destination soon enough. Just as she did not question the men who came to her door, she does not question this new turn of fate. More often than not, the system takes away. Moments of generosity are not to be analyzed, but grabbed and hoarded like the boxes of Cuban oranges that appear in the shop windows without warning.

You buy as many as you can afford, as many as you can carry, because you cannot know when they might appear again, if ever. You take more oranges than two people can possibly eat; you barter them for items you do need, toilet paper or socks; if you are enterprising, you swap some of the oranges for sugar, which you then use to make a loose marmalade of the remaining oranges. You keep the jars hidden in the bureau like golden coins, ready to be deployed in lieu of cash when noodles come along.

But, Miss Lasková Inspector Hrubý said, turning a jar in his hand. *I must object: you made it far too sweet, you eliminated the bitter edge, which is what makes a good marmalade. Tell me, who would want such sweet marmalade?*

He set the jar down, pushed a pencil toward her. *Write down their names.*

Now the Tatra reaches the Čechův Bridge, iced over, its statuary in disrepair. Though dawn is hours away, she can make out the graceful silhouette of Old Town. She prefers it at night. Sunlight is cruel, revealing lost tiles like rotten teeth; creamy surfaces varnished black by the sooty, cancerous winds that blow in from the north.

Against violet clouds, the buildings' regal contours assert themselves, and she feels a stab of kinship with these piles of wood and stone: beautiful, proud, soiled, secret.

"There is a group of Western artists visiting Prague," the Russian says. "I believe you are acquainted with one of them."

Her chest flutters. Yes, she is acquainted.

"In three hours, they depart for Vienna. They will convene outside the old synagogue before proceeding to the train station. You will approach your friend and explain that you have been discharged. You will express a desire to leave Czechoslovakia. You will display counterfeit travel documents and ask to go with her and her group, in order to provide cover. She will agree, because you have established a prior relationship with her. There is a recording of a conversation which took place between you, in which she is heard promising to work for your release. Am I correct, little bird? Do you remember she told you that?"

She will never forget it. She nods.

"Once in Vienna, you will go to the American embassy. You will describe the horrors of your confinement and offer to defect. To prove your sincerity, you will supply information about a novel design for a nuclear power plant to be constructed outside Tetov. You obtained this information from Doktor Jiři Patočka, a physicist with whom you have been romantic. I am sure you will have no difficulty describing your affair with him vividly. Allow me to introduce you."

She studies the black-and-white snapshot of a man she has never met.

"You will receive further instructions when appropriate."

She glances at her son.

"Yes, little bird, he comes, too. You understand we could not speak of this before. You have always been a loyal soldier. I admire that quality. But we had to give you a plausible motivation to betray us."

She understands perfectly. She prays that her son can understand, too.

Do you see, Danek, the purpose of our suffering? Or will you hate me forever?

"So?" the Russian says. "Happy? Faith is restored?"

"Yes, sir." Then she worries that she's given the impression that her faith was ever compromised. She says, "Hopeful."

The Russian laughs. "Even better. What is life, without hope?"

On Pařížská Street, he eases to the curb. Daniel throws open the door and dashes across the street toward the synagogue, gaping up at its serrated brow. The entire structure appears to be sinking into the earth, as though hell has opened its throat.

She gets out, hopping over a ridge of black slush.

Wide steps lead from the pavement down to a cramped, cobbled terrace. The Russian kicks aside wet garbage, clearing room to stand. Daniel explores pocks in the synagogue's exterior plaster, rising on his tiptoes in an attempt to grasp the column of iron rungs set into the wall, the lowest of which is still far too high for him. Her heart blossoms at this evidence that he remains a child, unaware of his own limitations.

He points to a peaked door at the top of the rungs, ten meters up. "What's that?"

"Really?" the Russian says. "Nobody has told you?"

Daniel shakes his head.

The Russian smiles at her mildly. "You can see for yourself why your nation is doomed. You lack pride." He says to Daniel, "This is an important part of Czech culture, little one. You have heard of the golem, surely."

The boy fidgets. ". . . yes."

"Are you telling the truth, or are you trying to avoid looking stupid?"

"It's not his fault," she says. "They don't teach useless fables in school anymore."

"Ah, but must everything have a practical application?"

She hesitates. "Of course."

The Russian laughs. "Well said, *soudružka*. Spoken like a true Marxist-Leninist." He smiles at Daniel. "I will tell you, little one: through that door is the synagogue garret. You know what a synagogue is? A church for the Jews. Their priest, he is called the rabbi. There was once a very famous rabbi of this synagogue. They say he made a giant from clay. A monster, made of mud, three meters high. Taller than I, and you can see for yourself how tall I am. Fantastic, eh?"

Daniel smiles shyly.

"Alas, the creature could not be controlled. It had to be stopped."

The Russian kneels, grasps Daniel by the shoulders with his huge hands, the fingertips and thumbs nearly touching. "But here's the interesting part. The golem is not dead. It is asleep, right behind that door. And they say that on certain nights, when the moon is full, it wakes up."

Daniel tilts his head back, searching the woolly cloud cover.

The Russian grins. "Yes. And if you are patient, and do what you must, you can draw it out. And if you say the right things, at the right moment, you can grab hold of it, and it becomes yours. It must do anything you command."

He gives Daniel's shoulders a squeeze and stands. "So? What do you make of that, little one? Do you believe it?"

Daniel's tongue protrudes in concentration. "Jews are dirty."

The Russian bellows laughter.

She says, "We don't speak this way about anyone."

"Your mother is right, little one. Dirty or not, you are going to be traveling among them, so you had better mind your mouth. Are you still hungry?"

The Russian looks at her. He wants his coat back.

She hands it over, and he fishes out a chocolate. Daniel begins to tear it open before manners kick in and he glances to her for permission.

"First say thank you."

"Thank you," Daniel says, and he crams the chocolate in his mouth.

The Russian says, "I hope you enjoy it very much."

"Are we to wait in the cold for three hours?" she asks.

"I will fetch the dossier," the Russian says. "Use the time to study it."

He bounds up the steps and out of sight.

She rubs her arms to keep warm, resentful that he took the coat with him. How long has she been free? Not an hour, and already finding something to complain about! Perhaps the Russian is right about the Czechs. But if they have no pride, it's because pride has been outlawed, per the dictates of men thousands of miles away.

He left her the hat and the gloves, at least.

She stamps and shivers, watching Daniel lick his fingertips. "Where did you learn to talk such rubbish?"

"Berta says so."

She starts to ask *who is Berta* before realizing he means Mrs. Kadlecová, the neighbor who has been caring for him in her absence.

What can she possibly say to that?

And what moral authority does she have to correct him? Not so long ago, she too might have said the same, without a second thought. *Špinavý žid*: dirty Jew.

Look at her now, enlightened, putrid, in tattered clothes.

"What else does Berta say?"

"That you are a collaborator."

Bitch. I entrusted my child to you.

"Do you believe her?"

He shrugs. "Collaborators should be hung from the lampposts."

"Did Berta tell you that?"

"Everyone says so."

"Who is everyone?"

He toes the ground, shrugs again.

My sweet boy, my cynical boy. Is that what you'd like to see? Your mother at the end of a rope?

She says, "I'm sorry I was gone so long. I didn't know it would turn out this way. It will be different from now on. I swear to you."

Silence.

He says, "It's my name day."

Of course it is. She had forgotten, wrapped up in her own shock. Of course it is this that makes a boy of six refuse to look at his mother—a simple error. With a simple correction. She could weep with joy.

"There are no calendars in prison, my love. You're right, though. You're absolutely right, and I apologize with my whole heart. I'll tell you what we'll do. As soon as we're settled, we'll throw the biggest party you've ever seen. Do you hear me, Danek? You won't know where to begin opening presents, there will be so many. We'll have a cake. What kind would you like?"

He looks at her uncomprehendingly.

"Over there, cakes come in many different flavors," she says. "Vienna is famous for its bakeries. Raspberry, lemon, marzipan, chocolate—"

"Chocolate," he says.

"Very well then, chocolate it is. And lemonade, too—no, hot chocolate, it's too cold for lemonade. Chocolate cake and hot chocolate, a chocolate feast, doesn't that sound marvelous?"

"How do you know?" he says.

"What?"

"How do you know they come in different flavors?"

"Because I've been there, my love. I've tasted them for myself."

His eyes widen. "You have?"

"Many times."

"When?"

When I was young. When I was beautiful. When I didn't know any better.

"Before you were born, darling."

She takes a tentative step toward him, emboldened when he does not retreat. She slips her filthy hand into his clean one, and for a moment feels clean herself.

"Well?"

The Russian clomps down the steps, greatcoat billowing, a leather satchel under one arm. He sets it on the ground and stands akimbo, puffing steam.

"Any sign of it?"

It occurs to her that although she has seen him many times, she has never really appreciated his entirety. In the hospital, lights were kept low, and it was inadvisable to look staff in the eye—a sure way to draw unwanted attention.

Now diffuse moonlight touches a long, pale, waxy face, a candle incised with the features of a man, at once handsome and ghastly and difficult to comprehend, as though his flesh is reshaping itself every second. His hair is the uncertain white of morning frost, his proportions an affront to common sense.

Stunted teeth, snaggled and blackly rimed, are the sole evidence of his humanity.

"Any sign of what?" she says.

"The golem," he says. "What do you say, little one?"

Daniel says, "I didn't see."

"Nothing?" The Russian squats, begins undoing buckles. "That *is* disappointing."

He opens the satchel and produces a fist-sized object wrapped in newspaper.

"Can I see the dossier?" she asks.

He begins peeling away layers of newspaper. "I must tell you: I lied."

The last layer comes away to reveal a small earthenware jar. The Russian gingerly sets it on the cobblestones and reaches into the satchel for another wrapped item, a flat disc. "A full moon does not have the first thing to do with it."

He unwraps a matching earthenware lid and places it on the ground.

"The artists left weeks ago, little bird." He cups the jar in the broad belly of his palm, then carefully slots the lid between thumb and forefinger, so that he is holding both, leaving one hand free. "They are home by now, in their comfortable American beds, fucking their comfortable American girlfriends and boyfriends."

For a third time, he reaches into the satchel, withdrawing a black-and-brown Makarov pistol. He flicks off the safety and stands up.

"Not the boy," she says.

"Of course the boy," he says, and he shoots Daniel.

Daniel collapses, shins bent under thighs, a black hole oozing in his forehead.

"Of course the boy," the Russian says. "That is the whole point."

She cannot find the air to cry out or the energy to move, and she knows without a doubt that he is right, she is doomed, they all are, because at least she ought to be able to summon a sense of outrage, but there is nothing, she feels nothing.

Gun in one hand, jar and lid in the other, the Russian stands with his eyes raised to the garret door, his lips moving like a housewife making a shopping list, murmuring.

After a while, he frowns at her. "My hat."

She stares at him.

"Take it off, please."

She does not move.

"I do not want to soil it," the Russian says.

She does not move.

"Never mind," he says.

He shoots her in the chest.

Flattened against the frozen stones, she tastes the warm salty gush rising from her ruined heart. The clouds briefly part, and then the Russian's winged shape looms forth to eclipse the moon.

HE WAITS FOR HER EYES TO DULL, then turns and watches the door, chanting softly.

Nothing.

He studies the whore's body. Still alive? To be absolutely certain, he shoots her a second time, slightly to the left. Her blouse shreds.

He looks up. Nothing.

Well, one can only try.

Try, and try, and try again.

Mindful of an irritating throb, he loosens his scarf to give his skin some air, probes the rising cairn of flesh. He tucks his gun in his waistband, sighs wearily, and kneels to rewrap the jar.

Freezing in horror.

The lid is cracked—a thin black line from edge to edge.

When did *that* happen?

He must have set it down too hard.

He was trying to do too many things at once. He only has two hands.

It's typical. He was sloppy, overeager, careless, an idiot.

He falls down onto his tailbone, rocking, shaking with rage.

Idiot, idiot, clumsy idiot, see what you've done, the mess you've made; stop crying, insolent little shit, don't stare at the ground, be a man and look at me, look me in the eye, look at me, *look*.

CHAPTER TWO

High in the garret above, through brick, and wood, and clay, seeps the gray.

She feels it before she sees it: an icy press, foul and consuming, rushing in like poisoned floodwaters to pry open her many thousand eyes, rousing her to fury, limbs stirring, writhing, wriggling.

She opens her armor, spreads her wings, takes flight.

It lasts one glorious moment and then she crashes into the clay ceiling.

She lands awkwardly, legs bent in six incompatible directions. Even with no one around to see it, it's more humiliating than painful.

Hissing, she rights herself for another try and once more bounces back as though swatted by a giant hand.

Now the pain is real.

On the bowl of her back, she rocks from side to side, managing to flop onto her belly. Flapping her wings slowly, she ascends cautiously in captive space until she touches a solid surface, the roof of her prison, river mud hardened to ceramic.

Tucking her legs in, she braces herself.

Pushes.

It is like arguing with a cliff. She struggles and struggles and meanwhile the gray has begun to drain, taking her strength with it, time running down.

No.

Abandoning caution, she begins slamming herself upward, again and again and again, at last settling on her side, exhausted, gutted by pain, shell split clean open, bleeding, jaws bent, wings shredded, watching the air as it steadily quiets, her eyes closing a hundred at a time.

Noting with satisfaction, before all goes black, a pale, slim fissure, a crack in the darkness of clay.

CHAPTER THREE

Detective Jacob Lev tracked the insect as it descended from the darkness between the rafters. The closer it came, the faster it circled, the buzz of its wings rising above the ambient rumble until it ducked down a row of steel shelves, out of sight.

Absently he scratched at the scar on his upper lip, then groped in his backpack for a flashlight, a clear plastic cup, and a fuzz-edged index card.

The Vollmer archive occupied one corner of a World War II–era hangar due east of Los Angeles, a vast sad wart on the back of crumbling El Monte Airport. For years the owner had been petitioning the county to rezone it for condos, a request never to be granted, because the place fit the bill exactly for local government agencies seeking to cheaply store their crap.

Regional Planning, Public Health, law enforcement from Long Beach to Simi Valley: the layout screamed territoriality, cubic miles of yellowing paper providing refuge for squirrels, rodents, snakes, not to mention an impressively varied insect menagerie. Jacob had personally evicted three generations of raccoons.

The vaulted, ribbed aluminum roof thwarted cell reception and created a microclimate prone to extremes, amplifying the summer heat and dripping in winter. Mushrooms fruited through the concrete. Bulbous metal halide lamps took half an hour to come to full strength, creating an unforgiving haze that reduced him to a specimen on a slide. He usually left them off and worked by the light of his computer screen.

Restocking was on the honor system. You needed a keycard for access, but otherwise nothing prevented you from carting off crates of supposedly sensitive material.

There was nobody to shoot the shit with. Nobody to make a coffee run. No roach coach outside trumpeting "La Cucaracha." In eleven months, Jacob had encountered nine other human beings—data hounds, lost souls.

His ideal work environment.

It hadn't always been this way.

More than two years had passed since the events that derailed him—events that he still did not understand, because understanding them meant agreeing to take them at face value, which he refused to do, because they were manifestly batshit.

More than two years since he woke up and found a naked woman in his apartment. She called herself Mai. She smiled at him and told him she had come down looking for a good time. Then she vanished into the morning.

More than two years since his first visit from Special Projects, an LAPD division he'd never heard of.

No one had heard of it. Officially, it didn't exist.

But it was real, or real enough, made up of strange, towering men and women who obeyed a code of their own; spoke their own, private truth; used Jacob for their own purposes. Real enough to reassign him. The division commander was a guy named Mike Mallick, an emaciated pedant who sent Jacob to Prague and England and back in search of a serial killer named Richard Pernath.

Jacob had caught him. Tracked down his accomplices, too. He'd done as well as you could ask of any cop, learning a lot of surprising things along the way.

He learned that his father, Sam, was descended from a sixteenth-century Jewish mystic.

He learned that his mother, Bina, wasn't dead, as Sam had led him to believe, but alive—if not well—in an Alhambra nursing home.

He learned that well enough for any cop was not good enough for Special Projects.

What they wanted, more than any criminal of flesh and blood, was Mai.

And Jacob learned that the naked woman from his apartment was no ordinary woman, but a creature of no fixed shape, capricious and alluring and terrifying, capable of breathtaking violence and breathtaking tenderness in the same gesture. No ordinary woman: she was drawn to him, over centuries, like a star spiraling toward a black hole.

Making him, in the view of Special Projects, bait.

It had come down to a bloody night in a greenhouse, Jacob gripping her by the hands amid a glittering lake of glass while the tall men drew near for the kill. *Stay right where you are* they warned Jacob.

He didn't.

He released her, and she looked at him and said *Forever* and flew away, sending Mallick and company into an unearthly fit of rage.

You have done a great wrong.

In the aftermath, Special Projects seemed divided on how to deal with him. Their initial response was swift and brutal, a short punt to a desk job in Valley Traffic.

But they still needed him, for the next time Mai turned up. They seemed convinced that she would, putting round-the-clock surveillance on his apartment.

And outwardly, they made a show of appreciation. Jacob had nearly died at Pernath's hands, and six months after his release from the hospital, he got a visit from Mallick's mammoth, dyspeptic deputy, Paul Schott, come to deliver a citation for outstanding work, along with a check for ten grand.

A "performance bonus."

LAPD didn't give bonuses.

It was hush money.

Jacob tore it up.

FOR THE NEXT YEAR, he went back to what was left of his life.

He drank. He ignored his father's pleading calls.

He hunched at his skimpy desk in Valley Traffic, typing up accident reports.

Then, on a dull December morning, a shadow stretched across his keyboard.

Without looking up, Jacob discerned the soaring point of the chin, the spindly frame. He anticipated the weary voice, eternally on the verge of losing patience.

Commander Mike Mallick said, "Afternoon, Detective. What're we busy with?"

A midday drop-in was a far cry from the cloak-and-dagger of their first encounter, in a vacant Hollywood warehouse with a bogus address.

Jacob supposed they were past the point of theatrics.

"Hit-and-run," he said.

"Who's the vic?"

"Brand-new parking meter."

"High priority."

"You said it, sir."

"Not too busy for lunch, I hope."

At that, Jacob raised his head.

Mallick had on aviator sunglasses and a lightweight suit, yards of gray crêpe in the legs alone. The silver tufts above his ears had thinned, like shed plumage. The necktie was interesting: no ten-dollar dry-cleaner special but a wispy charcoal snippet more befitting a wannabe screenwriter.

"New look, sir?"

Mallick smiled wanly. "Adapt or die."

THEY CLIMBED INTO THE BACKSEAT of a white Town Car. The air-conditioning was going full-bore. Jacob felt his eyebrows crackling as he leaned forward to clap the driver on the shoulder. "Looking good, man. Svelte."

"Trying." Detective Mel Subach patted his abundant gut. "Where to, sir?"

Mallick said to Jacob, "What's your pleasure, Detective?"

"Is Special Projects paying?" Jacob asked.

"We always do."

Jacob named a place on Ventura, a former greasy spoon refurbished by a pair of homesick Israelis. They'd kept the décor and overhauled the menu, serving up aromatic Middle Eastern fare to dark-skinned businessmen wearing large watches, and bewildered matrons who'd come in seeking a Cobb salad.

Subach stayed behind in the car while Jacob followed Mallick inside. The Commander strode past the WAIT TO BE SEATED sign, folding himself into a purple pleather booth and asking for recommendations. But after Jacob had ordered *shakshuka*, extra hot, Mallick closed his menu. "Nothing for me, thanks."

The waitress rolled her eyes and departed.

"You're missing out," Jacob said.

"I had a big breakfast."

"I thought you'd like this place, sir. It's kosher."

"How thoughtful of you. You do know I'm Methodist."

"I didn't, sir."

Mallick smiled. "You've started keeping kosher, then?"

"Not even close."

"Well. To each his own."

"I'm pretty sure you know my eating habits, sir. You have eyes on me twenty-four/seven."

"They don't search your fridge."

"They don't have to. I come home every night with hot dogs."

Mallick shrugged. "Those could be kosher hot dogs."

"From 7-Eleven?"

Mallick touched one silver temple. "The reports aren't that detailed."

Jacob laughed. "I appreciate the candor, sir. Nice change of pace."

The waitress brought Jacob's Diet Coke and a cup of ice water for Mallick.

She was pretty, with a no-nonsense ponytail and slender, muscular forearms that stretched to set out a small dish of pickled vegetables.

Jacob watched her disappear into the kitchen. "May I ask a question, sir? What are you hoping to accomplish? Your guys use the same unmarkeds over and over. It's the same cast of characters. I know you're there," he said. "And if I know, Mai knows."

"That may very well be."

"So who do you think you're fooling?"

Mallick raised his eyebrows. "I'm not trying to fool anyone."

"It's a waste of resources."

"I'll make that call, Detective."

"I'm sorry, sir. I meant no disrespect."

"Sooner or later," Mallick said, "she'll be back."

"And you'll be ready to grab her."

"You sound skeptical."

Jacob shrugged.

The Commander hinged forward at the waist. "I shouldn't have to convince you. You witnessed it yourself."

Jacob stifled a giddy laugh, remembering a horse-sized beetle exploding through a greenhouse roof.

Convulsions in the glittering dark.

A monstrous block of dirt.

Then: a sculpted female form, perfect.

The taste of mud flowing down his throat.

A bleeding gash on his arm cauterizing itself.

A black speck vanishing in the night sky.

Forever.

He said, "I'm still trying to figure out what I saw."

"I'm not asking you to take anything on faith," Mallick said. "I'm asking you to trust yourself."

"With respect, sir, that's the last thing I'm inclined to do."

Silence.

Mallick said, "How long since you went to a meeting? Talked to your sponsor?"

"Is this an intervention, sir?"

"It's me asking if you're okay."

Jacob stirred his soda. They could seem so sincere. Mallick, Subach. Even Schott.

What disturbed him wasn't that they *seemed* sincere.

It was that they *were* sincere, utterly convinced of their own righteousness.

Fighting the urge to bolt, he smiled at the waitress as she put out two sunny-side-up eggs wallowing in tomato sauce, a stack of warm pita bread for sopping. *Shakshuka* had been a favorite since his year in Israel as a seminary student. Normally, he'd have been salivating. His stomach had contracted to a hard sour walnut. *"Todah,"* he said.

"B'teyavon," the waitress said, and she left.

Mallick adjusted his sunglasses. "I'd much prefer if we could trust each other. We both want the same things."

"No kidding," Jacob said. "You want a pony, too?"

"I'm trying to make amends, Detective. How do you like life in Traffic?"

"It's dandy."

"I recall you saying that once before. I didn't believe you then, either."

Here it comes Jacob thought.

Returning to active duty raised issues he didn't want to begin to think about. The booze weight he'd shed during his convalescence was creeping back. He slept badly, waking with skull-splitting headaches from recurrent nightmares about tall men wielding knives, dust-choked attics.

A garden, lush, impenetrable.

He didn't feel stable enough to tackle any crime more daunting than assault with intent to inflict grievous harm on a parking meter.

Mallick said, "What I've got lined up for you—"

"Let's say, hypothetically, I don't want to take what you've got lined up."

"Mind your tone, Detective. I'm still your superior." Mallick reset his patience. "Here's a question for you. How many murders did we have last year?"

"About three hundred."

"How many in 1992?"

Crack, gang wars, race riots, an era of acute dividedness in a city where the disparity between the haves and the have-nots was a kind of perverse civic centerpiece.

In 1992, Jacob had been twelve. He said, "More than three hundred."

"Two thousand five hundred eighty-nine."

Jacob whistled.

"Of those, how many remain unsolved?" Mallick asked.

"A lot."

"Correct."

"All right," Jacob said. "Which one do I get?"

"All of them," Mallick said.

"I appreciate the vote of confidence, sir."

"You're not going to solve them. They're hopeless."

Jacob rubbed one eye, chuckled. "I appreciate the vote of confidence, sir."

"As of January first, we're required to begin converting our archives from hard copy to digital. Everything after '85 needs to be scanned. State-mandated."

This was how Special Projects sought to make amends? Glorified secretarial duty? He was already a desk jockey, had his cubicle organized just the way he liked it, no photos, no cartoons, no funny mugs. Bourbon in the bottom right drawer.

"Hire a grad student, sir. They're cheap."

"Can't. Technically, these cases are still open. It needs to be a cop."

"It doesn't need to be me."

"I thought you'd enjoy it."

"Why would you think that?"

"You're a Harvard man," Mallick said. "Consider it learning for learning's sake."

Jacob laughed and shook his head, picked up his utensils and cut cleanly through one of the eggs. Thick golden yolk oozed out.

Mallick said, "We'll set you up with everything you need."

"First I want you to do something for me."

"This isn't a negotiation, Detective."

"Call off your guys, please."

Mallick remained impassive.

Jacob said, "We both know Mai won't show herself as long as they're in place."

"They're not disturbing you," Mallick said.

"You want me to trust you? Trust me."

Mallick fooled with his skinny tie. "I'll think about it."

"I appreciate it, sir."

"In the meantime, if she does come back, you know what to do."

Statement, not a question. It saved Jacob from having to lie. He tore off a piece of pita and swiped it through sauce. "I had a knife," he said.

Mallick said nothing.

"A potter's knife. It belonged to my mother. It disappeared after Schott and Subach came to redecorate my place."

"Sorry to hear that," Mallick said.

"I'd like it back."

Mallick said, "You'll start after the New Year." He tossed down a hundred-dollar bill. "Take your time. I'll be outside."

ALONE, JACOB FINISHED HIS LUNCH at a leisurely pace. When the waitress came to collect his plate, he smelled *za'atar* and perspiration.

"Can I get you anything else?" she asked.

He tamped down the impulse to ask for her number.

It had been a long, long time.

More than two years.

But he remembered another night in his apartment, with an extremely ordinary woman whose name he never learned. They hadn't even made it to the bedroom. They were drunk, and naked on the kitchen floor, and the instant he went inside her, she seized to stone, her eyes rolling back in her head, not from pleasure but agony.

It felt like you were stabbing me.

And he remembered another night shortly thereafter, in England, a woman whose name he still thought about, because she had a nice soft face and a laugh to match. He remembered her body, welcoming his, and then the same poison. He remembered her huddled on her bed, shaking, fearing for her own sanity as she described what she'd seen.

She was beautiful.

She looked angry.

She looked jealous.

She was describing Mai.

The best he could do for any ordinary woman was to leave her alone.

"Coffee?" the waitress asked. "Dessert?"

"Piece of baklava to go," he said. "For my friend on a diet."

She brought it in a foam container, along with a bill for nineteen dollars. Jacob left the entire hundred and went out to the car.

WHEN HE GOT HOME that afternoon, the surveillance van was gone from his block.

The thrill of liberation was tempered by the realization that he was once again working for Mike Mallick. One way or another, Special Projects owned him.

He climbed the stairs to his apartment, where his answering machine blinked.

Jacob, it's me—

He hit DELETE, snapping his father's voice clean off.

Outside, dusk was gathering, streetlights glowing, moths and mayflies congregating, a pulsing vortex that raised in him an unsettling tide of nausea and arousal.

He yanked the curtains shut.

CHAPTER FOUR

The night before he began work at the August M. Vollmer Memorial Archive, Jacob went to Wikipedia to learn about its namesake.

Vollmer, it emerged, began as Chief of Police in Berkeley, introducing novel concepts like centralized records and the hiring of minorities. He had formalized criminal justice education and been among the first to equip his men with motorized vehicles. Flush with success, bursting with optimism, he'd come to Los Angeles in 1923 and promptly burned out, quitting after a year and returning to Northern California, where he later committed suicide.

Jacob shut the browser, wondering why anyone would choose to commemorate a guy whose career essentially proved what a shit-show LAPD was.

The next day, standing in a forlorn corner of the hangar, he took stock of his new digs and smiled without a trace of glee. He had his answer.

Rickety laminate desk. Rusty folding chair. Rusty gooseneck lamp. A black rotary telephone capable of inflicting blunt force trauma; a scratched scanner; a balky desktop with no Internet connection.

The archive was a repository for schmucks.

His Project was Special in the same way that certain Needs were Special.

We'll set you up with everything you need.

Not quite.

Jacob left the building, returning a couple hours later with a space heater, a gallon thermos of coffee, and four handles of Beam.

Adapt or die.

DESPITE THE MAKE-WORK NATURE of the assignment, he rapidly developed a taste for the solitude. Mallick didn't care about hours, as long as Jacob covered ground, and it suited him to show up when he felt like it and leave when he couldn't take any more.

He pulled down boxes. He put them back, striving to instill some form of order. He read. He coded entries on a prefab spreadsheet.

It was scut, but it did provide an interesting historical snapshot of the high-crime eighties and nineties, detectives barely able to keep pace with the torrent of drive-bys and street slayings, let alone whodunits.

In keeping with Jacob's experience at Robbery-Homicide, many instances everyone knew who'd done it. The family knew. The cops knew. The bad guy's name was in the murder book, circled and underlined. He'd threatened the victim in the past. He had a violent record. He had no alibi. But the evidence wasn't there to convict. Witnesses refused to come forth. They feared reprisal. They mistrusted the police.

And so the dead ends accumulated, the Coroner's map in the crypt unable to accommodate any more pins in its southern and eastern quadrants; squad room whiteboards filling inexorably with the names of young black and Hispanic males.

One by one, Jacob revisited them.

Omar Serrano, twenty-five, Boyle Heights, shot to death while stopped at a red light.

Bobby Garces Casteneda, nineteen, Highland Park, shot to death beneath the Arroyo Seco Parkway.

Christopher Taylor, twenty-two, Inglewood, shot to death leaving the In-N-Out Burger on Century Boulevard.

They weren't all male.

Lucy Valdez, fourteen, Echo Park, shot to death, a stray round passing through her kitchen window as she did her geometry homework.

They paraded past, the unsolved and the unsolvable, chanting the name of August Vollmer, Patron Saint of Wasted Effort; clamoring after Jacob Lev, his rightful heir.

Every so often, the desk phone would rattle, a detective ferreting out old links. Once, by sheer luck, Jacob had already cataloged the case, and he was able to hand-deliver the material to an astonished and grateful D. The rest of the time he heard himself trotting out excuses. Dates on boxes didn't match contents. Gappy murder books. Thirty years' worth of material; a jumble of nightmares.

The scorn came rolling over the line.

"What sort of bullshit racket you running?"

And while Jacob could point to the number of untouched shelves and tell himself he had miles to go before he slept, he knew they were right. He was drawing a DIII's salary, doing a clerk's job.

He'd been kicked way, way upstairs, up into the attic of the past.

Now, padding along in old sneakers, he played the flashlight between boxes marked PROPERTY CRIMES 77 ST 3/11/1990—

3/17/1990, VICE HOLLENBECK 07/2006, 1994–5 C.R.A.S.H. The insect's buzzing had ceased, and he paused in the middle of the aisle, watching his breath billow and dissolve, trying not to touch his lip, which itched like crazy in the cold, dry air.

He gave in and scratched.

From his left came a whisper of legs.

Six feet down the aisle, clinging to a half-opened box labeled HOMICIDE RAMPARTS APR 95: a beetle, its wings creasing and spreading exhaustedly.

Jacob edged sideways, cup poised.

Studded antennae bent—a premonition—

It skittered inside the box.

He hurriedly folded the flap shut and carried the entire box back to his desk, setting it beneath the spotlight of the gooseneck lamp.

Readying the cup, he opened the box and brought the trap down over the stunned bug.

Gotcha.

The beetle went berserk, throwing itself against the plastic pathetically.

"Shhh," he said. He slid an index card into place and moved the cup to the desk. "Take it easy."

While the prisoner continued to thrash, he paged through his field guide to insects of the West, eventually finding a match in *L. magister*, the desert blister beetle.

Native to the Mojave and surrounding areas. Typically they traveled in swarms. How a singleton had made its way into the archive, Jacob couldn't begin to guess.

Then again, he could ask the same of himself.

Maybe the little hothead had pissed off the beetle brass.

Maybe it was the August M. Vollmer of the chitin-wearing set.

Jacob lowered his chin and tried to make eye contact. "Lost?"

The beetle had simmered down and was glowering at him, drops of venom welling at its joints. Jet-black abdomen, head and thorax deep orange. Not a particularly sexy creature, the elytra pebbly and overlong, as if it was wearing poorly hemmed pants.

He was more interested in what it didn't look like than what it did.

He was more interested in what it might become.

It didn't look like her. And it didn't change. It was an ordinary bug, one of roughly a hundred hundred jillion. Compared to beetles, the sum total of every human being who had ever lived, from Adam to Einstein, was a rounding error.

He reached over and snapped off the lamp.

AT FOUR P.M., he saved his work to a flash drive. The weekend lay depressingly open, a problem solved by grabbing a handful of files from the box to take home.

He shouldered his backpack and sandwiched the cup and index card between his palms, causing the beetle to resume its frenzy.

"Chill out," he said. "You're gonna hurt yourself."

He'd arrived that morning before sunrise, and he stepped from the hangar into a disorienting midwinter twilight that made it seem as if no time had passed.

He hesitated before setting the beetle free, mildly concerned that it might turn on him in anger. That was what a human would do.

Surveying the tapestry of black, the glittering pinpricks, he recalled the taste of Mai's breath in his mouth as she spoke her good-bye.

Forever.

Promise; request; command.

But he could only swallow infinity in human doses, day by day, keeping his lonely vigil, stalking bugs with a plastic cup and an index card because he had no other way to be close to her.

He pitched the insect into the air. It shot off, all too happy to get away from him.

He had to smile. Beetles were survivors. They were high-strung. They spooked easily. Like all the most successful creatures—and they were successful—they lived strictly in the present, vengeance being memory's deadliest side effect.

Adapt or die.

CHAPTER FIVE

She floats on the night wind, watching him from afar.

He is searching the sky. Hunting for her.

In the kaleidoscope of her eyes, he appears as a thousand illuminated versions of himself, his color the dreary beige of loneliness. She loves each fragment equally, with fervor and futility, drawing comfort from knowing it is her that his heart breaks for.

Her heart would break for him. If she had one.

Forever she thinks, and she pretends that he can hear her.

A thousand versions of him toss as many beetles into the air; seconds later, the captive streaks past her angrily.

Thank you, friend.

The blister beetle doesn't pause but continues on toward the desert, uninterested in her appreciation. It did its job, it went where she wanted it to go, but not out of any special kindness toward her. She's a charmer, all right.

Below, a thousand car doors open, a thousand tailpipes chuff. He drives away.

Some nights she follows him home. From a distance, of course. They can't be seen together, and she doesn't want to alarm him.

But she worries. She can't help but worry. He has a nasty habit of drifting out of his lane, especially after a hard day, especially drunk. More than once she's had to nudge him back into line.

Other nights she makes a visit to a fig tree. She sits in its branches. She descends, to rest on the shoulder of an old friend.

Today is Friday. He'll be headed there himself, as he does every week.

So that leaves her at liberty, and—as she does every week—she circles down toward the building, entering through a gap in the roof panels, touching down and transforming into her truest self, standing nude at his desk, her skin pebbled with cold as she riffles through the open box, looking for the file she put there. Not wanting to be obvious about it, she placed it fourth from the top.

That was months ago.

True, he would have gotten around to reading it eventually.

Patience has never been her strong suit.

Tonight, at last, the file is gone.

Thank you, friend.

She ought to feel satisfied, but instead she's restless and reluctant to leave. The air still smells of him. She lingers, touching his chair, the desk, the surfaces where he has left his oils. On the computer screen, a golden shield bounces around a benign blue field: TO PROTECT AND TO SERVE.

An idea worth aspiring to.

He's left the space heater on. Another bad habit. She shuts it off and raises her arms to the false heaven.

CHAPTER SIX

Jacob sat facing the madwoman.

Like every other visit. Sitting. Staring. The two of them beneath a twisted fig, its branches fruitless, the adjacent concrete patio stained purple and brown by the decayed autumn crop.

The madwoman stared at the ground; at the branches; at her own twitchy hands.

In Jacob's direction, but never at him.

Her hair was dry steel veined with glossy black, a foot of waves tied into a staid bun. Tonight they'd dressed her in a navy-blue cable-knit sweater, tan flannel pajama pants, the fuzzy brown house slippers Jacob brought for her last birthday. An abrasive army surplus blanket draped her lap.

"Are you warm enough, Ima?"

He didn't wait for an answer. She wasn't going to answer. He wrapped the blanket over her shoulders like a prayer shawl. She didn't appear to notice one way or the other, pursing her lips, still full and red but chapped from long hours in the sun. Like Jacob's, her complexion was olive toned. Supposedly her own mother's side was originally Sephardic, Spanish-Jewish aristocracy dating back to the expulsion.

A tradition, a story, a rumor. You couldn't prove it, you couldn't disprove it.

She asked for you.

She hasn't spoken in ten years.

A decade of lies.

Following Sam's confession, Jacob began coming to see Bina every afternoon, desperate to claw back lost time, armed with his own bright ideas for drawing her out. Talk therapy. Touch therapy. Flowers, chocolates, trinkets; a blitzkrieg of love. Her only child, he would bring to the surface the maternal instinct seething like a century-old fire at the bottom of a coal mine.

Bina sat, stared, her unoccupied hands kneading the air.

Her doctors couldn't agree on the cause of the fidgeting. She'd been medicated off and on for Parkinson's. Well-intentioned nurses would give her whatnot to fuss with—a toilet paper tube, a stress ball with a pharmaceutical company logo.

There we go. Now she won't be so bored.

She had been a gifted and prolific ceramicist, once. Jacob asked the staff if they'd ever tried giving her clay.

They hadn't thought of that.

The following visit, he'd arrived with a package of Plasticine, seven rainbow-hued slabs stuck together. He pulled off a hunk of red, rolled it to warm it up, pressed it into her hands, and waited for the healing to begin.

She froze.

Ima?

Inert as the clay itself.

Maybe she wanted a different color? He tried orange. Same result.

He worked his way through the spectrum. Nothing. She was a waxwork. It unnerved him worse than the twitching. He took the clay and put it back in its pouch.

I'll leave this in your room in case you want it.

His visits thinned to every other day, then twice a week, once. The staff didn't judge him. On the contrary: they seemed to approve. At last he'd gotten with the program, accepting the basic worthlessness of his presence. The very model of a dutiful son.

She asked for you.

Another lie. More than two years, and his mother hadn't uttered a word.

"Who . . . wants . . . *meatloaf*?"

Her name was Rosario, and she was Jacob's favorite nurse.

"Looks good," he said.

Rosario, tying on Bina's bib, raised a penciled eyebrow. "I can get you some."

"I'm okay, thanks."

She peeled back the foil on a container of apple juice. "You're always saying how good it looks. I notice you don't eat it, though. You know what I think? I think you're a big talker . . . Am I right, honey?"

Bina pursed her lips.

"Yeah, exactly." To Jacob: "Need anything, I'm inside."

Alone again with his mother, he took a pair of challah rolls from his backpack and swaddled them in a paper napkin. He uncapped a mini-bottle of grape juice and filled the extra Dixie cup Rosario had supplied.

He cranked up a smile. "Ready, Ima?"

He began to sing *Shalom Aleichem*, the tune that welcomed in the Sabbath.

Peace unto you, ministering angels, angels of the Most High.

Peering through the knotty canopy of the fig tree, he pictured a pair of ethereal winged creatures crashing to earth, wondering what wrong turn they had taken to wind up on the rear patio of Pacific Continuing Care, a division of Graffin Health Services Inc.

Come in peace, angels of peace, angels of the Most High.

It was precisely because he didn't observe the Sabbath that he'd chosen Friday afternoon for his weekly visit. His father *was* observant, which meant Jacob could come by the facility without any chance of running into him.

While he was here, though, why not? Maybe the ceremony would touch some dormant spot in Bina's memory. Even if he felt foolish, mumbling the *kiddush* prayer, answering *amen* on her behalf, curling her fingers around the cup.

He watched his mother sip juice. Guided her tremulous hands to the rolls and made the blessing on bread and handed her a fork.

"You want seconds, speak up," he said, hating the rancor in his tone.

For a few minutes, Jacob watched her eat—robotic, each item delivered in methodical forkfuls. As always, he quickly grew bored. As always, he felt guilty for feeling bored. To occupy himself, he reached into his backpack for the files.

"Okay, let's see what we've got."

Hipolito Zamora, thirty-one, Westlake, stabbed to death outside a nightclub. No witnesses; no suspects.

"Outside a nightclub and no one sees. Gimme a break."

Bina finished one roll.

Roderick Young Jr., twenty-six, beaten to death in a schoolyard. Three men in dark jackets spotted fleeing the scene.

"That narrows it down. More juice, Ima?"

Bina finished her meatloaf.

Antonio East, twenty, and Jarome Jaramillo, twenty-nine, shot to death during a liquor store robbery. No suspects.

"Security footage?" Jacob said, paging to the end. "Height? Build? Clothing? Getaway car? Anything? Why should life be easy?"

Bina started in on her string beans.

"Okay," he said, stuffing the East/Jaramillo file in his bag. "Next."

Right away he spotted a problem with the fourth folder: it was the wrong color, the date scribbled on the cover off by nine years, 2004 instead of 1995. Hollywood division in a stack of Ramparts files.

Not the first example of clerical sloppiness he'd unearthed at the August M. Vollmer archive. But no less annoying. He'd be hunting for the correct box for days.

"Wonderful," he muttered, opening the folder. "Okay. So. Twenty-three-year-old black female, Marquessa Duvall; her son, five—"

The air went out of him.

Five-year-old black male, Thomas White Jr.

Bina had finished her beans. The fork rested in her hand.

She was looking at him.

He shut the file. "Eat your potatoes. I'll see if I can scare you up some dessert."

He found Rosario at the front desk, doing paperwork.

"Any chance you have a cookie back there somewhere?"

"Depends," she said. "Who's it for?"

"My mom."

"In that case, maybe," she said. "Cause you know you don't deserve a cookie."

"That's for damn sure."

She returned from the kitchen with a torn pack of Nutter Butters, two remaining.

"Seriously?"

She reached to take them back.

"Fine, fine, fine."

"You're welcome," she said.

In the dayroom, a handful of residents sat in chairs and wheelchairs oriented toward the television. *Jeopardy!* was on.

"Luckily for us, Max Brod disregarded this man's instructions to burn his writings after his death."

Jacob said, "Who is Franz Kafka?"

"Who is Kafka?" a contestant echoed.

"Shaddap," an old man said to Jacob.

"Literary Ks for six, Alex."

Jacob stepped out onto the patio and said, "Oh, no."

Pages were strewn far and wide across the concrete, in the bushes, in the dirt.

His mother had a folder open on her lap.

"For God's sake, Ima."

He crawled around, corralling the sheets before they could blow away. Big file, three hundred pages or more, now completely out of order.

He got up, brandishing the papers in one hand and cookies in the other, and came forward to retrieve the folder from his mother. Stopping short as he saw what she had in her lap: a gruesome crime-scene photo of a woman and a young boy.

Twenty-three-year-old Marquessa Duvall; her son, five-year-old Thomas White Jr.

Bina was staring intensely at the photo. The focus struck Jacob so sharply that he paused, fascinated by the new acuity. Then he came to his senses.

Gently, he said, "That's not for you, Ima."

He extracted the photo from her grasp, surprised when she did not resist.

"I'm sorry if that upset you." He put the file in his backpack, tugged the zipper shut. "I hope you're okay with these cookies—oh *come on.*"

Bina had jammed her fingers into her mashed potatoes.

"Ima. You're gonna make a—*Ima.* Give it here."

But she wrested the tray from him and resumed working the gluey mass, rounding it into a bell; raising, pressing, plucking, roughing out, her fingers flying, a vein in the center of her forehead throbbing manically.

Dumbstruck, Jacob watched the developing form. It seemed outrageous that it hadn't collapsed under its own weight.

Bina snatched up her fork and began carving out fine detail.

Then, all at once, she stopped. She lifted her hands and, sure enough, the shape imploded.

But the brief moment before it did was enough to demonstrate her gift. Enough to break Jacob's heart; enough for him to recognize the reedlike legs, the splayed toes.

The downy upraised throat of a little bird.

CHAPTER SEVEN

Barbara Reich says, "I'm going out."

Her mother frowns, dragging a wooden spoon through the simmering pot of *hovězí guláš*. The stew breathes savory and sour, oily and oppressive, turning the cramped kitchen to a swamp. "Where?"

"I'm studying with Cindy. We have a test."

"You must eat."

"I'll grab something at her place."

If Věra's frown deepens, it's to hide her approval. Barbara has left her knapsack carelessly undone, textbooks poking out—doorstops with titles like *Practical Biology: A Cellular Approach* and *Fundamental Principles of Organic Chemistry*.

"*Budes okradená,*" Věra says, closing the flap and buckling it. *You'll get mugged.*

"Anyone who wants to steal these deserves what they get," Barbara says.

Her mother clucks. "Very expensive."

"I'm kidding, Maminka."

"It is not funny."

Right Barbara thinks. *Nothing is.*

In the living room, her father is arguing with the *New York Times.*

"Bye, Taťka."

Jozef Reich slams the paper shut. Like most of his gestures, it lacks the intended punch: no satisfying bang, just a noncommittal crinkle.

CZECHOSLOVAKIA INVADED BY RUSSIANS AND FOUR OTHER WARSAW PACT FORCES; THEY OPEN FIRE ON CROWDS IN PRAGUE

TANKS ENTER CITY

Deaths Are Reported—
Troops Surround Offices of Party

SOVIET EXPLAINS

Says Its Troops Moved
at the Request of Czechoslovaks

Jozef's grin is sick and ironic as he hoists his shot glass of *slivovice.*

"*Socialismus s lidskou tváří,*" he says.

Socialism with a human face.

Before he has set the glass down, he's groping in the direction of the bottle. Barbara hands it to him and bends to kiss the vein in the center of his forehead. He smells like overripe plums and motor oil. Each day, he comes home from the garage slathered in grease, and Věra fills the kitchen sink and shampoos his woolly arms up to the elbow.

"Study good," he says.

"I will."

Outside it's so muggy the mosquitoes are complaining. Exactly the wrong weather for beef stew. Her mother's cookery is driven primarily by economics. Chuck roast is on special, twenty-nine cents a pound, they will eat *guláš*.

Barbara trudges down Avenue D in the direction of Cindy's house, rolling up her sleeves as she goes, aware of Věra watching from the kitchen window, staring down with that weird mix of suspicion and satisfaction. She can feel the knapsack imprinting itself in sweat on her back, the clasp of her brassiere biting into her spine, her blouse patching at the underarms. A group of boys wearing St. Vincent's ties and listening to the Yankee game wonder aloud what's hiding beneath her skirt.

Barbara pinches off a smile. *Use your imagination, if you've got any.*

She turns down Thirty-first, then circles back to Nostrand Avenue, where Cindy waits, tan and grinning, a one-woman conspiracy in a lime-green shift dress.

"Clockwork, baby."

The dress hits halfway up her thighs. Her feet are squished into matching lime-green go-go boots. Her handbag has bright pink flowers on the side. She looks like she's going dancing. She always does. It's how she comes to class. Beside her, Barbara feels like a dust mop.

Her own skirt comes secondhand. She tried raising the hemline, so it wouldn't look so dowdy. The first time she tried to walk out of the house, her mother screamed.

They will rape you.

It wasn't funny; nothing about her family life was, but Barbara struggled to keep herself from laughing. Because Věra made these dire predictions in her even more dire Slavic accent, trilling the *r* like a cartoon villain.

They—will—rrrrrrrRRRRape you!

Who were *they*, these rapists prowling the streets of Flatbush? The blacks? The Puerto Ricans? The young men of St. Vincent's Academy? In Věra's mind, it could have just as easily been the Nazis or the Communists.

Either way, it wasn't worth arguing about. Barbara went to her room and pulled out the stitching, leaving the skirt raggedy and misshapen.

Sometimes Cindy offers her stuff she never wears anymore. *It's not like you're up to the minute, baby.* Barbara declines. In the first place, her parents would never approve, of the clothes or the charity.

Plus she'd look ridiculous. As it is, Cindy's half a foot shorter than her. Two of her minis wouldn't begin to cover Barbara's tush.

"Oof," Cindy says, hefting the knapsack. "What's in here, bricks?"

"Books," Barbara says.

"I know you're going for *realism*, baby, but come *on.*"

Barbara smiles. She left the flap undone for effect. If her mother had been paying attention, she might have thought to question what class required textbooks for four different subjects. Or wondered how in the world Barbara could already have an exam when today is Wednesday and registration was on Monday.

Cindy drops the knapsack on the sidewalk and begins fiddling with Barbara's hair.

"You ought to use a little makeup, baby. You're so pale."

Barbara shrugs.

"I *wish* I had eyes like yours. You got it, flaunt it . . . you know what, hang on." Cindy rummages in her handbag for a bottle of liquid eyeliner. "Hold still."

As she gets to work, Barbara thinks what an odd spectacle they must make, the Groovy Gal and the Flying Nun. Last spring they shared a dissection table in Introduction to Vertebrate Anatomy, making up a full two-thirds of the class's female population. Of course Barbara ended up doing all the dirty work. Cindy couldn't bring herself to lift a scalpel, she'd get one whiff of formaldehyde and break for the ladies'. The next day, Barbara would hand her a copy of the finished report.

Thanks, baby. I owe you one.

As a premed, Barbara had to take VA. Cindy, on the other hand, was then a junior without portfolio, flirting with becoming a nurse, although that went out the window the minute she met Stan, cause, baby, he's the one. Not ashamed to want that, husband-house-kids, the whole shebang, she's no crazy man-hating feminist, no way.

You got a boyfriend? she asked Barbara.

No. Then, sensing this was the wrong answer: *Not yet.*

Don't worry, baby. You're young.

That's the problem. She's too young for her life.

High school was hard enough; she skipped two grades and still her parents called the principal weekly to complain she wasn't being sufficiently challenged. The schedule they set left little time for socializing, and she spent her first semester at Brooklyn College more or less alone.

Irrelevant, her parents say. You go to college for one purpose: to learn.

You learn for one purpose: to get a good job.

A good job ensures that you owe nobody nothing. It guarantees money. It guarantees your survival when civilization collapses, as it inevitably will. People will always need doctors. Even more so during the Apocalypse.

But it's her—not her parents—walking the halls, adrift in a sea of hormones and freedom, mismatched in every conceivable way.

Her sophomore math professor, an elderly Austrian, looked her up and down and said *The face is fourteen, but the body is twenty.*

She felt humiliated. She didn't know what to do. She told Cindy, who brayed a laugh. *You'll probably get an A.*

She got an A+.

Now, as Cindy continues to work on Barbara's right eye, foot traffic streams around them, folks barking to get off the damn sidewalk, quit blocking the steps.

"Shove it," Cindy says pleasantly. With a confident hand, she starts on the left eye. It's too bad she can't handle blood and guts; she'd make a terrific surgeon. "Sooo," she says. "When do I get to meet him?"

"Who."

"*Who?* Don Juan, dummy."

It's a reasonable assumption. The need for secrecy; the cover story.

Sure, why not? Her parents wouldn't approve of her real destination, either.

For that matter, neither would Cindy.

"I don't know," Barbara says.

"I dig, baby. You're feeling it out, right?"

"Right."

"He's your first, isn't he?"

"Mm."

Cindy sighs happily. "Nothing like your first."

The ground begins to tremble: the arriving train.

"I have to go," Barbara says.

"Almost done." Cindy steps back. "Voilà, baby. Jeepers creepers, look at them peepers. Before they were green. Now they're *green.*"

"Thanks," Barbara says, and she runs down into the station, praying Cindy doesn't forget to take the knapsack.

SHE RESURFACES AT BLEECKER STREET into the same steam, here charged with urgent energy. Faces are younger, pants are tighter, the music trickling from the windows earth-shaking bass and fuzzy guitars.

Hello, I love you, won't you tell me your name?

She's still unhip, although not as obviously. For all anyone knows, she's making a statement with her outfit, like those gals who don't shave their legs as an expression of solidarity with the Vietnamese.

Address in hand, she crosses the NYU campus, littered with fliers protesting the war; protesting the treatment of the people protesting the war outside the Democratic National Convention in Chicago. The news about Czechoslovakia is hours old, far too fresh to have permeated the collective consciousness. She can imagine the discomfort it will cause to those who like to talk about the humanity and beauty of the Soviet system.

Her own view is hopelessly colored by her parents, which makes her hopelessly square. Sometimes she'll disagree with her father about nuclear weapons or whatever, but without much heart. He gets so upset, turns red and pounds the table, spilling his drink, bellowing at her in Czech.

Tys tam nebyla.

You were not there.

How can she argue with that? She can't, that's how.

An American daughter cannot lay claim to suffering; her parents have gobbled up the entire supply, having endured the twin catastrophes of the Germans and the Russians. Věra was twelve when her mother, father, and younger brother perished in Theresienstadt concentration camp. She escaped to the countryside with her older brother, Jakub, sheltering with a friend of his from the Communist Party. During the purges, the same friend would denounce Jakub as a Trotskyite and a Titoist and a Zionist, sending him to the gallows.

Barbara has no memory of the event, which took place when she was an infant, after her parents had left Prague. Věra keeps her brother's photo on the mantel, and she lights a candle on the anniversary of his death, a rare concession to tradition in their godless home.

Her father's story is less well understood. He claims not to know his exact age, insisting people didn't keep track of things like that. Barbara guesses he's Věra's senior by fifteen years or more; his face is at once layered and eroded, like a fortress that has endured centuries of trial, centuries of repair.

This much she knows: he had another family before the War.

He never talks about them. But once, during a screaming match, Věra slipped up, demanding to know how she could compete with a ghost. He did not love her as much as Jitka, he could never love her as much as Jitka.

Through two closed doors, Barbara heard the slap, then weeping in two registers.

Later, much later, she asked her mother who Jitka was.

A friend of your father's.

Did you know her?

Věra shut her eyes. *Do your homework.*

The third girl in last spring's anatomy class was Japanese, quiet and shy, with a blunt-cut bob and discount eyeglasses that gave her the same anxious gawp as the frogs they cut open. Right away Barbara identified her as another child of immigrants; the deliberation, the wait-and-see, the rounded shoulders bowed under expectation.

When the instructor announced that it was time to pair up, the girl, whose name was Ka-something but who went by Kathy, looked hopefully at Barbara. Barbara felt intense heat, like she was confronting the sun in a mirror, and she turned away to partner with pretty, chatty, happy, incompetent Cindy Gorelick.

Kathy ended up working with a boy named Leon Fine, and Barbara spent the rest of the semester avoiding eye contact with her. But sometimes their paths crossed, and in the brief moments that they regarded each other, Barbara saw no disappointment, and certainly no surprise. Kathy, too, grasped the dog-eat-dog truth of the world; given the chance, she would've done the same to Barbara.

The lack of judgment made Barbara feel even guiltier.

It didn't change her mind, though.

THE AD IN THE *VOICE* led her to expect something grand, an art studio with nice light, but Minetta Street turns out to be a short, twisted passage lined with private homes. The door to number eleven is painted bright red. There's a note.

CLASS MOVED TO THE GARDEN →

Barbara retraces her steps to Bleecker Street, where the acute intersection forms a small, overgrown park. Through cascading greenery she spots a circle of people sitting cross-legged on the ground. She walked right past them.

"Welcome, sister."

The speaker is a white man in his midforties wearing a saffron robe. He has a shaved head and a dark, knife-point Vandyke. He beams at her.

"I'm looking for the pottery class," Barbara says.

The man raises his palms. *Behold.*

All she sees is a bunch of hippies. There are no tools, no tables, no wheels. Nobody has any clay.

"Please," the man says, "join us."

Confused, annoyed, Barbara settles herself awkwardly on the ground between two older women who shift to give her room. A couple wearing matching peasant shirts gaze at each other through dilated pupils.

No, her parents would not approve.

There's no word in Czech for *hobby.*

The fifth student is a tall, thin girl about Barbara's age. She's not a hippie. In fact, she's dressed like a Quaker, in a plain navy skirt that spreads around her generously and a long-sleeved white blouse buttoned to the neck. She ought to be burning up in the heat, but her skin is dry, and she sits up high and dignified.

Catching Barbara's eye, she tilts her head at the robed man, then raises a doubtful eyebrow, and Barbara smiles, knowing immediately that they're going to be friends.

NOT A QUAKER; not even close.

Her name is Frayda Gonshor, and she lives in the Grand Street Projects on the Lower East Side. Like Barbara, she was caught off guard by the announcement that payment for next week's class was due in advance.

The ad said free.

I share my wisdom freely the robed man said. He called himself Sri Sri Jivanmukta Swami. *The supplies cost three dollars.*

"Chutzpah," Frayda says as she and Barbara wait for the light to change.

Barbara agrees. All the same, they both coughed up the money. Three bucks isn't too bad, and she senses that she and Frayda share a common goal: escaping their parents.

"I wonder what his real name is," Frayda says.

"Probably something like Henry," Barbara says.

"Ralph."

"Mickey."

"Mickey," Barbara says, giggling. "Sri Sri Mickey Lowenstein."

"Guru Goldblatt."

"Swami Schwartzbaum."

The two of them teeter down Bleecker Street, arm in arm, in hysterics, exchanging information in a rush. Barbara has to force her long legs to slow down, as does Frayda, who is even taller than her, maybe the tallest woman Barbara's ever seen, high-waisted, with hands that flap excitedly, evoking nothing so much as a flightless bird.

"Have you ever made pottery before?"

"A little," Barbara says.

"I haven't." Frayda shrugs. "It said no experience necessary."

"I think that means Mickey," Barbara says.

Signs for the subway come into view, and Barbara feels herself slowing further, unwilling to part yet.

"Next week?" Frayda says.

"You bet."

Cindy is waiting for her on the corner of Nostrand and Avenue D, the knapsack slumped at her feet.

Barbara blows out an anxious breath. "Thanks."

"Yeah, baby, sure. So?" Cindy bites off a cuticle. "How did it go? Is it true love?"

"You bet," Barbara says.

THE SECOND CLASS MEETS indoors at 11 Minetta, in Sri Sri Jivan-mukta Swami's second-floor studio apartment. Again the group sits in a circle on the floor, which is really the only option, because Sri Sri doesn't own any furniture.

There's clay, at least—a little ball, the diameter of a nickel.

"All creation begins from a single point," he says.

They spend the hour forming tiny bowls by hand.

"You're really good at this," Frayda says.

Barbara shrugs.

Sri Sri presses his palms together. "The purity of the beginner."

Each week he allots a bit more raw material, until, by week eight, they are making vases using hand-turned wheels. Sri Sri shuttles back and forth, dispensing advice and mopping up gray water with a rag.

"Next week," he says, "we return to the garden to seek inspiration."

"And to protect your floors," Frayda mutters.

BARBARA'S PARENTS ARE HAPPY to see her taking her studies so seriously.

Cindy, on the other hand, is starting to get restless.

"I'm happy to keep covering for you, baby, but don't I deserve to meet him?"

"It's tricky," Barbara says.

"What, he's a secret agent?"

"Something like that."

The following Wednesday it's drizzling. Barbara and Frayda arrive at the park to find it deserted. On the door to number eleven Minetta hangs a sodden note, ink running.

CLASS CANCELED

They head to a café.

Frayda says, "I don't understand why he doesn't just put down a drop cloth."

"He's wearing it," Barbara says. She picks up her turkey sandwich but hesitates. Frayda isn't eating or drinking, and that makes her feel weird—observed. "You're sure you don't want anything? A cup of coffee?"

"No, thanks."

Barbara takes a bite, chews, swallows. Frayda has missed a couple of pottery classes due to a spate of Jewish holidays.

"You keep kosher," Barbara says.

Frayda nods.

"I'm sorry."

"That I keep kosher?"

Barbara laughs. "I don't want to be rude," she says, putting the sandwich down.

"Please," Frayda says. "Enjoy."

"You don't mind?"

"Why would I mind?"

"I don't know," Barbara says.

Frayda gestures to the carnival that is Greenwich Village. "A turkey sandwich," she says, "is the least of my concerns."

They talk about their families, about school. Frayda studies accounting at Hunter. She's nineteen, two years older than Barbara, but also a junior. With a detached air, she mentions that she's engaged.

"Cool," Barbara says, although she's amazed. "When's the happy day?"

"We don't know yet. We're not formally engaged. More like . . . *betrothed.*"

"That sounds fancy."

"It's not. We've known each other since we were five. Our families are friends."

Her accepting manner disquiets Barbara. "What's his name?"

"Yonatan. You could meet him sometime. You could come for Shabbos dinner."

"Sounds like fun," Barbara says, hoping she sounds more sincere than she feels.

"It really is," Frayda says. "You could come this Friday, if you wanted."

"Maybe." She promised Cindy they'd go to a movie. "I have to check."

"Sure."

There's a silence. Then Frayda peers at her suddenly.

"Do you have a Hebrew name?" she asks.

She does, but it's purely an abstraction. Talk of God enrages her father. He is clear: God perished in the camps. It is with barely contained disgust that he watches his wife light the *yahrzeit* candle for her brother. They eat pork, they drive on Saturdays, they socialize with other Czechs, Jewish or Christian, it doesn't matter, every last one of them is a devout atheist.

And yet he has chosen to live in Flatbush, surrounded by Jews. And when he drinks too much, he boasts. *Reich* is German for "rich," does she know that? They come from royalty.

They hate us because we are better.

Barbara looks across the café table at Frayda's cool, benevolent face, the temples tinged with premature gray. She decides she will cancel her plans with Cindy; she will go to Friday night dinner, if for no other reason than to please her new friend, a friend who asks questions and then actually listens to her answers.

Plus, she's curious. The concept of the Sabbath is foreign, and mysterious, and a bit naughty—an attractive combination.

"Bina," she says. "My name is Bina."

CHAPTER EIGHT

Rosario heard Jacob running toward the lobby and smiled without looking up.

"No more cookies."

"Something's wrong with my mother," he said.

Out on the patio, Bina was as Jacob had left her, fetal, sheened, the vein bisecting her forehead hideously engorged, neck a tendon cage, fluid hands shrunk to clubs. The remains of her dinner had been swept to the concrete, the tray pinwheeling, mashed potato skid marks.

Rosario took her blood pressure and pulse. She had a temporal lobe artery thermometer, which was a good thing, because Bina wouldn't open her mouth.

"Come on, honey. I need to look in your eyes."

Slowly, Bina's eyelids parted, allowing Rosario to check her pupillary response.

Like the rest of her vitals, it was normal.

While Rosario went off to page the on-call MD, Jacob paced, trying to talk his own heart down. The silence felt much heavier than usual, thrown into hard relief by his mother's burst of life.

For a brief moment, he'd seen her.

Now she was gone again.

"He'll be here as soon as he can," Rosario said, returning. She glanced at Bina, whose body had begun to lose its tautness, causing her to slide down, her head wilting over her chest. "She seems like she's okay now."

Jacob said, "You didn't see what I saw."

"What did you see?"

He didn't know how to answer that.

The doctor arrived inside the hour, by which point Bina had gone completely limp.

"We've got it from here," Rosario said. "Promise."

Jacob hesitated. "If you need to admit her, call me. Not my father. Okay?"

Rosario nodded, both of them knowing full well it was Sam's name on the proxy.

She touched his arm. "There's really nothing more for you to do."

He could take a hint. He'd done enough already.

THE FIRST AND ONLY TIME his father had accompanied him to the care facility, he'd led Jacob along a circuitous route—east through Boyle Heights, south through Downey. It was absurd, really, taking driving directions from a blind man, and Jacob had laughed, asking if they were being followed.

There was nothing joking in Sam's response.

You tell me.

The precautions went further than that: he'd registered Bina under a false name, going so far as to sign himself in as Saul Abelson.

Jacob still didn't understand exactly what, or whom, his father was afraid of. They'd never gotten a chance to discuss it. But Sam's sins didn't change the fact that he was a thoughtful man. If he deemed precautions necessary, Jacob would take precautions.

Tonight he performed his usual pre-drive check, feeling in the wheel wells and peering at the car's underbody for tracking devices. He made a few wrong turns, pulling over to flush out tails. Once on the freeway, he pushed the needle to eighty-five, his salivary glands pinching in anticipation as he neared the exit for his former favorite bar.

He wondered if they missed him. He hadn't been by in months. He wasn't looking for women, and he could drink alone, just as effectively and at half the price.

He imagined his face plastered to bourbon bottles across the state.

HAVE YOU SEEN ME?

Impulsively, he veered toward the off ramp—veering back as a horn blared.

One lane over, a middle finger waved.

"Yeah, okay, sorry."

But the guy wouldn't be placated, continuing to lean on the horn.

Jacob glanced over. Standard-issue asshole.

Thankfully, that was all.

There had been a period, the first four or five months after the madness in the garden, when he felt like an emotional antenna. He looked at people and saw—there was no other word for it—auras. Purple or blue or gray, gradated and shifting with every change of heart. He could walk into a room and know at a glance who'd fought with his wife the night before; who'd gotten laid; who could not let go, who could not hold on.

An exquisite, excruciating sympathy that would've made him a great therapist, but that turned freeway-driving into a terrifying ordeal. Every car became a plasma jar, lit up with the concerns of its occupants.

He couldn't tell anyone. They'd think he was losing it.

He thought he was losing it.

At the time, he'd been sneaking four or five Vicodin a day, nursing a cache accumulated during his hospital stay. He cut back. When that didn't help, he flushed the remaining pills down the toilet. The hallucinations persisted.

His GP gave him a mini-mental and sent him home with a psych referral. Jacob went so far as to make an appointment, canceling the morning of. He decided to tough it out, congratulating himself on his foresight and fortitude when, with time, the symptoms faded. Now he looked back and chalked them up to stress and detox.

Some days he even believed that.

One lane over, the guy was lobbing F-bombs.

Jacob fished out his badge and pressed it to the glass. The guy recoiled, yanking his steering wheel and nearly hitting another car himself.

IT TOOK SEVERAL HOURS to undo the havoc Bina had wreaked on the Marquessa Duvall file. Even after Jacob had gotten it in order, it remained incomplete: pages missing, pages waterlogged, pages nibbled by mice, pages from other cases mixed in.

Bottle of Beam in hand, he sat on his couch to read.

Early on the morning of December 20, 2004, a jogger completing his daily circuit noticed a human shape slumped in an alley south of Santa Monica Boulevard, between El Centro and Gower. That area, like most of Hollywood, had a large homeless population, and as the jogger explained, it was not unusual to come across people passed out, especially on a Monday, following a weekend of partying.

What was unusual was the person's size.

Mr. Sproul advised that he stopped to take a closer look. When I asked why, he stated that he was concerned it was a child. Mr. Sproul called out several times but received no response. He then proceeded to approach the person. He confirmed that the person appeared to be a black male between the ages of four and seven years old. The victim was propped in a semi-upright position against the wall on the north side of the alley. The victim did not appear to be breathing. Mr. Sproul stated that although he is trained in CPR, he did not attempt to touch the victim's body or to perform resuscitation. He advised that he could observe severe injuries to the victim inconsistent with survival. He stated, "I know a dead kid when I see one."

Mr. Sproul advised that he turned away from the body and took out his mobile phone to dial 911. In doing so, he discovered a second body, positioned opposite the child's body and facing it. The second body appeared to belong to a black female in her mid- to late twenties. She showed similar injuries and did not appear to be breathing.

Mr. Sproul advised that he did not notice the presence of the second body prior to then because it was blocked by a large trash container.

Mr. Sproul left the immediate vicinity to dial 911.

Marquessa Duvall, twenty-three years old.

Her five-year-old son, Thomas White Jr.

Jacob flipped through photos, advancing down the alley in shutter clicks.

The area was familiar to him from his days riding patrol in Hollywood Division: a trash-strewn corridor hemmed in on one side by commercial property, on the other by chain-link and pickets, cracked yards and lopsided parking pads. Yellow evidence markers flourished like an invasive species.

He kept going until he found what he'd dreaded and craved: a close-up of the boy.

A neat hole drilled in the center of the forehead. Crimson ribbons unfurled over his eye sockets, along the bridge of his nose, over his cheeks and his baby-fat double chin, throat shortened by the skeptical bend of his head, tugged down by gravity. His T-shirt collar, dyed red. He was dressed for activity, jeans and shoes with Velcro straps. His hands were folded in his lap.

I know a dead kid when I see one.

His eyes were wide open, making him appear polite and weirdly attentive. Jacob shuddered and shuffled rapidly to the next victim.

The fifty-gallon can used to prop Marquessa Duvall's body had been dragged there for that purpose; a group of identical cans lived down at the other end of the alley, behind a bakery. He pictured the killer struggling to keep her dead weight from toppling over, growing more and more irritated. The boy had been simpler; once wedged, his tiny frame stayed put. His mother had a large bust and a slim waist. She flopped around. Even in death, she wouldn't *cooperate.*

Like her son, she had a single gunshot wound to the forehead. It was easier for Jacob to estimate its size relative to an adult face. Small-caliber, probably .22 or nine-mil.

Her eyes were also open, and a medium-angle shot showed what he'd already inferred. Mother and child had been positioned as though staring at each other from across the alley, engrossed in a conversation never to take place.

It was this photo that Bina had gotten her hands on.

Of course it upset her. It was an atrocity.

Had context heightened the effect? She was sitting with her own son.

Wouldn't that be nice to think.

Someone was home, after all.

Sick, but nice.

He cycled through the stack twice more, searching for a trigger that might've led to the mashed potato sculpture. Dead bird, bird necklace, bird earrings, bird graffiti.

Nothing.

He checked the evidence log.

Candy wrappers.

Malt liquor bottles.

Cigarette butts by the score.

No shell casings.

No birds.

He was overanalyzing. The picture had freaked her out, and she'd resorted to the only form of self-soothing she knew: making something with her hands. As to her inspiration, who could say? Maybe a bird lived in the fig tree. Maybe she wanted chicken instead of meatloaf. You couldn't question an artist, certainly not a catatonic one.

He decided to wipe his mind of preconceptions, approach the case like any other.

Approach? Like it belonged to him?

Mallick's pronouncement rang loud in his head.

You're not going to solve them. They're hopeless.

Aren't we all.

Jacob went back to the beginning.

THE FIRST D ASSIGNED was a guy named Dan Ballard. His signature appeared on the reports until mid-2007, when a woman named Theresa Krikorian took over. For three years, she worked Ballard's leads and developed a couple of her own.

Then the paper trail dried up.

From what Jacob could piece together, there'd been no traction since. He did register the likelihood of stray documentation floating around in the system, lost on a hard drive or a shelf or a desk drawer.

He looked up Ballard, got an obituary.

He looked up Theresa Krikorian. Got another.

He could understand why cops would shy away from the case: it had already claimed two of them.

Dan Ballard had suffered a golf course heart attack.

Theresa Krikorian's family had established a fund in her memory, cancer research.

Killed in the line of duty could mean a lot of things.

Too many desk lunches. Too much nicotine.

Jacob drank to their memories, plunged back into the short lives of Marquessa Duvall and Thomas White Jr.

SINGLE WORKING MOTHER, her Culver City address a good nine miles from the dump site. Based on the absence of spatter or pooling, it appeared that the murders had gone down elsewhere, the bodies transferred to the alley.

On the questions of *where* elsewhere and *why* transferred, the file was mute.

Ballard described Marquessa's job as "hostess." Attach the right modifier and you came up with any number of activities ranging from banal to seedy.

Restaurant hostess? Hospitality hostess? Game show hostess?

I'll take Double Homicides for eight, Alex.

Maybe *hostess* meant hooker—a bit of respectful whitewashing on the D's part. Jacob hoped not. Euphemisms did no favors to anyone, least of all the victim. Anyway, Ballard's writing showed the hallmarks of a linear thinker.

JONATHAN KELLERMAN AND JESSE KELLERMAN

Jacob returned to the close-up of Marquessa's face. Death didn't improve one's appearance, and it was hard to look good with an extra hole in your face. But he could tell how beautiful she'd been. Lips, a coy invitation; waved hair, lush and streaked like macassar ebony.

He found himself searching for his reflection in her eyes. They were that big and dark and naïve.

And wrong. He couldn't pinpoint it.

He compared close-ups of both victims. Wide, wide open. Like there were invisible toothpicks stuck between the lids.

He dug out the autopsy report, which put Marquessa Duvall's time of death between ten p.m. and two a.m.—at least three hours prior to discovery.

Cause of death: gunshot wound to the head.

Lacerations to the right forearm and bruising of the right thigh.

No indication of sexual assault.

On a separate pathology page, he saw an enlarged facial diagram, arrows pointing to the eyes. A text box explained.

Victim's upper and lower eyelids

Jacob took a strong pull of bourbon before forcing himself to continue.

Victim's upper and lower eyelids were removed bilaterally with a sharp instrument. The precision of the cut and lack of cutaneous bleeding suggests mutilation took place postmortem. Search of the crime scene failed to recover the excised tissue.

The boy had been identically savaged.

Jacob went to the kitchen and stuck his head inside the fridge, lungs prickling. He had seen and could not unsee; and he felt sick all over again, imagining the trauma he'd unleashed on Bina, the horrors caroming around her hobbled brain.

The phone rang. The caller ID announced, "Lev, Samuel."

Jacob glanced at the microwave. Five-thirty a.m. For his father to call on a Saturday meant it was bad. Not many things overrode the Sabbath. Human life was one of them.

"Lev, Samuel."

If there was a true emergency, Rosario would have let him know.

The machine answered on the fourth ring. His father's voice came on.

"Jacob." He sounded calm. "Son. Please pick up."

Jacob wanted to. He missed his father, missed his complex, sometimes tortured logic. Sam was a Talmudist to the core, able to mine value from any idea, regardless of how bizarre it seemed on the surface. Jacob admired him for that.

He hated him for it.

"I don't want you to worry," Sam said, "but I got a call from the facility—"

Jacob disconnected the line.

He texted Rosario.

ok?

Her response came quickly. *doc says shes fine*

So why had Sam called?

As if she sensed the question, Rosario added two more lines.

i spoke to ur dad

he wants to talk to u

Good for him.

thanks he typed. *keep me updated*

of course

Sleep was now out of the question. Jacob took a quick shower, drank a cup of coffee, and officially kicked off his weekend.

CHAPTER NINE

He drove to the alley where the bodies had been left.

It was a wretched place to end up. The gentrification that had touched Hollywood's periphery had yet to soak this far into its flesh. He walked a grubby tenth of a mile, shooting video and photos on his phone.

The north side comprised the hind ends of a liquor store, a medical supplier, an art gallery, an ethnic market, an ethnic bakery, a sheet metal supplier, a glazier, a psychic. All were shuttered at that hour and presumably had been between ten p.m. and two a.m. on a Sunday night.

To his astonishment, he discovered the same collection of fifty-gallon cans—identical brand and color, at least, lined up behind the bakery, giving off an obscene vibe, lids ajar, black bags bulging, like deep-sea fish coughing up their own swim bladders.

Jacob wondered which one the killer had used to prop up his handiwork.

He supposed he could ask the psychic.

Throw in another $75 and she'd solve the case for him.

He made a second pass, concentrating on the residential buildings along the alley's south side, counting some four dozen windows with an unobstructed view.

Ballard hadn't recorded a canvass. One of the missing pages, maybe.

Jacob headed around to Eleanor Avenue. It was late enough to begin knocking on doors, early enough that he didn't expect to get a lot of answers. Starting with the El Centro Capri Apartments, he worked his way down the block, buzzing the manager's unit and, if he got no answer, playing call box directories.

There were nine addresses in all: six multifamilies, two detached homes, as well as an auto body shop fronting to Gower. By lunch-time he'd gained access to four of the apartment complexes. None of the occupants of the rear units had been living there at the time of the murder, though they didn't seem surprised to learn that one had taken place.

Nobody recognized Marquessa Duvall.

Nobody recognized her son.

Santa Monica was now open for business. He talked to bosses, employees, anyone who'd stick around to listen.

Zip.

He hadn't eaten solid food in over thirty hours. He headed for the bakery, concluding a futile interview of the counterwoman by buy-ing a pair of mushroom *pirozhki*. Beneath a corkboard papered with fliers for piano and violin lessons, he sat on a bench, balancing the file on his thigh so he could read as he ate.

The pastries were earthy and filling, made of humble ingredients brought together out of necessity but elevated by human ingenuity; exemplars of the cuisine of poverty that had recently become trendy, and therefore expensive, and therefore self-defeating.

"Delicious," he told the counterwoman.

She nodded brusquely.

Neither Ballard nor Krikorian put much stock in the idea of a crime of passion. The scene was too well thought out—at once clinical and grandiose.

That in itself didn't necessarily indicate a stranger murder. Marquessa had had a number of boyfriends. Ballard had questioned, swabbed, polygraphed, eliminating them one by one, including the boy's biological father. Thomas White Sr. had the best alibi possible: he was in county lockup, serving out a nine-month sentence for possession.

Theresa Krikorian began the tedious task of sorting through known sex offenders. She hadn't gotten very far. In 2007, the California registry was in its infancy, and it wasn't at all clear that it would survive challenges to its constitutionality.

More to the point, she didn't know where to begin looking. The alley was not the scene of the crime. The same problem applied to the search for witnesses.

How many gunshots went off on a given Sunday night in the greater L.A. area?

How many of those went unreported?

If the murders had taken place even a few blocks west, any caller reporting shots would've gotten routed to the sheriffs. LAPD might never have heard about it. Either way, the tapes would be long erased.

Time for some human intelligence.

"Excuse me, please," the counterwoman said.

Thickset, lantern-jawed, she frowned ostentatiously at the ceiling and drummed the softened marble countertop.

He realized he had the file open to a photo of Thomas White's brutalized face.

"I have customers," she said.

Strictly speaking, it wasn't true: they were the only people in there, unless you counted the infant girl pictured on the box of chocolate bars beside the register.

The counterwoman cleared her throat. "Mister."

Jacob took his lunch to go.

DAN BALLARD'S OBITUARY STATED that he was survived by his mother, Livia. Back at his apartment, Jacob searched for her on his home computer and got another obituary.

A lifelong bachelor? Or estranged from his ex, his kids?

Jacob felt an unwelcome sense of kinship.

He phoned Theresa Krikorian's widower, a retired firefighter out in Simi Valley, and introduced himself.

"The file's pretty thin," he said. "I figured maybe she mentioned it to you."

"Huh," the husband said. His name was Ray, and he sounded like every firefighter Jacob had met: gregarious and mellow and sheltering, a cop without the jaded edge. "I'd love to help you out, but I really don't remember much. Mind if I ask what made you guys decide to reopen it?"

"It was never officially closed."

"Honestly, it's kinda hard to talk about those days. It happened right around the time she got sick."

"I'm sorry," Jacob said.

"It is what it is." Ray paused. "I always thought that was a dumb thing to say. You know? Anyhow . . . Terri always did have trouble leaving her work at work, and that case really got to her. From what I recall, it was pretty heinous."

"It was."

"We have a daughter about the same age."

Today she'd be fourteen or fifteen. Crushes, first kiss, crystallizing sense of self.

Stages Thomas White Jr. would never attain.

Ray had fallen silent again. To draw him out, Jacob asked about his daughter.

"Phoebe? She's terrific. Sharp, like her mom."

"Any other kids?"

"A boy, Will. Twelve." Ray laughed. "He'll be happy driving a shiny red truck."

"Who wouldn't?"

"Yeah, well. He talks about the Marines, too. I told him to save his back. That's what finished me off. Disc degeneration."

"You served."

"Desert Storm." A beat. "I will tell you that when Terri caught the case, it was a big step up for her. Till then, she'd done auto theft and burglary. She was psyched to work her first homicide. I don't know why they thought it was smart to give her this one in particular. I mean, Christ, they knew she had young kids at home. Maybe they thought they were doing her a favor, tossing her into the deep end."

"Sure," Jacob said, although he considered it more likely that the mechanism behind Terri Krikorian's case assignment was like everyone else's: indifferent.

"It changed her," Ray said. "Before that, she was never the overprotective type. The opposite, actually, easygoing. She and I were both busting our butts, trying to get ahead, working these crazy hours. We used to leave our kids with the neighbor. But once Terri started working the mother-son thing, her attitude did a total one-eighty, it was, 'No, it's not safe, one of us needs to be home.' Have you ever been out to Simi Valley?"

"Once or twice."

"Then you know, it's not the mean streets. You got kids running around in their front yards, playing together. The biggest danger is peanut allergies. Terri, she starts asking me to cut back on my shifts so I can do day care. We fought about it a lot. I was like, 'Why should I be the one to adjust? It's your job, yadda yadda.' Looking back, I can't believe what a big deal I made about it."

The remorse in his voice pinched Jacob's heart.

"You get stuck believing certain things are so important, and they're vanity and bullshit. Tell me she'll be gone three years later, you think I'm standing my ground?"

"You didn't know," Jacob said.

"Yeah." Ray laughed sadly. "Whoever said what you don't know can't hurt you was the biggest idiot that ever lived. What you don't know is *exactly* what beats the shit out of you."

AROUND DINNERTIME, Jacob phoned Pacific Continuing Care to ask about his mother. The nurse who picked up sounded casual. Appetite normal, vitals normal, not a peep in the last twenty-four hours.

He'd never expected to feel relieved to hear that Bina was nonresponsive.

"Can you please tell her I'll swing by tomorrow?"

"Sure."

"And if she does anything unusual, you'll let me know?"

"Unusual like what?"

He hesitated. "I'll be by tomorrow."

For form's sake, he checked the fridge. One-third of a six-pack. He pretended to feel disappointed in himself, then set out for his daily dose of nitrates.

The guy working the 7-Eleven register was the owner's son, a tubby Asian-American named Henry who greeted Jacob, as always, with a listless fist-bump.

"What's the good word?" Jacob asked.

"Not much," Henry said. He seemed distracted.

Jacob let him be. He knew about tough days; he was having one.

He got his hot dogs, piled on toppings, couple bottles of Beam to wash it down.

Usually Henry cracked wise about Jacob's drinking, knowing it wouldn't make a difference: an addict is an addict. Tonight he rang up the bourbon without comment.

"D'you see that car?" he asked.

"Which one?"

"Green Nissan. There."

A patchy sedan, black in shadow, sat parked along Airdrome on the far side of Robertson.

"It's been there for two hours," Henry said.

"Maybe he's picking up someone at the rec center."

"It was here yesterday, too."

"Sitting there, doing nothing?"

Henry nodded.

Jacob squinted, unable to make out the driver. "Did you call the cops?"

"They said no law against parking."

Jacob used his cell to zoom in and snap a picture of the license plate. It came out too blurry to read, the driver's face obscured.

He left Henry his card. "Anything more, call me right away. Don't be shy."

The clerk nodded skeptically. "Thanks."

Jacob took his dinner and his clanking plastic bag of booze and exited the convenience store. Crossing Robertson, he saw that the car was indeed dark green, a Mazda rather than a Nissan. The driver hunched behind tinted windows and a hoodie.

Jacob strolled by, eating a dog, noting the shape of a second person in the backseat. He memorized the tag number, jotting it down once he'd rounded onto Wooster.

Henry was right. A parked car, no matter how sketchy, would elicit no serious response. Even in this relatively quiet stretch of West L.A., the cops had more pressing matters to deal with. All the same, Jacob felt on edge as he walked home.

His tension ratcheted up fast at a hulking, dark shape lurking on the landing outside his apartment door.

He set his bags down in the driveway, gripping a bottle of Beam by its stubby neck and quietly mounting the steps.

The bulb on the landing had been dead since April. Again and again Jacob had mentioned it to his landlord and gotten the same response: *right away.* He could've dealt with it himself, but the issue had hardened to a matter of principle.

Vanity and bullshit.

The man leaning against Jacob's front door was muscular, the back of his thermal shirt straining as he fiddled with a phone. Its blue glow limned a black scalp shaved clean.

Nathaniel, one of Mallick's, sometimes took the late-night surveillance shift on Jacob's block, parked in a fake plumber's van.

Nathaniel had never come to his door. No watcher had.

Transferring the bottle to his dominant left hand, Jacob stopped halfway up the steps and barked, with as much macho hostility as he could muster, "Can I help you?"

The man jerked and gasped and spun around, and Jacob found himself looking up at a familiar face: Nigel Bellamy, his father's caretaker.

Terrified.

Jacob realized he was inches away, hefting the bottle like a weapon.

"Crap." He lowered it. "I'm sorry, man. I didn't realize it was you."

"Who'd you think it was?" Nigel had his hand pressed to his chest and was breathing hoarsely and rapidly.

"I don't know. I wasn't thinking. I'm really sorry." Jacob unlocked the door to the apartment, then ran back to the driveway to collect the other bottles.

In the interim, Nigel had sunk to the living room sofa, still huffing, massaging his sternum, rubbing a small gold cross. His lips were dry, his color worrisome.

"You can't sneak up on a man like that," he said. "I'm no kid."

Jacob apologized again. The adrenaline was wearing off, and it disturbed him that his perception had gotten so out of whack, nearly leading him to clobber a good man. Nigel was as close to saintly as anyone Jacob knew. He'd been tending to Sam since Bina's death—

Jacob caught himself. He made that mistake a lot.

Tending to Sam; leave it at that.

Since banishing his father from his life, Jacob had been out of contact with Nigel, as well, and he noted changes: the thickness was there in the trunk, but the arms had shrunk a degree or two, the crow's-feet grown entrenched.

"You didn't tell me you were coming," Jacob said.

"That's right, Yakov Meir," Nigel said. "Blame the victim."

Jacob went to the kitchen, snuck a quick bolt of liquor, filled a glass with water, and returned to the living room, hurrying to clean up the blizzard of crime scene photos and police reports.

"Long time no see," he said.

"Your dad asked me to drop in."

The phrasing was telling: not *sent me* but *asked me*. Sam never could get comfortable in the role of ward. The fact that Nigel's salary was paid by a wealthy friend, Abe Teitelbaum, didn't help matters. Abe took great pains to reframe his charity, employing Sam as the superintendent for one of his rental properties and calling Nigel Sam's assistant. The act grew less and less convincing as Sam's weakening eyesight demanded greater and greater maintenance.

Jacob wondered how bad it had gotten since they'd last talked.

He wanted to ask.

He kept his mouth shut.

Nigel said, "He's been trying to reach you for a while."

He finished his water, set it down, sat up straight and tall.

Jacob felt a nervous flutter. Could he be one of them, too? In his most paranoid moments, anyone over six feet tall fell under suspicion of working for Special Projects.

He'd have to suspect himself, then.

Where did it end?

Nigel said, "Would it kill you to talk to him?"

"That's a lousy standard for decision-making."

Nigel opened a palm. "'Bear with one another and if anyone has a complaint against another, forgive each other; just as the Lord has forgiven you, so you also must forgive.'"

"Sounds New Testament."

"Colossians."

"Lucky me," Jacob said. "Not my book."

"Good advice is good advice, no matter who's giving it."

Jacob shrugged.

Nigel said, "You two got your differences, it's not my business. But I do know—"

"Hang on a minute," Jacob said.

"He's suffering, and you know he's had enough suffering in his life. That's something you ought to be able to appreciate. He's a good man, one of the finest I know. You get a little older, you realize how rare that is."

Jacob pressed the heel of his hand to his forehead. "You have no idea, do you."

"I told you, not my business."

"What did he tell you happened? He must've told you something."

"I asked why you haven't come around, he said you won't talk to him."

"He didn't tell you why."

"No, and I didn't ask."

Jacob hated himself for what he was about to do. It had to be done, though.

"Every week," he said, "you drive him to Alhambra. To a long-term care facility."

"Wednesday."

"You don't go in with him."

"I drop him off," Nigel said. "Pick him up in a couple hours."

"You've never been inside."

Nigel shook his head.

"Who does he say he's going to visit?"

"A friend."

"What friend?"

"He never saw fit to mention it," Nigel said. "It's his business."

"It's my mother," Jacob said.

Nigel seemed to short-circuit. His head jerked, his forehead clumped into wrinkles. "Your mother's dead."

"Not as of six o'clock yesterday, she wasn't. I talked to her myself. In person."

". . . I don't—"

"He buried a box," Jacob said. He didn't have the energy to raise his voice. "Then he lied about it. He lied to you. More important, he lied to me, for close to half my life."

Nigel grimaced, felt for his cross, squeezing it as though to draw strength. "I know your father. He doesn't do things without a reason."

"Can you come up with one?"

"I haven't had a chance to ask him."

"Start there," Jacob said. "Then you can feel free to lecture me."

Nigel's lips shook. He rose, stooping as he walked to the door. Turning the knob, he looked back at Jacob, then left without a word.

CHAPTER TEN

BROOKLYN, NEW YORK
APRIL 3, 1969

Barbara stops on the fifth-floor landing to remove her shoes, climbing the last flight on the balls of her feet. Outside her parents' apartment she pauses again. The crack at the bottom of the door is dark, the silence beyond sleepy and settled. Above her, a fluorescent tube buzzes; insects hurl themselves against it in worship.

She slides her key into the lock, one ridge at a time.

Her father's voice, in Czech, harsh: "You are late."

Both her parents are up, occupying opposite ends of the sofa, like counterweights. Lights doused. Very clever. What in the world made her think she could fool them? For God's sake, they survived the Holocaust.

Jozef says, "Sit."

Barbara obeys, cursing her own stupidity. She got careless, telling them she had to study three, four, sometimes five nights a week. Or maybe Cindy sold her out, annoyed because she never gets to meet "the boyfriend," fed up with Barbara's excuses.

*He's shy . . . under the weather . . . it's his birthday, he wants to
spend it with me . . .*

Dumb, dumb, dumb.

"Do you know the time?"

"About three-thirty," she says in English.

He replies in Czech: "Three. Forty. Three."

She hadn't realized. Enjoying herself, she'd lost track of time.

"Why are you coming home so late?"

"I'm sorry."

Jozef grunts. "I did not ask you to apologize. I asked why you are
so late."

"It took a while for the train to come."

He switches on the floor lamp, causing her to flinch. He's wearing his coveralls and cap, a bath towel beneath him to protect the
sofa from grease. His name patch blackened: JOE. A blunt Ameri-
canism no one uses. Věra wears a prim dress, faultlessly smooth, as
though she has ironed it to mark the occasion.

Jozef says, "Where are you coming from?"

"I said I'm sorry."

"You keep apologizing. Nobody is asking you to."

"I am anyway."

"Why?"

"Because you're mad."

"And how do you know this?"

She fights back sarcasm. "You're waiting up for me."

"Yes?"

"So, I'm assuming you're mad."

"This is your problem," Jozef says. "You assume."

Barbara says nothing.

"Where are you coming from," he says.

"Manhattan."

"What is in Manhattan?"

She can't help herself. "Pigeons."

"*Neopovažuj se*," Věra says. *Don't you dare.*

"Why did you go there?" Jozef says.

"To see a friend."

"Don't lie," Věra says.

"I'm not," Barbara says.

"You went to see a boy," Věra says.

Jozef says, "Who is this friend?"

"You don't know her."

"She has a name."

"Frayda."

"Frayda what."

"What difference does it make? You don't know her."

"Answer your father."

"Gonshor. Okay? Happy?"

"Frayda Gonshor," Jozef says. "Where did you meet Frayda Gonshor?"

"Around."

"Around where."

"Just around, okay?"

"What kind of friend is she?"

Bina rolls her eyes. Only they would ask a question like that. "A good one."

"A good friend does not keep you up until the morning," Věra says.

But they're wrong. That's just what a good friend does.

———

IT BEGAN at that first Shabbat dinner.

Barbara arrived early, nervously crushing a bouquet of flowers as she climbed the stairs to the Gonshors' third-floor walk-up. The door was open and she stepped into silken light and raucous laughter and the soft golden aroma of fresh challah.

And people. So many faces smiling at her, names thrown at her like rice at a wedding. Frayda was the fourth of six. Her older siblings lived in the neighborhood and had brought their own small children, as they did every Friday night. Barbara smiled politely, struggling to memorize the full roster: Elie, Dina, Ruthie, Danny, Benjie, Shoshie, Yitzchak, Menachem, Little Sruli, who plucked the flowers from her hand.

Yonatan, Frayda's quasi-fiancé, was a sturdy, well-proportioned fellow with a reddish beard and an abstracted mien. He acknowledged Barbara, saying how much he'd heard about her. Then he went back to his book.

Don't mind him Frayda said, leading her to a table set with white beeswax candles.

Barbara copied her: gathering the light, covering her eyes. She tripped through the blessing, a syllable at a time. The Gonshors' unit faced the airshaft, and Barbara could see dozens more flames waving. The building was half-Jewish, Frayda explained—down from what it had once been, as families gained a financial foothold and relocated uptown.

Mrs. Gonshor took her hands. *We're so happy to meet you.*

Three folding tables of unequal height stretched from the kitchen to the front door. The chairs didn't match; the couch had been pressed into service. There was no art, just yards of books on sagging shelves. Frayda's sister Naomi shrieked as her daughter lurched for the window, cracked to relieve the heat pouring from the kitchen, the heady smell of yeast now mingling with chicken soup and garlic and vegetables roasted a deep caramel. Everyone talked at once. Despite the hubbub—because of it—the space felt more expansive than her own home, choked with the unspoken.

Mr. Gonshor clapped his hands, summoning everyone to their seats. Frayda had gotten her height from him. A towering man, six-six, at least, and like his daughter, thin as a thread. He taught social studies at PS 110 but dressed like a Hasid, black hat and satin coat belted at the waist, black beard meticulously barbered.

The singing began—noisy, joyously out of sync. People swayed, people stood still. There seemed to be no rules, yet Barbara felt she was breaking one simply by existing. A little white booklet appeared in front of her. She stared at Hebrew, blocks and blocks of incomprehensible Hebrew. For all she knew, she was holding it upside-down. She felt like a dunce. She wondered how bad it would look if she ran out. She would've, except it was raining, and she didn't know where they'd stashed her coat, and her mother would kill her if she came home without it.

Frayda's hand slipped into hers, squeezed. *Relax.*

They sang another song. Mr. Gonshor blessed each of his children, one by one.

And welcome, Bina.

Nobody had ever addressed her by her Jewish name. She smiled back self-consciously. *Thanks for having me.*

Mr. Gonshor recited a blessing and distributed silver thimble cups of wine. The family rose en masse—the sound of chairs scraping the parquet was earsplitting—and filed into the kitchen to wash their hands at the sink. Scarred pans covered the range, the countertops, the table, the chairs. There was a single dented oven, hardly bigger than a shoebox. That it had produced so much food seemed nothing short of biblical.

Like this Frayda said, showing her how to wash her hands from the ritual cup.

Back at the table they broke bread, and in short order courses began flying out of the kitchen. Barbara tried to help and was shooed away, leaving her sitting with Mr. Gonshor, who amiably peppered her with questions. What did her parents do? Where did they come from originally? Did they change their names when they emigrated?

The more she answered, the more specific he got.

Stop interrogating her Mrs. Gonshor said, handing him a platter of potatoes, which he promptly passed along.

I'm not interrogating, I'm making conversation.

The meal was simple, tasty, massive. Five or six conversations ran in parallel, currents weaving and tangling. Barbara's neck began to hurt from turning to address this person, then that. A fight broke out between two of the youngest children. A peace was brokered with chocolate layer cake.

The racket would have driven her parents up the wall. At home, they could eat an entire meal without so much as a request for salt.

Yonatan got up to bus his plate, leaving his book open at his seat. Barbara stared at it as though it might leap up and bite her.

Frayda pointed to a spot in the text and read: *"These are the generations of Noah. He was perfectly righteous in his generation."*

She slid her finger to a paragraph at the bottom. *"Some of the Rabbis interpret this favorably: if he lived in a righteous generation, he would have been even more righteous. But others see it negatively: only in his evil generation did he stand out."*

She smiled at Barbara. *Context is everything.*

A second round of desserts arrived. Barbara noticed that Frayda hadn't touched her cake. She'd barely eaten, in fact. The same went for Mr. Gonshor. Barbara had to wonder how you got to grow that tall on a diet.

They recited the Grace After Meals, Frayda pointing to the words in the booklet.

When they were done, she kissed the cover. *Would you like to stay awhile? We could learn more.*

Thanks Barbara said. *I don't want my parents to worry.*

Or to call Cindy's house. She thanked Frayda's parents and walked to the subway, her mind inflated with sweet wine and filled to capacity with strange, intoxicating words.

SOON AFTERWARD the pottery class came to an abrupt end. Sri Sri announced that he was moving to California to be with his (much older, much richer) girlfriend.

Fly free, little chicks he said.

Barbara traded the hours devoted to working clay for sitting in the Gonshors' apartment, practicing letters in a composition book.

Bet *looks like a* bayit, *a house.*

Yod *is a hand raised up in the air.*

Nun *makes a nose.*

Hay, *a little man hides inside.*

Writing her own name brought her unexpected pleasure, and by spring she was devoting as much energy to learning Hebrew as she was to her coursework.

On days when she'd had enough book learning, she and Frayda would take walks around the Lower East Side, dissecting their dreams, talking anthropologically about boys. Or they simply sat in the kitchen, Barbara eating cookies, reveling in the presence of people who—gasp—talked! And smiled! Wanting badly to feel like she could give something in return, she loaned Frayda copies of her favorite books.

An inky, creased edition of Kafka's *Metamorphosis*.

The Bell Jar, bristling with dog-ears.

Should I be worried? Frayda asked.

Happiness snuck up on her. Barbara had never doubted the correctness of the school-work-job-money-safety equation. She'd never felt anything missing from her life. Certainly she didn't see herself on a spiritual quest.

The Gonshors gave her permission to want joy, instead of merely avoiding pain.

It was as though she'd been starving without realizing it.

That evening was Passover. She sat at the Gonshors' table and sang the Four Questions. It was a role traditionally reserved for the youngest child, and as the family rose to give her a standing ovation, she felt that she had indeed become newborn.

Now she says, "They invited me for Seder."

When her father speaks, his voice has dropped to a low, dangerous place.

"We do not do this."

"Speak for yourself," Barbara says.

Her father says nothing.

"It's my right, Taťka."

Věra slaps her thighs and whoops. "Listen to this. She has rights."

"I'm eighteen in a month," Barbara says. "So, actually, I do."

"Oh, very good. What a big girl you are. What a *grown-up woman*."

"I don't get what the big deal is."

"You will go to your room," Věra says.

"You've never given it a chance," Barbara says. "I love Frayda's family. I love their life. It's beautiful."

"We do not do this," her father repeats. But the fight has gone out of him; he sounds mangled.

"I'm sorry if it upsets you, Taťka, but it's what I choose."

"I will count to ten," Věra says.

What is she, four years old? She didn't expect the conversation to go well and it hasn't. They're not even trying to understand. She may as well drop the hammer.

"I've changed my mind," she says. "I'm not going to summer school. I'm going to Israel."

She waits for the explosion that does not come. Her father has turned deep red, a thick cord pulsing in his forehead, as if his skull might cleave in two. Barbara nods at each of them and goes to her room.

THE COUNTERATTACK COMMENCES the next morning, Věra leading the charge.

"We forbid it."

Barbara places her knapsack on the kitchen floor.

"You will take physics, as planned."

Barbara slides aside the plate of toast and reaches into her knapsack for the box of *matzah* the Gonshors gave her. With her parents watching in stunned silence, she takes out a cracker and puts it on a napkin.

"Can you please pass the marmalade?"

Věra doesn't know what to do; she hands Barbara the jar.

"Thank you," Barbara says.

The scrape of the knife against the *matzah* is deafening.

Věra, collecting herself, says, "You will not go to see this person anymore."

The crunch between Barbara's teeth is even louder, bombs bursting in her head.

Jozef has his unshaven face buried in his hands and is muttering.

Barbara says, "May I please say something?"

"No," Věra says.

"Fine." Barbara finishes her breakfast. She stands up, kisses her father on the crown of his head, and leaves for class.

OVER THE ENSUING MONTH, her mother's arguments grow progressively more desperate. Who will pay for this trip? How can Barbara live on her own? Doesn't she read the news? Israel is a terrible, dangerous place. A war zone.

Věra seems not to appreciate that in asking these questions, she's tacitly conceding that the decision is not hers.

"It's a women's seminary," Barbara says. "Frayda's uncle is the rabbi, and he's giving me a scholarship."

"Scholarship . . ."

"It's only for the summer, Máma."

"Plenty of time for you to get blowed up."

"It's in a very safe part of the city."

"There *is* no safe part."

"It's safer than Brooklyn," Barbara says. "There's no street crime. People don't lock their front doors."

"Yes, it is perfect." Věra looks ready to spit. "And how do you know so much?"

"Frayda told me."

"Ah, I forgot, *Frayda*. Frayda knows everything."

"She wouldn't bring me with her if she felt it was dangerous."

"Wonderful, she's going, too."

"What's that supposed to mean?"

"It means this person, she's making you crazy."

You're making me crazy. "We're going to be study partners."

"You have enough to study."

"This is important to me."

"What? What is so important?"

"My heritage. My—"

"Dej mi pokoj."

"Stop it, Máma."

"You never cared about this before."

"Because I never knew about it. I'm completely ignorant. That's the point."

"You will fall behind."

"I have more than enough credits. I could graduate next fall, if I wanted."

"Then do that," Věra pleads. "Finish your classes, and then we discuss it."

"I need a break, Máma."

"From *what*."

"From school. From everything."

The implicit coda—*from you*—hangs.

Věra says, "You will break your father's heart."

"Will you please, *please* stop being so melodramatic. I'm not dying. I'm going away for the summer. Most normal kids start doing that when they're six."

Věra raises a triumphant finger. "You are not six."

"Uuuccchh. You are missing the p—"

"You are not normal."

"Gee, thanks."

"You are special," Věra says. "You are our daughter, our only daughter."

"And I still will be in September. I'll just have a tan."

Věra says nothing.

"I'm happy," Barbara says. "I wish you could be happy for me."

An endless silence.

Věra says, "I will talk to him."

"Thank you, Máma."

"You must be very careful."

"Of course I will."

"You must write."

"Every day."

Věra says, "Don't make promises."

WHATEVER VĚRA SAYS or does not say to Jozef makes not the slightest difference. In the weeks leading up to Barbara's departure, he refuses to speak to her. If she enters the room, he gets up and leaves; if she tries to catch his eye, he shows her his back.

She tells herself that he'll calm down eventually. But as the cabbie loads her suitcase, her mother comes downstairs and shakes her head.

Barbara raises her face to the sixth-floor window. Maybe he's watching.

She says, "Tell him I love him."

She looks at her mother. "Will you tell him?"

"He knows."

"Tell him again," Barbara says. "Just in case."

They embrace.

"Please don't cry, Máma. I'll be back in ten weeks."

Věra wipes her face and smiles, her cheer brittle and false and fearful.

"Yes," she says. "Ten weeks."

She doesn't seem to believe it, though, and looking back, Barbara would come to wonder if her mother had unknowingly experienced a brief flash of prophecy.

CHAPTER ELEVEN

Sunday morning Jacob got up early and drove out to Valley Traffic. The squad room was quiet, and he borrowed a colleague's computer, combing the databases for crimes matching the Duvall/ White homicide.

He kept widening his parameters, finding nothing even remotely similar.

He was surprised, and disappointed. He assumed that this was not the killer's first rodeo. Mutilation that precise required practice. And the staging spoke to an internal logic, however warped.

He'd heard of serial murderers cutting out eyes. A typical profiler's interpretation would be: rage, followed by shame, the bad guy unable to bear the gaze of his victims.

With Marquessa and Thomas, the opposite seemed true. He *wanted* them to watch him. He took pride in his workmanship.

Who were they to him?

Who were they, period?

Ballard's notes included the name of Marquessa's mother, address in Watts, and a phone number that rang twice before a young girl picked up.

"Duvall residence."

"This is Detective Jacob Lev, LAPD. I'm trying to reach Mrs. Dolly Duvall."

"Hold, please."

An older, sharper voice came on. "This is Mrs. Duvall."

Jacob reintroduced himself, saying he'd come across Marquessa and Thomas's file and was hoping to ask a few questions.

"I've answered all the questions," Dolly said. "Too many times."

"I'm sure you have, ma'am. I hate to bother you."

"It's my daughter and my grandson," Dolly said. "It wouldn't be a bother, if I believed you had something new to offer me. What does that mean, you 'came across' their file? That sounds like it happened by accident."

Aware that he was talking to a woman with an exquisitely tuned BS detector, he took care with his words. "I've been reviewing open cases, and theirs hit me square in the chest. I can't promise I'll solve it, ma'am, but I'll give it my best."

Silence.

Dolly Duvall said, "It's not a good time. We just got back from church and I have to start on dinner."

"Is there a day that works for you this week?"

"You can come tomorrow at noon."

"I appreciate it."

"Another thing." Dolly exhaled. "The previous detectives brought photographs. Please don't do that."

BEFORE LEAVING THE STATION, he ran the tag of the green Mazda near the 7-Eleven. It came back stolen, taken from the owner's driveway in La Mirada.

He called the mini-mart. Someone other than Henry answered.

"Tell him Jacob said if he sees the car again, he should phone it in right away."

"Okay, boss."

"You'll make sure he gets the message."

"Yeah, boss."

"Jacob Lev."

"Yeah."

MARQUESSA DUVALL'S LAST KNOWN address was a pink stucco cottage on Berryman Avenue, in Culver City. Like the rest of the houses on the block, it'd had some money pumped into it during the most recent boom. The roof looked new. Geometric topiaries flanked a short front walk. It might have been a nice place to live, save the fact that it backed up to an eighteen-foot cinder-block wall, behind which roared the 405 South.

The noise would make it easy to miss a couple of shots.

Forensics of the residence had come up blank. No blood. No forced entry. No sign of struggle. No foreign DNA, or none that could be linked to anyone on the suspect list.

As a crime scene, it was arid.

What Jacob wanted was a launching point for sympathy.

If he was totally honest, he had nowhere else to turn.

The house's current occupants, a young couple with a kinetic Shetland sheepdog, had never heard of Marquessa. Jacob's presence alarmed them, so after a walk-through, he left them in peace.

The next-door neighbor was a mid-sixties man named Jorge Alvarez.

"I remember her," he said.

He invited Jacob in and settled himself in a melon-green La-Z-Boy. The living room smelled like cat.

"She wasn't here long," Alvarez said. "Year, year and a half. Nice gal, great smile. The boy, TJ, he was cute, too. Very bright."

Jacob mentally cataloged it: she called him TJ. A simple fact that made both mother and child that much realer.

That was good, and that was awful.

Alvarez said, "I used to throw the ball around with him. I felt bad knowing his father was out of the picture."

"Were there other men around?"

"Oh, sure. She was a good-looking woman. A knockout, truth be told."

"Anyone who stands out?"

"It's not like I was keeping records," Alvarez said. "For a while there was a limo coming to pick her up. They used to block my driveway."

Not in the file. "Did you mention that to the police?"

"I really can't remember," Alvarez said. "Probably I did. I'll tell you, Detective, I didn't appreciate the way you guys handled it, storming in here, crawling all over the place. I'm not sure what I was asked and what I wasn't. A few times I offered my help and got the feeling I was being a nuisance."

"A limo," Jacob said, writing it in his pad, wanting this talkative man to know he was being taken seriously.

"Whale of a car," Alvarez said. "She'd go out in a tight dress. The dress I remember because it was shiny. Shiny little gold thing."

"Did you see who was driving or riding?"

Alvarez shook his head.

"Any idea where they went?"

"I didn't ask."

Jacob said, "Who took care of TJ while she was out?"

"She took him with her."

"In the limo?"

Alvarez nodded.

"What did you make of that?"

"What do you mean?"

"It's not necessarily what I would expect."

"Did you grow up with a single mother?" Alvarez said.

Jacob nearly replied *single father*. He shook his head.

"I did," Alvarez said. "I know the sacrifices they make. So, no, I didn't think it was strange. I figured she was doing what she needed to do. It wasn't that often. Couple times a month, maybe."

"What time of day did they leave?"

Alvarez skimmed a hand over his pate. "Now you're making me think. Evening, I guess. And don't ask me when they came back because I never saw that. I go to sleep early. I'm retired."

"From what?"

"I was a teacher over at Stoner Avenue Elementary." Alvarez smiled at the memory. "Math and science, fifth and sixth grade."

Jacob hesitated. "I need to ask this, sir: did you ever get the impression Marquessa was charging for her services?"

Alvarez said, "I couldn't say."

"But not a definite no."

"Look, I was her neighbor. That was it. I don't judge people. What she did with her free time wasn't my affair. The limo? Maybe she took her son because she had a rich boyfriend who was okay with that. In that case, more strength to her."

"Anything else you'd like to tell me?"

"Only what I told the detectives a few years ago," Alvarez said. "I can't imagine anyone who'd want to hurt that woman."

———

JACOB WORKED THE REST of the block without success, finishing as the sun sawed into the horizon. Avoiding a freeway dense with red lights, he navigated Venice Boulevard, slowing as he came up on the apartment complex where Dr. Divya Das lived.

He couldn't blame her for the long stretch of silence between them—longer, in fact, than the freeze between him and his father. There had been no official reason for her to get in touch. She worked at the Coroner's, and he no longer worked murders.

She belonged to Special Projects, and to Mallick.

Still, she could have called. She could have checked up on him during those early months when he nightly thrashed himself awake; could've sent the occasional e-mail. Her withdrawal felt personal, and while his attraction to her had largely faded, her rejection continued to sting.

I'm not like you, Jacob.

Understatement. She was tall and smart and charming and beautiful, and ultimately untrustworthy. He'd made the mistake of allowing himself to think of her as a friend, probably because she was the best actor in the troupe.

He hadn't contacted her, either.

Vanity and bullshit.

Tonight, he pulled over outside her building. He thought about buzzing up, called instead and got her voicemail.

"Hey," he said. "I'm in your neighborhood, wondering if I could drop by. No worries, though. Hope you're well."

HE ARRIVED AT THE CARE FACILITY after seven, stopping to retrieve the packet of Plasticine from his mother's nightstand. Out on the patio, Bina sat beneath the fig tree, gazing up at the branches, her tray of food finished and awaiting removal.

"Hey, Ima."

An extraordinary thing happened: her hands stopped fiddling.

She turned to face him.

He stood still, his heart shouting with wild hope.

Because damn if she didn't look surprised.

It wasn't his regular day.

Surprise implied expectation. Expectation implied awareness.

Awareness implied more than anyone had given her credit for.

"Ima," he said.

She looked back up at the tree.

Desperate not to lose her, he hurried over to the bench, dropping his backpack on the ground. "Hey there, hey. How are you? I wanted to see you. See how you're feeling."

She was slipping away, cheeks slackening, eyes going hazy.

"It's cold out here. Do you want another blanket? Ima? I can get you one. Ima. A nice warm blanket . . ."

He kept yammering. He wanted to shake her, to scream in her ear: *come back.*

Limp. Mute. Gone.

Gutted, he slumped on the bench, and for a few moments the two of them were equally vegetative. Then her hands resumed their hollow march.

A passage of Talmud, memento of a previous life, leaked into his mind.

Since the destruction of the Holy Temple, prophecy was taken from the prophets and given to children and fools.

"Marquessa," he said.

No reaction.

"Marquessa Duvall," he said. A click in his throat. "Ring a bell?"

Bina knitted air.

"Thomas White? TJ? He was Marquessa's—"

Why was he doing this?

"He was her son."

Nothing.

He pressed on: "You saw their pictures."

Silence, broken by the distant blare of a car horn.

"You saw the pictures. Ima, are you hearing me?"

He ripped off a chunk of Plasticine and began softening it between his palms. It had dried out, colors mashed together to produce a dirty brownish swirl.

"You made a bird."

He pressed the ball of clay into her jittery right hand.

"Do it again. Please. Make me another beautiful bird?"

He let go of her fingers. They fell open and the wad plopped to the ground.

He tried again. She wouldn't hold on.

He had the file in his backpack, the crime scene photos.

He asked himself a brutal question: did he want to help her or use her?

Use her to what end, though? The more he thought about her outburst, the more convinced he felt that it had been nonspecific. Showing her the photos would be pointless.

Pointless, and cruel.

He needed to get out of there before he did or said something he'd regret.

"I've gotta go," he said, standing. "I'll see you Friday."

CHAPTER TWELVE

BOIS DE BOULOGNE

16EME ARRONDISSEMENT, PARIS, FRANCE

The *police scientifique* had begun to pack up, affording Capitaine Théo Breton his first opportunity to think without distraction. He crouched at the center of the clearing, unwarmed by his anorak and scarf, covering the cough that kept insisting up his throat, reading the trees and tasting the emotional nature of the scene, the hole in the canopy like the roof of a pagan temple.

From his left, from his right, the obscene stare of woman and child fell relentlessly upon him.

They were markedly underdressed, she in a ruffled white shirt and a black miniskirt, the opaque tops of her pantyhose peeking out. Oily black hair draped the left half of her face. A gunshot wound marred the center of her forehead. The boy wore jeans and a Hugo Lloris jersey, and he had the same wound, as though it was an inherited trait, a black cavity standing out against the rest of his skin, which had gone a violent, chemical blue.

It disturbed Breton to realize that he had already begun to conceive of them as mother and son.

A whistle: Dédé Vallot, waving to warn him: the prosecutor had arrived.

Breton stood, knees popping. He had a backache, an auger boring into his kidney. He coughed into his elbow, smiling at the dapper man waddling over to offer a soft hand.

The prosecutor said, "*Bonjour*, Théo."

"*Bonjour, monsieur le procureur.*"

Breton did his duty, walking him around the crime scene. Animals had mucked the area up, and the ground had since refrozen, leaving a veneer of ice and no footprints. The man who had discovered the bodies, a pensioner hunting winter mushrooms, was hospitalized with a panic attack, unable to remember if he had touched anything.

The prosecutor's name was Lambert. He was bundled up in a cashmere coat, like a spoiled child, his cheeks bright red. He said, "I must tell you, Théo, I've had complaints that your boys are not helping the situation. 'Tramping around like a Mongol horde' was how the criminalist put it."

Breton said nothing. He had gotten adept at concealing displeasure. Smart *procureurs* knew their rightful place: behind a desk. They knew what they were and more importantly what they were not. Not cops, not psychologists, not television stars.

Lambert said, "You ought to keep them on a tighter leash."

"I'll bear it in mind."

The *procureur* breathed on his hands. "Press been by?"

"Not yet."

"This sort of thing, they can be helpful for identifying the victim."

And for getting your fat face in the paper. "Of course."

"You've begun your canvass."

"Martinez and Berline are out as we speak."

"I suggest that they focus their efforts on the Allée de Long-champ."

"Most of the prostitutes scattered before we could talk to them."

"Then come back tonight, when they've returned," Lambert said. "Someone will recognize her."

"No one has so far," Breton said.

"You said yourself: they ran off. Keep at it."

"I've never known a prostitute to bring her son to work," Breton said.

"Maybe she couldn't find a babysitter. Ballistics?"

"Nothing yet."

"The bullet might be embedded in the ground. Or in a tree."

"Mm."

"He must have picked up the casings."

"Or it was a revolver," Breton said.

"Yes, as I was going to say. You know, Théo, you might consider the possibility that they were killed elsewhere."

Breton was getting tired of this guy. He was getting tired of every-thing. His insides churned, his mouth felt cottony, his skin raged with itches and areas of needlepoint sensitivity.

"They were definitely shot elsewhere," he said. "There's no spatter."

"And," Lambert said, warming to his theme, "there was more than one killer. You can't move two bodies a great distance on your own."

You couldn't, you slob.

Then again, Breton had to admit that neither could he, these days.

Lambert squinted through the trees in the direction of the road. "They drove up, dragged them here, drove off. Twenty minutes, maximum."

"Longer than that," Breton said.

The prosecutor frowned at being contradicted. "What makes you say that."

"It's a hundred twenty meters over rough ground. The bodies were staged carefully."

Lambert spiked a lawyer's finger. "Which proves my earlier point. That amount of commotion, the whores must have noticed something. It's inevitable."

He bent, putting his face level with the woman's. "Any sense of how long they've been here?"

Breton shook his head.

"They're very well preserved."

"It's been cold."

"No nibbling, I mean," Lambert said, straightening. "Well. You may continue to investigate it *en flagrance*, for the moment, anyway. We'll revisit the question once we've heard what the pathologist has to say."

Breton nodded. That, at least, was decent news. Once the case became an official inquiry, he would lose control.

Lambert had turned to stare at the boy. "What is he? Five?"

Breton shook his head. He lacked a point of reference, but Pierrot Martinez, who had two boys of his own, had guessed six or seven. Registering the anxiety in his voice, Breton had taken pity and sent him out to canvass.

Lambert sighed. *"Monstrous,"* he said.

Inwardly, Breton agreed, but he found the *proc*'s stage-bound tone distasteful.

"Don't you find it uncomfortable? Why doesn't someone shut their eyes?"

Breton said, "You're welcome to try."

Lambert glanced at him uncertainly.

"He sliced their eyelids off," Breton said.

With grim satisfaction, he observed the Prosecutor's jowls twitch.

"Is that—really . . ." Lambert fumbled for a cigarette, fired up, sucked in a breath, offering the pack to Breton as an afterthought.

"No, thanks."

"You quit? Since when?"

Breton did not answer.

Lambert took another deep drag. His fingers still shook a bit. "Anyway. It's . . . But—you're well, otherwise?"

"Superb," Breton said.

"Busy."

"Always."

"I understand. There's no need to be a hero."

Breton looked at him.

Lambert said, "We can agree that the Crim is better equipped to handle this."

"I'm sure I don't know what you mean, *monsieur le procureur*."

"Don't be so sensitive, Théo."

Breton said, "They're busy at the Crim, too."

"Yes, of course. Big cases. Media. I wouldn't want you to feel overwhelmed."

"That's nice of you."

"Of course. I only want to help." The *procureur* checked his watch. "My appointment book is full. *Au revoir*."

When he'd gone, Dédé Vallot ambled over, scratching his goatee. "That guy's a twat."

Breton clapped him on the arm. "Go back. Start checking missing persons."

Vallot nodded and departed.

The attendants were getting ready to remove the bodies. Breton watched them cover the woman and place her on a stretcher. He did not watch them deal with the boy.

AN HOUR LATER, as Breton was about to leave the scene, Lambert had his revenge.

"Bonjour, Capitaine."

She offered her ID card, presumably to show him that she, too, was a captain. Her name was Odette Pelletier, and she was young, trim, nice looking, with dyed blond hair and slanted dark eyes that parsed him like a supermarket scanner.

"The *proc* sends his regards," she said. "He's asked me to assist you."

As a rule, Breton adored women. He had known a fair number of them in his day. He fancied himself something of an expert. His own mother was a woman! But he didn't want them on his team. They complicated the dynamic he'd worked so hard to cultivate: the coffee and smoke breaks, evenings at the cinema watching American and Japanese action movies, Saturdays at his cottage outside Auxerre, kicking around a flappy football.

Your boys Lambert had called them. And so they were. Around the division they were known as *les Bretons*, as though he had personally sired every one of them.

As far as family went, that would have to do.

Odette Pelletier tossed back a shelf of hair. She was wearing a leather motorcycle jacket and black jeans, a bright green scarf tucked in at her throat, a crescent of paper-white skin visible at her neckline. Around her wrist was an odd, chunky bracelet made of matching green rubber. Breton wondered at it before grasping that it was one of those fitness trackers, the kind that buzzed at you when you'd completed your daily death march of ten thousand steps. He felt a mild pulse of contempt.

"So," she said. "What do I need to know?"

"We should meet later," he said. "You're not dressed for the cold."

He even disliked her teeth when she smiled. Too white, like a print ad.

"I'll survive," she said.

As he had done for the *procureur*, Breton led her in orbit around the scene, pointing out the location of the bodies, now gone, and describing their positioning.

She asked to see his camera. He watched her thumb through, her face placid and emotionless. It was worse than he'd realized, far worse: she was one of those women who thought she was a man.

"Lambert feels we should be looking for a missing prostitute," he said.

"And you feel differently."

"The women don't recognize her as one of their own."

Pelletier peered at the camera. "She's not dressed like a hooker."

Now that she was agreeing with him, Breton felt compelled to adopt the opposite stance. "That depends on what you want in a hooker," he said.

"Looks like a uniform to me. A maid, or something."

"Some men like that," he said.

"Do they."

"It's a type of fantasy."

"If only I had you with me all the time," she said. "To help me navigate the tangled jungle of the male mind."

He smiled thinly.

"If you'd like," she said, "I could have a word with the girls along the Allée de Longchamp. They might be more forthcoming with a woman."

"They're not shy," he said.

"Not while doing business. They might be in this situation."

"My men know how to seduce a witness."

She raised an eyebrow, returned to the camera.

"It's personal," she said. "Don't you think?"

He shifted to see what she was looking at: the boy.

"The *proc* called them mother and son," she said. "Do we know that for a fact?"

"DNA will tell us."

She handed him the camera. "I'm not any happier about this arrangement than you are, Capitaine."

"I doubt that."

"Think whatever you want. It's not a promotion for me."

Wind blasted through the trees, shattering branches. Breton hunched into his anorak—a reflex he regretted when Pelletier did not flinch.

"Here," she said.

She was offering him a tissue.

"I'm fine."

"You're not," she said. "You've got a nosebleed."

His face had gone numb; he didn't feel it running down his lip, but then it reached his mouth and he tasted the liverish tang. He grabbed the tissue and pressed it to his nose.

"Tilt your head back," she said. "Pinch."

"I know," he said irritably.

"Maybe you want to step aside," she said. "To avoid contaminating the scene."

He gave a grunt but moved to the edge of the clearing. Thinking that it was an accurate, if unsubtle, symbol. How long before he was completely marginalized?

Odette Pelletier said, "It's the dryness. I get them, too."

The blood was slowing to a trickle. Breton waved off a second tissue.

"Anyway, I'm here," she said. "You may as well make the most of the opportunity. Or whatever it is to you."

He gestured haphazardly at the acres of snow and dead wood. "Why don't you take a walk? See what you can find. It's a big park."

"Very well." Giving him a mock salute, she tramped off, a bright green anomaly in the monochrome. Then she vanished altogether, and Breton felt minimally better.

He pressed the pad of his thumb to his nose, checked for blood. Negative.

He cupped his hands and yelled to Sibony that he was heading out.

He hiked back through the trees and up the road to his unmarked. It would have been just as easy to walk from the commissariat, but he was exhausted.

He drove a kilometer south from the scene, pulling over near a barren copse. From the glove compartment he took a beige vinyl case with a zippered top. He opened it and shook out a disposable lighter and a plastic bag containing seven marijuana cigarettes.

He selected the fattest one and lit up. He adjusted the seat back, shut off the police radio, and switched on France Musique. They were broadcasting live from the Umbria Winter Jazz Festival. Abdullah Ibrahim was playing "Damara Blue."

CHAPTER THIRTEEN

Dolly Duvall met Jacob at the door to her house, an outlier on an otherwise ramshackle block of 113th Street. Fresh paint along the trim; flower beds brimming with bright winter annuals to match her yellow floral-print skirt suit, which in turn matched yellow lizard-skin pumps.

"Please come in, Detective."

Jacob stepped into the living room, where the same level of order prevailed, not a doily askew. Ceramic doodads lined up in height order. A wall tiled with photographs of children and grandchildren—Marquessa and TJ at its center.

"Punctual," Dolly said. "I appreciate that."

He'd arrived early in order to knock at noon on the dot. He was operating on stolen time. The weekend was over, his extracurricular activities—that's what Marquessa and TJ were, a side project—eating into the massive task that awaited him at the archive.

It felt good to stick it to Mallick, however trivially.

Sinking into a champagne-colored brocade sofa, he accepted a cup of coffee, reaching for a slice of crumb cake out of politeness; then reaching for seconds.

Dolly regarded him with amusement. "You like my baking."

"Yes, ma'am. Outstanding."

"I'm glad. You should be, too. It's a privilege not many people get to enjoy."

"I appreciate it." He wiped his mouth. "And, Mrs. Duvall, thanks for seeing me. I know revisiting this has to be tough."

Dolly shifted, looked away, as if readying herself for an injection. "Go on, then."

He opened his notebook. "First off, let me ask if there's anything you'd like to share with me about Marquessa."

She didn't answer.

"Unless that's too—"

"I'm thinking, Detective. It's not easy to sum up your own child."

Jacob nodded.

"She was my baby," Dolly said. "I didn't *baby* her, mind. Everyone else did, though. She had a way about her that made you want to sweep her up. Her brothers and sisters used to pass her back and forth like she was a rag doll. They called her Dolly Two, because she took after me."

Dolly Duvall had smooth skin, regal bone structure, elegant calves—a glimpse of Marquessa's uprooted future.

"How many in the family?" he asked.

"Five boys and four girls, and I raised them on my own after my husband passed. Marquessa was eighteen when she had TJ. He was like one of my own. Then they moved all the way across town."

Dolly took a sip of coffee. "I taught my children to choose their own paths. My other girls live up the corner. My boys, too. Their children. Everyone comes over on Sundays." She pressed her lips together. "Marquessa chose to leave."

"Did you get to see them much?"

"I don't drive."

"I'm wondering why they moved. TJ's father—"

Dolly cut him off with a shake of the head. "He never came around. I wouldn't let him in the house."

"Were he and Marquessa in touch?"

"I was given to believe that Thomas Sr. wasn't considered a suspect."

"No, ma'am, he's not. I ask because romantic relationships can be relevant in different ways."

She snorted. "There's nothing romantic about a silly young girl falling for an older boy with a fancy car. I never understand about cars. A fellow comes into some money, that's the first thing he runs out and spends it on, a new ride."

Her scorn put *I don't drive* in a new light—staking out the moral high ground.

She said, "I don't see how he could've hurt her, though. He was incarcerated."

People had friends. Nasty guys had nasty friends. He said nothing, though.

"No," Dolly said, "I never will believe it was him. He was lazy and crude, but I never saw him show a temper."

Having checked Thomas White Sr.'s record, Jacob tended to agree. A whole mess of drug offenses, but nothing violent. On top of that, both Ballard and Krikorian had worked the personal angle exhaustively. Still, Jacob knew that a neglected question could prove disastrous.

He said, "How come Marquessa moved away?"

"She couldn't get what she wanted living here with me. I told her, 'Fine, then, you go and get it your own self.'"

"What did she want?"

"Money. She always had an eye for nice things. She'd cut out pictures from her sisters' fashion magazines and strut around the house. Everybody laughed and gave her attention. It was cute when she was four. Then she grew up, and we started rubbing up against each other. Do you know how you get to be after you raise nine kids?"

Jacob shook his head.

"Tired," Dolly said. "You get bone-tired. Marquessa, I loved her, but she was an arguer, and I was done arguing. More coffee?"

"Please."

She was gone longer than necessary, and when she came back from the kitchen, he noticed retouched lipstick.

"Marquessa talked about wanting to be an actress," she said, sitting down. "I asked why she needed to move so far, and she told me she had to get close to the action."

"Action, meaning . . . ?"

"Movie people, I guess. And she did work, I'll grant her that. She never asked me for help. She paid her own bills."

"Acting."

"Mostly it was modeling. Nobody could say she wasn't something to look at. That was the trouble."

He waited in vain for her to expand. "Besides TJ's father, were there men in her life?"

Dolly stiffened. "I've talked about all this before to those other detectives."

"I know, ma'am."

"Once she left my house, she could do as she pleased."

"What about an agent? A manager?"

"She didn't discuss it with me. Her sister might know. They were close. I can call her if you'd like."

"Would you mind? It'd be helpful."

Dolly left the room again, allowing him to sneak a third piece of coffee cake.

"Farrah will be by shortly," Dolly said, returning. She glanced at the half-empty plate. "I can see you've got a healthy appetite. Take another."

"Thanks. I really shouldn't."

"Well, you do what you do."

He let her ease into talk of simpler things—the weather, gardening. Ten minutes later, the front door opened and a woman stepped in. Farrah Duvall was heavier than her sister but still striking. Three small boys scurried in behind her. They saw Dolly and came to attention.

"Hello, Gram."

"Hello, Gram."

"Hello, Gram."

Dolly inspected them, fussed with them, gave them each a piece of cake on a napkin, and sent them to the backyard. Once they'd gone, she aimed a scowl at Farrah. "You didn't say nothing about bringing them kids."

"Mama. What'm I supposed to do? Leave them so they can destroy my house?"

Dolly shook her head. "Have some cake."

"I'm not hungry," Farrah said.

Dolly rolled her eyes.

Farrah sat in an armchair. "My mother said you asked about an agent," she said, handing Jacob a wrinkled silver business card.

A² TALENT

A URL but nothing more. Commerce in the Internet age.

"Can I hang on to this?" he asked.

Farrah nodded.

"Thanks. Any idea what sort of modeling Marquessa did?"

"Clothing," Dolly said. "I have some of her catalogs."

"In the file it says she also did some hostessing," he said.

"I guess," Farrah said.

"We're talking parties?" He was thinking of the limousine Jorge Alvarez had described. "Events?"

"She made sure I knew she was living the good life," Dolly said. "Getting paid for standing around and looking nice. 'That's all I have to do, Mama. Look hot.'"

"Was she dating anyone?" he asked Farrah.

She gave a noncommittal shrug, but Jacob noticed her squirm. He wished Dolly would go outside to supervise the boys—he could hear them raising hell—so he could speak to Farrah unchaperoned. But when one of the boys began to wail, she sighed and got up and went to check.

Dolly said, "More cake?"

HE LEFT WITH A FULL STOMACH, but unsatisfied. Started the Honda, began to back out.

Farrah came hustling out of the house, carrying a plastic shopping bag.

He rolled down the window.

"She wants you to have the rest of the cake," she said.

Despite himself, Jacob laughed. "Thanks."

Farrah smiled nervously, shifting from foot to foot. "I don't like to talk about it in front of my mom, cause it makes her upset. But a couple of months before it happened, Marquessa started acting strange."

"Strange how?"

"Not strange," Farrah said. "Erase that. More like—okay, she always liked to brag, this and that. But all of a sudden, she's got bank to back it up. Don't ask me where she got it from. I'd tell you if I knew."

"A neighbor of hers told me a limo used to come pick her up," Jacob said.

"Wouldn't surprise me. She used to work those events, like you said. She told me about it. Like, they put her in a string bikini and she stands up on a table, sticking her butt out. I remember one time she brought me this bag they gave her, and it had a ton of stuff in it, gift certificates, and a three-hundred-dollar pair of headphones. And it was like a *nice* bag, not some piece of plastic. I still have it. The card I gave you, that was in there, too. I was like, 'They just give you this? For *free?*' She told me all the models get them. And I was like, 'Damn, I need to lose me twenty-five pounds.'"

"Running with a rich crowd."

"Absolutely."

"Did she mention any names?"

"I asked her sometimes—like, did she know anybody famous? But she just got all high and mighty about it. 'I can't tell you that.'"

A breeze stirred. Farrah hugged herself. "I'm sorry. I know how I sound. I used to feel angry. I thought it was her fault she got herself into trouble. Now I'm just sad."

Jacob nodded.

"My sister," she began, before falling silent.

She said, "My sister had dignity. She expected people to treat her like a princess, so they did."

A curtain parted in the front window. Dolly's face appeared. She rapped sharply.

"I need to go," Farrah said, and she double-timed it up the front walk.

Jacob held up the shopping bag, mouthed, "Thank you," at the window.

Dolly let the curtain fall back into place.

CHAPTER FOURTEEN

For the next few days, Jacob went back to the archive to resume his routine of reading and typing and forcibly liberating bugs. Marquessa and TJ were never far from his mind. He took the file with him when he left the hangar. Not to read; he'd been over it enough. Just to have. To remind himself that he was still a detective.

On a chilly Wednesday, he heard footsteps coming up the aisle, and a familiar, dancing voice called out his name.

"Over here," he said.

Six-plus spectacular feet of Divya Das materialized from the shadows like a struck match. She was dressed in white linen slacks—gutsy choice for a pathologist—and a silk blouse in her preferred orange. Black hair buried one shoulder. Her eyes were huge and glittering, her mouth amused as she took in his sad little fiefdom. "So this is where they've got you."

"I've always considered exile romantic."

"It's bloody freezing in here. How do you stand it?"

He indicated the space heater.

"Those things are terrible fire hazards," she said.

"Let's hope so." Waving at the acres of paper. "Save me a shitload of work."

Divya laughed. "Have you taken your lunch?"

"Nope."

"Want company?"

"You buying?"

"Cheek. Well, fine, I'm in a benevolent mood."

"Good deal," Jacob said. "I'll drive."

"No," she said, switching off the space heater. "I believe I'd rather."

HE REMEMBERED HER OLD CAR, a silver Toyota sedan dating to the turn of the millennium. The upgrade shocked him.

Orange Corvette, chrome rims, a discreet little spoiler.

She laid a loving hand on the hood. "It improves the commute."

Jacob just managed to buckle his seat belt before she peeled out, spitting gravel.

The howl of the engine made conversation a nonstarter, so he settled back. It was hard not to see Mallick's hand in her drop-in. The voicemail Jacob had left her mentioned nothing about his assignment, yet she'd tracked him down easily enough.

As excited as he felt to see her, he could not lose focus on the fact that, in the end, she was still one of them.

Taking city streets at dangerous speeds, she arrived at a strip mall on Rosemead.

"Your bonus," he said, after she'd cut the motor.

"Pardon?"

"After the Pernath case, I got a check for ten grand." He tapped the dash. "Not that that would cover the down payment on this."

Divya shrugged. "I heard you didn't cash yours."

"It costs more than that to buy me off."

"So cynical. Why not just see it as a reward for a job well done?"

"I understand why they'd bribe me," he said. "I'm supposed to pretend what happened didn't happen. But why you?"

They had pulled up in front of a restaurant called Flavors of Bombay. Divya continued to grip the steering wheel, stacks of glass bangles tinkling on slender, cinnamon-colored wrists.

"I've told you before," she said. "We're not all the same."

"No?"

"No. And frankly I'm insulted that you continue to act as if we are."

"You take orders from Mallick."

"As do you," she said.

He said nothing.

"You need to learn who your friends are," she said.

Jacob glanced at the restaurant. "This place any good?"

"Yelp seems to think so."

"You don't have to take me for Indian food. I wouldn't take you for gefilte fish."

She drew the key from the ignition. "Thank God for that."

THE DINING ROOM WAS PACKED. A waiter handed them menus, but halfheartedly, knowing full well they were going to opt for the $8.95 buffet.

"You go first," Divya said. "I'll watch our things."

Jacob joined the line, piling a plate with rice, dal, saag paneer, lamb tikka masala.

In his absence, a basket of naan had appeared on the table, along with two plastic tumblers of water. He spread his napkin on his lap, waiting for Divya to take her turn at the buffet. She didn't budge.

"Start," she said. "It'll get cold."

"Don't make me eat alone," he said.

She got up to join the line, came back with a basically bare plate.

"I'm sorry I missed your call the other day," she said. "I was out."

"It's not like I gave you any notice."

"What brought you to my neck of the woods?"

He grinned, spooning spinach onto a triangle of flatbread. "That didn't take long."

"I'm making conversation, Jacob."

"Perhaps the mysteries of Culver City entranced me."

"Might I point out that you called me? I'm exhibiting normal curiosity."

It was true. She'd never done anything to cause him to distrust or resent her.

Still: one of them.

She said, "I know you've had a damned hard time of it. How could you not? What you saw that night—there's not a person on earth capable of holding it in their head. Even you."

He snorted.

"Don't undersell yourself," she said.

"Oh, but that's part of my charm."

She smiled. She reached across the table and took his hand. He was too surprised to move away, and once they were touching he saw no reason to let go.

He said, "I've got a case I'm looking into."

She nodded as though she already knew.

Maybe she did.

But her skin felt warm and comforting, embers at the end of a long night, and right then, he didn't care if she was manipulating him. Right then, he didn't give a shit about anything but a dead woman and her son.

Divya said, "Do you want to talk about it?"

He did.

"THAT'S ALL I've got so far."

The restaurant had emptied out. Jacob had finished his food, gone up for seconds.

Divya had yet to unwrap her silverware, was staring over woven hands at her untouched plate. She said, "Kids always get to me."

He nodded. "Any thoughts?"

She seemed reluctant to speak. Shook it off. "The mutilation," she said. "Your description put me in mind of someone with surgical experience."

"I had the same thought. Doctor, dentist, nurse, vet. The file doesn't mention anyone who meets the criteria, but it's far from complete. Have you ever heard of anything like that? Just the eyelids gone?"

"Thankfully not."

He said, "When I was at the scene, I had this weird idea. Kids, you know how they'll set up their stuffed animals?"

"As an audience," she said.

"Exactly. I'm not sure what it means. Marquessa was a model, so she had experience with being looked at. Posing."

"Your bad guy was reversing the process?"

"Maybe. I don't know. I've been calling the modeling agency, but they keep putting me off. I'm going to go over there in person as soon as I get a chance."

He stirred his cup of rice pudding. "I'd appreciate if you told Mallick that I'm diligently applying myself to my day job and nothing else."

"Will do."

He said, "I want so badly to believe you."

"Then believe."

Jacob smiled sadly. He chinned at her tray. "Don't you ever eat?"

"Your case ruined my appetite."

That he most assuredly did not believe. Generally speaking, crypt doctors had the strongest stomachs around. You saw bags of Doritos lying open on autopsy tables.

"Not just now," he said. "Not just you. All of you. Mallick. Schott. I bought Mel Subach a piece of baklava last year and he made a huge deal about how he couldn't touch it cause he's on a diet."

"And so he should be," she said. "He's a tub."

"Apparently not from excess calories," he said.

She snatched a shred of naan from the basket and stuffed it in her mouth, chewing with effort, her long neck convulsing, her eyes watering as she worked to get it down. He began to worry she would choke. "Hey," he said. "Take it easy."

She gagged, pounded her chest.

"Are you okay?"

She reached for her water glass, took a spiteful sip, and showed him an empty mouth.

"Happy?" she said.

She sounded hoarse and close to tears.

Taken aback, he said, "I didn't mean you had to—"

"Leave off," she said. "Please."

Silence.

"I'm sorry," he said.

She took out a twenty. "Don't worry," she said. "I earned this myself."

CHAPTER FIFTEEN

The El Al stewardesses pin their little hats on with one hand, using the other to hold back the crush of bodies in the aisle.

Children wail and adults shove and bags rain from the overhead bins. Fourteen hours in the air, and Barbara hasn't slept one second. Dazed, dehydrated, she clings to Frayda's sleeve, and together they inch toward the exit.

When they finally step out, they're hit with a blast of heat and light. Barbara hesitates at the top of the steps, blinking, and receives a swift elbow to the back from the octogenarian behind her.

Nu!

She stumbles her way down to the tarmac. The welcome committee consists of a pair of rust-bucket minibuses belching exhaust. A few people have already climbed aboard and are tapping their feet impatiently, waiting to be driven to the arrival terminal. Many more of the passengers have fallen to their hands and knees, pressing their lips to the cracked, oil-stained ground. They weep and chant prayers of thanksgiving.

Bless you, Lord, our God, Ruler of the universe, Who has given us life, and sustained us, and enabled us to reach this moment.

Frayda drops to her knees.

Barbara shakily sinks down beside her. Gravel bites into the flesh of her palms.

She kisses the earth.

Her first impression of the land of Israel, ancestral home of her people, will always be smarting hands, the astringent stink of jet fuel, sacred dust coating her tongue.

THE SULAM WOMEN'S SEMINARY is located in the West Jerusalem suburb of Bayit V'Gan, atop a hill that forms the third point of a triangle with Sha'arei Tzedek hospital and the Yad Vashem Holocaust memorial.

Sulam, Frayda explains, means "ladder" in Hebrew.

Bayit V'Gan means "a house and a garden," and that's essentially what the place is, or was, before Frayda's uncle Rav Kalman bought it: a shambling pile of Jerusalem stone plopped down at the end of a dirt cul-de-sac.

Barbara drags her suitcases into a stuffy foyer dimmed by metal shutters, the air vaguely redolent of noodle soup. She starts looking around for food, but there's nothing doing, and within a day or two she will come to realize that the whole school smells that way, all the time, an aroma equal parts salty human sweat and floury baked paper, finished with a glaze of bookbinding glue.

Books huddle three deep on cinder-block shelves.

Books on the tables, on the chairs; books the upholstery of cast-off furniture.

Books the only adornment, unless you count the small tapestry hanging from a nail in the dun-colored plaster, a verse embroidered in golden thread.

And you shall meditate on it, day and night.

Books, a landscape in flux, like the city of Jerusalem itself. Put one down and leave the room and it might very well materialize elsewhere, opened to a different page. The same principle of communal ownership applies to hairbrushes, pencils, socks, cosmetics—a loosening of the boundaries between *yours* and *mine*.

The student body consists of seven girls, including her and Frayda, the others a pair of Israelis and three from England. All except Barbara were raised religious. All except Barbara speak Hebrew.

As such, she is an object of fascination. Why has she come? It's not a challenge, just friendly interest. They know the literal answer. She came because Frayda brought her, and Frayda came because her uncle runs the place.

But *why*?

Upstairs are two bedrooms, shockingly inadequate by American standards. Some miraculous geometry has enabled Rav Kalman to fit three beds in each room. The Brits—Wendy, Dafna, and Margalit—bunk together, and Barbara moves in with the Israelis, a pair of warmhearted girls from old Jerusalemite families. Allegedly this arrangement will help her practice her Hebrew, although her roommates refuse to speak anything but English to her, so that they can practice their English.

"I am so exciting to meet you," Zahava says.

"Excit*ed*. 'I'm so excit*ed* to meet you.'"

"Ah, yes?"

"Please," Shlomit says, "you like *petel*?"

Barbara warily sips the cup of scarlet liquid, sweet to the point of bitterness.

"Yum," she gasps.

"Take more," Shlomit says, pouring.

Barbara has most of the bureau to herself. She packed light, but the Israelis—all the other girls, for that matter—own nearly nothing, content to wear the same skirt two weeks running. Barbara tries to emulate them, to simplify. In the shower, she shuts off the tap while shampooing, in order to conserve water.

Soap runs into her eyes; she wipes it away and looks down and screams.

"What it is," Zahava says, running in. "What."

Barbara can only point at the giant roach that has crawled out of the drain.

"Ah, yes," Zahava says. "One moment."

She calls Shlomit into the bathroom.

"Wow," Shlomit, "look this *juke*."

"Kill it," Barbara yells. She is sudsy, smushed into the corner. *"Kill it."*

But the Israelis are admiring the insect, using their hands to estimate its size.

"This *juke*," Zahava says philosophically, "is a finer *juke*."

"Kill it *now*."

With a sigh of regret, Shlomit removes her sandal and slaps it down, splattering shell and guts.

AND YOU SHALL MEDITATE on it, day and night.

There is no curriculum, no real schedule. By six-thirty a.m., everyone's awake and praying—all except Barbara, who stands with her *siddur* open, eyes blurring at the muddy field of words.

Afterward they breakfast on sliced cucumbers, feta, tea. Rav

Kalman's wife, Rivka, serves as mother hen and cook. She and her husband make up the sum total of the staff, unless you count Moshe, the ancient Yemeni fixit who pedals around the neighborhood on a rattling bicycle, dropping in to patch leaks or unclog toilets. There's a sense of adventure, of life improvised, like they're camping indoors. Everyone has to pitch in, and the girls rotate helping out in the kitchen.

All except Barbara, who doesn't know the ins and outs of keeping kosher. On her third day, she causes a minor kerfuffle by using a meat fork to break off a piece of cheese, resulting in the whole precious chunk going in the trash, and the utensil being whisked outside for purification by burying.

Frayda lays a comforting hand on her shoulder. "It's okay. You didn't know. You'll learn."

Barbara fights back tears of humiliation. That's why she's here: to learn.

But how?

Trial and error? Until every last fork is jutting up out of the dirt?

Dear Máma and Taťka, Israel is amazing, and I am having a wonderful time.

During the morning session, the girls pair off to pore over passages of Talmud and commentaries. Officially, Barbara is the third wheel attached to Frayda and Wendy. Really, she spends the majority of the three-hour block floating around the room like a homeless electron, awash in Aramaic and Hebrew.

The others do their best to include her, and she puts on a show of gratitude, all the while sinking deeper into despair.

Dear Máma and Taťka, every day I learn something new.

What was Frayda thinking, bringing her here?

What was she thinking, coming along?

And you shall meditate on it, day—

At eleven, Rav Kalman appears, smiling beatifically through a luxuriant gray and black beard that spills like moss from the great tawny cliff of his face. He is a tall man, his shirtfronts tested to the limits. Whenever Barbara sees him, she instinctively cringes, afraid a button's going to come shooting off and take out her eye.

"My dear, holy daughters, good morning."

The girls rise out of respect. Then they gather around the dining room table for his lecture—also in Hebrew. Barbara can tell he's going slowly, for her sake. But it's still a torrent. Even with Frayda continually translating in her ear, she's absorbing at most half a percent, and she feels bad for interfering with Frayda's comprehension.

"I'm fine," Frayda insists. "And how else are you going to learn?"

Good question.

Dear Máma and Taťka—

Lunch is more vegetables and cheese, followed by an afternoon of free study, the girls recombining into new pairs to review the Bible or Prophets.

They're on their own for dinner. As a group they tramp down the dirt road to the neighborhood falafel stand, where thirty *agorot* buys a soft, fresh pita stuffed with shatteringly crispy chickpea fritters, stiff hummus, and watery tomatoes, washed down with a can of Tempo Cola.

Barbara stands at the side of the road, chewing and gazing out at the sunset, honey over the bleached limestone faces. To the north, Mount Herzl swells through the haze raised by a citywide frenzy of construction.

"Right, then," Wendy says. "What d'you make of it? Some place, no?"

Barbara smiles and tries not to cry.

———

ON A THURSDAY NIGHT, hopeless and exhausted after yet another day of floundering, she slips from her bed at four in the morning.

Bayit V'Gan; a house and a garden.

The garden behind Sulam is a rude dirt patch, sunk into the steep hillside and accessible via a rickety ladder. Nothing grows there except a stark, gnarled tree with oblong gray leaves. Sometimes she skips the afternoon session to sit under its branches, brooding and planning her escape.

The hardest part will be the look in her father's eye when she admits failure.

She backs down the ladder in the moonlight, touching bottom and feeling immediate relief: she can sob in peace.

Except she can't.

Rav Kalman sits at the base of the tree, a book in his lap, a penlight in one hand.

His eyes are closed, his barrel chest rising and falling steadily.

She turns to leave, quietly placing her foot on the lowest rung.

"Bina."

"I'm sorry," she says. Her heart is in her throat. "I didn't mean to wake you."

"Not at all. I wasn't asleep." He closes the book, pats the earth. "Please, join me."

She hesitates, then settles on the ground near him, leaning against the buckling retaining wall.

"Trouble sleeping?" Rav Kalman asks.

She nods.

"Me too." He holds up the book. "I could read to you. Put you right out."

She smiles weakly.

"What have you got there?" he asks.

She regards the packet in her hand with surprise. She forgot she was carrying it. "Clay."

"I see," he says. She can't tell if he disapproves.

It's not real clay. It's Plasticine. She tossed it in her suitcase at the last moment.

"My niece tells me you met in a pottery class," he says.

"Yes."

"She says you're very gifted. 'Brilliant' was the word she used."

Barbara shrugs. "It's just a hobby."

"You're being modest," he says. "That's fine. Maimonides says, everything in moderation, except humility. There's nothing wrong with being aware of one's talents, though. We all have them. God is generous."

"What's yours?" she asks.

"Lucky me: I have two. The first, you see, is a talent for spotting talent." He smiles, gestures to the Plasticine. "That's how I know it's more than a hobby for you."

She shifts uncomfortably. "And the second?"

"A strong stomach for adversity."

That much she can confirm. Whatever Barbara's feelings about her own place at Sulam, its very existence constitutes an act of bravery.

Men's yeshivas are commonplace. Frayda's fiancé, Yonatan, is in Israel, too, studying at a revered institution called the Mir. But the concept of advanced religious education for young women is virtually unheard of, and, to some, deeply threatening. The previous week, someone put a brick through the back window, along with a note quoting from tractate *Sotah*.

Rabbi Eliezer says: whoever teaches his daughter Torah, teaches her obscenity.

The incident seemed especially frightening given that Frayda's description of Jerusalem as free of crime has turned out to be largely accurate. Young children wander the streets unaccompanied by adults. There are outbreaks of Arab-Jewish friction, remnants of the Six-Day War, but they are sporadic and confined primarily to the eastern parts of the city. To have violence jam its snout into their mild, book-strewn corner of the universe horrified Barbara.

Frayda, on the other hand, was unbothered, either by the brick or by the idea. *The Talmud is lecture notes. Every opinion gets recorded, even the stupid ones.*

She dropped the note in the trash along with the swept-up shards.

Now Barbara regards Rav Kalman, the easy manner concealing a well of sadness. In a way he reminds her of her own parents—the unstoppable, grinding will to exist. He and Rivka live on the grounds in a small converted stable; childless, they have given Frayda the room that would have belonged to a son or daughter.

Barbara asks what he's reading.

"See for yourself."

She takes the book, sounds out the title: *"Dorot shel Beinonim."*

It's unlike any text she has encountered in the last month, consisting not of paragraphs and chapters but page upon page of elaborate, hand-drawn diagrams, labeled in Hebrew, but also Latin, Arabic, Chinese . . .

"Yes," he says. "A little different, *n'est-ce pas?* You won't find us studying it in class, at any rate. Not many copies in existence. I consider myself fortunate to have one."

She wants to keep reading, but he is waiting, and she returns the book to him.

"Thank you," he says, wrapping it inside his jacket. "I know this has been difficult for you. A journey of a thousand steps, yes?"

"I'm not learning anything."

"Nonsense. I've seen myself how much you've grown."

Searching for a new subject, she asks what the tree is.

Rav Kalman glances up at the weathered branches. "An olive. A friend of mine who knows such things told me it's a thousand years old."

"Can you eat the olives?"

"It doesn't give fruit. It never has."

"It might have at one point, if it's that old."

"True."

"Or it might in the future. Don't lose faith," she says.

Rav Kalman laughs heartily. "Touché. And what a day that will be."

He sweeps his hand over the slumbering hills, dotted with orange light. "You've arrived at an auspicious moment. For the first time in centuries, we control our holy places. It would be a shame if you left before you had a chance to experience it."

She hasn't said a word about leaving. She thinks about it nonstop, though.

Gawd, it's pathetic, how transparent she is.

He says, "Do you know the story of Rabbi Akiva?"

She shakes her head.

"There lived a man, one of the wealthiest in Jerusalem. His name was Kalba Savuah. I should point out that names are vitally important in our tradition. They reveal a person's character. Your own name, for example."

Her mouth twists. The irony is lovely, just lovely: *Bina* means "understanding."

"'Kalba Savuah' means 'satisfied dog.' The Sages say that anyone who entered his home ravenous as a dog left satiated. Though, of course, there are other interpretations, not all of them as complimentary."

Barbara enjoys the wryness in his tone.

"At any rate, Kalba Savuah had a daughter, Rachel, who fell in love with one of his shepherds. Now, this fellow, Akiva, was illiterate, from the lowest class. Yet Rachel looked beneath the layers of ignorance. She saw his soul."

"A talent for spotting talent," Barbara says.

Rav Kalman claps his hands delightedly. "Yes. Exactly. It's a skill we all possess when it comes to the person we love. Akiva and Rachel became secretly betrothed. Think of Rockefeller's daughter eloping with . . . eh . . ."

"Steve McQueen?"

A belly laugh. "Maybe Steve McQueen's poorer cousin."

"What does 'Akiva' mean?"

"Good question. It derives from 'Jacob,' which itself comes from the word for 'heel,' because our forefather was born holding Esau's heel. Jacob, too, was a shepherd with a difficult father-in-law. And 'Rachel'—who was both Jacob's and Akiva's beloved—means 'ewe.' The words, the themes, they repeat, time and again. That's a fundamental principle. The cycle of history."

Barbara has friends back home who dabble in Eastern religions. The notion wouldn't sound weird coming from them. But she's surprised to hear it from a rabbi.

"When Kalba Savuah found out about the engagement, he threw Rachel out of the house and disowned her. Think of the fortitude required for her to remain by her husband's side: she went from bathing in golden tubs to selling her own hair for money. Akiva, naturally, lost his job, but Rachel insisted that he forget about getting another and devote himself to learning Torah. He left and studied for twelve years, beginning with the alphabet and rising to become the greatest sage of his generation."

"While his wife supported him."

"Yes."

"Classy," Barbara says.

Rav Kalman's eyes twinkle darkly. "I thought American girls believed in a woman's right to work . . . In any event, at the end of twelve years, Akiva decided to pay his wife a visit."

"How generous of him."

"As he walks up to the door, he overhears a neighbor taunting Rachel, saying her husband has abandoned her. Rachel says, 'If it were up to me, he'd stay another twelve years.' So he does. He turns around and goes back. He never steps foot inside the house. Never even says hello. What do you think of that?"

"I think," she says, "that's incredibly cruel."

Rav Kalman nods slowly. "Perhaps it is."

"I think that Rachel is the real hero of this story."

"That is without a doubt true. When Rabbi Akiva came home at last, after his second twelve years, he brought his disciples with him, numbering twenty-four thousand. They arrived in his village, and a wrinkled woman came running out to greet him. The students started to push her back. They had no idea it was his wife. Rabbi Akiva said, 'Let her be. Everything that I know, and everything you know, belongs to her.'"

Silence.

"There's a happy ending," Rav Kalman says. "Kalba Savuah apologizes and gives them half his estate."

"Of course he does," Barbara says.

Rav Kalman chuckles and twirls his beard. "You're very cynical, you know that?"

"I guess."

"It won't help you here," he says.

"It doesn't hurt, either," she says, but she feels ashamed.

"I don't pretend that real life is simple," he says. "That's why we tell stories."

The sky hints at dawn.

Rav Kalman says, "Let's see if we can't figure out a way to help you get a foothold, eh? In the meantime, you should get out a bit, see the country. Make art. The bottom line is to do whatever it takes to make yourself feel at ease."

"What if nothing makes me feel at ease?" she says.

He rises, dusts himself off. "Then, my dear, you are human."

MONDAY AFTERNOON, she sits beneath the tree, creating and destroying a series of shapes. She forms a giant cockroach, squashes it; raises and demolishes a ladder. She hasn't been to class in four days. She spends her nights in the garden, sleeps through the morning session, skips meals, rising to action only when Frayda comes to warn her that the solar heater is running low; better hurry up if she wants a hot shower.

She has an idea that she will never be this lonely again.

The odd truth: she will miss it.

"Hello?"

A male voice, not Rav Kalman's.

Barbara sets aside the bird she has been shaping and rises on tiptoes to peer over the retaining wall.

A young man of about twenty-five stands halfway up the slope. For a second Barbara wonders if he's drunk: he's tottering, arms out for balance, a book in each hand. Painfully thin, with a long, curious face and a close-cropped beard, he wears a large black knitted yarmulke, pale blue polyester slacks, a short-sleeved white button-down shirt, and cork-soled sandals. He peers at her through dense eyeglasses.

"Bina?"

Without waiting for an answer, he drops to his haunches and scoots downhill toward her, triggering an avalanche of pebbles. "They said you were out here."

She backs away as he descends the ladder.

"I'm not interrupting you, am I?"

"Who are you?"

"Right," he says. He hops from the bottom rung. "I'm Sam. Rav Kalman asked me to come. He thought maybe I could show you the ropes."

She appraises him coolly. "Ropes."

"With Hebrew, or just in general. Anyhow, sorry for barging in. We don't have to start—I can come back tomorrow. Or never, it's really up to you." His eyes shift. "Wow. That's incredible. Did you make that?"

Once again he's moving before she can reply, striding toward her bird.

"Don't," she shouts.

Sam goes rigid, his arm outstretched. He's paler than a moment ago, if such a thing is possible.

Feeling a little bad, she explains that it's Plasticine, not real clay. "It doesn't dry hard, so if you don't handle it carefully—"

She makes a squelching noise.

"Got it," Sam says. He cranes over, studying the bird through those thick, distorting lenses. "What is it?"

"Uhm. A bird."

"Right," he says. "But what *kind*?"

She's at a loss there. Her models are the tiny creatures who visit the olive tree, delicate brown and orange bodies that flit through the leaves.

"It looks like a finch," he says.

"Are you a bird person?"

"Not in the slightest," he says.

"Then how can you know what it is?"

"I don't." He grins. "That's the first thing you learn in rabbinical school: how to pass judgment with complete confidence, especially when you don't have a clue what you're talking about. Anyway . . . Marvelous."

Barbara bites her lip.

"Right," Sam says. "Like I said, I'm here to help if you want."

"You're wasting your time."

"Not the first person to tell me that," he says, sitting cross-legged in the dirt.

After a moment, she joins him, waiting for him to open the books. Instead he smiles at her. "How about we start like this? *Shalom,* Bina."

She rolls her eyes. "*Shalom.*"

"*Toda raba,*" he says.

"You're welcome."

"*Ma shlomech?*"

"Fine, thanks."

"Right on," Sam says. "Now you try."

She thinks a moment. *"Slicha,"* she says, leaning over to shove him playfully.

Sam falls back on his hands, gaping at her, and in an instant her pleasure curdles. Frayda has warned her about avoiding physical contact with religious men. Barbara forgot; she was just beginning to feel comfortable in Sam's presence, she wanted to impress him with her Israeli street savvy.

She starts to stand. "I'm so sorry."

"No no no no," Sam says. His hand on her arm, gentle but insistent. "Really."

His glasses have slid to the end of his nose.

She must have pushed him harder than she thought.

She is half up, half down.

"Please don't go," he says. "Please stay."

Barbara chooses down.

"Thanks," he says. "I appreciate your tolerance. But: question? What did you mean by that, *'slicha'*?"

"That's what people say on the bus when they knock you out of the way."

Sam explodes in laughter.

"What?" she says.

"Slicha," he says, "means 'excuse me.'"

"Really?"

"Really."

"Oh my God," she says, starting to laugh, too. "I thought it meant 'push.'"

"Welcome to Israel," he says.

They laugh and laugh, and she watches it leaving her, the loneliness that has become her companion, she watches it spread its wings and rise, good-bye, good-bye, you've been a good friend; a second

self, undiscovered, rising to fill the void; and she finds herself forming her own question, almost unconsciously.

"Sam what?" she asks.

"Lev."

"That means 'heart.'"

"There you go," he says. He smiles. "You know more than you
think."

CHAPTER SIXTEEN

Marquessa Duvall's former modeling agency occupied a suite in a mid-rise on Wilshire and Gale, a few blocks west of the Beverly Hills city limits. Scanning the lobby directory, Jacob counted no fewer than three plastic surgeons, which had to be extremely convenient for the models.

He rode up and badged the receptionist, an unimpressed, emaciated redhead sucking Diet Coke through a straw. "And this is about?"

"I've left several messages."

She told him to feel free to have a seat.

Beside the agency logo, a flat-screen scrolled through glamour shots and magazine covers of the female clientele. The sole recurring male presence was a tan, handsome man with a three-day beard, posing with celebrities: courtside with Jack, bro-hugging Kanye. He had one or more women on his arm at all times.

The receptionist hadn't bothered to pick up the phone. Jacob walked back to her desk and waited for an image of the tan man to cycle up. "Who's that?"

"Uhhhh. That's *Alon*."

"The boss?"

"Uh, *yeah.*"

"Tell him I want to talk to him, please."

"He's in a meeting."

"When will he be free?"

"It's tough to say."

"Now, when you say that," Jacob said, "do you mean it's literally tough for you to say? As in, he'll be free at six, but you have a speech impediment—a lisp, say—and pronouncing 'six' is difficult for you? Or maybe you don't actually know. In which case, it's not tough to say. It's impossible to say. Right?"

She stared at him.

"Or—I'm thinking out loud here—maybe you have the capacity to tell me, but you're not *supposed* to tell me, so in that sense it's tough for you, because while it's physically possible for you to articulate that information, it entails overcoming a certain amount of apprehension."

He smiled. "Which one is it?"

She said, "It's tough to say."

"Okay," he said, and strode past the desk.

"Excuse me. Excuse me. *Sir.*"

He walked directly to a door at the end of the hall, which—while standing at the desk—he had pegged as the leading candidate for the biggest office, with the best view.

Alon Artzi

Jacob did him the courtesy of knocking once.

Handsome and tan, Alon Artzi stood beside an expansive glass desk, his jeans down around his ankles, getting head from another, equally handsome man. For one spellbinding instant they both sort of levitated, leaving the carpet before settling into decidedly more prosaic and awkward postures: Artzi rocking back on his bare ass on the bare glass, his fellator springing backward into a minimalist floor lamp, entangling himself in the cord that yanked out of the wall with an audible crackle of voltage.

"Shit," the receptionist was saying. "Shit shit shit shit shit shit shit—"

Jacob said, "Bad time?"

Artzi had managed to plant his feet and was hopping around, trying to get his pants on, bellowing in a thick Israeli accent.

"Am-*berr*, what the *fuck*."

"I'm so so so sorry, I told him to wait, he just came like running in."

"Call to the security. Go. *Go*."

The receptionist hustled out, the second man close behind.

Artzi zipped up his fly and assumed a martial arts posture. "Fuck you, you shitfuck, who the fuck are you think you are?"

Jacob showed his badge. *"Mishtara,"* he said.

Artzi sagged, rubbed one scruffy cheek. He pushed the intercom button.

"They're on their way," the receptionist's voice said.

"Call them back," Artzi said. "Never mind."

A FULLY CLOTHED ALON ARTZI glanced at the blowup of Marquessa Duvall's DMV photo. "Of course I know her. The police come to interview me."

"There's no record of it in the file," Jacob said.

"This is not my problem."

"What did you tell them?"

"I say it's sad." Artzi turned the photo facedown on the desk and leaned back in his Herman Miller chair. "But I don't know nothing."

"Who did she work with?"

"Lot of people. She was very beautiful girl."

"What type of gigs did you get her?"

"All type. Photo shoot, magazine, parties, everything."

"Anyone who stands out? Repeat customers?"

"I don't remember."

"Can I get copies of her contracts?"

"There is nothing you can learn from this. What can you learn? Tell me."

Jacob mentioned the limousine that had come to pick Marquessa up.

"One week," Artzi said, "you know how many limousines I am going in?"

"I'm not saying it was you," Jacob said, although it then occurred to him that he hadn't bothered to evaluate Artzi himself as a suspect. "Somebody out there liked her."

"Yes, okay, so what?"

"And maybe she didn't like him back."

"This is the world," Artzi said.

"You must've been asked to make arrangements."

Artzi feigned incomprehension.

"Sex," Jacob said.

Artzi scoffed. "I am running a talent agency, not . . . eh. How you say? *Beit zonot*."

"You expect me to believe that not one of your customers has ever tried to put a move on a girl?"

"My customers, if you knowed who they are, they're not need to beg. They get anything they like. There is girl who says no? Okay, fine, *b'seder*, they take different girl."

"It's the things people can't get that they want the most," Jacob said.

Artzi smiled. "Yes, okay. But still I don't know nothing."

From the file, Jacob took a picture of TJ and set it on the desk. "Her son. He was murdered with her."

He watched the tan bleed from Artzi's face.

"You didn't know she had a son."

Artzi shook his head.

"He was five. His name was TJ."

A picture window showed a gull-gray sky, tatty clouds migrating across the glassy surface of the Flynt Publications tower, an umber oval outthrust like a disembodied thigh. Traffic throttled the streets. For some reason, Jacob found the view sad, and his thoughts slid toward his mother.

He'd forgotten to pick up challah and wine. The kosher markets closed early on Fridays; he'd have to scrounge.

"Why someone does this?" Artzi asked.

Jacob shook his head.

"The other cops, they didn't say nothing about this boy." Artzi turned TJ's photo facedown, as well. "I am tell you the truth. She work for many, many people."

"Let's focus on six months before she died. I need your records from then."

"I don't have them here. They go to storage."

"How soon can you get them out?"

"I don't know, I'm busy."

"Send your secretary. She's not."

Artzi slid both photos right up to the edge of the desk, getting them as far away as possible. "I try, okay? Now, please."

Jacob thanked him. He put the photos away and headed for the door.

"Hey, but—where you're learn to speak Hebrew?"

Jacob shrugged. "Where'd you learn to speak English?"

"The movies," Artzi said.

EN ROUTE TO THE CARE FACILITY, he stopped to pick up a bag of onion rolls and a bottle of Welch's, the closest substitute for traditional Shabbat fare that the Alhambra Vons had to offer. As he stepped into the lobby, Rosario intercepted him.

"We need to talk."

She led him to an unoccupied office, locked the door.

"Your mother was talking in her sleep. I recorded it."

She took out her phone, hesitated. "It's not easy to listen to."

Jacob made an impatient noise. She pressed PLAY.

The file began abruptly—in the middle of a shriek that tightened Jacob's scalp.

The sound died, replaced by faint moaning and recording hiss.

"I heard her from the hall," Rosario said. "I went in to check on her."

New sounds: footsteps, an unoiled doorknob; the moans growing louder and more distinct, his mother's voice, ropy with dread, evolving into a chant, low and frantic.

"What's she saying?" Rosario asked.

Jacob shook his head. It sounded like *Michael*, or *Micah*.

He could hear the bed's steel feet stamping, limbs whipping against sheets.

A second voice joined the mix: Bina's roommate, yelling at her to shut up. And then Rosario's soothing contralto, close to the microphone.

It's okay, Mrs. Abelson.

At first Jacob thought she was comforting the roommate. Then he remembered that was the name the staff knew Bina by. Another piece of his father's deceit.

Be quiet, you stupid bat.

Go back to bed, please, Mrs. Delaney.

Tell her to be quiet.

Micah Bina moaned.

Shutupshutupshutup.

Mrs. Delaney, please.

She woke me up.

I know she did, but—

Micah.

I can't sleep with her squawking like that.

I—one second, please. Mrs. Abelson. Listen to me. You're okay. Shh. Shh.

Micah. Micah. Micah. Micah.

Shh. Shh . . .

A final shriek, the speaker distorting and crackling, and then the sound cut off.

Jacob was bent over, palms pressed to thighs, sweat-soaked from the waist up.

"I'm sorry," Rosario said. "I shouldn't have—I'm sorry."

". . . no. I needed to hear it."

She nodded doubtfully.

"Does anyone else know? Besides Mrs. Delaney."

"No. I didn't tell the MD."

"Good. Let's leave it like that for now, okay?"

Rosario nodded. She blotted her eyes on her sleeve. "I couldn't help her."

He managed to find a smile for her. "You did what you could."

OUTSIDE, Bina was on her bench, her dinner tray clean. Jacob sat beside her.

"Ready?"

Same ritual. It felt more futile than usual, which was saying something: he sang in a low voice, raced through the blessings, watched her pick at the onion rolls.

He refilled her cup with grape juice. "I understand you've been having some trouble sleeping."

Bina slurped, reached for the roll.

"Ima? Who's Micah?"

The roll stopped moving, hovered a few inches from her lips.

"You said it in your sleep. 'Micah.' Is that someone you know? Who is he?"

Bina's lips pursed in and out and in and out.

"Does he have something to do with the bird you made?"

Her nostrils flared. Would he kill her if he didn't stop? In a sense, she was already dead. He wouldn't be a murderer; he'd be a reviver. Like a last-chance emergency surgeon. Win some, lose some.

Or he was simply a bastard.

Bina's head turned, her eyes crossing as she stared at the roll in front of her face.

She crammed it into her mouth.

"Ima," he said.

Her cheeks bulged, crumbs spilled down her sweater. Her chewing was almost comically loud, her face purpling, the vein in her forehead beginning to writhe. She had turned to stare straight at him, her expression ripe with purpose, and he could hear her banging at the walls of her mind, demanding his attention through the luminous, vibrating air. Her ferocity terrified him and he groped for the water bottle.

"You're going to choke," he said, uncapping it and raising it to her lips.

She swatted the bottle from his hands, sending it skipping across the concrete.

With a sickening grunt, she swallowed.

Stared at him.

Waiting.

He said, "Take it easy—"

She snatched up the second roll and tore into it like an animal.

The vein stood out like scar tissue. The muscles in her jaw swelled and hardened, determination and pain in every bite.

"Ima—"

A wet gag trickled out of her.

She began clawing at her throat.

"Shit," he said. "Oh, *shit*."

He ran behind her, fought to get his arms around her midsection. Her head lolled, and she stared up at him, never losing eye contact even as drool streamed from her mouth and over her chin and down her neck.

He shouted for help, and a pair of nurses burst from the dayroom.

"She's choking," he yelled.

They were all over Bina in an instant, wrestling her upright. But she pried herself free and lunged forward off the bench, stumbling to the center of the patio, where she turned and faced them, bending at the waist like a ham actor and bearing down. From ten feet away, Jacob heard a series of moist pops, the cartilage in her throat buckling and unfolding, moving the huge mass of dough down, like she was giving birth in reverse.

She stood up, sucking air. Looked Jacob in the eye.

Opened her mouth.

Stuck out her tongue.

She'd swallowed.

One of the nurses said, "Are you okay, honey?"

"She doesn't talk," the other nurse said.

"Are you okay? Nod if you're okay."

Bina could breathe, that much was clear; she was heaving, eyes pegged to Jacob.

"She bit off more than she could chew," the second nurse said, giggling tensely.

Jacob took a step forward. "I don't understand, Ima."

The first nurse said, "We're going to need to write this up."

Rosario came hustling out. "What's going on?"

"She's fine," the second nurse said. "She got it down."

"Jacob?" Rosario asked.

The first nurse said, "I need to go write it up."

Jacob said, "Can I have a minute alone with my mother, please?"

Rosario frowned.

He faced her. "One minute. Please."

"Yeah. Yeah, okay, come on, let's go," Rosario said, and she ushered the other two nurses inside, leaving Jacob and Bina standing together.

"I don't understand," he said. "Please help me."

She was swallowing saliva, head craning forward and retracting, like a pigeon.

"Do you still have something stuck?"

Her face fell. Wrong answer.

She began shuffling back to the bench.

"Hang on," he said. "Don't—wait."

She plopped down. Jacob hurried, knelt before her, snapping his fingers. "Ima. Hello? Clay? Do you want some clay? I can get it for you."

But the ebb was nearly complete, her back rounding, her shoulders soft; and he felt a stab of panic. Abandoning the clay idea, he grabbed his backpack instead.

"You know what, here. Here's a pen. Write it down. Write what you're thinking."

He clutched her right hand, zigzagging spastically.

"Look. Look. 'Micah.' I'm writing it for you. M—"

The pen was dead; he tossed it aside and tore through the bag for another.

"M-I-C-A-H. See? What's his last name? Wri—take the pen, please. Ima. Would you please take the pen? Take it. Take—Ima. *Take the fucking pen.*"

She dropped it.

Silence.

"Shit," he said quietly.

He picked up the pen and winged it into the fence.

"Shit."

Rosario stuck her head out.

He held up a hand. "We're fine."

He hoisted his backpack, stooping to whisper into Bina's ear. "I'm going. I don't know when I'll be back."

Bina's dull eyes aimed at the sky, her hands danced without rhythm, the skin on her neck undulating as she swallowed nothing, over and over again.

CHAPTER SEVENTEEN

The cold that had preserved the bodies made the pathologist reluctant to fix a date of death. Based on weather reports, he gave a range of one to seven days.

Hoping to buy time, Breton attempted to steer him toward the lower end of the estimate, but the fellow was oblivious to subtlety, adding with disappointment that there was no evidence of sexual assault to either victim. The mutilation of the eyelids had caused minimal bleeding, indicating that it had taken place postmortem.

Leaving the morgue, Breton made the obligatory call to Lambert to relay the findings. He didn't much feel like talking to him but neither did he want to give the *procureur* any excuse, procedural or otherwise, to snatch the case away.

Breton asked if they should continue to treat it as *en flagrance*.

Lambert waffled. He had to think about it. In the meantime: how was it working out with Odette Pelletier? Did Breton find her perspective useful?

"I can't thank you enough," Breton said.

"Don't be childish, Théo. We're searching for the truth, not fighting over a bone."

The truth was that Pelletier had vanished. Breton hadn't seen her since batting her away in the park. If she was as smart as the prosecutor claimed, she'd know when she was not needed or wanted. Probably she was out getting a manicure.

Breton had bigger problems. DNA confirmed that the victims were mother and son, but further identification proved difficult. Dédé Vallot was camped out at his desk, sifting through missing persons reports, his search radius bloated beyond Paris proper. Berline hit nightclubs, bars, restaurants, shops; Sibony and Martinez focused on schools. They started in the Sixteenth and worked outward from there, the Fifteenth, the Seventeenth, the Seventh. When that failed to pan out, Breton sent them over the river. The woman was dressed for service; maybe she worked for a bourgeois family in Neuilly-sur-Seine or Nanterre.

A brief item in *Le Figaro* brought a tidal wave of dud tips.

Each dead end had to be written up in triplicate and added to the quickly swelling dossier. Ordinarily, a fat file buoyed Breton's spirits. Now he regarded the thing on his desk as a malicious parasite, feasting on his ignorance. It filled him with disgust and despair, and he stalled as long as he could before sending it to Lambert.

It could not be helped, though. Ten days in, they had yet to name a viable suspect. The office of the *juge d'instruction* called, summoning Breton to the Palais de Justice on a Monday morning.

He climbed up to the fifth floor, pausing at the top to catch his breath and prepare excuses. Juge Félix could be a bit of a prig, and Breton expected a mild dressing-down.

He didn't expect an ambush.

"Théo. How nice to see you."

Félix was in his early fifties, with lank hair and eyes perched distressingly wide, giving the impression that he was endeavoring mightily to look backward, and succeeding to a frightening degree.

"Come in," he said. "Sit down."

Breton lingered in the doorway before taking the open chair, between Lambert, flapping his necktie like an obscene sensory organ, and Odette Pelletier, coiffed, sharp, a magazine rolled in her lap, like she was on vacation, getting ready to head down to the pool.

He should've known. He hadn't, and he felt foolish.

The *juge* himself was in shirtsleeves, a beautiful powder blue rolled up to the elbows, his wrists resting on two worn spots in the desk leather. Flanked by imposing stacks of files, overhung by a glittering wall of commendations, lit by a fine Art Nouveau lamp, he presented the very picture of bureaucratic noblesse oblige.

"I apologize that it's so stuffy," Félix said. "Caroline has complained, but I fear that we are shouting into the ether. Make yourself comfortable, we're not formal."

Breton smiled stiffly, shifting in his bulky sweater, bulky coat. "I'm fine, thanks."

"We were just starting to hear about your excellent progress. Odette?"

Pelletier opened the magazine on the desk, turned pages. "As I was saying, we felt that the victim's uniform might be relevant. The name of the brand is Dur et Doux. Nine shops in Paris carry it. Although we can't discount the possibility that it came from elsewhere or was ordered directly from the manufacturer."

"Or that it was acquired secondhand," Félix said.

"Yes, *monsieur juge.*"

The magazine was in fact a catalog. Pelletier had stopped on a two-page spread of maid's outfits and was pointing to a black dress and frilly white apron. Her nails were slick and red, Breton noted. He'd been right about the manicure, at least.

"Unfortunately, most of the managers I spoke to indicated that it's one of their bestselling items." Pelletier smiled. "Apparently, it's popular with housewives, too. I'm told that's a fantasy some men have."

"A hooker dressed like a maid?" Lambert said. "Or a maid dressed like a hooker?"

The *magistrats* turned to Breton.

"The *capitaine* prefers not to speculate," Pelletier said.

Speaking for him. As if he was a deaf-mute.

"What about the boy?" Lambert said.

Breton found his voice. "It seems he may not have been enrolled in school."

"If they're Gypsies, he probably wasn't," Lambert said.

"There's a group camped at the southern end of the park," Pelletier said. "They couldn't recognize either victim from photos."

"You know as well as I do that Gypsies are incapable of talking to police without lying," Lambert said. "It's part of their culture."

As the discussion turned to the victims' ethnicity, Breton tuned out. He now knew what Pelletier had been up to in her absence. Why she'd share credit was harder to fathom.

"Considering the obstacles you're facing, I'm pleased."

Breton realized Félix was speaking to him. "Thank you, *monsieur le juge*."

What else could he say? He was being commended for his fine work. Only he and Pelletier knew how little he'd contributed.

He had to admire her cleverness. She could've mounted a frontal assault, complaining he'd sidelined her, insulted her status as a member of the Brigade Criminelle, et cetera. That would only give the impression of a territorial squabble.

Much more destructive, Breton decided, to undo a person from the inside out.

Yes, he admired her.

A shock of cold hit him.

"Théo?" Félix asked. "Are you all right?"

Breton shoved his trembling hands in his pockets. "Too much caffeine."

"I can imagine you haven't been getting a lot of sleep. Well, look, I'm not going to step on your toes. Unless there's something you need from me?"

"We'll want the invoices from the uniform shops," Pelletier said.

"Right," Félix said. "Caroline?"

The secretary finished typing out the *commission rogatoire*.

"Anything else that occurs to you," Félix said, signing it, "please let me know. Jean-Marc, if you can remain behind a moment?"

"Certainly," Lambert said. "Keep it up, you two."

"*CAPITAINE*. WAIT."

The crowded corridor made it socially unacceptable for Breton to ignore her. He allowed her to catch up, then humped down the stairs, Pelletier close behind.

"You can't seriously be angry," she said. "I didn't have to play it that way."

"No, you didn't."

"Is it so incredible that I might be trying to help you?"

He said, "I'd already asked Dédé to check into the uniform."

"I'm sure you did."

"He hasn't had a free moment."

"I'm sure he hasn't. I have. Otherwise, tell me what you'd like me to do instead."

"I have an appointment," he said. "I'm going to be late."

They reached the boomy marble lobby, polished with gray winter light. Breton dodged robed *avocats*.

"What's your appointment?" Pelletier asked.

"I'm visiting my father."

"Can you give me a lift back to the commissariat?"

"It's in the other direction." He waved at her fitness tracker. "Anyway I wouldn't want to deprive you of steps."

Traffic was going to be horrible, he ought to leave the car and leg it himself. The walk to the Institut was less than two kilometers. He felt so tired, he was winded, fuzzy around the edges. He hadn't eaten in hours. He had no appetite. He needed a fucking joint.

He stopped, rubbed his sweaty forehead.

"Follow up with the uniform suppliers," he said to her. "After that, start calling domestic service agencies." He paused. "Unless you've already done that, too."

"Next on my list," she said. "Thank you."

"Take Dédé with you," he said. "He could use the fresh air."

AT HOME THE NEXT EVENING, he put on *Friday Night in San Francisco* and boiled spaghetti, wrestling with a jar of tomato sauce amid applause and warring guitars. He wiped his clammy hands on a towel but the lid refused to turn, and he swore and threw the jar into the sink, hoping it would shatter and provide some sort of catharsis.

It thudded dully against the plastic, intact.

He sank down, his head a loose pile.

Each time he finished a treatment, some nice pretty nurse would offer to wheel him to the elevator, help him flag a cab. No need, he said; his girlfriend was meeting him in the lobby. The nurses did not press. They understood that he wanted to walk out of the clinic alone, under his own power. Or perhaps they assumed it was the notion of the girlfriend, that prideful fiction, that mattered to him.

At one point it had been true: during his first go-round, five years ago, Hélène would hold his head in her lap while they rode back to his place in Belleville. She would prepare plain pasta with a sliver of butter, a light salad without dressing, no meat or cheese because he couldn't keep them down.

One day she announced she couldn't take the stress anymore. The awful joke was that his latest scans had shown no trace of relapse. She'd survived the worst of it, they both had, now she could stay and they could be happy. But she'd made up her mind. Within days, she'd moved in with a guy who sold high-end stereo systems.

She and Breton still kept in touch. The set of speakers through which he was listening to Paco de Lucia had been last year's Christmas present. She'd sent them along with a card that said she was grateful to have him around. He knew what she meant but found her choice of words macabre and amusing.

They were really nice speakers. Breton had looked them up on the Internet. They retailed for eight hundred euros, about half his monthly salary. Obviously Hélène hadn't paid that much, if she'd paid for them at all. Knowing their value, Breton made a sincere effort to keep them in perfect condition, so that when he died she could take them back to her boyfriend and he could resell them without a problem.

Slumped on the kitchenette floor, he watched steam rising from the pot. The energy required to stand, lift it, tip it into the colander . . . He could not begin to think.

"Frevo Rasgado" came on, his favorite of the album's five cuts. He felt his stomach starting to rebel and leaned sideways to avoid vomiting on himself.

Since he had eaten nothing, next to nothing came up. In a way that made it worse: whatever did come up was part of him.

The battery-operated pump attached to his venous catheter came loose of his belt. The pump looked like an alien grenade. He was perpetually anxious about rolling over in his sleep, accidentally kinking the line and giving himself an aneurysm. They told him it wasn't possible, but he knew impossible things happened every day. The first two cycles, he'd sat up until the morning nurse came to remove the pump and flush the line.

He supposed he would do the same tonight. Then he would go to work, dressed in a bulky sweater and bulky coat to cover the lump of the catheter through his shirt. It was a good thing he was always cold, he could leave his layers on indoors and no one would be the wiser. To forestall the question of *why* he was so cold, he'd pried the cover off the thermostat in his office and stabbed it in the guts with a screwdriver until it bleeped surrender. Now the office was a polar ice cave.

Nobody asked why he couldn't get the thermostat fixed. The answer to that was self-evident. They couldn't afford paper clips.

Three cycles, nine to go.

The present regimen was far more intense than its predecessor, five medications in combination instead of one. His oncologist said they couldn't take chances at this stage, they had to be aggressive. Studies showed a doubling of the median survival rate. Breton asked what the median survival rate was and learned it was five and a half months. Leaving him with less than a year.

With luck, he would have found the killer of the mother and child by then.

Nausea rose again, and he crawled from the kitchenette to shut off the music. He was thinking of that scene from *A Clockwork Orange*. He didn't want to develop an association between the song, which he loved, and the sickness. The stereo was next to the futon mattress, both on the floor. He'd moved everything important to the floor.

He hit the power button and collapsed on his belly.

Knocks came through the sudden silence.

"Théo. Are you there?"

It was Odette Pelletier.

"Fuck off," he said.

"Théo. Open up."

"Fuck off," he said again, louder.

Hearing him, she began to pound. It felt like she was punching him in the eyes and ears.

"Open the door or I'm going to kick it in."

Her tone threatened that she might actually do it. He crawled over to the door.

Out in the hallway, she stood with hip cocked. She peered down at him, clucked her tongue. *"Pauvre chou."*

She stepped over him and shut the door; crouched, hooked her hands under his armpits, and dragged him to the mattress, flopping him into the nest of rank sheets.

"Have you eaten?" she asked.

"Go away."

In his blurry periphery, he saw her mopping up vomit, draining the pasta.

"Where do you keep your olive oil? I won't put in too much. Never mind, got it."

She eased down beside him, propping him up with one arm while she twirled spaghetti on a fork. "Eat," she said.

"You don't exist," he said.

"Eat."

He choked down a few bites before vomiting again, avoiding the mattress but speckling her shoes.

He croaked a laugh.

"Don't be an asshole," she said.

"I give the orders," he said.

"You weren't in today," she said. "Someone had to take charge."

"Go to hell."

"I thought about it. I said to myself, 'Something's up, here. He doesn't seem like one of those lazy shits you so often find running the show at DPJ.' Then I thought about your father, who you went to visit yesterday. And I wondered, 'Why would he do that? It must be serious, if he's going to run off in the middle of a busy investigation.' I asked Dédé. I figured he'd know. He loves you, you know; you're like a father to him."

Breton felt sick again in a different way.

"'What's wrong with Capitaine Breton's father? Is he ill?' 'No, no, you must be mistaken, his father died years ago.'

"Then I thought about your bloody nose and how you reek of pot. I thought maybe there was harder stuff, too. Nobody is going to tell me that, of course, they don't trust me, certainly not Dédé Vallot. I can only guess what you've been saying about me behind my back. I poked around in your records. Surprise! You're clean as a choirboy. I wondered if you had been in treatment but managed to keep it quiet. I called my partner at the BC and had him ping you in the CPAM database," she said. "Voilà."

With a groan, he pushed away the forkful of spaghetti headed his way, detaching himself from her embrace and rolling over, mindful of the pump.

"At least I don't have to arrest you," she said.

She got up and began walking around the room, toeing sodden clothes. "Although I should do it anyway, you live like a pig. What do you pay for this shithole? Not more than six hundred, I hope."

She knelt beside him. "They really don't know? Nobody on the whole team? How did you keep it from them for so long?"

"You should be looking for the killer," he said. "Not harassing me."

"The only explanation I can come up with is that they must be very dense. I met you two weeks ago and I knew immediately something was off. But if you ask me, it's not fair of you to lie to them. They deserve better. *Beurk*, it stinks like a reggae concert in here."

She pried up a window. Cold air howled in. Breton gasped.

"Fuck off," he shouted, or tried to shout. He sounded so small.

"Poor Théo," she said. "Do you want to know my good news? Maybe you'll feel better after you hear it. I spoke to a uniform supplier in Oberkampf. Six months ago, they sold a batch of those very maid's outfits to the Russian embassy. Do you know where that is?"

He knew.

"It's on Boulevard Lannes," she said. "Right over the road from the Bois de Boulogne. Under a kilometer from where the bodies were found."

She bent over, stroked his shoulder. "You really should stay in bed tomorrow. You're not well enough to come in. Don't worry. I have everything under control."

CHAPTER EIGHTEEN

The buzzer sounded as Jacob entered 7-Eleven.

"Did you get my message?" he asked.

"What message," Henry said. He looked fried.

"That car, it's stolen. If it shows up again, you need to call it in, stat."

"It was here last night," Henry said. "It drove through the parking lot. In one side and out the other."

"Did you get a look at the guys?"

"I told my father we need a gun. He's too fucking cheap."

"Listen to me. I need you to be smart about this." Jacob paused. "Henry?"

"Yeah."

"I'm going to call over to West L.A. patrol and let them know there's a stolen vehicle floating around here. I can't promise they'll be here if the car shows up again, but it's a step we can take to get them focused on this area. But you have to promise me you won't do anything dumb."

The clerk stared through the storefront. The green Mazda's spot was taken up by a benign-looking station wagon without anyone at the wheel. It was nine-thirty a.m.

Jacob asked, "You go off shift soon?"

"Half hour."

"Go home, get some rest, try to relax."

Henry nodded reluctantly. "You need anything? A hot dog, or . . . It's on me."

Jacob considered where he was headed next. "Beer wouldn't hurt."

MOST SATURDAYS, he avoided going out in the morning, when the streets of Pico-Robertson were crowded with young families bound for synagogue. He dreaded running into an old classmate, the pitying looks.

He wondered for the umpteenth time if he should move. His relationship with his father was what had kept him around, and that was gone.

But he'd tried to leave before. It hadn't taken. The most important lesson of his disastrous marriages was that he couldn't feel at home, here or anywhere.

He was an unbeliever who spoke the language of belief. Having clawed his way out of the bubble, he'd gotten stuck to its exterior, condemned to slide around its shimmering surface, gazing in at a way of life he'd rejected.

He left the 7-Eleven. Most of the foot traffic was headed toward Pico Boulevard, and Jacob fought upstream against a righteous tide of double strollers. Sam Lev eschewed the larger congregations, which he considered too political, too much about keeping up with the Katzes. Instead he favored a prayer quorum that convened in the grungy basement of a commercial building owned by Abe Teitel-baum. It was an austere place: ocher lino, folding chairs, only a plywood Torah ark to distinguish it from a small bingo hall.

Growing up, Jacob had been the youngest congregant by decades, and he remembered the atmosphere as more or less tolerable, depending on the odors seeping in from the upstairs tenants. The good era was a caterer (roast beef, lemon meringue pie). Bad were the beauty salon (peroxide, acetone, burritos) and the pet groomer (wet spaniel). In any event, he remained keenly aware that his peers were elsewhere, at the big *shuls.* Swapping rumors and Bazooka Joe gum and checking out girls.

Now he loitered beneath a bus stop, drinking beer and watching the entrance to his father's *shul* from fifty yards away, waiting for the service to wrap up.

He was into his third tallboy when Sam emerged arm in arm with Abe. The two of them schmoozed on the sidewalk for a bit. Then Abe put on his fedora and crossed Robertson, headed back toward his triple-lot Beverlywood home.

Sam unfolded a white-tipped cane.

Jacob's chest knotted up. *That* was new. While he knew perfectly well that his father's deteriorating eyesight had nothing to do with their breach, the guilt reared up regardless.

He cracked open another beer, trailing as Sam tapped his way homeward, jogging to close the gap as they neared the building.

"Abba."

Sam stopped and turned slowly. The picture he presented from up close was shabby: untrimmed gray beard, caved cheeks, drooping eyes, flaking lips.

Before he could speak, Jacob said, "Let me be clear. I'm not here to make up or to console you. I need information. If you can give me that, great. If not, I'll go."

Sam sagged. But he nodded.

They stepped onto the abraded concrete patio fronting Sam's apartment. While his father felt for his keys, Jacob stashed the last two beers behind a dead potted plant. For later.

THE INTERIOR WAS CLOSE AS EVER, dust saturating the air between the boxes of books that defined his father's world. It gave Jacob a pang to see the dining table preset for a meager Sabbath lunch. Challah rolls like the ones Jacob brought his mother, tap water and grape juice in foam cups, a solitary paper napkin folded into a decorative triangle. The plastic place setting included a coffee spoon that would go unused.

A mistake, coming here. Jacob could feel his resolve weakening.

He begged himself to remember: his father had lied.

Sam said, "Can I offer you something to eat?"

"No, thanks. You go ahead, though."

Sam recited the *kiddush*. Jacob resisted the reflex to answer amen.

As his father hobbled to the kitchen to wash his hands, Jacob took his customary seat at the table. His heart was threatening to explode.

He said, "I'm sorry to barge in on you like this."

You're not sorry. You've done nothing wrong.

Sam reappeared with a tub of tuna fish. He made the blessing on the challah, tore off a chunk, and dipped it in salt and ate. "I'm just happy to be near you."

"Don't do that," Jacob said.

Sam appeared genuinely perplexed. "What did I do?"

Ignoring him, Jacob said, "I've been to see Ima."

"I know. It means a lot to—"

"*Stop.*"

Sam flinched.

Jacob exhaled in a tight stream. He stood up. "It's stifling in here."

In the kitchen, he pried up the window sash and stuck his head out. He'd consumed enough alcohol to feel edgy, not nearly enough to round that edge off.

He checked the refrigerator for wine.

The damn thing was bare.

"When was the last time Nigel brought you food?" he called.

"Wednesday, I think."

Jacob puckered with resentment, reading his father's poor condition as an act, orchestrated to pluck at a son's conscience.

That wasn't fair. Sam hadn't known he was coming.

Fuck fair.

He came back to the dining room, putting a seat between them.

"How do you know Divya Das?" he said.

"I don't," Sam said.

"Bullshit. When she visited me in the hospital, you recognized her. I saw it."

"I've never spoken to her, other than that day," Sam said.

"Please, please don't bullshit me. *Please.*"

"I'm not," Sam said. "I don't know her, specifically."

"What's that mean, specifically?"

Sam got up from the table.

"Where are you going?"

"One second."

Sam bushwhacked to the far corner of the living room. Jacob heard him shifting boxes. Upon return, Sam had swapped his dark glasses for his magnifying spectacles, and he took advantage of the moment to get closer, sitting next to Jacob and sliding him a decaying hardcover.

"Bear in mind that this is an old copy," Sam said.

The book was thick as a dictionary, its cover unmarked.

Jacob flipped to the title page.

Dorot shel Beinonim.

The Generations of the Middle Ones.

If it was a sacred text, it was unlike any he had seen.

No scripture. No commentary. Just spiderwebbed diagrams, inked by hand on thick vellum. Alien characters filled the first twenty or thirty pages before giving way to Sanskrit, Hebrew, Greek, Arabic, Latin, Cyrillic, pictographs.

Jacob pointed to an unfamiliar script. "What is that?"

"Ge'ez. From Ethiopia."

"Abba."

Sam looked up, his eyes ludicrously enlarged. "What?"

"You can see."

"Enough."

"You're walking around with a cane."

"Drivers pay better attention when they think you're blind."

Jacob shook his head, went back to reading.

There was a system. That much he could tell. He jumped ahead ten pages at a time, groping at comprehension. Dotted lines, wavy lines, broken lines, lines that ran to nowhere: he was looking at the relationships between husbands and wives, parents and children, siblings. Where a line touched the margins, a number appeared. He could turn to the corresponding page and find its continuation.

It would be possible, he realized, to tear out all the pages and piece them together.

Creating a single, enormous family tree.

The final entry, before the pages went blank, was in his father's handwriting.

"For your mother's sake, I tried to keep track of them," Sam said.

Jacob shut the book. He felt the beginnings of a migraine. "Keep track of who?"

"You won't believe me. It's just a theory, anyway."

"Humor me."

Sam sighed. He went back into the stacks, returning with several more books.

The first was familiar enough to Jacob: the Bible.

Sam opened to the sixth chapter of Genesis, reading aloud in the original Hebrew.

"'And it was when men began to multiply on the face of the earth, and daughters were born to them, the sons of Elohim saw the daughters of men, that they were good, and they took them as wives. And God said, "My spirit will not judge in man forever, for that he is also flesh. His days will be a hundred and twenty years." The fallen ones were on the earth in those days, and also after that, when the sons of Elohim came to the daughters of men, and they bore to them.'"

He stopped reading and looked up.

"That's it?" Jacob asked.

"'The sons of Elohim.' 'The fallen ones.' Surely you've wondered what those things mean."

"I've wondered."

"And? What's your interpretation?"

"My interpretation," Jacob said, "is that it's a myth, written a long time ago by guys sitting around a campfire who smelled like sheep and believed in magic."

Sam shrugged. "Fine."

"*You* were the one who told me that."

"I said it was a myth?"

"You said—I can't believe you don't remember this. I came to you and asked how it was possible that God had a hand. For smiting. You remember what you said?"

"That it was a metaphor, I assume."

"Yeah. A metaphor. Which is a very hard concept for a six-year-old to grasp, by the way. You got me in a shitload of trouble at school."

For the first time, Sam smiled.

"'Elohim' means 'judges,'" Jacob said. "It's saying there were powerful men and they took the best women for themselves. It's no different nowadays."

"You know very well that's not the primary meaning."

"If you're going to tell me it means 'gods'—"

"I'm telling you that you have to look at the context," Sam said. "Not Elohim. 'Sons of Elohim.' As a phrase that has its own distinct definition. It's like what Mark Twain said about the difference between 'lightning' and 'lightning bug.'"

"You don't think you're being kind of literal?"

"Quite the opposite," Sam said. "You know who the sons of Elohim are. I know you know. We learned it, together."

Jacob knew.

Angels.

"If you'll bear with me," Sam said, reaching for a second book, "I'd like to show you some other sources—"

Jacob held up a hand to stop him.

"That's fine," Sam said. "We can look at it later."

"I don't need to look at it."

"I don't know why you're getting upset at me, Jacob. You asked me a question. I'm attempting to answer comprehensively. I told you you weren't going to believe me."

"What's upsetting to me is that *you* believe it."

Sam said nothing.

"Divya Das is a doctor," Jacob said.

"And so she is."

"She works for the Coroner."

"Yes, she does."

"Mike Mallick is a cop."

"Yes, he is."

That Sam had not asked *who's Mike Mallick* unsettled Jacob.

He plowed on: "Mel Subach is a cop. Paul Schott is a cop. These are people with jobs. They have houses and cars and kids."

"People can be more than one thing," Sam said.

"They're still *people.*"

"I'm not disputing that," Sam said. "In a sense." His voice was hypnotic, indifferent: he didn't care if Jacob believed him. "That's what the '*Beinonim*' in *Dorot shel Beinonim* refers to: they're not exclusively one or the other. They're both."

"Angel-human hybrids." Jacob heard himself laughing, trying far too hard.

Sam was unfazed. "The verse itself says it. 'The sons of Elohim came to the daughters of men, and they bore to them.' Listen. Listen to this."

He was reaching for another book, *The Dead Sea Scrolls of Qumran.*

"You can read me quotes all day long," Jacob said. "That doesn't make it true."

Sam cleared his throat, took a sip of water. "Part of the problem is that these topics, by their very nature, tend to attract a certain kind of person, given to superstition and speculation. The literature is cluttered with misinformation."

"But you know better."

"My ideas have been cobbled together over years. But I've noticed patterns, yes."

"Such as."

"Obviously, they're extremely tall," Sam said. "A common alternative translation for 'fallen ones' is 'giants.'"

"Obviously."

"They don't eat, or very sparingly."

"Giant anorexics. Gotcha. Anything else?"

"They're goal-oriented, but they have limited power over the affairs of men. Mostly they work through pressure and intimidation."

"So, giant, anorexic middle management," Jacob said.

"They refuse to enter a synagogue."

"Hey, maybe I'm one of them."

"Not possible. I'm not, and neither is your mother."

"That's, that's, wow, a really huge weight off my shoulders. Thanks."

"You would know better than I do," Sam said. "You've witnessed firsthand."

That spiraled Jacob back to hideous recollection.

The greenhouse.

Mai contracting to a black point.

Mallick and Subach and Schott, three tall men, advancing on him, expanding into a shrieking legion. Accusing.

You have done a great wrong.

Then as now, Jacob felt his mind yawning open and he clenched his eyes and pressed the chasm shut.

When he looked again, he felt tired and dry. The light on the wall had mellowed. His father sat quiet as a well.

Jacob said, "They call themselves Special Projects."

"Fitting."

"What do you call them?"

Sam opened a third book—*The Books of Enoch*. The margins were heavily annotated, one word in particular underlined whenever it appeared.

Irim.

The Wakeful.

"They want to kill her," Jacob said. "Mai."

"Again, you'd know better than I would. But I don't think they do. The way I understand it, she's like a subcontractor." Sam paused. "Perhaps that's the wrong word."

"She's a hit woman," Jacob said.

"Well, yes, I assume that's part of the job description. The form she takes, the task, depends on time and place. I suppose you could say they loan her out. What is a golem but a vessel? Her spirit—*that* is eternal. That's what they're afraid of, Jacob. Ultimately, they're responsible if she gets loose."

Silence.

"In Prague," Jacob said. "I saw a clay figure. In the attic of the Alt-Neu Synagogue. The caretaker said it was the Maharal. But it looked like you. Exactly like you."

"I've told you," Sam said. "I'm not the important link."

Jacob remembered the tombstone of the Maharal's wife, whose name was Bina's middle name. A disquieting thought struck him.

"I'm descended on both sides," he said.

He stared at his father. "You and Ima. You're cousins."

Sam hesitated. "Not close."

"How close is not close?"

"There's nothing to worry about," Sam said. "Royalty did it all the time."

"You're not royalty."

"I should also point out that it was not unusual among first-generation immigrants. Couples often met at family circles."

"You're *not* a first-generation immigrant."

"What I'm getting at, son, is that plenty of these unions have taken place—"

"In Alabama."

"I intended to tell you. I wanted to. We haven't been speaking."

"Don't even," Jacob said.

Sam studied him with concern. "Are you all right?"

"You mean other than the fact that I'm inbred?"

"Don't denigrate yourself," Sam said. "You're an heir. Twice over."

"Which makes me a magnet for her. And them. And here I thought it was my good looks. Anything else you'd like to share?"

Sam got up from the table again, bypassing the library and continuing on into his bedroom, returning soon with a small object that he set on the table.

A clay bird.

CHAPTER NINETEEN

Bina sorts the mail.

Bills, bills, junk, and then a surprise: the familiar flimsy blue-green paper of an Israeli aerogram, nearly impossible to open without damaging its contents.

She lights the stovetop, fills a kettle, waits for the water to boil.

Jacob, strapped in his high chair, his face plastered with marinara sauce, says, "Eeeeeeeeeeeeeeee."

It's an eerily accurate impression of the kettle's whistle, good enough to draw a call from the living room:

"Bean? Are you making tea?"

Sam enters, a book in each hand.

"Eeeeeeeeeeee," Jacob says.

He stops squealing and grins. Sam and Bina break into laughter.

"Very good," Sam says. He kisses Jacob on the head.

Meanwhile the real kettle has begun to pipe. Bina waves the aerogram through the steam to loosen the glue. "You can have the water when I'm done."

"Who's it from?"

She shakes her head. No return address. For the first few months following their departure from Israel, she and Sam kept up a lively correspondence with their friends. It abated as everyone accepted that the Levs weren't coming back.

These days it's rare to find anything *but* bills in the mail. The irony is that they came to Los Angeles hoping to ease the financial strain.

The old joke had it: how do you wind up with a million dollars in Israel?

Start with two million.

After Sam got the job offer—pulpit position, two-year contract, option for a third—they weighed the spiritual loss against the gain in security. If they saved diligently, they could return to Jerusalem with a nest egg. Enough, perhaps, to buy an apartment.

Eight years later, they're still in L.A., living in a rented duplex without air-conditioning, scraping by. Bina looks at her son, drumming the tabletop with his rubber-coated spoon, and she's amazed to realize how naïve they were.

In L.A., you need a car. Gas. Maintenance and repairs. Then there are doctors' bills. Rent. The mind-boggling American cost of living.

Bina works open the aerogram's curling flap—a delicate operation, with her nails cut painfully short. In a perfect world, she'd prefer to leave a little length. But clay gets trapped underneath, making her look like some unwashed orphan out of a nineteenth-century novel. No amount of digging with the nail file gets it out. It dries, shrinks, and falls out on its own, shedding everywhere—tiny moons, immune to vacuuming, forcing her to crawl around the apartment, picking them out of the carpet fibers.

Who has time for glamour? She has a toddler to care for. And her husband—her kind sweet husband, with his head jammed in the clouds—he thinks she's beautiful, perfect, just as she is. He tells her so, often.

Sometimes she wishes he would stop.

Bina manages to open the aerogram without shredding it.

"It's from Frayda," she says. "She's coming to visit."

"Wonderful." Sam decants the boiled water into a mug. "When?"

"She gets in on Monday." Bina folds the damp paper in half. "She could have given us a bit more notice."

"You know how long those things take to arrive," Sam says. "She probably mailed it a month ago." He sits at the breakfast table, dunking a tea bag with one hand and petting a happily babbling Jacob with the other. "What's the occasion?"

"Fund-raising for Sulam."

"Ah," Sam says, blowing on his tea. "I should introduce her to Abe."

"You don't have to do that. She's staying with us, that's more than enough."

"Whatever you want," he says.

What does she want? She wants him to be more annoyed. He can't help being decent. She loves him *because* he is so decent.

Still, it's not always fun, living with a saint.

She says, "I have no idea what I'm going to say to her."

"I'm sure it'll be easier than you think," he says.

He takes a single sip of tea, checks his watch. "Oops, gotta run. Study time with Dr. Prero." He kisses Jacob. "Bye, bubba."

"Bah, Abba."

Once he has gone, Bina moves the mug to the fridge, setting the tea bag on the windowsill to dry out for a second use.

———

FRAYDA KNEELS in the center of the living room, her hands plastered to the sides of her face in astonishment. "Look . . . at . . . *you*."

Jacob hides behind Bina's legs. She gently pries him loose. "He's not usually so shy."

"Oh, please." Frayda smiles. "I'd be scared of me, too."

She stands, stretching like a tree. "So much *space*, you have."

"You're kidding."

"Tch. You've forgotten what it's like. For Jerusalem, this is a mansion."

Coming from anyone else, it might sound petty, but Frayda is truly happy for her.

"Where do you do your art?"

"On the roof."

"No. Really?"

"There's a small deck."

"What about when it rains?"

"It doesn't rain in Los Angeles."

Frayda laughs. "I told Sari Wasserman I was going to stay by you, and she asked me to bring her back an autograph."

"Whose?"

"Anyone, as long as they're famous."

"One of Sam's congregants invented a new kind of dental floss."

Jacob has scuttled behind the arm of the sofa, his blond head poking up, observing them in that somber way of his. It reminds Bina of no one so much as Věra.

"So," Frayda says, "here we are."

Their second embrace is longer, silent, warm, ending as Sam struggles through the front door with a plaid suitcase.

Frayda says, "I know, I overpacked. If it's any consolation, I brought presents."

A knitted yarmulke for Sam, silver jewelry for Bina, Hebrew books for the both of them to share. To Jacob go the greatest spoils: handmade wooden toys, chocolate, children's books, a T-shirt with the *Sesame Street* characters in Hebrew.

The display of generosity overwhelms Bina. The Cohens aren't rich. She recalls her peevish reaction to the news of Frayda's visit and blinks back guilty tears. Forcing brightness into her voice: "You must be starving."

HOVĚZÍ GULÁŠ, heavy and brown, totally inappropriate for the summer heat.

Chuck roast was on sale.

It's official: she has become her mother.

Frayda passes around a photograph of her children, who range in age from eleven years to fourteen months.

"Dov, Shlomo, Tamar, Reuven, Hadassah, Aliza."

"Beautiful," Sam says.

"It's not hard for you to leave them?" Bina asks.

"Are you kidding?" Frayda says. She points to the gray, now spread beyond her temples. "The hard part is going to be convincing myself to go back."

In the photo her children are posed at the edge of the Mitzpeh Ramon crater, an Israeli version of Our Gang.

Bina squints at the youngest boy. "He's six? He looks like he's twelve."

"He takes after me," Frayda says.

Los Angeles is the last stop on her U.S. tour. She has been to New

York, Miami, and Chicago, scaring up funds for the seminary's pro-
posed dormitory expansion. Over the last thirteen years, Sulam has
blossomed, with fifty-one girls in three classes. Yonatan runs day-to-
day operations, while Frayda teaches Talmud. Perhaps the greatest testament to the institution are the dozen other women's yeshivas that
have sprung up in its image.

"And Rav Kalman?" Bina asks. "How is he?"

Frayda presses her lips together. She looks down at her plate.

"Oh, Fraydie," Bina says. "When?"

"Right after Pesach."

"We had no idea," Sam says.

"I should've told you sooner. I didn't want to burden you."

Bina touches her friend's arm and recites the traditional pallia-
tion: "May the Omnipresent comfort you among the mourners of
Zion and Jerusalem."

"He spoke about you often," Frayda says. Her smile is small,
askew. "You always were his favorite."

Embarrassed, Bina laughs and reaches for the serving spoon.
"More?"

"No, thanks," Frayda says. "It's delicious."

Her plate is untouched, though. As usual. When does she *nourish*
herself?

"And you," Bina says, "always were a horrible liar."

"I WAS SORRY TO HEAR about your parents."

Midnight, they sit together on the living room floor, talking by
candlelight. Sam was right. It was easy to reconnect. However much
Bina has changed—and she has, in every way—Frayda remains
essentially the person she was at nineteen: quick to laugh and to

praise, alternately flippant and pious, optimistic despite the stress of life in Israel.

"Honestly," Bina says, "it was a relief. They suffered."

"Still. It's not easy."

Bina nods. Somehow she knew exactly how they would go: Věra first, swiftly, diagnosis to funeral inside of three months; Jozef stubborn, dissatisfied, swearing in Czech at the staff of the Hebrew Home for the Aged.

Another irony: her father finishing out his days surrounded by trappings of the religion he detested. There was no choice. He qualified for a special survivor's rate. Otherwise it would have been a Kings County facility.

The end, when it came, was apt. At the communal Passover Seder, a well-meaning volunteer tried to put a skullcap on Jozef's head. He lashed out to swat it off, fell out of his chair, hit his head. Bina didn't know whether to be amused or appalled when she learned that the last earthly thing he'd heard was the Four Questions, sung by Mrs. Gerber, at seventy-nine the baby of the bunch.

At the time, Bina was three months along. On the flight back from JFK following the funeral, Sam asked if she wanted to name the baby for her father, if it was a boy.

She didn't want to talk about it. Talking about it was bad luck. They didn't need any more bad luck.

And sure enough, she lost that pregnancy, too, and the pain and disappointment dragged her over the edge. She did something— she's ashamed to think of it, now—she screamed at Sam that it was his fault, that he had done this to her.

What was the *this* that he had done, though? Drawn her to religion? Married her? Taken her to Los Angeles? Gotten her pregnant, again and again?

What else could she blame him for?

It never was a fair fight between them. Her anger would foam over, and he would stand there and take it, waiting for her to come to her senses, which infuriated her further. In her unhappiest moments, she came to believe that his calm was actually a form of character flaw, proving that, on some level, he did not love her as much as she loved him.

His unwavering faith drove her batty.

It will happen when God wills it.

Shut up, shut up.

Like it or not, he would always be her teacher; she would always crave his approval. She read and reread the sources. Sarah, Rachel, Hannah, Ruth—the Bible offered no shortage of barren women. They were heroines. Women of valor. Each had her prayers answered, eventually.

But by then Bina had studied enough to know that you couldn't lean on easy interpretations. No character felt as familiar to her as Michal, volatile daughter of mad King Saul, first wife of King David.

She had died childless.

It wasn't merely Bina's body in revolt. Her mind, too, began to betray her. Concentration faltered. Sound arrived on a half-second delay. Food became dull; sex a cruel joke; an expanding cavity displacing desire. Anything could and did set her off. The tagline of a pet food ad (*Take care of them like they take care of you*). The sad truth of a soap droplet, pirouetting in a dirty cereal bowl; the world's infinite, unrealized shapes.

She got so accustomed to crying for no reason that she was glad to have the hormone treatments as an excuse.

Waking before dawn, dread stomped her chest like a paper bag, and she slipped from the room, hauling her supplies in a citrus crate up to the roof. She spread her drop cloth on the tarpaper, took clay in hand, kneaded it gently to avoid disturbing her husband, snoring righteously below.

The community supported her as best they could, commissions trickling in. Wedding gifts, bar mitzvah gifts, cups and platters and bowls. Sam tried to buck her up. See? People appreciated her talent.

Bina saw the orders for what they were: pity.

She worked on them during the day.

But at night, in the jaw of melancholy, she created figures meant for no one else, rendering in three dimensions the citizenry of her nightmares, blackened bodies. She pinched out the smug faces of the ravens that strung the telephone wires like a firing squad. She smoothed the innocent necks of the pigeons that roosted in the eaves.

Invariably she did not fire these pieces to completion. She threw them off the roof to explode in the street. She left them to crumble in the merciless sun.

Those days are behind her. Now she has no time to brood, nothing to complain about. She has a son. A beautiful boy, named not for her father, but for her mother's brother, a young man ripped from the world before he could start a family of his own. She wields her contentment as a shield against the sadness that turns up in the small hours, soliciting at the door of her mind. She has what she wanted: she is no longer alone, never, not for one instant. How wicked of her, to miss it so much.

THREE IN THE MORNING, they're still talking, and Bina is starting to feel the weight of the approaching day, chasing Jacob around on no sleep.

Frayda says, "You know what I was thinking about? That class where we met. With the hippies."

Bina laughs. "Sri Sri."

"I remember the first time I saw you create something," Frayda says. "A tiny bowl. Like a thimble. Do you remember?"

"Of course."

"Do you still have it?"

"The—bowl? No. No, it's long gone."

"What a shame."

"It was just a silly little thing," Bina says.

"Mine was silly," Frayda says. "Yours was perfect."

"I'd like to think I've improved since then."

"You're not listening," Frayda says.

Her vehemence catches Bina off guard. "All right."

"You need to face up to the nature of your gift," Frayda says. "It's irresponsible not to. There are things only you can do."

Bina lets out a short laugh. "It's not hard to make a bowl. I bet even you could learn."

But Frayda isn't smiling. She has drawn up tall, and when she leans in, it is with a frightening momentum, so that Bina shrinks back, crazily afraid of being crushed.

"I saw God that day," Frayda says.

She seizes Bina's hands and raises them like an offering. "Here. In your hands. That was what I saw."

The candle has burned down to a nub, changing Frayda's face.

"We need you to do something," she says.

The oddness of that sentence, its plural subject and directionless verb, leads Bina to make assumptions. *We* are Frayda and Yonatan; they want her to *do something*, which is to say, make a piece for them—a *kiddush* cup, maybe, to auction off, raise money.

"Of course," Bina says. "Anything."

Frayda remains clutching Bina's hands. "Two months from now, a group of Jewish artists will be traveling to Czechoslovakia as part of a cultural exchange."

"Okay."

"We need you to go with them."

Bina blurts another laugh. "Pardon?"

"Your grant application has already been approved. You'll still need to write to the Czechoslovakian consulate for a visa. That I can't do for you."

". . . Frayda—"

"Request expedited processing. We'll cover the fee."

"Frayda. Frayda." Bina smiles. "What in the world are you talking about?"

"If it were up to me, I'd go, too. I tried. They won't permit it. They said I have no role to play."

"Who won't per—you're not making any sense."

"I'm telling you so you won't think I've abandoned you," Frayda says, and she finally lets go of Bina's hands and begins digging in her bag. "I need you to understand how deeply I care about you. For me, it's never been about this moment. You've always meant more to me than that. I am your friend. We all are. We always will be. You must believe that. Here. Look."

She produces a snapshot of a tree with silvery leaves. After a moment, Bina recognizes it as the old olive in the garden outside Sulam—the one that has never fruited.

Its branches sag beneath the weight of a bumper crop of fat black orbs.

What a day that will be.

"Turn it over," Frayda says.

On the back of the photograph is a note, written in Hebrew.

No evil will befall you, and no plague shall come near your
tent for He will command His angels to you, to guard you in
all your ways.
   Go in peace.
   Kalman Ovadiah ben R. Nachum Gonshor

Frayda points to the date in the upper left corner. "He wrote it the night before he passed. He said you'd understand, once you saw."

Bina says nothing. She wants so badly to fit this conversation into a rational framework. She knows the horror of feeling her own mind slipping; to watch it happening to her best friend is worse still.

"Don't worry about packing your tools," Frayda says. "You'll get everything you need on site."

Bina sets the photograph aside, fighting to keep her voice even. "If you want me to . . . I mean, I can make you whatever you want. Just tell me and I'll get started."

"No. We need you to be physically present."

Bina doesn't know how to respond, except to play along. "What about Jacob?"

"You'll only be gone a couple of weeks. He'll be fine."

"A couple of—Frayda. He's *two*."

Why is she arguing? It makes her sound as if she's considering accepting, which of course she isn't, because the whole situation is preposterous. She will tell Frayda, flat-out: *you need to get help*.

But then Frayda leans in once more, her shadow rearing up, madly out of proportion in the damaged candlelight.

"All those years," she says, seizing Bina's hands again, "when you could not conceive. When you were in pain. When you thought you were alone."

The shadow spreads like a canopy, menacing, inhuman, advancing beyond physical limits, so that Bina must suddenly wonder if in fact she's the one going mad.

"You were not alone," Frayda says.

Words of comfort, they boil like a threat.

Kindness has an inverse.

What is given can be taken away.

"You were never alone," Frayda says, squeezing Bina's hands tighter still. "We did not forget you."

"Frayda. Please."

"We did not cease to pray, not for one instant. We prayed for you, Bina Reich."

"You're *hurting* me."

"We have acted with kindness, and now you will show kindness in return."

The pain grows—her hands, they mean so much to her—but Bina can't pull away, and the shadow continues to loom, sopping up light, gobbling the oxygen until the candle snuffs itself out and darkness clamps down. She hardly knows her own, feeble voice.

"What will I tell Sam?"

At once Frayda releases her. Bina draws her arms into her body, like a wounded bird.

"Tell him what every young mother says," Frayda says. "You need a vacation."

CHAPTER TWENTY

Jacob cupped the clay bird in his palms, as if cradling a living creature.

It was difficult to compare it to the one Bina had recently made—mashed potatoes didn't make for a precise medium—but the general dimensions and shape matched.

He said, "Where did you get this?"

"She made hundreds of them," Sam said. "They were an obsession of hers. So far as I'm aware, there's nothing special about this one in particular, other than it survived."

"Survived?"

"She destroyed the rest."

All at once, the clay bird felt malignant as lead. Jacob set it down. It rocked slightly, as if bobbing on a lake. Sam laid a finger on its spine to still it, removing then his magnifying spectacles. His eyes were red and loose.

"She went to Prague," he said. "She was never the same after that."

A fist through Jacob's midsection. "When?"

"You were very young," Sam said. "You'd just turned two. We had a visit from an old friend of ours. She mentioned to your mother a mission of Jewish artists traveling to Prague, giving lectures and workshops and that sort of thing."

He paused. "This woman, Frayda, she's one of them. I didn't know that, then. If I had, I never would have done what I did, which was to encourage your mother to go."

"Why did you?"

"I thought it would be good for her to get out of the house. She'd been struggling. We didn't call it depression. Certainly, there weren't signs of mania yet. She just had the blues. Her father, rest in peace, he was probably depressed his whole life. That generation, the subject was taboo. Everyone knew someone who'd been put away, but it was considered shameful. We—I—should have known better. But your mother was young, healthy, educated. I figured she'd take a break, it would pass, she'd be normal again."

Sam's lips trembled. "She was supposed to be gone for two and a half weeks. I didn't hear from her once she left, but it didn't worry me. Remember, this is long before cell phones or e-mail. The eastern bloc . . . It might as well have been another planet.

"About ten days in, I got a call from the foundation that had organized the trip. There had been some trouble in Prague. The mission was being cut short. They were arranging to get the group out of the country on various flights, but they were having problems reaching your mother. They were very vague. I think they wanted to keep me from panicking, which of course had the opposite effect. Finally they admitted that she'd been unaccounted for, for several days."

He lifted his water glass, the rim knocking against his teeth.

"It was chaos. I stopped sleeping. I think I lost ten pounds in the first week. As I mentioned, communication was next to impossible. I tried the U.S. embassy in Prague, but the phone would ring and ring. Finally I got through to them and they started calling hospitals

on my behalf. I went to the police. I went to the FBI. The best anyone could do was to take a statement or refer me to a different agency.
I went to the Federal Building and walked up and down the halls,
pushing you in the stroller, knocking on doors. They thought I was
out of my mind. And I was, I was petrified.

"The community rallied behind me. They took care of you when
I couldn't, they scared up some local media. For the most part, we
were ignored. Reporters got confused, they thought your mother
was a refusenik.

"I wanted to apply for a visa to go to Prague myself and look for
her. The Czechoslovakian consulate wouldn't grant me an appointment. Abe got me a meeting with a congressman, and a few days
later the consulate says, all right, you can have your visa appointment, the soonest opening is March. This was November.

"A month without contact, people began to talk as if she was
already dead. I actually had someone suggest I should start saying
kaddish.

"Then the embassy in Prague called. Your mother had turned up
at their door. She'd had some kind of breakdown. She was covered
in blood and she was raving. They tried to call an ambulance for her,
but she began screaming incoherently. They had to have her forcibly
sedated.

"When I finally got to speak to her, she sounded as if she was at
the end of a tunnel. It wasn't just a bad connection. Her voice—I
didn't recognize it.

"Another week went by before they got her on a flight home.
They had to drug her, and they sent a doctor along on the plane, to
keep injecting her so she'd stay calm.

"I met her at the airport. I'd brought you with me, and several
people from the community had come along, as well. They were

cheering as she came through customs. She was being pushed in a wheelchair. Jacob, when I saw how she looked . . ."

He shut his eyes against the memory.

"I tried to hand you to her, but she wouldn't move. She sat there, with a TWA bag on her lap, staring into space. I tried to kiss her, to hug her. I could feel her bones."

Nauseated, Jacob fingered the faint patterns in the tablecloth.

"People expect an explanation," Sam said. "They expect their heroes to be heroic, and their victims to suffer in a way that they can understand. Your mother would not oblige on either count. She was absent. In the beginning, we had all sorts of people coming by, to say hello, drop off food. She would lock herself in the back room. Do that enough and they stop coming.

"I was just as bad—just as entitled. I can admit that, now. It hurt me to sleep apart. She wouldn't undress in front of me. If I tried to ask her questions, she simply shut down. Whatever was happening to her was happening behind closed doors.

"I dragged her, against her will, to see a psychiatrist, but the moment she saw him she began shaking and ran out of the office. The same thing happened again and again. It was clearly torture for her, so I backed off. In those days we were living in the place on Doheny. She kept her studio on the roof. That was the only thing that gave her any peace. She spent hours alone up there, making those damned birds.

"Anger I could deal with. Fear. But what can you do in the face of blankness? I've replayed that period a thousand times and I still can't find an opening. It's my fault for not looking harder. She was in pain and I didn't want to make it worse. I believed she would open up when she was ready. And I know it sounds like an excuse, but I was simply so grateful to have her back.

"The hardest part was watching her relationship to you change. Suddenly it was agony for her to be near you. She loved you. She never stopped loving you, you must know that, Jacob. But any sign that you were in distress overwhelmed her. If you started crying, it was as if the volume was louder for her than for anyone else. She fought and fought, but eventually she couldn't handle it. She had to escape.

"I wish you had gotten the chance to know her as I did. Her life—her real life—began the moment you came into the world. She had seven miscarriages before you."

Jacob said, "You never told me."

"Why would we? Who would that help?"

"You never told me any of it."

"I'm sorry. Does it matter that I'm sorry?"

Jacob said nothing.

"That level of stress—you can't grapple with it every waking moment. You block it out, because you need to buy groceries. My major achievement was that I managed to get her on lithium, which allowed a minimal level of functioning, as long as she remembered to take it.

"Looking back, it was crazy to think you weren't affected. It was my fault; I treated you like an adult. That's how you seemed. Grave, and wise. You tried so hard to be good."

Sam pinched the bridge of his nose. "About six months after she returned, I went up to the roof to bring her a cup of tea and found her bleeding at the wrists. I have to assume she wasn't serious, because she could've just as easily jumped. And she didn't cut the right way, thank God.

"Perhaps I should've kept her hospitalized longer than I did. They tried to give her ECT, and she began shrieking as if she was being torn apart. I undid the straps myself and took her home.

"The summer you stayed in Boston," Sam said. "That was her second attempt. I was supposed to be teaching a class, but it got canceled, and I came home early."

Alone in an otherwise empty Harvard dorm, listening to his mother's last words to him, a voicemail left the day she'd supposedly died.

I'm sorry, Jacob.

Sam said, "She'd cut the right way."

His face was riven with anguish. "I let my guard down. It had been so long by then. I fooled myself into thinking we were safe. We were a family, we'd made a life. Maybe not somebody's ideal, but what is ideal? There is no ideal. You can get used to anything. You have a strong incentive to forget. One terrible month, in the course of a lifetime—it's nothing. A blip.

"And we were happy, sometimes. That's what I thought. Was I wrong? I was wrong to think we were out of danger. I've been wrong about so many things.

"I don't expect this to mean much to you. And I know you don't want more excuses. But when I told you she died, it was only half a lie. Because she did die, to me."

The room had grown dim.

"Who's Micah?" Jacob asked.

Sam shook his head.

"She screamed that name. She was screaming it in her sleep."

"I don't know, Jacob."

"You put her away."

"I couldn't take care of her any longer. She was too sick. She stopped talking, she fought taking her medication. It was a matter of time before she tried again. I couldn't keep vigil over her day and night. My eyes . . . I couldn't handle it, Jacob. And I worried, constantly, that they'd come for her again."

"Special Projects."

"I was trying to protect her. Both of you."

"Don't you dare put that decision on me."

"I'm not—" A rare glint of anger, quickly stifled. "I'm not blaming you for my decisions. You're my son, Jacob. I wanted you to live free of burdens. I stuck my head in the sand. Whatever that makes me, I accept it. If a fool, then I'm a fool."

"That's not the word that comes to mind."

Sam did not reply.

"You could have told me," Jacob said.

"You never would have believed me," Sam said.

"Maybe not right away, but you could've said something, at some point."

Sam seemed not to agree. But he said, "I'm sorry."

Silence.

"Two years ago," Jacob said. "Did she really ask for me?"

"I wouldn't lie to you about that."

"Well, excuse me, Abba, but I don't quite get how you draw the lines."

Sam looked away, chastened.

"I see her every week," Jacob said. "I've never heard her speak."

"I give you my word. She said your name."

"Prompted by what?"

Sam rubbed his temples. "It happened shortly before Rosh Hashana."

Jacob said, "Around my birthday."

"Yes. I suppose so."

"I turned thirty-two that year," Jacob said. "Meaning, thirty years since her trip."

Silence.

"You tried to stop me from going to Prague," Jacob said. "You thought the same thing would happen to me."

Sam hesitated. "Did it?"

The memory pierced Jacob. An infinite climb up a trembling finite ladder. A cloak of dust. The voice of Peter Wichs, the synagogue sexton, urging him upward.

Every moment since then had been different.

He said, "I guess we'll find out."

CHAPTER TWENTY-ONE

Leaving his father's apartment, Jacob felt as though he had been poured full of poison, then punctured all over and drained hollow.

At home he turned on the television, staying in front of it through Sunday and most of Monday, arising only to get a new bottle or to pee. Finally, to answer the doorbell.

A courier handed him a binder stamped with the logo of the A² agency.

You can't grapple with it every waking moment.

You block it out, because you need to buy groceries.

Jacob tossed the binder on the couch and went to take a shower.

Maybe Alon Artzi felt guilty, or maybe he was just a decent guy. Either way, he'd overdelivered: Jacob had asked for info on the half year before Marquessa's death and gotten her entire booking history, along with a portfolio and several sets of headshots.

He began laying the material out on his living room carpet.

The first headshots were blurry and amateurish, probably home-made. Marquessa perched on the edge of a park fountain in jeans, platform shoes, and a white tube top that contrasted brilliantly with her glowing brown shoulders.

She'd attached a résumé listing work experience at Burger King. Cashier.

Her pluck impressed Jacob, as did the conviction shown by the agency in taking a chance on her. While she was a nice-looking girl, L.A. was full unto sickness with physical beauty.

Her first pro gig was a shoot for *Ventura Blvd* magazine. It paid two hundred dollars, of which the agency took a twenty percent cut.

A hundred sixty take-home.

Better than seven bucks an hour for flipping burgers. And how validating, to get paid for being pretty—for being herself.

For a while, jobs came in dribs and drabs, never paying more than five hundred, typically far less. Then her luck changed. She landed a swimwear catalog, and more lucrative offers began rolling in. At her peak she'd been netting around a grand a week.

Good enough to move out of the house.

Some of the income stream came from photo shoots, but an increasingly sizable chunk came from what A²'s filing system referred to as "personal appearances": charity galas, red carpets. She had served as ring card girl at a boxing match.

Mostly she worked trade show booths, repping ceiling fans, industrial lubricants, network servers, skin cream, high-efficiency washer-dryers. For interacting with attendees "in a friendly and informed manner," she earned between thirty and fifty dollars an hour.

"Mood modeling" for VIP parties paid three times as much.

The dry language of the contracts was mute on what she did once the party ended.

Her final six months were comparatively jam-packed. It took Jacob several days to winnow the leads down. Remembering Farrah Duvall's words—*all of a sudden, she's got bank*—he homed in on elite jobs, ending up with four strong candidates.

Annual conference for financial managers.

Launch party for a "new-generation" fragrance.

Luxury car premiere.

Movie producer's seventieth-birthday party.

He began with the perfume, finding plenty of PR-firm flackery archived on the Web. The brand name was SPF, which stood for "So Phreakin Fun." The celebutard who had allegedly cooked it up claimed to be inspired by "corn dogs and suntan lotion—you know, everything that makes summer awesome."

Jacob scrolled through images. A platoon of models in cleavagey orange satin cocktail dresses used oversized atomizers to spritz party-goers.

Marquessa stood near the end of the bar, the only black girl.

She seemed to be having the time of her life.

He poured himself a drink in her honor, then e-mailed the distributor, asking for the guest list. He doubted it would bear fruit, but it was a start.

The producer's birthday party had warranted a smattering of gossip mag reportage. On a blog Jacob found mention of the A-listers in attendance: an actor couple, a rap star.

Caught canoodling! Hannah Hollowskull and Trent Numbnuts!

Referring back to the contracts, he saw that both gigs had been booked by Chiq Party Design and Catering.

He looked them up.

Defunct: your basic L.A. story.

Searching the state business directory, he came up with an expired LLC registered to a Marlee Watchorn, phone number and an address in Silver Lake.

Jacob called her. She was cheerful enough at first but turned bitter when he asked if she still had the guest list.

"I don't have anything," she said. "Roberto took it all."

"Roberto being . . ."

"My ex-husband. Ex–business partner. Ex-you-name-it."

"Do you think he might have held on to it?"

"I don't think about him," she said, "ever."

"Can I get a current phone number for him?"

"Is he in trouble?"

"I wouldn't assume that," Jacob said.

"I'm not assuming," she said. "I'm hoping."

ROBERTO NOW RAN a party planning business of his own. He confirmed that the feeling was mutual.

"Under normal circumstances I wouldn't release a guest list. To you or anyone. We cater to clients who cherish their privacy. However. Seeing as it's Marlee who made the deal, and she's the one responsible and who would suffer if that information should happen to get out, I would love to give it to you, and in fact I'm going to encourage you to share it with every single person you meet on the street. I'm out of the office for the rest of the week but I'll e-mail it to you first thing Monday."

"Thanks."

"It's my complete pleasure."

Gathering intel on the other two events proved trickier. The financial managers' conference was a massive, four-day affair attended by representatives from scores of banks. He wrote to the organizer, hoping for a response while praying he wouldn't need it.

That left the luxury car premiere, where he ran smack into the opposite problem.

No photos. No press releases. No blogs.

No coverage whatsoever.

The name on the contract, Seta Event Management, maintained a far slicker profile than the flaming mess that had been Marlee and Roberto. The home page drew itself in black and magenta curlicues, framing a rotating gallery of glittering stills. Lusty electronica slithered through the miniature speakers on Jacob's computer.

He muted it, moused over the menu bar, clicked CLIENT LIST.

As Southern California's leading event management and luxury lifestyle firm . . .

He scrolled down.

Some of Our Clients Have Included:

LVMH MoËT HENNESSY • LOUIS VUITTON SE

ROLEX

NBC

BVLGARI

APPLE

VAN CLEEF & ARPELS

Rarefied company for a girl from Watts.

According to the contract, Marquessa had worked an event for Gerhardt Technologie AG. They made high-performance sports cars, more akin to low-flying rocket ships than anything earthbound. A video clip on their home page showed a blood-red blur screaming around a racetrack; Jacob had to watch it three times before he managed to spot the car. The company motto was *Geschwindigkeit—ohne Kompromisse,* which Google translated as *Speed—without compromise.*

Anyone who could afford a Gerhardt probably didn't have to do a lot of compromising. The base price was $1,345,000. "Options" kicked that up rapidly.

He called Seta Event Management. Predictably, they stonewalled him.

"All I'm asking for is an idea of who was invited," he said. "You don't have to give me names, just a general sense."

"I can't give that information out."

"This is for a murder investigation."

The woman sighed. "Like I've never heard that before."

Click.

WITH LITTLE TO LOSE, he wrote directly to Gerhardt. Then he had another idea. He went to the website for the LA *Times.*

The automotive columnist was named Neil Adler. Jacob e-mailed him asking for a phone interview and got up to take a leak. Thirty seconds later he ran out with his pants unbuckled, snatching his cell phone before it buzzed off the edge of his coffee table.

"Hello?"

"This is Neil." Boyish, excitable voice.

"Hey. Thanks. Wow. That was fast."

"You're a cop."

"Yeah. I—"

"Buy me dinner."

"Pardon?"

"Kings Road Café, twenty minutes. What do you drive?"

"An Accord," Jacob said.

"What year?"

"Two thousand two."

"Make it thirty minutes, then," Adler said, and hung up.

CHAPTER TWENTY-TWO

The restaurant was dark, crowded with endomorphs in skinny jeans. Among them, Adler constituted a different species: motorhead meets egghead. He took off a Bugatti baseball cap to reveal a shaven scalp; a wide jaw widened out to a muscular neck, widened further to massive shoulders, his chest busting out of a blue sport shirt with a Porsche logo on the breast pocket. He adjusted tiny rimless eyeglasses, fiddled with a bow tie as he contemplated the menu for three and a half seconds.

"Protein Power," he said. "Over easy. Side of sausage. Triple espresso."

The waitress looked at Jacob.

"I'm good, thanks."

"You're paying," Adler confirmed.

"I said I would."

"Okay." The journalist reached into a battered messenger bag (LEXUS) and took out a stack of glossy Gerhardt pamphlets. "Which model?"

"Eh—it came out in 2004, so—"

"The Falke S," Adler said, and he began shuffling through the pile for the correct document. Even before he'd found it, he was rattling off stats: 9.0 liter W16 engine (pointing to the cap on the table: "that's one liter bigger than the Veyron"), five turbochargers, 1,100 horsepower at 8,300 RPM with a redline at 8,500, giving you a zero-to-60 of 2.34 seconds and a top speed of 253 MPH.

"That's assuming you wouldn't achieve liftoff or have your DNA recombine, so officially they limit it to two twenty-five."

"Awesome," Jacob said. "What I wanted to ask you was—"

"Pre-preg carbon fiber Kevlar hybrid body, shaving a solid five kilos off the Model G, which is like performing lipo on an Ethiopian child. They had to use solid-state electronics throughout because during the initial testing it shook so fucking much the soldering broke apart. I sat in one, once. I thought I was going to come."

"Did you?" Jacob said.

"Custom boar-skin interior," Adler said. "Hand-stitched. I restrained myself."

Jacob asked about the premiere event. Adler recalled it without hesitation:

"I wasn't invited."

Jacob's heart sank.

Adler went on, cheerily peeved. "Assholes. I'm free publicity. I'm not ashamed to admit it. That's why I'm there. They allow me to live out a fantasy and I give them a write-up. Everybody wins. Gerhardt, they make a great car, but they're a bunch of pricks. I think they wanted to up the cachet factor by being hush-hush."

"That's not standard practice."

"Hell no. Most manufacturers will rent out the Petersen, bring in a band, girls, food, champagne. Not this time. I had to drive way the hell out to an industrial park in East L.A. Unmarked building, security."

"You weren't invited and you went anyway," Jacob said.

"Crissake, I'm still a reporter. I got a master's from USC Journalism. First time in my career I can actually get a *scoop*. There was chatter on the message boards about when and where it was going to go down, so I took my chances."

"Did you get in?"

"They wouldn't even give me a T-shirt. Buncha Nazis."

Jacob decided that the dinner comp wasn't that unreasonable a request after all: the guy had gotten used to not paying.

Adler was shaking his head. "It was gonna be my Pulitzer moment."

The waitress brought his espresso. He threw it back and asked for another.

"Anyway," he said, "I found the whole thing incredibly obnoxious. You buy a million-dollar car, that's cachet aplenty, stop pussying around."

"Who's the clientele for something like that?"

"The Gulfstream–megayacht–private island crowd. Toss in a few more billion for petty cash. There's this Saudi who has four hundred cars, every single one has a gold-plated bidet."

Jacob said, "Not for use while driving."

Adler laughed. "Nobody *drives* these things. The point is to own a toy nobody else has and then say, 'Look at me, I don't give a shit.' The Falke S, they made eighty, to celebrate old man Gerhardt's eightieth birthday. Snapped up in preproduction."

"What's the point of the party, if not to promote?"

"Mutual congratulation," Adler said. Contemplatively: "It's a circle jerk, really."

"Where're the cars going?"

"A lot of them end up in the Middle East. Wouldn't surprise me if bidet guy was there that night. Or one of his cousins. China, once upon a time, although they don't have the cash for it these days. Here in the States? Anywhere there's that level of dough—Beverly Hills, New York, Greenwich, Florida. And Russians. Oh my God, Russians can't get enough of that shit. They armor-plate them, which if you ask me is a fucking travesty."

"The company's based in Stuttgart," Jacob said. "Why have the party here?"

"There were rumors about them building a more affordable 'green' car—think seven-figure plug-in. They changed their mind later, but it was a live topic back then, so they timed the party to coincide with the L.A. Auto Show. Everyone who counts was in town."

Jacob pictured it: dozens of alpha males, paddling in a tank of pure testosterone.

"Tell me about the women at these events," he said.

"There are no women."

"You said—"

"I said *girls*. What do you want to know?"

"They hang out and talk to the buyers."

"Sure."

"Go home with them?"

Adler pitched forward, alert. "That's who got killed? One of the honeys?"

"Can't get into that."

"I'm still looking for that scoop."

"I'll do my best. You think you'd be able to find out who owns a Falke S?"

"Doubtful. I'll give it a shot, though. And you'd only be talking original buyers, right? Which could get complicated. Stuff at that level changes hands all the time."

"Where?"

"Sometimes at auction. I read the catalogs from Gooding and RM regularly and can't remember one coming up. So I'd have to say private sales. No record. No taxes."

"Once the car was registered, they'd have to pay—"

"No no no no. You don't get it. Why spend the extra hundred fifty bucks to register something that never leaves your private museum?"

Dinner arrived: a grilled chicken breast, two quivering eggs, a scoop of cottage cheese, the sausage on a separate plate.

Jacob said, "So you'll try to find out? About the buyers."

"Why the hell not? Nice to apply my talents to a mission of substance." Adler stabbed a sausage, grinning as he chewed. "Eat the rich, right?"

AROUND TWO A.M., Jacob felt his eyes drying out and decided to call it quits. He'd thrown as much as he could at the wall; now it was a matter of seeing what stuck.

He opened a kitchen cabinet, alarmed to discover himself fresh out of liquor.

He checked the recycling bin. Four empties.

How long since you went to a meeting?

Talked to your sponsor?

He put on sneakers and a lightweight jacket.

Outside he paused to admire the insects mobbing the street lamp.

"Evening, ladies."

As he walked, he thought about Marquessa, a human *objet*, circled by men unaccustomed to hearing *no*. Her brief life a line that shot up optimistically, only to plummet to zero.

There were gaps, too. TJ the biggest of all.

Why the boy?

I can't imagine anyone who'd want to hurt that woman.

Jorge Alvarez had said that in an offhand way. Turning the corner onto Airdrome, it occurred to Jacob that the words might contain a deeper truth.

Maybe nobody wanted to hurt the woman.

So far, he'd understood Marquessa as the target, TJ as collateral damage.

The opposite was equally possible.

In a certain way, it made more sense. Anyone who'd slaughter a child, mutilate him, and prop him across from his mother—that wasn't the tantrum of a guy denied game, even if that guy was an egomaniac. Jacob had studied enough homicides to recognize the patience underscoring the depravity, the disquieting overlap of rage and devotion.

He was nearing 7-Eleven when a loud report broke his train of thought, the telltale skinny pop of a Saturday night special.

He took off toward Robertson in a sprint.

CHAPTER TWENTY-THREE

The robbery was in progress.

From half a block away, he could see the green Mazda parked parallel to the 7-Eleven storefront, its headlights on. As he ran, he ordered priorities: Henry; Henry could be dead, he could be shot but alive, he could have fired the shot himself.

Jacob felt on his hip for a gun he did not have. He didn't take it with him every time he went out for booze. He went out for booze a lot.

He kept running.

Reaching the eastern side of Robertson, he saw the counter untended under bright lights, the door to the boiler room wide open. They kept the safe back there.

The Mazda honked a frantic tattoo. He'd been spotted.

He barreled into the crosswalk, shouting *police don't move don't move* at a man with a bandana over his face who busted through the front doors swinging a plastic shopping bag with the orange and green 7-Eleven logo. The guy threw himself into the car and the tires spun and the worst part for Jacob was knowing that he'd failed; he'd seen it coming for days, just as it was playing out in drip-time, the streetlight winking in the side mirror and the scrape of the fender as the Mazda lurched over the sidewalk and slammed into the street, fishtailing on the asphalt; the bones of his feet pounding in sneakers and the rattle of untrained lungs; his upper lip, buzzing, crescendo.

A piece of the night sky tore loose.

Black light, jagged, intent. It rocketed down, punching the driver's door.

Steel buckled like a sucked-in cheek. Four tires lifted. The car rolled and skipped sideways, turning a half-dozen revolutions before landing on its roof, seesawing in a pool of shattered glass, tortured metal, the hiss and pop of ruptured lines.

Sounds of human pain leaked feebly through gape-mouthed window frames.

Stunned, Jacob scanned the sky for the source of the assault.

Nothing.

But he knew, and he felt a stab of gratitude, before he remembered Henry and ran into the store.

HE FOUND HIM in the boiler room, wrists zip-tied to a steam pipe beside the open safe, blood trickling from his ear.

"Are you okay? Are you shot?"

"He hit me," Henry said. He sounded drunk.

While dialing 911, Jacob did a quick check for entry wounds, finding none. He gave the dispatcher his badge number and asked for an ambulance and a black-and-white, then went behind the counter to fetch a pair of scissors and a cup of ice. One of the fridges had a hole blown it, blue Gatorade dripping down the interior glass.

"I heard a shot." He knelt to cut Henry free, pressed the ice to his head. "The drink case? Is that what I heard?"

"My father's going to shit himself," Henry said.

"Stay here," Jacob said. "Don't try to stand up."

He ran out to the street.

The Mazda had stopped rocking. Jacob approached in a wide, careful arc.

"Police," he said. "Get out of the vehicle. Hands where I can see them."

No response; no movement. He crouched level with the windshield. It was streaked with blood, broken but hanging in place, the safety glass distended.

"Are you okay in there?"

Fire Station 58 was two blocks north. Already he could hear the siren. He crab-walked around to the driver's side, holding his cell phone out with both hands.

"I'm going to approach your vehicle," he called. "I don't want you to move. If you move, I will shoot you. Do you understand? Don't move. I'm coming. Here I come."

The bravado of Mr. No-Weapon. He scooted forward rapidly.

Inside the car, a mess of limbs, bloody money, glass.

He tucked his phone in his pocket and intercepted the arriving EMTs.

"These are the bad guys. They don't look too hot. The good guy's inside, he got whaled on a bit."

One EMT broke off to follow Jacob toward the store, glancing back at the overturned car. "The fuck happened?"

Jacob shook his head.

"You didn't see it?"

"Just the result."

Jacob led the EMT to the boiler room and watched him check Henry's pupillary response. Normal. He patted Henry on the knee and went out to await the squad car.

By TEN A.M., he was back at his desk in the archive, doing his duty.

"Morning, Detective."

The arc lights had yet to come up to full strength. Commander Mike Mallick's starched shirt shone dully as he came forward and bent to examine Jacob's stack of files.

"I would've thought you'd be further along than this by now." Mallick closed a folder and straightened up. "Happy to see me?"

"I'm always happy to see you, sir."

"Alas, I can't say the same, today."

Jacob had expected a visit; just not so soon. "I take it you saw the incident report."

"Everything you do ends up on my desk."

"I meant to call you," Jacob said.

"But you didn't."

"I didn't see how it would help. It's over. There's no emergency."

"The *emergency*, Detective, is that someone—although there seems to be a bit of controversy over *whom*—is bowling with cars."

"I apologize, sir. I should have called you sooner."

"Yes, you should've. Because now we've got a story problem. You told the EMTs you hadn't seen anything. Then you told the responding officers that it was a hit-and-run."

"How else would you describe it?" Jacob said.

"I would describe it as a clusterfuck. We have two lowlifes in the hospital who might not live, and if they do, they're going to swear up and down that there was no other car in the vicinity."

Jacob had never heard Mallick use profanity. "They were fleeing the scene of a robbery, sir. Not much credibility."

"That doesn't mean they deserve to die."

"No, sir. Of course not. All I mean is, I saw the shape they were in. There's no way they'll remember anything but impact."

"What if she'd hit another vehicle? What if she'd hit a pedestrian?"

"The road was clear—"

"What about the woman pumping gas on the other side of Airdrome?"

Jacob paused. "I didn't notice that, sir."

"A piano teacher. With superb credibility."

"Is she okay?"

"She's fine," Mallick said. "In fact, she was so fine that she was able to provide a detailed statement. She said the car started rolling"—he went hand over hand, and for a moment Jacob had an image of him, leading a conga line—"like it was hit by a missile. But she didn't see a missile. She didn't see a flame. She didn't see an explosion. She said—this is a quote—'It just jumped up in the air and went crazy.'"

Jacob had to admit that it was an accurate description.

"You don't think that's going to raise some questions?" Mallick said.

"Look," Jacob said, "it was dark, there's—"

"Forget her. What she does or does not say is secondary. What's crucial now is preventing a repeat performance. This can never, ever happen again. Clear?"

"I can't control her, sir."

"You promised me you would not let her get away again."

He hadn't; he had been careful never to make that promise. "There was nothing I could do. It was over in less than a second."

"I want you to describe what *you* saw," Mallick said. "Everything. Don't skimp."

As Jacob talked, the Commander's face grew more and more

deeply furrowed with distress. He had perched on the edge of the desk, long neck wilting.

"Before it happened," he said, "you weren't in manifest danger?"

"Not immediately, no. The threat wasn't toward me. If I were you, sir, I'd think that's cause for optimism. She's taking chances."

Mallick shot him a withering look. "She chose to show herself. Why?"

"They were getting away."

"How many times a day does someone get away with something awful and she doesn't do a thing about it? She did it for *you*. You were angry. She saw a way to help."

"How would she know what I'm feeling?"

"How do you think? You're like a goddamned Roman candle to her."

His aura.

The liminal waves of color that he had perceived surrounding others, that had his doctor referring him to a shrink. They'd begun after Mai transfused him and faded as his body healed. "Sir? Can you see it, too?"

"Wise up, Detective. If I could, do you think I ever would've agreed to take surveillance off you?"

Mallick began to pace. "She's taking risks because she can. Every day she's free, she gets stronger."

"Until?"

"I have no idea. She's never been out of custody this long before."

Jacob said, "You're getting weaker."

Good guess. Mallick flinched.

"I saw the book," Jacob said. "*Dorot shel Beinonim.* My father has a copy."

The Commander sat there, chewing his cheek. When he spoke

next, his voice was low—almost ashamed. "It occurs at a slower pace. Generation to generation, rather than day to day. But, yes, sooner or later we're going to reach the point where we can't readily contain her on our own."

"I think you're already there," Jacob said. "That's why you need me."

"We need you because, whatever our capacity to deal with her once we have her, she can simply continue to stay out of sight."

"You don't know where she is."

"Of course I don't," Mallick said irritably. "I'm not a prophet."

"Nobody's taken the time to explain the rules to me."

"Ask your father. I'm sure he'd be willing to fill you in."

"I did. He showed me the book. He also told me what you did to my mother."

Mallick stiffened.

"You destroyed her," Jacob said.

"That's not correct."

"You used her the way you're using me."

"What happened," Mallick said, "was extremely regrettable."

Jacob began to laugh. "Honestly, sir? Right now, I'm trying not to say something extremely regrettable myself."

Mallick folded long arms across his chest. "It did not occur on my watch. And we've revised our policies since then. Your safety is of the utmost importance to us."

"Horseshit," Jacob said.

Silence.

"I was supposed to retire," Mallick said. "Did you know that?"

"No, sir, I didn't."

"Mel organized a collection for the party. I had my watch picked out. Then . . . *this*."

Jacob said, "So that's your strategy for dealing with her. Containment."

"Ask yourself what you'd do in my position."

Jacob said nothing.

"I know you're fond of her," Mallick said. "But please believe me: it's not safe to have her free in this world. For anyone. You. Most of all, for her. She's a danger to herself. If you care about her, you'll help us."

Then, dialing up a new demeanor, he laid a waxy hand atop the stack of files. "Find anything interesting?"

The sudden bout of agreeability bothered Jacob. He assumed that Divya Das had relayed the contents of their conversation, and that Mallick already knew about his side interest in the Duvall murder. But the Commander's curiosity sounded authentic, and tinged with regret, as if he was just now coming to appreciate the punitive nature of the archive assignment.

"There's a case I've been taking a closer look at," Jacob said.

"Really. And what would that be?"

"Double homicide. Mother and child. Ugly stuff."

"I see."

"I could use some time to work on it."

Mallick was silent a moment. Then he said, "I suppose you'll need a new setup."

Special Projects, making amends for making amends?

Or changing the subject, diverting Jacob's anger over Bina?

Whatever the Commander's motivation, Jacob wasn't about to argue. He much preferred the relatively human horror of murder. "That'd be helpful, sir."

"I'll have it sent to your apartment. Anything else?"

Jacob remembered a white credit card with seemingly unlimited credit—but only for certain items. "Expense account?" he asked.

Mallick stooped to tie a shoelace. "You want to work like everyone else, you'll submit reimbursement forms just like everyone else."

Jacob said, "What's going to happen with the piano teacher?"

"Let us worry about that."

"What are you going to do to her?"

Mallick straightened up. Fixed him with a stare. "I hope you're not implying what it sounds like you're implying, Detective."

Jacob said nothing.

"We're the good guys," Mallick said. "Don't ever forget that."

CHAPTER TWENTY-FOUR

Stoner Avenue Elementary School sat half a mile from the house where Marquessa and TJ had lived. Jacob flashed his badge briefly at the receptionist and introduced himself as a truancy officer on an administrative call.

She told him to head on inside while she paged the principal.

Patricia Eubanks was a black woman in her early fifties. She shut her door, fretting as she shook Jacob's hand. "You must be new."

He said, "I'm here about TJ White."

She recoiled. "Pardon?"

He handed her his ID, adding that he'd meant to be discreet.

She appraised him before giving an appreciative nod.

"I've been asked to revisit the file," he said. "I didn't want to create a disturbance."

Eubanks nodded. She sat at her desk and began opening and shutting drawers. "I haven't thought about TJ in a long time. For a long time, I thought about nothing else."

"Whatever you can tell me would be helpful."

Eubanks found what she was looking for: a neon-green stress ball, which she began to squeeze rhythmically. "Unfortunately, I don't think I can add much. I try to establish a personal connection with each one of my students, but that takes time, and I never got the chance to know TJ or his mother. They were new to the area."

She paused. "I do remember where I was when I heard the news. That I will never forget. It was a Thursday evening, day before Christmas Eve. I was wrapping presents and my phone rang. One of our former teachers lived on their block."

"Jorge Alvarez," Jacob said. "I spoke to him."

Green foam swelled from her fist. "I'd known Jorge ten years, but till that night I'd never heard him cry."

Jacob considered Alvarez's emotional state during the most recent interview—less extreme, but consistent with the natural ebb of grief. "Did the police ever talk to you?"

"No."

"His teachers?"

"Nobody came to the school, Detective, except for the community relations officer. We held a meeting for parents in the gym." Eubanks paused. "I suppose they could've spoken to Susan over the phone."

"Susan . . ."

"Lomax. TJ's teacher. We have two kindergarten classes. One slot, we can't keep someone there more than a couple of years; it's a revolving door. The other class belongs to Susan. She's been around longer than I have. We had an emergency staff meeting the day after Christmas to figure out how we were going to talk to the students about what had happened. Susan was at the center of the discussion, because it was her kids most directly affected. In the end, we tried to use it as an opportunity to learn."

"About death?"

"About life," she said.

She put down the ball.

"That poor, poor little boy," she said. "Everyone, and I mean everyone, was a wreck. We came back for spring semester, and it felt ten degrees colder."

"If it's all right with you, I'd like to speak with Mrs. Lomax."

"It's certainly all right, although you'd be better off not calling her that."

"What should I call her?"

"Ms.," Eubanks said. She glanced at her computer. "Recess is in seven minutes."

She left, clutching the stress ball.

Eight minutes later, the door opened and in walked a stout woman in khaki cargo pants. Susan Lomax stood around five feet, but her entrance dramatically shifted the room's gravity, prompting Jacob to sit up a little straighter.

She said, "I've been waiting ten years for you people to call me back."

LOMAX AND JACOB sat facing each other.

She said, "We keep a sign-in sheet posted on the wall of the class-room. There's a space for morning drop-off and another for pickup. It's important for us to know who's taking which child and when, and to have a record of it. TJ's mother kept forgetting to sign him out. It was an ongoing problem. At the end of the week, I have to submit the attendance sheet to the principal, and in TJ's row there would be five blank spaces, highlighted where his mother hadn't signed."

Realizing she was taking a dead woman to task, she toned it down a degree. "I didn't like to pester her about it, because I knew she was a single mother, and she always looked wrung out. About halfway through the fall semester—early November—a man came to pick TJ up instead of her."

"Can you describe him? Age, race, height, build?"

"He was white. Big, and tall, although frankly, everybody looks big and tall to me." Lomax grimaced. "I'm not being very helpful, am I."

"You're doing great."

"I feel responsible to get it right," she said.

Her eyes grew unfocused as she walked back in time. "It's hard to say how old he was. People age differently. He wore a hat, one of those—you know, fur, with earflaps. He was totally overdressed. That struck me. He looked like he was getting ready to land on the moon. Overcoat, scarf, gloves. Then I heard him talk and thought, 'Well, he's Russian, that's why.'"

A spike of excitement. "How do you know he was Russian?"

"My mother-in-law is from Petersburg," she said. "I recognized the accent. And TJ called him *dyadya*. 'Uncle.'"

"TJ knew him."

She nodded. "And liked him, I could see that. He said TJ's mother was busy and had asked him to help her with pickup. But he wasn't on the authorized list. I told him sorry, I couldn't allow it. He started arguing with me. 'Just for today.' I told him to tell Ms. Duvall to come get TJ no later than six, and that she'd be responsible for the fee."

She paused to explain: "We do an after-school program. You have to be enrolled, and TJ wasn't. It costs eight dollars a day. Less back then, but we need every penny."

"What happened?"

"He took out a hundred-dollar bill and waved it in my face. 'For the fee,' he said."

Jacob stopped scribbling and looked at her.

"Your basic bully," she said.

"Did you get his name?" Jacob asked. "Maybe when you checked the list?"

She looked despondent. "I'm . . . I don't remember. I—"

She broke off, her eyes big and round. "Something else. I just thought of it. He was wearing a ring."

"What kind of ring?"

"I don't know. It wasn't gold, that much I can . . . Black, I think, and huge. He'd taken off his glove, to get at his wallet, and he was waving the money in my face. I thought he might punch me. Does that help at all?"

"Absolutely," Jacob said.

"I'd draw it for you," she said, "except there's really nothing to draw. It was just a big piece of metal, almost like brass knuckles. Vulgar. Black, though. Definitely black."

Jacob said, "That's excellent. Thank you."

"I'm sorry I can't remember his name."

"It's all right," he said. "What happened next? After he waved the money at you."

"I asked him to leave. He walked out and I never saw him again." She paused. "TJ's mother came to get him that evening. She was pretty clearly annoyed with me.'"

Disapproval had crept back into her voice.

"It's the child's welfare I'm concerned about, first and foremost," Susan Lomax said. "Parents don't always understand that. It can be very frustrating."

Jacob asked if she had told any of this to the police.

Like a lighthouse beacon, the disapproval swung around in his direction.

"I tried," she said. "Nobody ever called me back. Can you explain that to me?"

He said, "Wish I could."

"At least you're honest. How hard is it to return a call? I even went down to the station in person, but they told me I was at the wrong department, they couldn't help me."

She shook her head, glanced at her watch, worn with the face on the inside of her wrist. Jacob figured it for a habit born of too many job-related casualties.

"Recess is over," she said.

She didn't get up to leave, though. She said, "He was a sweet child."

Jacob nodded. "So I hear."

"Some boys come into a room and immediately go for the first thing they can destroy. It's not malicious, it's just the age. TJ wasn't like that. He was thoughtful, cautious. Young for the class. He preferred to play with the girls. He liked to draw. He liked to build. A bit of a loner, but I respected him for that."

She reached for the tissue box on the principal's desk.

"I've been doing this job since I was twenty-three," she said, wiping her eyes. "I'm forty-seven now. Except for my mother's death, I've never taken more than a week off. I timed both of my pregnancies to give birth over the summer. I love what I do. But I'll tell you something, Detective. That spring, I came close to quitting."

"You didn't, though," Jacob said.

She evaluated him for sincerity. Nodded, and set the crumpled tissue down, watching it slowly expand. She started to cry again, without fanfare. "I felt I had to set an example for the children."

CHAPTER TWENTY-FIVE

He phoned Neil Adler from the road.

"Christ, you're impatient."

"I need Russians," Jacob said. "That narrow it down for you?"

"Lot of Russians in this universe."

"Do your best."

"I expect another meal out of this," Adler said.

"You got it."

"And an exclusive."

"No promises," Jacob said, clicking off.

Fighting his way to Hollywood along side streets, he pulled into the body-dump alley and stopped behind the bakery.

Two slots, filled by a white delivery van and a tan Sentra. He blocked both and entered the bakery through the rear door, walking a hallway crammed with cleaning supplies.

Dry heat radiated from the kitchen, where a pair of Hispanic men in hairnets toiled, one painting a sheet of dumplings with egg wash, the other tilting a fifty-pound sack of flour into a mixer. Neither man looked up as Jacob passed.

The same counterwoman was on duty. She did a double take, quickly returned her attention to the customer at the display case.

Jacob got in line.

While he waited, he scanned the corkboard, covered with bilingual fliers. English and Russian. He read the labels in the case, written in both Latin and Cyrillic characters.

Syrniki. Vatrushka. Bird's Milk Cake.

The customer was an old woman. She left a smudgy trail on the glass as she indicated various piles of cookies.

"Dva . . . Pyat . . ."

The counterwoman dutifully filled a box, her eyes occasionally darting to Jacob.

"Okay," the old woman said. *"Chorosho, dostatochno."*

The counterwoman reached up to tug string from a reel bolted to the wall. The old woman counted coins from a beaded purse. Jacob's eye snagged on the girl depicted on the box of chocolate bars beside the register.

Like TJ, a child who'd never age.

The old woman finished paying for her cookies. Said, *"Spasiba,"* and tottered out, activating an electric chime.

The counterwomen said, "Can I help you?"

Unmistakable now, the guttural *h.*

Ken I chelp you.

He was starting to take out the case file when the door chimed again. A man in a gray suit and no tie got in line behind him, shifting his weight impatiently.

The start of the lunch rush. Jacob ordered a cup of coffee and a couple of mushroom *pirozhki* and sat on the bench beneath the corkboard, eating. He waited for the gray-suited man to leave with his sandwich, then set his cup down, walked to the front door, flipped the sign around from OPEN to CLOSED, and threw the dead bolt.

"Excuse me please," the counterwoman said. "What are you doing?"

Jacob took out the file, selected a close-up of TJ with his eyelids cut off, and slapped it on the marble counter.

"Look," he said.

As she'd done before, she averted her face toward the ceiling. He'd thought then that she was reacting to the brutality of the image.

I have customers.

Now he knew better. She'd looked away because she was afraid.

"Look at him," Jacob said.

The woman's lips bunched. "Leave my shop, please."

"Not until you look."

"I will call police," the woman said, loudly.

He held up his badge. "Be my guest."

She said nothing.

"Look at his face."

"I do not need to."

"I think you do."

"I have nothing to say."

"I hear that a lot," Jacob said. "Nobody ever says it unless they have something to say."

"I want lawyer."

"You're not under arrest. We're talking."

She said nothing.

"You have kids," Jacob said.

She blinked, but didn't answer.

"They're probably grown up by now. Do they have kids? Are you a grandmother?"

A rattle at the door—a pair of men in work clothes, trying to enter the bakery.

"He has a grandmother," Jacob said. "You want to meet her? I could bring her by."

The men began to knock.

"I have business," the woman said. "Please."

"You'll get back to it, soon enough." Jacob wagged a finger at the men. Pointed to the CLOSED sign.

Consternation, then shrugs. The men left.

One of the bakers poked a floury head out. "Zina? *¿Todo bien?*"

"Tell him to get lost," Jacob said.

There was a small dent in the counterwoman's jaw, just to the left of her chin. She rubbed at it, as though trying to smooth it out. *"Vete fuera,"* she said.

The baker didn't move.

"Rafael, tambien," the counterwoman said. *"Ahora, por favor."*

The baker disappeared; Jacob heard the back door open and shut.

"Ten years ago," he said. "And you still think about it."

She was twisting her apron.

"But it wasn't your fault. Was it? I don't think it was. I don't think you had anything to do with it. I think you were afraid, just like you are now."

"Please," she said. "I don't know."

"Then why won't you look at him?"

"Because I don't want to see," she said shrilly.

"You think I like looking at it?"

She shook her head, disgusted. "You are making problems."

"For who? Him? He's dead. His mother's dead. That's never going to change. But me? I'm a policeman. It's my job to make sure the person who did this doesn't do it again, to anybody, ever. That means I have to ask you questions, again, and again, and again, until you talk to me."

She began to laugh. "Okay, mister."

"That's funny?"

"*You* are funny," she said. "You know what's policeman? He comes to your house in middle of night. He bangs down door. He spits in your face. He breaks your bones," she said, pointing to the divot in her jaw. "He puts you in cell. You don't know what you did. You don't know how long you will be. *That* is policeman," she said. "You? You are *nothing.*"

She crossed her arms and nodded to herself.

Jacob said, "That's not how it works here. That kind of law doesn't last."

Another customer was rapping, hollering through the glass.

The woman said, "I know nothing."

Jacob picked up the photo of TJ. He tacked it to the corkboard, along with his business card, and left via the back.

CHAPTER TWENTY-SIX

Bina blearily follows the group off the plane to the gate, where two men await them. The first is sallow and trim in a brown polyester suit, smiling blandly over the shoulder of a compact, bushy-headed fellow in snug blue jeans and a hairy green turtleneck.

PRAGUE WELCOMES
INTERNATIONAL ALLIANCE OF JEWISH ARTISTS

They number eighteen, hailing from points across the United States, plus a token Canadian to make the alliance international. Strangers when they convened in the international terminal at Kennedy, they now share the peculiar, mildly delirious intimacy that comes of long distance traveled at close quarters.

The man in the turtleneck folds his sign and addresses them in clean English.

"Honored guests." Black eyes gleam above tracts of five o'clock shadow. "I am Ota Wichs. On behalf of the Jewish community, it is my privilege to be the first to say: *vítejte!*"

Mumbling: *hello* and *thank you*. Bina catches herself before she replies in Czech.

"My friends, we have eagerly anticipated your arrival. There is much to do and see. Before we proceed, however, it is my added privilege to introduce to you my esteemed colleague Mr. Antonín Hrubý, religious undersecretary of the Ministry of Education and Culture, without whose support this opportunity to host you would not have been possible."

He begins clapping loudly. Confusion passes over the group before they get the message and join in. The man in the brown suit takes a shallow bow.

"Friends," Ota Wichs says, "please, come with me."

They proceed down the arrivals corridor, bunched uneasily, like sheep. A souvenir vendor offers tin buttons imprinted with the Czechoslovakian flag. Other carts stand idle, covered in heavy plastic tarps and chained, though it is midday. Bina counts more soldiers than passengers, and while the place has the correct layout, the correct stale plasticky odor, something about it feels misaligned— theoretical, the result of asking someone who'd never been in an airport to build one.

A sandy-haired photographer from Seattle uncaps her camera, drawing Hrubý's instant attention. He brings the group to a halt.

Ota Wichs clears his throat. "For reasons of security, we ask that you refrain from taking photographs inside the airport, please."

Hrubý puts a hand out.

There's a tense moment before the photographer pops open her camera, removes the film, and gives it to him. He pockets it and walks on.

"Please continue," Wichs says.

Bina hears her father's old rebuke.

You were not there.

She's here now.

To avoid an immigration line three hundred strong, Hrubý herds them down a side corridor to a cramped office, where he calls roll and checks passports against a preprinted list. Nervous chuckles as they answer *here* like schoolchildren.

To offset the coarseness of the process, Ota Wichs makes sure to smile at each of them individually.

"Bina Reich Lev," Hrubý reads.

Wichs meets her eye. "Welcome."

Hrubý looks up from his clipboard. "Bina Reich Lev?"

"Here," she says.

He crosses off her name and moves down the list, leaving Bina to reflect on the fact that Wichs knew who she was before she'd spoken a word.

They board a tour bus. Bina takes a row at the back, putting her legs up to ward off company. Thus far she has succeeded at keeping mostly to herself, and the group has tacitly designated her resident oddball, with her long skirt and her head scarf and her kosher airplane meal.

As they merge onto the highway, the faulty seal around her window begins to stream cold air. Not the worst thing, as several people have lit up, the cabin growing hazy. Bina watches the passing countryside, orange farmhouse roofs licking at a pitted gray sky.

Ota Wichs blows into a microphone. "Testing. Testing . . . Okay. Now, friends, I must ask if anyone has been to Prague before."

Bina nearly raises her hand. But she has only false memories. Ghost stories.

"Then I welcome you again. Please, to your left, you may see the nature preserve of Divoká Šárka, named for the lady warrior, wild Šárka. According to our legend, many years ago these lands were ruled by women. You see, my friends, our people are very progressive, we had female leadership long before it became fashionable in the West . . ."

There are few other cars on the road until they reach the outskirts of town. In a bid to distract them from the increasingly grim landscape, Wichs keeps up his patter, clutching at a seat back as the bus sways between stacks of concrete painted harsh primary colors.

"To your right, you may see the military hospital."

Everything from shoes to street lamps has been designed with function foremost in mind, and the sunlight that worms through the clouds serves mainly to harden angles and expose seams.

"To your left, a brand-new gymnasium . . ."

Bina doesn't care about the accomplishments of the state.

She's looking up at the apartment buildings.

Behind one of those dingy curtains, her mother is chopping vegetables.

She's looking at the bent-backed man, smoking on a park bench: her father, following a fourteen-hour day, not yet ready to face his family.

I'm here now, Taťka.

The city's brutalist shell begins to crack open, a foot at a time, giving way to Old Town, the architectural elegance that remains because no one has bothered to dismantle it. Traffic congeals. After thirty minutes trapped on the Hlávkův Bridge, suspended over a river Vltava crawling thick with pollutants, a vote is taken to walk the last half mile. They drag their bags over cigarette butts to the musty lobby of the Hotel Důlek. Wichs distributes room keys, allotting them a brief break to freshen up before the welcome reception.

IT TAKES PLACE at the old Jewish town hall and is attended by community leaders as well as a cadre of local artists. Before the meal come greetings, expressions of fellowship, and a speech from the chief rabbi of Bratislava, who has taken the train in for the occasion and who talks at length about the Torah's connection to the class struggle.

"We observe that many religious rules have a socialist character," Wichs translates, "such as the abrogation of property rights every seven years, during the *shemittah* year, so that in a real sense we may regard Moses as a forerunner to Marx."

Undersecretary Hrubý leans against the wall, taking notes.

The window nearest Bina overlooks the scabby roof of the Alt-Neu Synagogue. On the way over from the hotel, Wichs paused outside the *shul* to provide a thumbnail biography of Judah Loew, the Maharal. Were they familiar with the golem of Prague?

Everyone was, although no one perhaps as intimately as Bina. Sam is a devotee of Loew's, introducing his ideas into most Shabbat table discussions. She's heard the golem legend and its variants too many times to count.

Someone asked if Wichs had ever been up to the garret.

He placed his hands on his heart. *I regret to inform you that there is nothing but broken furniture. But we will learn more tomorrow. For now let us move on, please.*

The rabbi from Bratislava wraps up, drawing tired applause. Teenagers acting as waiters distribute bread baskets and pitchers of water and beer.

Joining Bina at her table are five locals, an installation artist from San Francisco, a painter from Dallas, and, to her left, a dour Brooklyn lithographer who drinks pint after pint of pilsner, growing more slurred and more insistent as he tries to engage the Czechs on politics, while they smile awkwardly and attempt to steer the conversation back to art.

Dinner arrives: a platter of sausages, wallowing in fat.

"I'm not saying I was *happy* Reagan got shot," the lithographer says, sliding a sausage onto his plate.

"Hello, my friends." Ota Wichs drags a chair over, inserting himself next to Bina, moving the platter along before she can take food. "We are enjoying ourselves?"

"I don't like it if anyone gets shot," the lithographer says.

Wichs claps him on the shoulder. "Yes, of course, this is tragic, this is no way to celebrate, we must talk about more pleasant things."

He fills the nearest glass.

"To art," he says. "The universal language. *Na zdraví.*"

"I thought love was the universal language," the lithographer says.

"Love, art," Wichs says. "To an artist, they are the same thing, yes?"

The sausages have migrated halfway around the table, coming to rest in front of a Czech writer, who is telling the Dallas painter that she has lovely lips. Bina waves to get their attention and is startled by Wichs, murmuring in her ear.

"I understand that you observe the kosher laws."

Bina looks at him.

"I believe it said so in your application," he says. "Unless I am mistaken."

"No," she says slowly. "I do."

"Then you will not want to partake of the meat."

"It's not kosher?"

"Unfortunately, our community lacks a butcher. However, I have arranged for a special meal."

"Thanks."

Wichs beckons a waiter. "Don't thank me until you've seen what it is."

A limp, undressed salad; an extra bread roll and a pat of margarine.

"Please accept my apologies," Wichs says. "The beer is quite tasty, though."

"I don't drink," Bina says.

"I've never met a Czech who didn't drink."

She raises an eyebrow at him. "I'm not Czech."

"Your application said you spoke the language."

"What else did my application say?"

A wry smile. "You ought to know. You wrote it."

She didn't, though. Frayda did. "My parents spoke Czech at home."

"Ah. And did they drink?"

"My father," she says, tearing open a roll. "Too much."

Wichs presses his palms together. "Again, my sincerest apologies."

"Forget it," she says, spreading margarine. "Excuse me."

In the restroom, she washes her hands, stepping outside to make the blessing. When she returns to the table, Wichs waits for her to make the blessing on the bread and take a bite, allowing her to speak again.

"What must it be like for you," he says, "to come home."

The bread is chalky; she sips water to wash it down. "I was born in New York."

"But your soul is from Prague."

"Was that on my application, too?"

He laughs. "No. But I can see your nature plain as your nose." He tilts his empty glass, laced with foam, toward her paltry dinner. "It's the way of our people to accept their fate without complaint."

Nineteen sixty-eight, Soviet tanks grinding through Wenceslas Square.

Her father, throttling the newspaper.

"I'm also Jewish," she says. "Jews love to complain."

"Yes, that's true. I suppose I've offended you, reducing you to one aspect when clearly you have many sides."

"We all do," she says. "Did my application mention that I observe the Sabbath?"

"It did, yes. Friday night you will dine with me and my family."

"That's very kind of you."

"It is kind of you to come." He rises. "I hope you will find your visit inspiring."

THE NEXT DAY, everyone else is hungover, pulling coats against the seven a.m. chill. Last night brought a bit of musical beds. Bina lay awake until two, listening to laughter and grunts through the thin walls, and now cigarettes and sheepish grins go around.

"Good morning, my friends."

Ota Wichs wears the same clothes as yesterday, a fresh crop of stubble already rising. He inquires after their accommodations, exclaims approval, and announces the day's itinerary: a tour of Josefov, the former Jewish quarter.

They proceed on foot through wet, cobbled streets. Wichs peppers them with a mixture of statistics, Communist rhetoric, and hoary Tales from the Ghetto. It's unclear to Bina how much he believes what he's saying, and she feels saddened by this caricature, so at odds with the Prague she inherited from her parents, a city at once profound and everyday.

All the same, she can appreciate the need for caution. Leaving dinner, the Czech writer gripped her by the arm, whispering that her hotel room was bugged. He offered to take her home instead, which did throw his motivation into question.

Their first stop is the old Jewish cemetery. Official visiting hours don't begin until nine-thirty. Undersecretary Hrubý is there to open the gates.

Behind them lies a mess of broken stones and unchecked vegetation, bottles and spent condoms, moss and rotting leaves.

"To the naked eye," Wichs says, "not very large. But remember: the dead lie twelve deep. In terms of luminaries per square meter, you will not find a more illustrious resting place in Europe."

He leads them along the perimeter path, pointing out the grave of the astronomer and mathematician David Ganz; the grand monument to financier Mordecai Meisel.

Hrubý trails them, taking notes.

"And here we come to our most famous resident, Rabbi Judah Loew, the Maharal."

They crowd around a formidable marble tomb framed by cartouches. Wichs launches into a lengthy discourse on the headstone's motifs—the grapes, the lion—as well as the inscriptions detailing Loew's literary achievements.

"And beside him for eternity, his beloved wife, Perel."

Bina has to smile. Just another rabbi's wife. Some things never change.

"Now that we have paid our respects to the individuals," Wichs says, "we shall proceed to the Alt-Neu Synagogue, where, it is said, the famous golem was given life."

He plucks a pebble from the ground, places it atop the monument, and walks on.

Bina lingers, waiting for the group to dissipate. Sam would want her to pay respects. She kneels to get a pebble of her own.

"Excuse, please."

Hrubý stands on the path, frowning at her.

"Sorry," she says. "I was just . . ."

She gets up, brushing herself off, laughing self-consciously. "Sorry."

Hrubý flips to a new page in his notebook and begins to write.

Bina hurries to rejoin the group. Not until they have exited the cemetery does she realize she forgot to place the pebble.

THREE DAYS GO BY, three days of sightseeing and workshops, capped by long indulgent evenings in wine bars or beer halls, hashing out meaningless points of aesthetics in order to get to the real goal: determining that night's couplings.

And all the while, Bina hovers at the edge.

They visit the Alt-Neu and stand in the antechamber listening to a pro forma lecture on Gothic architecture. Bina looks at the Maharal's chair. She looks at the Torah ark. She peers through slots cut into the wall at the shuttered women's section. She rubs the pews' soft wood, waiting in vain for the heavens to call to her.

They visit the site of Theresienstadt concentration camp, where

Věra's family died, where the memorial plaque commemorates *35,000 Czechoslovak citizens* without mention of Jews. Bina puts her ear to the wind and hears nothing.

She sits on a panel discussion about craft and class without opening her mouth.

Hrubý takes notes.

Alone in her dingy room, she pleads yet again with the hotel operator to grant her a connection to the United States.

"I'll pay for it in advance," she says. "Please."

She hasn't spoken to her husband or son in four days.

What is she doing here?

She wants to consider her decision to come to Prague as a form of temporary insanity, caught from Frayda. But she needed weeks to get ready. She had to get the visa, secure child care. So she isn't insane, or else it wasn't temporary.

On the morning she left, Sam accompanied her to the gate at LAX, making a puppet of Jacob, waving his hand. *Good-bye, Ima! We'll miss you!* She leaned in to kiss them and Jacob lunged out and clung to her. His nails bit into the nape of her neck. They grow so fast, and Sam is helpless with the clipper. She mumbled something about an emery board in the bathroom; she freed herself from her son's arms, and walked down the Jetway to the sound of his screams.

Clearly you have many sides.

Never has she been aware of so many of them simultaneously; never have they felt so at war. Artist. Jew. American. Czech. Wife. Mother. The tide in her head builds to a roar as the operator informs her, for the fourth day in a row, that it is not possible to call abroad at the moment.

Bina slams the phone down.

———

Thursday, October 28, is a national holiday, the anniversary of the founding of the independent Czechoslovak state. Along with thousands of others, the group boards the tram to the parade grounds at Letná Plain. Weather balloons bob, numbered by city district, the sections further subdivided by employer: the Skoda automobile factory, the Ministry of Information. Members of the Workers' Militia usher folks amid a tossing sea of tricolors. Scratch at the patriotism, though, and find mischief; a torn cup becomes a megaphone, used to direct a question toward the bandstand.

"Here I am, Mr. Husák," the man yells, addressing the absent Prime Minister. "Where are you?"

The International Alliance of Jewish Artists has its own private section, set up with chairs so that they can observe the proceedings in comfort. A nice surprise is the presence of Ota Wichs's family: his wife, Pavla, an angular woman toting a picnic basket, and son, Peter, who's nine but looks five, with elfin features and a thatch of shiny black hair. His shy smile gives Bina a dull ache in her chest.

Wichs's attempts to translate are drowned out by overloud cheers. Then follows a lively display of strength, intelligible in any language: MiGs thunder overhead, soldiers march, a military band blares. The national anthem starts up, and thirty thousand people lift their voices, and Hrubý climbs up onto a chair, waving his arms like a conductor. Words Bina thought she'd forgotten fall from her mouth like tears.

Kde domov můj? Kde domov můj?
Where is my home? Where is my home?

They sang it, her parents and their friends; potlucks in Prospect

Park, the adults drunk at midday and telling sappy stories. *Where is my home?* Bina understands, now.

It's not a question, but an accusation.

Where is my home?

What have you done with it?

The festivities last for hours, district divisions breaking down, people trampling the vast brown lawns, toasting, singing, dancing, hugging. They share sandwiches, a precious bottle of wine. A stranger hands Bina a cucumber, which he boasts was grown by the sweat of his labor on his allotment garden. He insists that she eat it, watching her with a squint of profound pleasure; when she finishes, he kisses her cheek and runs off.

As dusk falls, she has put nothing else in her stomach except acrid water. Her bladder is bursting. She goes off in search of a bathroom that turns out not to exist. Men and women alike are simply doing whatever they need to do, wherever they can find room to do it. Bina weaves between the locust trees, her feet squelching. Over the plain roll accordion music and the urgency of sexual congress. Fireworks explode. She's going to want a long, hot shower.

Finding a suitable clump of privet, she waits for the night to fade to black before gathering up her skirt. To the west, the turrets of Prague Castle are lit red, white, and blue—a hilariously romantic view for peeing. She starts to giggle.

"Prominˇte."

Bina shrieks and leaps up.

A whistle lances the sky, light bursts, and she discerns the shape of a boy.

"Excuse me," Peter Wichs says. "I did not mean to scare you."

Her heart is racing, a stray drop of urine trickling down the inside of her thigh. She feels vaguely assaulted. She reminds herself that he's a child.

She asks in Czech if he's lost.

"Please come with me," he says, and he slips off into the night.

HE MOVES QUICKLY, playing a weak flashlight through the trees, short legs pumping.

Bina hurries to catch up. They've gone some distance before she realizes they're headed in the wrong direction.

"We should go back," she says. "Your father will be worried."

"My father sent me."

"To do what?"

"Bring you."

"Bring me where?"

"You can speak English," he says. "I know how."

They stumble along the paths sloping toward the Vltava.

"Peter." She assumes her most maternal tone. "Peter, let's stop for a second and you tell me what's going on."

"Can you walk faster?"

They reach an unpeopled area. The edge of the city comes into view.

"That's enough," she says, grabbing at his sleeve.

He regards her with weary patience. "I thought you would go sooner."

"What?"

"To the bathroom," he says. "I was waiting all day. What took you so long?"

He removes her hand. "We're late."

———

CROSSING OVER THE ČECHŮV BRIDGE, graffiti shouting from its rusting balustrades, Bina finds herself starting to speed up, and then to outpace him.

She knows where they're headed.

In the wan moonlight, the Alt-Neu *shul* broods like a bird of prey.

"My father will be here as soon as he can," Peter says, reaching into his shirt.

He tugs out a key on a necklace of twine.

They enter the synagogue and step down into the antechamber, chilly, resonant. She follows Peter along the hall. He unlocks a door and reveals an unlit stairway.

"I'll wait here to give you privacy," he says, handing her the flashlight.

He offers no further explanation. Bina makes her way down carefully, fingers brushing the wall for balance. The stones grow slippery, the air damp and fungal.

She reaches bottom, a candlelit room with a small bureau, a stack of fraying towels, a camp shower in a plastic tub. Through an arch, she sees a second room. More candles dance in the rippling surface of a ritual bath.

There's no one to supervise her. No wise husband to teach her, no friend making obscure demands.

We need you to be physically present.

She is here. She could not articulate why she is here. Yet the moment is calling to her, like a song in a forgotten language.

She strips, showers off, and immerses, finding the *mikveh* pleasingly warm. She dresses and heads upstairs, reaching the top just as Ota Wichs arrives.

He bolts the front door and comes to join them. "Okay?" he asks.

"Okay," Peter says. "No one saw."

Ota kisses him on the head. "Well done." Turning to Bina, he says, "I apologize for the secrecy. Obviously, we have had to be extra careful. Hrubý—you have seen enough of him to know what type of fellow he is. His father was a hammer, his mother, a sickle. But it's all right, he'll be drunk tonight."

He smiles. "Shall we ascend?"

CHAPTER TWENTY-SEVEN

The Commander asked me to bring this by."

Detective Paul Schott stood on the landing outside Jacob's apartment, a laptop dwarfed by his huge hands.

Jacob stepped back to admit him.

Of all the members of Special Projects, it was Schott, with his strong whiff of zealotry, who unsettled Jacob most. Fat, red-cheeked Mel Subach had a sense of humor and could give as good as he got; Mike Mallick was driven and condescending but a pragmatist at heart.

Schott made no attempt to disguise his contempt as he lumbered in, carelessly Frisbeeing the computer onto the couch. He'd shaved off his mustache, which elongated his face and emphasized his frown.

"I'd offer you a drink," Jacob said, "but you're going to turn me down."

Schott waved impatiently. "Fine, you know. I know you know. Congratulations. I'm going on record that I don't trust you."

"Join the club," Jacob said. "Call my ex-wife, she's the president."

"Which one?" Schott grinned, a bulldog contemplating steak. "Yeah. I know all about you, too, Lev."

"Everybody needs a hobby," Jacob said.

"You could take up pottery," Schott said.

"You," Jacob said, "can shut the fuck up."

The big man started.

"You don't mention her," Jacob said. "You don't allude to her. Ever. Got it?"

Silence.

Schott said, "That all, Your Highness?"

"Yeah. Leave me the hell alone."

Schott snorted. "Best of luck."

HAVING DECENT RESEARCH TOOLS felt like coming up for air. For the next twenty-four hours, Jacob reran names, combed databases.

His relief faded fast. He could find nothing with a matching MO, not even close.

He turned his attention to the owner of the bakery. Her name was Zinaida Moskvina. Her record was spotless, free of so much as a parking ticket, and he felt affirmed in his hunch that whatever had happened, she hadn't been at the center of it but dragged along.

Her daughter was a different story.

Ekaterina Moskvina, twenty-seven, had racked up three DUIs in the last four years. Additional busts for coke, shoplifting, chucking a drink at a police officer. She called herself Katie on her Facebook page and declared herself "dat bitch u dont fuk wit." Her posts consisted of announcements that she was hitting the club and sHiT gOn GeT kRaYzEe KrAy.

Jacob agreed with her there.

He spent that night staking out her Van Nuys apartment in an unmarked. She was disappointingly well behaved, in by seven and lights out by ten. The same went for the next several days. But he persisted, and late on Friday night, he got his reward.

Eleven p.m., the hour for shit getting krayzee kray fast approaching. He'd skipped his visit to Bina and was composing a guilt-stricken text to Rosario when Katie emerged in circulation-choking jeans and a black halter top.

She got into her Kia and sped off.

Jacob tailed her to a dive bar on Magnolia. His breath quickened as he stepped inside, walking past Katie's booth to occupy a stool at the end, scalloped wood a comfort beneath his backside.

"What can I getcha?"

Jacob tore his gaze from the blocky amber silhouette of the Jim Beam bottle and asked for a Bud Light. Moderation of a kind.

Behind him, Katie & Co. were whooping it up, a multiethnic team, all wearing identically skimpy clothing: *Girls Gone Wild* meets the United Colors of Benetton. Over pitchers of margaritas, they debated hotly where to take the evening next.

"Here you go, buddy."

Jacob had begun salivating well before he took the first sip. He white-knuckled through the urge to drain the bottle in one go.

Katie seemed unencumbered by any such doubts. For the next hour, Jacob kept a refill count. He figured it wouldn't take long. She was petite, five-three without the platform heels. Though she did have Russian genetics. And there was another variable: the strength of the margaritas.

For the sake of research, he ordered one for himself. Medium.

An hour later, he felt confident she would blow well over the limit.

Now he had to hope that she'd offer to drive.

"I'll drive," she announced, pitching back a half-full glass.

Like ducklings the women filed out of the bar, went through the leggy contortions of fitting into Katie's tiny car.

He followed them over Laurel Canyon to the Strip. She'd had a lot of practice driving drunk. No twenty-mile-per-hour trepidation, no reckless lane changes. You could screen a video of her in driver's ed as an example of road courtesy. They had that sad fact in common, he and poor Katie: both functioned better with a certain amount of intoxicant in their systems.

Finally, at Sunset and Fairfax, she made an illegal U-turn, and he clamped the light on his dashboard and switched on the flasher.

The compact lurched. Making a run for it?

No. She was pulling over.

When he reached her, her eyes were full of tears, her mouth full of breath mints. He asked her to step out of her vehicle.

She blew a .129 and immediately demanded a blood test.

"You got it."

He drove her down Sunset, turning onto Wilcox toward Hollywood Station but stopping a block shy to veer into the parking lot of a Staples. He cut the engine and turned around.

"Listen," he said. "You're fucked. You know that, right?"

Her mascara was running in streaks. "I want a blood test."

"I'm trying to reason with you, first."

"Lawyer. Lawyer."

"Pipe down a sec."

"Lawyer. Lawyer. Lawyer."

He said, "There's another way."

Her eyes got big. "What?"

"Help me out and this doesn't need to happen."

She said, "You're fucking disgusting."

Jacob burst out laughing. Even in his heyday, he maintained some minimal standards of hygiene. Katie Moskvina had *vector of infection* written all over her.

"Don't flatter yourself," he said.

"Fuck you," she said, crying harder.

"Do yourself a favor," he said. "Shut up."

"I'm going to sue your ass."

"Listen to me carefully. This is your last chance. You can help me out or we can drive over to the station and they'll jab your arm. Fourth DUI in four years? You're looking at sixteen months, mandatory minimum. I tell the judge how you spit at me, it'll be worse."

"I *never*—"

"—especially after you grabbed my arm. Especially after you threw that drink at that cop. That's called a pattern of aggressive behavior toward the police."

"You're a *fucking liar.*"

"And you're a drunk," he said.

Katie began to weep quietly. "Asshole."

"Great," he said, dialing his cell. "Now that we're on the same page."

He put the ringing phone on speaker. "Tell your mom to get over here. Speak English."

WHEN ZINAIDA MOSKVINA ARRIVED, Jacob allowed her a look at her daughter, cuffed and stuporous in the back of his car. Then he led her off a ways, to a splotch of deathly yellow light on the parking lot blacktop.

"That speech about the police banging on your door in the middle of the night? Very powerful stuff. Definitely gave me a few ideas."

She shifted her glare from him to the unmarked.

"She must drive you up the wall," Jacob said. "Hardworking woman like you, you give her opportunities, and she just keeps screwing up."

Zina's temples bulged.

"I don't want to lock her up. I don't think that's the place for her. Rehab, maybe. But, a girl like her, at County? She'll get eaten alive."

He stepped toward her. "I know you're frightened."

"You don't know nothing."

"Talk to me," he said. "I can keep you safe."

She laughed. "You can't touch him."

"Who?"

She laughed again. "You think I'm stupid?"

"I think you're scared. I saw how you looked when I showed you the boy's picture. I can see what it's doing to you, keeping everything inside. You're going to feel better if you tell me."

Silence stretched.

"I was not there," she said.

"Who was?"

Another silence, longer and denser.

"Remember what he did to a child, Zina. He's going down, whether you help me or not. The only question is if you're going to let your own child go down in the process."

He paused. "I mean, I don't know. Maybe *she* had something to do with it."

Zina looked up sharply. "No."

"Whatever," he said. "I'll find out one way or the other."

He started walking back toward his car. "I'll make sure she gets her lawyer."

He got in and slammed the door hard, jarring Katie awake.

"What's—what the fuck," she said.

"Time for that blood test," he said, starting the engine. "Mother knows best."

He shifted into drive.

Katie flopped onto her back and began screaming and kicking at the door.

He stomped the brake. *"Knock it off."*

She had rolled off the seat and was lying on the floor, tangled up, sobbing.

He swore quietly. Now he had to actually book her.

Bullshit. Paperwork. Testimony. And no lead.

He swung the unmarked toward the exit, was about to turn when he heard a shout. In the rearview mirror, Zinaida Moskvina was running after them, waving her arms.

CHAPTER TWENTY-EIGHT

Even then, she wouldn't say the name out loud.

"We had a deal, Zina."

She had turned pale. She took his pen and pad with trembling hands and wrote.

Тремсин

Jacob said, "English?"

She hesitated, then added *Tremsin*.

"That's good," he said. "That's his last name?"

Nod.

"First name?"

She scrawled.

Arkady.

"Arkady Tremsin."

A violent tremor ran through her.

"All right," he said. "Now tell me what happened."

"I told you, I was not there."

"You must have seen something or we wouldn't be having this conversation."

Zina glanced at Katie in the unmarked's rear window. "Night, I am cleaning oven. There is knock. 'Go away, we are closed.' Knocking, knocking. I go out, man is there."

"Tremsin."

She shuddered. "Another."

"Who?"

"I don't know him."

"What does Tremsin have to do with it, then?"

"He works for him."

"You know that because . . ."

"People say."

"Which people?"

"No one," she said. "Everyone. It's ten years ago."

"So you let this other guy in."

"He was not asking permission."

"Why did he come to you?"

She said, "He was coming few times before. To buy food." A tart smile. "He says he is here with his boss, on vacation. His boss says I make *vatrushki* like home."

"Did he threaten you?"

"He told me, 'Go home.' I went."

"Did he give you anything? Money?"

Zina bit her lip. "No."

He didn't believe her, but he didn't want to shut her down. "Okay. Go on."

"In morning I come to work, there are many police cars."

"He used one of your garbage cans," Jacob said. "To prop the mother's body."

"I never saw nothing."

"Why didn't you tell the cops about him?"

She stared at him. "You're crazy."

"What did he look like?"

She shook her head. She had begun to withdraw.

"Did he kill them inside the bakery?"

"I don't know."

"Was there blood?"

"No," she said.

"What did—"

"No more," she said.

He started to press, but her face had hardened and she was look-ing toward the unmarked. She said, "I can't save her always."

He'd hit the limit. "All right," he said. "I'll give her to you."

"She won't like this," Zinaida Moskvina said. "She will like you better."

BACK HOME, he opened the laptop, the bourbon he'd earlier denied himself tucked between two couch cushions. It was two-thirty in the morning.

He typed in *Arkady Tremsin.*

The sheer number of hits gave him a sense of the scale of Zina's fear.

Arkady Lavrentyevich Tremsin, age sixty-three, founder of Met-allurgy TechAnsch ZAO, one of Russia's largest refineries. Wikipe-dia, citing *Forbes*, put his net worth at $850 million.

Three years ago, he had abruptly resigned and moved to Paris. The reason for his departure was subject to enthusiastic conjecture, everything from a sex scandal to financial hanky-panky. He'd kept a low profile ever since, shunning public appearances and giving no interviews. The past spring, the Russian government had frozen his assets and seized a controlling share of TechAnsch, citing failure to pay tax. Lawsuits were ongoing.

However much money he'd left behind, the presumption was he had hidden plenty more in offshore accounts—enough to ride out exile in luxury.

Image search returned a pinkish man with melting features. It was not so much that he was fat, but that he lacked foundations; the underlying structures were sunken, resulting in a flat, indistinct mien. More recent photos were pixelated, long-lens shots of a white head, surrounded by bodyguards, as it ducked into a limousine.

Susan Lomax might be able to positively ID him. In the meantime, Jacob reviewed the notes from their conversation.

Big and tall; ugly black ring.

Nestled amid the shoulders and elbows and marble faces, Tremsin was about the same height as his bodyguards. No shots of his hands, but no big deal. Appearances changed. In the end, it was his pattern of behavior that carried the most weight.

Jacob began excavating the past.

THE GUY WAS NOWHERE, and then everywhere, and then nowhere again.

Prior to 2002, he seemed not to exist. Then his name began popping up on finance blogs and in industrial trade journals, most of them in Russian. Jacob hobbled along, leaning on translation websites, e-mailing Mallick to request an interpreter ASAP.

The mother lode came in the form of a fifteen-thousand-word profile, originally published in *Novaya Gazeta* in 2006, later serialized by the British *Financial Times*.

It opened with a description of the flat Tremsin had grown up in, twenty-eight square meters in Moscow's Kapotnya District, over-looking the mammoth oil refinery where his father worked. As a child, he had suffered lung problems and for a period was confined to bed. His mother left a bookkeeping job to care for him full-time, enforcing a grueling regimen of calisthenics and rote memorization, so that little Arkasha returned to school physically robust and three years ahead of his peers.

The arrangement of the murder scene rose up in Jacob's mind.

Mother and son, in wide-eyed concentration; a lesson in progress.

What kind of pressure pushed a child that far out in front of the pack?

The author of the piece, Natalia Honcharenko, struggled to contain her distaste for her subject, writing in a tone that periodically flared from cynicism into outright paranoia. An inevitable flaw, Jacob thought, of a culture so long lied to.

At some point, though, even she had to cop to Tremsin's brilliance. His former instructors at Moscow State University recalled him with awe. At twenty-three, he'd earned a first-level doctorate in applied chemistry, an unheard-of feat.

Jacob examined the inset photo.

Kandidat Tremsin wore mutton chops and boxy eyeglasses.

In 1975, he moved to Leningrad, ostensibly to take up a teaching position. Honcharenko claimed otherwise, citing an anonymous source who put Tremsin at the 401st KGB school. It was there, she wrote, that he had met and befriended the man who would later enable his vault to the top of the food chain.

> Dr. Tremsin and President Putin found multiple points
> of common ground. Both men enjoyed the outdoors, and
> colleagues remember them as frequent walking companions

in the Alexander Gardens. Sometimes these walks would turn into contests of strength—races, or wrestling matches.

"They had a bit of a rivalry," says a former classmate, speaking anonymously.

"Most of the time it was good-natured. You must remember that the KGB is a very competitive place, attracting the most competitive people and encouraging that trait."

Asked which man was the dominant personality, the classmate says, "I would say it's a matter of perspective. Putin gave the orders, he gave orders to everyone. At the same time, Arkasha could get under his skin in a way that nobody else could."

One incident stands out as exemplary.

"It must have been late January," the classmate continues. "The Neva was frozen solid, and the boys were talking about getting together to cut holes in the ice and take a swim.

"Putin declined, giving the excuse that he had gone the previous week. As he said this, Tremsin got a mischievous look on his face. He said, 'But, Vladimir Vladimirovich, when did you go? I was with you Sunday, we had work the rest of the days. Maybe you meant the week before? But that can't be, that was New Year . . . Did you go at night? No, that isn't possible, you'd never be so foolish, you could have an accident and nobody would be there to pull you out . . . So when did you go?'

"Putin turned a frightful color. He said nothing, but we could see how furious he was.

"The next day, Tremsin shows up with his arm in a sling, a bruise on his face. He could not stop laughing about it.

"This sort of thing happened on several occasions. The funny thing was, it didn't seem to harm their relationship.

Soon enough Putin would be laughing, too. Not many people could make him laugh."

Indeed, this talent would stand Tremsin in good stead in years to come . . .

Starting in 1977, he went to work for Norilsk, the Soviet government's gigantic nickel concern. His official title was research scientist; he was the principal author on dozens of papers, coauthor of dozens more. In 1978 he earned a second-level doctorate, becoming a corresponding member of the Russian Academy of Sciences and receiving a civilian medal for "contributions to the development of techniques leading to greater efficiency in the electrolytic refinement of copper."

Honcharenko dismissed the Norilsk job as a cover. His real work, she alleged, took place at Laboratory 12, the KGB's division for poisons and chemical weapons.

As before, her proof was thin. A handful of KGB files had been opened to the public, but most remained classified.

One indication of Tremsin's special status lay in his freedom of movement, far greater than that of the average Soviet citizen. His name turned up on the rosters of chemistry conferences across the globe; he'd spent academic year 1978–79 in Paris, lecturing at the Université Pierre-et-Marie-Curie, as part of a Franco-Soviet exchange program.

A brief marriage produced no children and ended in divorce. Lingering acrimony prompted his ex-wife, who worked at the Ministry of Information and Press, to denounce him as a homosexual—a crime punishable by up to five years' hard labor.

Somehow, Tremsin avoided this more serious fate. In April 1981, he was dismissed from his post at Norilsk, and within the week had left Moscow for Prague.

CHAPTER TWENTY-NINE

Jacob stared at the screen, which seemed to be molting, letters falling like scales.

She went to Prague.

She was never the same after that.

He shifted the laptop to the table, killed the bourbon, headed to the kitchen. Along the way, the empty slipped from his grasp, thudding to the carpet.

Uncapping a fresh bottle, he took slow, steady drafts until the liquor hovered waist-high in the bottle. He set it on the counter and returned to the sofa.

The screen saver had kicked in, LAPD shield bouncing from corner to corner. He touched the space bar and the text reappeared like a slap.

Honcharenko could locate no official record of Tremsin's activities in Czechoslovakia. She had, however, managed to track down a requisition form bearing his signature, from a Prague psychiatric hospital called Bohnice. A former nurse at the facility—speaking on condition of anonymity, like every other source—named him as the head of the inpatient ward, starting in the spring of 1981.

When I asked how Dr. Tremsin, a Russian chemist with no formal medical education, had come to occupy a position of authority at a Czechoslovakian hospital, the nurse laughed.

"His qualifications were irrelevant. He was brought in for one purpose alone: to tighten the taps."

I asked what she meant by that. She explained that the previous director had released a patient of whom he was unduly fond.

"As it turned out, he had been duped. The patient was KGB, a *vlaštovka*, and after she got out, she proceeded to defect. The administration was humiliated. Moscow was furious. They blamed the Czechs and demanded action. They sacked the old staff and replaced them with their own people. I survived the purge only because I spoke Russian well. They needed at least a few people who could communicate with the patients."

Perhaps the nurse was scared, or else she had things on her conscience that didn't sit well: she declined to detail Tremsin's work on the ward, leaving Honcharenko to indulge in more suggestive speculation.

Whatever project occupied Dr. Tremsin's time in Czechoslovakia, it seems he attained enough success to make him valuable to Moscow once again. In January 1983, he was reinstated at Norilsk, where he became involved with

Jacob went back.

Eighty-one through eighty-three.

Overlapping Bina's visit.

She was never the same after that.

———

THE REMAINDER OF THE ARTICLE covered the periods pre– and post–Berlin Wall; Tremsin's patient accumulation of friends and resources; the rise of the first wave of oligarchs under Yeltsin and their dismantling at Putin's hands. Between 1999 and 2004, the list of Russia's richest men turned over completely, leaving Tremsin bobbing comfortably in the middle of the pack.

All the same, he maintained a relatively modest lifestyle. It was chemistry that Tremsin loved; the fact that his passion happened to generate reams of cash was immaterial. Honcharenko played up the contrast between his childhood home and his current residence, a seven-bedroom flat on Moscow's Ostozhenka Street that sat unoccupied most months. Typically, Tremsin preferred to stay at his dacha, driving distance to the TechAnsch campus in Shchyolkovo. Foremen cited him as a frequent visitor to the refinery floor.

Jacob had a hard time seeing him as the driver of a Gerhardt Falke S.

Maybe he'd brought it to a friend's house for dinner, in lieu of wine.

Please enjoy these eleven hundred horsepower as a token of my gratitude.

Published several years before his fall from grace, the article ended on an ambivalent note.

What will become of Russia if it is populated by men like Tremsin, men for whom nothing is too costly, and for whom nothing has value?

Hoping for follow-up, Jacob opened the *Novaya Gazeta* homepage, clicked the little British flag to bring up the English-language edition. He typed Natalia Honcharenko's name into the search box.

The first item that came up was from 2008.

Not by Honcharenko, but about her.

JOURNALIST'S COLLEAGUES REMEMBER, CELEBRATE HER BRAVERY

MOSCOW, May 21—Somber and frightened, angry and grieving, they gathered in the basement of the Bar Ogonek to pay tribute to their fallen colleague.

One year ago, thirty-two-year-old Natalia Romanovna Honcharenko, an award-winning journalist for this paper, was gunned down outside her apartment.

The case remains unsolved.

"We thought about using the church around the corner," said Alexei Kozadayev, an editor who worked with Honcharenko on a series of articles exposing corruption in Moscow's Department of Urban Development.

"We decided that this would be more to Natka's taste. She came here often after work. And we should remember that she was not one to bow to authority."

Several of the evening's attendees echoed this theme: Honcharenko's unrelenting thirst for truth.

"She ruffled their feathers," remarked Renata Givental, a fellow journalist who has written for *Novaya Gazeta* and *Nezavisimaya Gazeta*. "They want us to be afraid."

Givental declined to specify who "they" were, adding, "Anyone with half a brain can figure it out."

While Honcharenko's friends and coworkers may consider it obvious who is responsible for her death, police maintain a more circumspect attitude.

Praporshchik Yury Filippov, speaking on behalf of the GUVD, said, "We continue to examine all possibilities."

Jacob scrolled down the list of articles to find when the story broke.

June 2007, about nine months after Honcharenko's profile on Tremsin first appeared.

A masked man rode up on a motorcycle as she left her building. He pulled a handgun, shot her once in the back of the head, twice more when she fell, and drove off.

No shortage of suspects. Therein lay the problem. She was an investigative journalist in the new Russia. Threats came with the territory, and pissing off powerful people was her stock-in-trade. Among those she had vivisected in print, Tremsin was neither the most prominent nor the most notorious.

Jacob searched for hours without finding further information about Tremsin's tenure in Czechoslovakia. It stood to reason that few writers would want to tackle the subject, given what had happened to Honcharenko.

He needed that interpreter, badly. He sent Mallick a second request, then returned to the *FT* profile, reading and rereading the Prague section, scrutinizing every turn of phrase with Talmudic fervor. He felt like he was tilting a photograph, trying to fudge the angle: it was all tantalizing surface. He googled TechAnsch, Norilsk, Laboratory 12. Plenty to read. Nothing of substance.

He googled *vlaštovka*.

The first line of the first hit bounced him out of his seat.

Native to every continent except Australia and Antarctica, the barn swallow is the most common species of swallow in the world.

Sweating, he clicked the link.

The Web page showed a picture of a little bird, perched delicately on a branch.

Mashed potatoes, rising to life.

His mother, choking on bread.

Swallowing it down.

She had been talking to him all along.

He hadn't been listening.

A hot tide rose in his own throat.

He stumbled to the bathroom and heaved up fifty dollars' worth of booze. He rinsed his mouth until it stopped burning; tore off his shirt and ran a cold washcloth over his body.

In the bedroom he lay down on the unmade sheets. He gave himself ninety minutes to sleep, setting an alarm for eight-thirty in the morning, late afternoon in Prague.

JACOB HAD LIEUTENANT JAN CHRPA's number listed in his phone under *Czech Detective*. He didn't know if it was current. The voice that answered *ahoj* sounded different, free of wheezy edge. But the background track was identical: kids, screaming.

How long had they been at it? Two years running?

Jacob said, "Can't you turn on the television or something?"

There was a pause.

"This is the problem," Jan said. "They fight about what to watch."

A bark in Czech, a dip in the noise, a return to full strength within moments.

"Hold please," Jan muttered.

Jacob stretched out on his couch. He'd taken four Advil and eaten a piece of dry toast; physically, he felt a little less horrible, but his nightmares continued to reverberate.

An attic, a garden, Bina's twitching hands.

As he listened to the bickering fade, it occurred to him that he knew next to nothing about Jan's personal life, other than that he had a sister. Originally he'd assumed the kids to be Jan's own. Later he'd changed his mind and decided they were younger siblings. He still didn't have the answer. He didn't know if Jan was married or gay or lived with his parents or what. They'd talked on the phone a couple of times and spent a single morning together, reconstructing a brutal crime.

Yet he knew that Jan would remember him. What they shared was indelible. More than victory, it was trauma that united men.

Jan came back on the line. "I'm happy to hear from you."

"Same here. You sound good."

"I'm okay, yes."

Jacob was glad to take a few minutes to shoot the shit. He asked after Jan's sister, Lenka, and got an annoyed sigh in return.

"She is becoming a police officer."

"No kidding. She went through with it?"

"I told her this is a terrible idea. She doesn't listen. For this I blame you."

"Me? What did I do?"

"After you left, she was talking about you very often. I told her, forget this guy, he is bad news."

"I'd like to be offended, but you're probably right."

"Of course I am right. You are dangerous. You come to Prague, you ask questions I don't want to answer. I answer you anyway. Then you leave and I don't hear jack shit."

"Your English has really improved," Jacob said.

"Why didn't you call?"

"After the case broke, they shut me down. I couldn't get anywhere near it."

"Cockblock," Jan said.

Jacob laughed, releasing some of the tension in his chest. "I wanted to call. They were monitoring my phone and e-mail. I didn't want to cause more problems for you."

"It's okay. I forgive you. But, Jacob, it was a very weird thing. Before I met you, I was in a lot of trouble."

"I remember."

"Then, two, three months after you went, my boss, he called me to his office. 'Congratulations, you are getting a promotion.'"

"Huh."

"Yes, but it is more weird." An uptick in Jan's breathing, a hint of the former rasp. "Before, I was *poručík*, lieutenant. After this comes *nadporučík*. My boss, he tells me they are making him *major*, and I will be *kapitán*. This is not normal."

"After I was pulled off the case, they gave me ten thousand dollars," Jacob said.

There was a pause before Jan asked, "Who are these people?"

Jacob didn't like lying to him. He said, "I don't know how to answer you," hoping the distinction between that and *I don't know* would be lost.

Jan grunted. "I never learned who killed this person."

Jacob recited LAPD's official version of the story: acting with an accomplice, Richard Pernath was responsible for the murder of a former accomplice, Terrence Florack. Scotland Yard, accepting this explanation, had closed the file on the slaying of yet another accomplice, British national Reggie Heap, on foreign soil.

"I don't think you're telling me everything," Jan said.

Jacob said, "Believe me: it's for your benefit."

Jan was silent a moment. "The person who did it. He's getting punished?"

Jacob thought about the sorrow in Mai's eyes in the instant before she left him.

"No doubt about it," he said.

JAN ABSORBED THE DETAILS of the Duvall/White homicide without comment.

Jacob said, "This guy Tremsin was in Prague in the early eighties. He ran a psych ward at a place called Bohnice."

"I know it," Jan said.

"It's still there?"

"Yes, yes. They have many crazy people."

"Can you get in touch with them?"

"I will try. You wonder if Tremsin's doing the same thing here."

"It's a question worth asking."

"I agree. But it will not be simple to learn. After Communism, there is a lot of confusion. The files are not complete, many were destroyed."

Jacob pictured the Vollmer Archive, writ huge. "I get it."

"This is terrible," Jan said, "the mother and the son."

Jacob saw Bina cradling the photo of Thomas White Jr.

The mutilated face.

The endless stare.

She recognized it.

She'd seen it before.

"What I think," Jan was saying, "is to talk to ÚDV. This is the division for special cases that could not be investigated before, for political reasons."

"If Tremsin was working for the KGB, he probably had local protection."

"Yes, no, maybe. We have the files for StB, not KGB. There was not a lot of cooperation, they did not like each other. Did you ask the Russians?"

"I'm waiting on a translator. I have a feeling they're not going to talk so easily."

"I think you are right."

"Do me a favor? Ask around anyway. Anything helps. Whatever you can dig up."

"You are coming back to Prague?"

"To be honest, I hadn't thought about it. I'd love to, though. Someday." Jacob laughed. "I still owe you a beer."

Jan said, "Now you owe me two."

CHAPTER THIRTY

As Jan had suggested, the next logical step was to call the Moscow police. Tremsin had spent the majority of his last thirty years there.

In the end, it was the simplest stuff that got you: Jacob couldn't figure out which number he wanted. He tried a few at random and got nowhere.

He e-mailed Mike Mallick a third time.

He e-mailed Neil Adler, updating him with the name.

He made coffee and began slogging through Russian news sites, searching for mother-child murders, mutilated eyelids, eliciting a barrage of pop-up ads for discount plastic surgery. By noon, he'd gotten to the point where he could sound out the characters in Cyrillic. He still didn't know what any of it meant, though.

The doorbell rang: his interpreter, arrived at last.

Officer Anna Polinsky was a petite redhead in LAPD blues. Jacob had her wait outside while he hurried around the living room, depositing bottles in a trash bag, a clinking indictment he stashed in the bathtub. He brushed his teeth and smoothed down cowlicks, apologizing for the mess as he let her in.

"I'm totally the same way," she said in a voice that made clear she was not at all the same way.

The colonel they reached at Moscow CID was determined to give them as little information as possible while simultaneously sucking Jacob dry.

"What I want to know is if they've got anything with a matching MO."

Russian Russian Russian.

"He says it's impossible to determine. Moscow is a big city."

"I don't expect him to give me an answer off the top of his head," Jacob said. "He's going to have to hunt around for it. Have him call me back."

Russian, Russian, Russian Russian Russian.

"He says it's not his responsibility."

"Then who should we be talking to?"

"First he would like to know what proof you have against Arkady Tremsin."

"That's exactly why I'm—"

Russian Russian *Russian* Russian.

"He would like to know," Polinsky said, "if there are other crimes you suspect Tremsin may have committed while on U.S. soil."

"Tell him no and ask him about the Natalia Honcharenko homicide."

Russian, Russian, Russian Russian Russian.

"He says he does not recall."

"It was front page for three months."

Russian.

"There are no suspects."

"Now he remembers?"

Polinsky shrugged.

"Was Tremsin ever in the picture?"

"He can't answer that."

"What can he answer?"

"First he would like to know what steps you plan to take."

"Jesus Christ, it's an ongoing—okay, tell him I'm not taking any steps yet."

Russian Russian, Russian Russian.

"If you're not taking steps," Polinsky translated, "then why are you bothering him?"

Three more hours calling various branches; three hours of evasion and dismissal.

"You don't happen to speak French, do you?" he asked Polinsky.

"Sorry," she said. "Not my pay grade. Anyhow I'm going on shift soon."

He was glad to hear it. They'd been sitting together long enough that he was going to have to offer her a bite to eat soon, which would entail disclosing that he didn't *have* a bite to eat, which would in turn necessitate running out to 7-Eleven. He thanked her for her help and the two of them called it a day.

He didn't call it a day.

Instead he shifted his aim to Paris, where Tremsin now lived, working late into the night before coming up with a hit.

QUI EST LA FAMILLE-X?

A brief item from a Parisian daily, dated winter of last year. A woman and a young boy had been found murdered in a park. The cops were reaching out to the public for help identifying the victims.

Oddly enough, there was no photo, which he would've thought useful in making an identification. He assumed they'd withhold anything unprintably gory, or of evidentiary value—missing eyelids, say, or gunshot wounds to the forehead.

The statement released by the prosecutor's office waxed dramatic.

To depreciate a mother and child so is the greatest evil conceivable. We will not rest until we brought-have this monster to justice.

Wondering what nuance he was missing, Jacob tried retranslating the sentence, a word at a time. *Avilir* meant "to depreciate."

It could also mean "to debase."

As good a term as any to describe what had been done to Marquessa and TJ.

A second piece, a month later, implied that investigators had hit a brick wall.

Captain Odette Pelletier of the DRPJ stated, "There are many avenues left to explore for us."

It was about eleven a.m. in Paris. Persistence led him to a guy who spoke heavily accented English and offered a limp assurance that he would locate Pelletier's division and call Jacob back.

"After lunch," he said, and clicked off.

Jacob lay down on the couch.

The sun was up when he next opened his eyes.

He looked at his phone: 6:48 a.m. No missed calls in the last five hours.

One hell of a long lunch. He redialed.

"Allo?"

"Sorry if I'm interrupting dessert," Jacob said.

The guy said, "She will contact you."

"When?"

"Later."

To Jacob's surprise, the call came within the hour. He was further relieved when Odette Pelletier introduced herself in crystalline English.

"This is a rare event," she said. "To what do I owe the pleasure?"

He described the Duvall homicides.

"May I ask what prompted you to assume there would be similarities to our case?"

"There were no photos of the victims in the paper."

"Naturally. That would be disrespectful."

"Then how'd you expect anyone to recognize them?"

"We hoped that someone would be looking. A friend, a boyfriend, a grandmother."

"No one stepped forward."

"Unfortunately not."

"The statement said the victims were debased."

"Procureur Lambert isn't one to avoid hyperbole," she said.

"Debased how? Their eyelids?"

"Surely you can appreciate that I cannot discuss this over the phone."

"How about in person?"

She laughed.

"I'm serious," he said. "I've got time."

"You'd have to send your request to the *juge*'s office in writing."

"My victims were each shot once in the forehead. Small-caliber. Does that match?"

"As I said—"

"If you tell me they were strangled, I'll hang up right now."

Silence.

"They weren't strangled," he said.

"I never said that."

"You're still here," he said.

A beat. "Anything else, Detective?"

"What about a suspect? Any luck?"

Another beat. She said, "We never got that far."

"Thank you."

"And you?"

"Just Arkady Tremsin." He waited for a reaction. "Did that name ever come up?"

"No."

"But you know who he is."

"Only by reputation."

"Which is?"

"He's very rich," she said. "Like most very rich people, he values his privacy."

"You could take a look at him now," Jacob said.

"That's up to me and the *procureur*."

"The procu—what is it?"

"*Procureur.* Prosecutor."

"He's like the district attorney."

"Of a sort. Technically I answer to him."

Sensing another point of entry, he said, "That must be a pain in the ass."

"Lambert and I have a good working relationship."

"Well, sure. I'm just saying, if you think Tremsin deserves a look—"

"I never said that, Detective. You did."

"I'm trying to make your life simpler."

Pelletier asked, "Is there anything else?"

"The victims," he said. "Any progress since the article?"

"Very little. We pursued the matter for several months. Their prints didn't show up in our system or Interpol. The pathologist believes they're Eastern European."

"Based on what."

"The mother's features weren't typically French."

"What's that mean, 'typically French'? She wasn't carrying a baguette?"

"This isn't America. People wear their identities."

"Eastern European could be Russian."

"I suppose it could be, yes."

"Arkady Tremsin is Russian."

"I fail to see how that's relevant," she said. "Unless that's how it works in America? People only kill their own kind?"

"I was hoping you might be able to get me in touch with him," he said.

"I'm flattered you think I could obtain an audience."

"You could get a warrant."

"The *juge* would want a compelling reason to issue it."

"Let me send you the pictures of my crime scene," he said. "Maybe that'll convince you."

"Do as you like. Don't expect a response any time soon."

"That's fine. I'll call you later."

"What for?"

"I like your voice."

He said it to keep her on the line, but as it emerged he realized it was true. "We don't have to talk about murder. We can talk about something else."

"Such as?"

"Anything," he said. "Except soccer. I don't like soccer."

"It's not a game for the impatient," she said, and she hung up.

CHAPTER THIRTY-ONE

Talking to Pelletier had been strangely invigorating. That seeped away over the next few days, as he recontacted potential witnesses.

He e-mailed a photo of Tremsin to Alon Artzi, Farrah Duvall, Jorge Alvarez, Susan Lomax.

Nobody recognized him.

"He never got out of the limo," Alvarez said when Jacob called him. "He might've stuck his head out once or twice, but I don't think I ever got a solid look at him."

"Put him in a fur hat," Susan Lomax said. "Can you do that? Photoshop one on?"

Jacob sent the photo to Zinaida Moskvina. She didn't reply, which he'd half-expected: she'd already said it was a flunky who came to see her, not Tremsin himself. He doubted he could get much more out of her, even if he rearrested Katie.

Discouraged, he got in his Honda and drove to Culver City.

DIVYA DAS OPENED HER DOOR. Arched a thin black eyebrow. "This is a surprise."

"Pleasant one, I hope."

She motioned him in. "I'll let you know once I've decided. Tea?"

He nodded and took a seat at her kitchenette pass-through. "Thanks."

She put on the speed kettle. "I'm afraid I don't have much to eat."

"Well, *yeah*," he said.

She looked at him, startled, and then they both started laughing.

"I usually keep something around," she said, rummaging in a cabinet, "in case of unexpected—ah. Here."

She triumphantly displayed a faded box of Wheat Thins. "Let no one say that I am not a gourmet."

She shook crackers onto a plate, poured the tea and slid it to him, pulling up a seat on the other side of the pass-through. "May I ask what brings you by?"

"Nothing in particular," he said. "I'm spinning my wheels, so."

"And how did you know I'd be home?"

"I didn't. I took a chance. But your car's in your spot. It's what we in the police biz call a 'distinguishing mark.'"

"Too true," she said, adjusting her bathrobe.

Only then did he notice that she was dressed for bed, the robe over scrubs.

"I've just come off an all-nighter," she said.

"Shit. I'll go."

"Don't be daft. You just got here. What's bothering you? The mother and child?"

He filled her in on his halting progress.

"When I asked the French cop about her victims' eyelids, she didn't say no. I know," he said, "she didn't say yes, either."

"How did she respond?"

"By changing the subject, which to me means I touched a nerve."

Divya said, "It would be nice to confirm that this Tremsin fellow was actually in Los Angeles at the time of the murders."

"I contacted ICE for immigration records." He bit down on a cracker: dust and must. "Meantime I'm floating around in a fact vacuum, surrounded by all sorts of fun things to play with."

"Such as?"

"Susan Lomax said the guy who came to TJ's class was wearing a big black ring. I found some blogger who hinted that Tremsin used to be a member of a KGB group called the Zhelezo Circle. I'll bet you can figure out what '*zhelezo*' means in Russian."

"'Big and black'?" she said.

"Close. 'Iron.'"

"Iron circle," she said. "Cute."

"Not cute. They were a torture squad. A bunch of psychopaths with PhDs."

Divya bit her lip. "My God."

"It's a blog," he said. "Proves nothing. But you wonder, right? And Zinaida Moskvina insisted that the guy who came to the bakery was one of Tremsin's men."

"Mm," she said.

He eyed her. "What."

"You're quite persuasive," she said. "And I don't want to be a wet blanket."

"Just say whatever it is you're thinking."

"This baker," she said. "She's the one who set you after Tremsin to begin with. Have you considered that she might be stringing you along?"

"Her? No way. She was practically shitting herself, she was so scared."

"All right. But does it have to be him she's scared of? Perhaps the real danger is from someone local, and she's throwing you Tremsin's name because it's relatively low-risk. He's halfway around the world. He's never going to hear about it."

Smart girl.

"Is she in trouble?" Divya asked. "Does she owe money?"

"Don't know about debts. Her record's clean."

"Well," she said. "If I were you, that's where I would start."

He flicked his mug morosely. "Crap."

"I'm sorry," she said. "I'm not trying to discourage you."

"Don't be. That's why I came. I've been holed up for a week talking to myself."

He got up, paced. "Last night I got sidetracked, reading up on Cold War stuff. Crazy, what went on. They had these female spies, swallows, trained to seduce men. They'd develop a relationship with a mark and pump him for information. Sometimes it went on for years, the suckers convinced they'd found true love. There were even marriages. Forget Us versus Them. It was *Them* versus Them. The Soviets, the Czechs, the East Germans—they were all spying on each other. That was a major part of their undoing."

"Without trust, there's nothing," she said.

He felt a twinge of annoyance, unable to tell if she was admonishing him.

"The first time Special Projects called me out to Castle Court," he said. "It was just you and me. You knew it was Mai."

She hesitated. "I wanted to tell you up front."

"But."

"Commander Mallick thought she would respond better if you were frustrated."

He shook his head. "You people are amazing."

"We people?"

"You know what I mean."

"Besides," she said, taking his mug to the sink, "you can't claim Mallick wasn't correct. It worked."

Jacob said, "I'm frustrated now."

Her back to him, she said, "I hope that passes." A graceful pivot. "I really do."

"You know what, I should let you get some sleep."

"You don't have to run out the minute I show concern for you."

"I'm not running out," he said. Then he said, "*Do* you sleep?"

She laughed.

"Don't act like that's a ridiculous question," he said.

"Not ridiculous. Just strange. I don't understand you. First you say we're full of it. Now you're talking to me like a true believer. Which is it?"

"Both," Jacob said. "Neither."

"Make up your mind, would you? And for the record, yes, I sleep."

"All of you? Or does some part remain on alert?"

Her voice dropped low: "Detective Lev, let's not get bogged down in theoreticals."

It was an eerily terrific impression of Mallick.

Jacob said, "Does he know you can do that?"

She laughed. "Absolutely not. You can't tell him, he'd thrash me."

She leaned in conspiratorially, her robe dipping open, dark dagger of skin.

"You know," she said, "sometimes I even feel myself starting to get hungry."

"Really. Then what?"

"I wait. It passes."

"I find that sad."

"Do you? I imagine most people would love to be able to have the ability. Put it in a pill and I'd make a billion dollars. You could call it Resolvex."

"I'm not talking need. I'm talking want."

"Desire is tyranny."

"I'm living proof of that. But I still wouldn't get rid of it. No light without heat."

She said, "That's not a completely foreign sensation to me."

She gathered up a bolt of hair, securing it with a rubber band. Her neck was smooth, an invitation, and he turned his face to look at everything but her.

Shabby carpet.

Walls blistered by water damage.

Posters of gods and goddesses, blanched and peeling at the corners.

Such a glorious creature. Living in such a grungy little place.

But then she was coming around the counter, coming toward him, and he could see her, only her, her mouth opening to his, blinding, burning.

CHAPTER THIRTY-TWO

While it was happening, Jacob kept waiting for it to end—waiting for the cry of agony, the eyes rolling back in the head, the muscles locking up. His heart ran fast and rudderless, terror piled on top of arousal, needing her and needing to escape before he shredded another woman's psyche.

Divya Das was no ordinary woman.

Astride him, her black eyes glistened. She did what she wanted, rolled off, positioned him on top of her as if he was tissue paper, bracketed her legs around him and held him fast and clawed his back and kissed him with force enough to incinerate the breath inside his lungs.

Afterward, she lay back.

He said, "Are you all right?"

She turned on her side, grinning.

Smug, even.

She reached for him again.

On the drive home, the world blared hyperreal.

Divya was one of them.

She was immune.

But was he? He kept leaning forward over the dash to peer up at the darkening sky, expecting retribution.

The unseen fist, streaking down, to send his car tumbling end over end.

Was this how it was going to be, for the rest of his sexual life?

He could only sleep with the members of Special Projects?

Member. Singular. Schott and Subach and the men in the vans, not his type.

His laugh was brittle, forestalling the next wave of anxiety.

Another mile. Nothing happened.

He was now the protagonist of a cheesy ballad.

Send me an angel.

Send me an angel . . . hybrid.

He made it back to his place in record time, parking on a slant and sprinting upstairs, eager for the mock safety of ceiling, walls, and floor.

HE SHOWERED, drank till he was right, fixed himself a batch of Paleolithic mac and cheese and ate from the pot, standing by the range. Using his free hand to work the laptop, he burrowed into Zinaida Moskvina's history.

Opened the bakery in 1998.

Silent partners? Men who wore big vulgar rings?

Naturalized in 1999.

A debt with roots in the old country?

All he could do was wonder. Nothing close to a concrete suspicion.

Her daughter remained her most glaring weakness.

The coke bust was for a small quantity that classified it as personal use, not dealing. It had occurred after her first DUI, before

Katie had established herself as a chemical dependent. She pled out, no time served.

No bankruptcies, no credit issues, no defaults.

The icon for an incoming e-mail popped up, interrupting his train of thought. Thinking it might be from Divya, he opened his inbox.

It was from an ICE agent.

Subject: Query TREMSIN Arkady

Jacob scanned the first line and grabbed his phone.

Divya answered, groggy. "Hello?"

He said, "He was in the country. Tremsin. He entered through LAX customs on a six-month visa, July 11, 2004. The victims were killed the night of December 19, discovered the next morning. His exit stamp was December 22." He paused. "Hello?"

"I'm here," she said.

"Okay. So? Interesting, isn't it?"

"Very," she said, yawning.

Her lack of enthusiasm irritated him a bit. Then he remembered her overnight shift. "I woke you up, didn't I."

"Indeed you did." She yawned again. "I'm glad for you, Jacob. Well done."

"Thanks," he said. "Are you all right?"

"Why wouldn't I be?"

"I mean, everything's . . . okay."

"If you want to have a *talk* talk—"

"No need here."

"Then let's agree that it was a nice thing that happened and leave it at that."

"It was," he said. "Nice."

"Well, I thought so."

He laughed softly. "Go back to bed."

"Aren't you going to get some sleep yourself?"

He glanced at the clock. Eleven p.m. For the last couple of weeks, he hadn't gotten more than four or five hours a night. That he didn't feel tired awakened a dormant fear: in a manic phase, his mother would stay up for days on end.

His laptop sat open. More work to do, threads to pull.

He said, "Stay on the line with me?"

"Hurry," she said, yawning.

He didn't bother to brush his teeth. He stepped out of his shoes, out of his clothes, and got into bed. He put the phone on speaker and set it on his chest. "Still there?"

"Barely."

For a few minutes, they said nothing, sinking into the silence together. Then he said, "Good night, Divya," and she said, "Good night, Jacob," and he tapped the screen and rolled over.

IN HIS DREAM, the garden has changed.

What was once gold and green has been leached to mud gray, leaves of stone and tendrils of graphite, dead and depthless.

Flitting from a distant corner of his consciousness:

Forever.

The ground trembles and smokes, and he turns, looking for her. *Mai?*

You said forever.

He still can't see her. *Can you come out, please?*

You lied.

The air shimmers dangerously.

You need to understand how this is for me he says. *I'm a human being. I'm alone.*

When she replies, her voice is full of quiet menace.

What do you know about loneliness?

Mai. He starts to walk toward the sound of her, but a hellish wave of heat drives him back, and he blinks at the garden, rippling beyond a curtain of invisible flame.

Let's be reasonable about this he says.

A wild laugh. *Oh, no. Oh, no, no no no. I'm not going to let you get away with* that *again.*

Get away with wh—

You think because you're good with words you can talk your way out of anything.

I don't think that.

"I have loved you forever and I will love you forever still."

Mai. I don't know what you're talking about.

You think I don't remember? "I need you to come home to." Lies.

I never said those things to you he says.

Yet the text is familiar, a lesson from the womb.

If I did he says *then I apologize.*

No answer.

I'm sorry he says. Then shouts it.

But the heat closes in, and amid the stench of broiling hair, blackening flesh, he perceives that he, too, is aflame.

JACOB SEIZED AWAKE.

His upper lip itched like mad.

Every smoke detector in the apartment was howling.

He charged out of bed and ran toward the bitter clouds billowing from the kitchen.

The leftover mac and cheese, sending up a pillar of smoke.

He threw up a window, wrapped his hand in a towel, dumped the pot in the sink, ran cold water, thermal shock crackling the aluminum.

The upper left burner, cranked to high, screamed with blue flame.

He remembered shutting it off, before heading to bed.

He wasn't sure, now.

He twisted the knob down.

A cold gust passed over his naked body, and he turned and saw the living room window, cracked an inch.

He was sure: he'd never opened it.

He walked over.

Outside, the streetlight, insects coalescing, an electric dandelion.

He slammed the window down, latched it, yanked the curtains together.

He checked every inch of the apartment, finding nothing else amiss.

Returning to bed, he sat with his damp back against the wall.

He said, "I don't know if you can hear me. I'll assume you can." Silence.

"I'm not going to call Mallick," he said. "In case you're worried about that. I'd never try to hurt you."

He imagined her reply: *Promises, promises.*

"I don't think you really want to hurt me, either."

He thought that was true. She could have easily done much worse.

"You need to think about it," he went on. "What if the batteries in my smoke detector were dead and I never woke up?"

Shivering, he drew the blanket up to his chin.

"I had one decent pot," he said. "You ruined it."

Eventually the sun rose, slashing open his bedroom. He started to get dressed, thinking he ought to get on with his day.

The bed began to vibrate.

He bunched with dread.

His phone buzzed its way out from under his blanket.

The screen showed a mass of digits—a foreign number.

Odette Pelletier, having second thoughts?

But it was a man's voice, barely, that said, "*Allo.* Police?"

"This is Detective Jacob Lev. Who am I talking to?"

A rattle of phlegm. "Capitaine Théo Breton."

The man began speaking in a hurried whisper.

"Slow down, please. I can't understand you."

"Pelletier," the man said. "She is bullshit."

"Pe—are you a cop?"

There was a commotion on the other end of the line.

"Hello? Hello."

A rustling sound came over the phone. Then a rush of incoherent anger, growing louder until Breton managed to croak out a single, hoarse word.

"Tremsin."

Before Jacob could respond, a woman came on and began reprimanding him in blistering French. The line went dead.

Jacob pulled up the number on caller ID.

"*Institut Curie, bonjour.*"

"Hello, English?"

"Yes, *monsieur.*"

"I just had a call from you," he said. "I got disconnected."

"With whom you were speaking, *monsieur?*"

"Mr. Théo Breton. I'm a colleague of his."

"Pardon?"

"From the police department."

"One moment."

The line rang and rang and rang. He tried several more times before giving up.

Jacob sat on the edge of the unmade bed, thinking.

The smell of smoke was still fresh in his nostrils.

After a few minutes, he fetched down an overnight bag from a high shelf in his closet. He filled it with a variety of clothes, suitable for a variety of tasks. It was December, so he grabbed all three of his sweaters. Then he began looking around for his passport.

THE SOONEST FLIGHT to Paris was a red-eye that evening. He bought the last remaining coach seat and sent an e-mail to Mallick.

Late in the day, packed and ready, he wondered if he had enough time to visit his mother. In the end, he decided not to go. What could he say that didn't risk harming her?

He phoned Sam instead, bypassing *hello* and getting right to the point.

"Did Ima ever mention the name Arkady Tremsin?"

"I don't believe so. What is it?"

"Tremsin. Think, Abba. It's important."

"I don't remember that," Sam said. "I suppose I could ask her when I—"

"Absolutely not," Jacob said. "Do *not* do that."

Silence.

"Forget I mentioned it," Jacob said. "I mean that."

Sam said, "As you wish."

"Promise me."

"I promise."

"Okay," Jacob said. He wanted to believe him. "Here's something you can tell her: I'll see her soon as I'm back."

A distressed inhalation. "Back from where."

"Paris. Not sure how long I'll be gone."

"Jacob?" Sam said. "Can I give you *tzedakah* money?"

It was an old custom: giving a traveler charity money to protect him from harm. Sam had made the same offer before Jacob's trip to Prague.

A lot of good that had done.

Jacob said, "No, thanks."

When the honk sounded from the street, he hefted his carry-on, pausing by the door to address the empty air:

"Try not to burn anything down while I'm gone."

Not a cab idling by the curb, but a silver Town Car.

Jacob approached, slowly.

The window buzzed down.

Jacob said, "You're kidding."

Behind the wheel sat big Paul Schott. He patted the front seat and gave a dour smile. *"Mais oui."*

CHAPTER THIRTY-THREE

Later, Bina will remember the ascent to the synagogue garret in fragments.

Moving through the women's section, stepping into a wood-paneled room the dimensions of a phone booth, she and Ota Wichs and the boy Peter pressed bodily close, the dampness of her hair against her neck.

A rope dangled from the ceiling. Ota reached for it, pausing to suggest she shut her eyes.

She complied, and a blast of dust filled every crevice in her head. Four hands guided her to the rungs of a ladder, urged her upward into lightless infinity.

Then nothing.

Now she lies on the attic floor, Wich's shining face bobbing like a lure.

"Breathe," he says.

Croak of inhalation, tinged with death rattle.

"Now out. Good. In again. Thank you."

Father and son raise her up to a seated position.

Her surroundings appear in expanding circles of awareness.

A pulsing lantern. A pile of rags.

And beyond, a wondrous vision unfurls: a sunken garden, the hills of Jerusalem, the Jerusalem she remembers, its golden green horizon, dry and verdant.

The olive tree, in full bloom.

She cries out in amazement. Her voice cracks.

But Ota is forcing her to drink from a flask. "You have had a difficult ascent," he says, and she sputters and swallows the water along with the dust, which mingles in her throat to become mud. She chokes it down, eyes watering.

When she looks again, the city is gone.

The tree, the garden—a bright promise, broken.

She cries out again, in grief.

"A memory, nothing more," Ota Wichs says, holding her. "You are here, now, Bina Reich."

She wrenches free and stands unaided, peering into the unending clutter, cobwebs and shadows, rafters ghoulishly looming.

Ota says, "Whenever you're ready."

The garret stretches the length of her imagination.

Purpose settles over her like a past life.

She says, "I'm ready."

THEY WALK FOR WHAT seems like hours, covering an immense distance that does not square with the building's exterior dimensions. Peter carries the lantern, avoiding obstacles invisible to Bina until she trips over them. The floor is slick with frost, uneven beneath a sea of junk: listing coatracks, steamer trunks, fossilized shoes, oxidized candlesticks, orphaned eyeglasses.

All that and more, mixed with enough ritual objects to stock ten synagogues; prayer shawls, candles, velvet scraps of Torah covers, wine bottles ringed in sandy purple, books and books and books.

Ota says, "Almost there."

Squeezing between two wilting stacks of chairs, they arrive into a kind of clearing, a semicircle fanning out from an enormous rectangular object pushed flush to the wall and covered in a canvas sheet.

Arrayed on the floor are the components of a makeshift pottery studio. A low three-legged stool; a wooden handwheel; rags; a leather tool roll; a galvanized bucket filled with water beginning to ice over.

Wrapped in blotchy muslin, a football-sized lump.

Modernity pokes its head up: a portable propane stove.

You'll get everything you need on site.

Peter Wichs lights the stove from a match and hefts the bucket over the burner.

Bina kneels before the pottery wheel. It's old, the wood split and warped. When she gives it a spin, it wobbles.

"I don't know if I can use this."

"Try," Ota Wichs says.

"I can't do anything if the clay won't stay on the wheel."

"It will."

She frowns, shifts to inspect the leather roll. Inside are two dozen tools of varying sizes and shapes. Spearheads, spoolies, fettling knives. Metal parts look new but wooden handles are well-worn, the grain enriched by oil from human skin.

She selects a potter's rib and her thumb settles perfectly into a notch rubbed smooth, as if she has been using it for years.

Ota says, "Originally they belonged to the wife of the Maharal. They have been passed down from maker to maker. Now they are yours."

You need to face up to the nature of your gift.

It's irresponsible not to.

There are things only you can do.

"Her name was Perel," she says. "Not 'the wife of the Maharal.'"

Ota gives a shallow bow. "Were she here, I'm sure she would say the same."

Peter has nearly finished untying the ropes that hold the canvas sheet, standing on tiptoes atop a stack of crates to release the topmost. His father gathers up a corner of the cloth and counts: *"Raz, dva, tři."*

They pull.

A giant cloud engulfs them.

When the dust clears, she beholds a massive piece of furniture. It might be an armoire, except for the many holes drilled into its sides. Ota Wichs unlatches the doors, which swing open on wooden hinges. The shelves have holes drilled in them, too, and they are littered with shards of ceramic.

It's a drying cabinet, used to store pottery before firing.

Back home, she has one of her own, much smaller and made of steel mesh.

Ota reaches in armpit-deep and withdraws a jar about the size of a softball. When he holds it to the lantern light, the clay appears translucent, with subtle gradations of color swirled in, like a sheet of mica.

"It's fine work," she says.

"As will yours be."

"You've never seen my work," she says.

"Your reputation precedes you," he says.

He tilts the jar, revealing a hairline crack in the lid. "As you can see, it has already begun to deteriorate. Once that happens, we try to replace it as soon as possible. But tell me, please. The clay—is it enough?"

"For one jar? That's plenty."

"No, no. More than one. As many as you can." He scratches at his shaggy head, calculating: "You can work for a few hours tonight. Tomorrow is Shabbat, then four nights next week before your flight leaves . . ."

He tenses. Glances at his son. "I sincerely hope that yours will last longer than the last batch. So if you think you will need more clay, tell me, I will send Peter to the riverbank."

The boy is toiling silently, wiping down the work area. Bina hates to think of him running through the streets of Prague in the dead of night, lugging a bucket of mud.

"Why don't we start and see how it goes?"

"Very well."

She puts her hand out for the jar. "May I?"

Ota hesitates, then places it in her palm.

Her skin tingles. She feels warmth, and a slight pulse, as though the clay is alive.

An overwhelming desire fills her: lift the lid.

She starts to reach for it.

Ota catches her by the wrist, not exactly gently.

"Better not," he says.

But the clay is singing to her.

She says, "I need to look at the interior if I'm going to be able to copy it."

He hesitates again. "I will do it, please."

He takes the jar from her. Gingerly he raises the lid.

Inside the jar, an enormous roach lies belly up. Jet-black, with a great tusk erupting from its head, it reminds her of the *juke* that crawled out of her shower drain so many lifetimes ago.

But bigger. Twice as wide.

Not a roach at all. A beetle.

She ought to recoil, but she finds herself suffused with peace, fascinated by the reflections in its hard underbelly. She wants nothing more than to touch it.

Her hand begins to move through liquid space.

Legs stir.

Ota hurries to clap on the lid, nearly pinching her finger.

"You must never do that," he says.

She stares at the jar, blinking.

"Bina Reich. Are you hearing me? It must never be allowed to get out. Under no circumstances can it leave this building. Do you understand?"

She nods, thinking vaguely that he got her name wrong again.

"The ones who sent you," he says. "They didn't tell you what to expect."

She shakes her head.

"What did they tell you?"

"Just that I needed to make a piece."

His laughter devolves into a sigh. "I'll never understand them. But I suppose they don't much understand people, either."

He returns the jar to the cabinet, pushing it as deep as he can, beyond her reach.

SMALL BUBBLES HAVE BEGUN to break the surface of the water in the bucket. As Bina sets the clay next to the stove to thaw, Ota excuses himself: he must return to the park before Hrubý notes his absence. He will come to collect her before dawn.

"Peter will remain behind, to assist you."

She glances at the boy, a toy soldier, awaiting orders. Truthfully she'd rather work alone, without his hovering over her. But she nods.

Ota bows and departs, his footsteps receding.

She prods the clay. It isn't getting softer. At this rate, it could take an hour.

"What we need is a pot," she says.

Peter runs off.

Clanking and shifting.

He returns with a tarnished saucepan.

"That should work," she says. "Well done. We're also going to need a color TV."

He hesitates, then starts to go.

"Wait, wait. I'm kidding."

He smiles uncertainly.

Bina rests the saucepan atop the now-simmering bucket, creating a double boiler. As the clay warms, it separates, parts of it becoming dry and crumbly, others slimy.

She moves the bucket off the fire; scoops up a handful, and begins kneading it to fuse it back together, wedging it against the floorboards.

"You see what I'm doing?" she says. "This forces air out, and redistributes the water, which is important when you're dealing with clay that has been frozen. We'll have to let the piece dry thoroughly. Otherwise you get pockets of steam that expand when the piece is fired. What do you imagine happens then?"

Peter thinks. "It cracks."

"Exactly," she says. "Very good. Here—you give it a try."

He takes some clay from the saucepan, mushes it between his palms, then slams the mass down, repeatedly, with startling ferocity.

"Good," she says, a bit alarmed by his violence. "You don't want to overwork it, either. Actually, that looks about right."

She wets her palms and rolls a ball, assessing the clay's character. How forgiving it is; how stubborn. As many personalities as man.

"Once I get the wheel going, I need you to make sure it doesn't stop. And you're in charge of making sure the water doesn't freeze, either. But you can't let it get so hot that it burns me. You'll have to keep moving it on and off the fire." She pauses. "I know that's a lot to concentrate on. Do you think you can handle it?"

Peter nods.

She sets the pliant clay in the middle of the handwheel. "Here we go."

At speed, the wheel loses its wobble, flattening out in the horizontal plane. Already her arms feel tired. At home she uses a kickwheel, and the cold has tightened her muscles.

She pokes the crown of the clay, forming the beginnings of an interior. Peter keeps the wheel going with methodical strokes, his lips moving as he counts the rhythm. Watching him, she feels the distance to her own family, and she briefly surrenders to longing, blotting wet eyes in the crook of her elbow.

He stops counting, looks at her curiously.

She smiles. "Come on, now. Don't stop, please."

He resumes turning the wheel.

Bina rewets her hands. "Do you go to school?"

"Of course."

"What's your favorite subject?"

"History."

"That's a good one," she says, wondering which version they teach in Czechoslovakia. "Do you help your father out a lot?"

"I have to." Peter sits up, dignified. "It will be my job to take care of the synagogue when he dies."

"I see," she says. "What about your brothers and sisters?"

He shakes his head. "It must be me."

"You're an only child."

He nods.

"My son is an only child, too," she says. "Only children are special."

He shrugs.

She deepens the hollow, forming the sides of the jar. "Your father must be very proud of you. Your mother, too."

"My mother is dead."

"The woman I met at the picnic—"

"Pavla is my stepmother," he says. "My real mother died when I was five."

"I'm sorry to hear it."

He listlessly traces the edge of a floorboard.

"My parents died a few years ago," she says. "They were older. I was older. But I still miss them."

Peter nods.

"What was your mother's name?"

"Rachel."

"That's a pretty name. An important name. In the Bible, she was the wife of Jacob."

The boy grins. "You told my father not to call Perel 'the wife of the Maharal.'"

Bina laughs. Scoots back from the wheel. "Would you like to try?"

"My father wouldn't like it."

"Then it's a good thing he isn't here."

Peter smiles. He crawls over.

"Let's get your hands wet . . . Okay, now, the less you move, the better. The clay will shape itself. Your job is to encourage, not to control."

She gives the wheel a couple of pushes, guides him into position.

"Like this. See? See how it's growing?"

He is wide-eyed, delighted and petrified in equal measure.

"You're doing great . . . Whoops. Okay. Don't worry. We'll fix that . . . All right. We're losing speed. Let me work awhile, then you can try again."

He keeps the wheel turning, keeps the water temperate. Bina thought that she would need to refer to the old jar, but as she sinks into concentration, her fingers take up a march, the cadence confident, innate. The clay feels wonderful, at once pliable and strong and responsive. She presses herself: Can she make the walls thinner? How thin, before they fold? And the lids—it's the lids that take the longest. To ensure a perfect fit, she labors over them by hand, scraping, smoothing.

By the time Ota returns, she has completed a pair of jars, setting them on a shelf to dry.

He inspects the results, smiles at her with evident relief.

"I knew you would succeed."

He leans in, his nose inches from the surface of the clay. "I'm tempted to make the transfer right here and now."

"You'll still need to fire them," she says. "And they need to dry first."

He nods reluctantly.

Peter begins straightening up, dousing the stove, rewrapping the remaining clay.

"Yes, very good," Ota says. He worries his chin. "Now, if you can make a hundred more, we'll be fine."

THE NEXT NIGHT is the Sabbath eve. With no events scheduled, the rest of the group scatters to various wine bars and beds across the city.

Boarding the tram to Prague 11, Ota Wichs remarks to Bina that Hrubý must be having a fit, trying to figure out whom to follow.

Shabbat dinner at the Wichs home is a stripped-down affair, in keeping with its setting: fifty square meters on the sixth floor of a joyless concrete monolith. Husband, wife, and child share a bedroom, a toilet, and a combination kitchen/dining/living space. For the sake of economy—and to stave off claustrophobia—furnishings are minimal.

Ota and Peter and Bina sit on the floor around the coffee table, while Pavla Wichs ceaselessly shuttles to and from the counter, bringing alternating courses of brown bread and cheese in an attempt to create the impression of variety.

When the last crumbs are gone, they recite the Grace After Meals. Pavla does not participate, and as she bends to collect her husband's plate, a small crucifix swings free of her blouse. Catching Bina's eye, she smiles and gives a helpless shrug.

The singing ends.

"Děkuji vám," Bina says. "Everything was delicious."

Pavla excuses herself and disappears into the bedroom.

While Peter begins doing the dishes, Ota retrieves a photo album from a shallow pressboard bookcase. His knees crick as he settles on the floor, paging through black-and-white snapshots with scalloped edges.

He stops at a picture of two men, early twenties, shirts unbuttoned three deep, sleeves rolled. It's a moment of intimacy, a private joke.

The taller man wears his dark hair swept into glossy waves; he faces the camera without noticing it, crease-eyed in laughter, taut cheeks drawn back to the molars.

His companion is squarely built, balding, his expression contented as he cocks his hip and gazes out of frame. Smoke leaks from the butt between his fingers.

Wichs taps the smoker. "Karel Wichs, my father."

He slides his finger over to the other man. "Your uncle Jakub."

Well, but—no. Bina knows better. She knows what her uncle looked like. His portrait sat on her parents' living room mantel.

"Here," Wichs says, prying the photo up at the corners.

Sure enough, the date on the back is wrong: *3. květen 1928.* Her mother was born in 1927. Jakub was five years older, making him six at the time of this picture.

"I think you're mistaken," Bina says. "He was a child when this was taken."

"Ah. Of course you are confused. This is your father's brother, Jakub Reich. Not your mother's brother Jakub. Yes, confusing. Two Jakubs. Like the Holy Roman emperors, all Ottos and Henrys." His smile falters. "I thought you would be pleased."

"No," she says. "I am. I'm . . ."

What? Part of her is filled with gratitude. Another part, a surprisingly large part, swells with resentment. The man in the photo looks far too happy to be her relative.

She says, "My father never mentioned anyone named Jakub."

"That does not prove he did not exist. I assure you, he did. My father spoke of him often. They were dear friends. They fought together in the resistance. Jakub was shot attempting to bomb the tracks to Theresienstadt."

Maybe he's her uncle after all. He shares the futility gene.

And if he had succeeded?

Perhaps her mother's family would not have died. Perhaps Jozef would not have come to America. Perhaps she would not exist.

Ota says, "To me, it is good to know these things. It takes away some of my loneliness—to know that we are not the first, we will not be the last. It was your uncle who made the last batch of jars, when my father was the sexton. There was a connection between them, and now between us. We both have sons—"

Bina says, "Please don't talk about that."

The kitchen sink shuts off; the faint swish of the dish towel.

She says, "I should go home."

Ota nods disappointedly. "Of course. You must be tired."

He remounts the photo. "I shall escort you to the tram."

"I was planning on walking."

"Then we will walk together. For your safety."

"Everyone says the streets are safe."

"This is true. Very little to steal. Still, it is not chivalrous to let you go alone. Don't argue, please, I insist."

"Can I come, Papa?" Peter asks.

"Certainly not."

"Then who will walk back with you?" Peter says. "It is not chivalrous."

His father, bested, sighs. "Put on your scarf."

THEY DON'T GET VERY FAR. It's waiting for them, right outside the building: a black snub-nosed car, engine running, coils of exhaust snaking toward the sky. Behind the smeared windshield sits a bulky shape, black paws resting on the steering wheel. The passenger door opens on agonized hinges and Undersecretary Antonín Hrubý gets out.

He's wearing the same brown suit.

Bina wonders if he ever takes it off.

"Good evening," he says. "If you wouldn't mind coming along with me, Mrs. Lev. You too, Mr. Wichs."

"My dear sir," Wichs says. A servile smile. "I wonder, is it possible for me to please understand the purpose of this request?"

Hrubý's head yaws. "Is it *possible . . . ?*"

Lazy traffic rumbles along the highway.

Ota touches Peter's shoulder. "Go home. Tell Pavla I'll be back soon."

The boy does not move.

"Listen to your father," Hrubý says, holding the rear door. "He's a clever man."

CHAPTER THIRTY-FOUR

Jacob twisted in a coach seat designed by sadists.

A filmy sleep had settled over the dimmed cabin, buckles biting into hips, sticky necks bent at angles that predicted morning misery. He'd passed out during takeoff but awoken for dinner, and now, feeling restless, he unlatched his seat belt and high-stepped over his seatmate, who opened an annoyed eye.

He moved up the aisle, parting the nubby curtain separating coach from business. Unchallenged, he proceeded through the next layer of social stratification into first class, where eight lucky souls snoozed in individual pods.

Seven lucky souls, and one Something Else.

Paul Schott curled up fetal, the blanket across his rump like a postage stamp on a rhinoceros, the very opposite of wakeful.

He was dressed in supersized travel casual: circus-tent jeans, a flannel shirt large enough to move the price of cotton. A pair of battered brown cowboy boots, kicked off. He shifted and the pod's plastic housing begged for mercy.

No food, yet he looked like that. Did he work out or was that part of the angelic package?

A deep snore. Obviously, they slept.

Waking him up was going to feel good. Petty, but good.

Jacob poked him in the shoulder. "Hey."

The big man jerked up on one elbow, ripped off his eyeshade, blinking. "What. What. What." Then: "You're not supposed to be up here."

"Just stretching my legs," Jacob said. "I don't think Mallick would be pleased to learn you're nodding off on the job."

"There is no job right now. We're over the goddamned Atlantic."

"I thought you were supposed to keep an eye on me."

"I'm here," Schott said evenly, "as your interpreter."

"I didn't request one."

"You should be grateful to have a native speaker."

"Native to where."

Schott regarded him warily. "Montreal."

"You don't say. Hockey player?"

Schott said, "You and me? We're not friends."

"How come you get the royal treatment?"

"I need the legroom."

"And I don't?"

"You're one entitled son of a bitch," Schott said.

He lay back, drawing the shade over his face.

Ninety minutes before touchdown, as Jacob was sawing open a wooden croissant and bitterly imagining the omelet growing cold on Schott's china plate, a flight attendant swished down the aisle, bearing a tray.

"A gentleman in first class would like you to have this," she said, swapping out Jacob's breakfast for one that drew envious stares.

Tucked between the salt and pepper shakers was a note. Jacob unfolded it.

goalie

Smiling, he scooped up a bite of still-warm eggs.

———

SCHOTT'S LUXURY ALLOWANCE ended on the ground. They took the bus from de Gaulle, chugging beneath a leaden, sway-backed sky.

"Thanks for breakfast," Jacob said.

Schott grunted.

"Goalie, huh?"

The big man flexed his lats. "Better believe it."

He wiped at the window condensation. "Always wanted to see Paris."

They plunged beneath a densely graffitied overpass.

Schott said, "So far it's ugly."

Jacob said, "I assumed you'd been."

"Nope."

"You've been to Prague."

"That was for business."

"I was here once, with my ex-wife," Jacob said. Adding: "The second."

A romantic Hail Mary, culminating with a drizzly spring night spent walking the banks of the Seine because Stacy had locked him out of their hotel room.

"Take it it didn't help," Schott said.

"In retrospect, the money would've been better spent on a decent divorce lawyer."

Schott clucked his tongue. *"C'est la vie."*

TRAFFIC GREW SULLEN around the *banlieues*, low-rent outskirts oozing their way into the city proper. The bus listed, gasped, collapsed at Gare de Lyon. They changed to the Métro, resurfacing at Saint-Paul and proceeding along the Rue de Rivoli through slush, Schott cursing as his roll-aboard bounced and snagged on the cobblestones.

Jacob's cell had found a local carrier and was showing a time of eleven a.m., though it felt like evening, ashy light caulking a cityscape in contradiction. Plastic mauve signage bolted to five-hundred-year-old stone; barren planter boxes hanging from immaculate Art Nouveau ironwork. Soggy undernourished teenagers huddling in their screens, blue-faced as drowning victims. Whiny mopeds and lurid commercialism, stripped trees forming a picket line against svelte women tottering in heels, shopping bags and hips swinging. Jacob could smell chestnuts.

It would be Christmas soon, he realized.

In the alleyway behind a *boulangerie*, an African man in an apron stomped fruit crates to pulp, venting the rage of generations.

Jacob and Schott dropped their stuff at their hostel, a shabby affair in the Marais, set on a narrow run of cobblestones called the Rue des Mauvais Garçons.

"Bad Boys' Street," Schott translated.

"Like the modern classic buddy comedy," Jacob said, "starring Will Smith and Martin Lawrence."

Schott gave him a strange look.

Jacob chucked him on the arm. "You and me, dude. BFFs."

THE INSTITUT CURIE was not one but several buildings bunched together in the Fifth Arrondissement. Smokers congregated on the hospital steps, like some sort of breeding program for future patients.

They tracked down the correct ward. A nurse informed them that

Monsieur Breton already had a visitor, they had to wait. They signed the register and Jacob went off in search of coffee.

Forty minutes later, a man with a frail blond goatee stumbled through the lobby, looking lost, twitchy fingers referring to a pack of cigarettes stuffed in his breast pocket. He did a double take at Schott before getting into the elevator.

The nurse reappeared to beckon them forward.

At a hall closet, they paused to gown and glove up. Schott, his hands suffering inside a pair of extra-larges, flailed around, trying to catch hold of the gown's strings.

"Suck in," Jacob said.

Schott glared but complied, producing enough slack for Jacob to tie a knot, leaving the back of the gown looking like a corset.

Outside Breton's room, the nurse paused to whisper.

"He's very ill," Schott translated. "Even talking exhausts him."

Jacob nodded, and the nurse knocked softly.

Capitaine Théo Breton lay with eyes half-shut, arms slack and bruised, bedsheet tented at his hipbones, knees, ankles. Only his head had any mass to it; it sagged into the pillow, grotesquely large at the end of a stemlike neck.

"Bonjour, monsieur," the nurse said. *"Encore de la visite pour vous."*

Breton's chest rose and fell shallowly in time to the monitors.

"Bonjour, Inspecteur," Schott said. *"Excusez-nous de vous déranger."*

Jacob leaned back on his heels, surprised to feel uncomfortable. He'd witnessed more than his fair share of decline, in much more depressing venues. He supposed the environment's sterility made its true function that much starker.

The nurse said, *"Vous avez vingt minutes,"* and exited.

With one eye on the clock, Jacob introduced himself, asking how

Breton had gotten his number. Schott's translation got no response; Jacob moved on to the Duvall case, pausing occasionally to hold up a crime scene photo before Breton's unseeing eyes.

At the mention of Tremsin's name, the heart rate monitor jagged, and Breton began sliding sideways on the pillow.

"Easy now," Jacob said.

Carefully, they righted him. Breton's tongue probed the air. *"Eau."*

Jacob poured water from a jug on the nightstand, inclined the bed a few degrees higher. The sound of Breton's swallowing was sharp and painful, a kinked hose. Water dribbled down his chin as he spoke in a quick, desperate rasp, Schott hustling to catch up.

"He asked the judge to put a . . . *Comment on appelle ça?* Okay. He wanted to tap Tremsin's phone. The next day his boss has him in for a talk about mandatory retirement. That's when the woman took over."

"Odette Pelletier," Jacob said.

"Menteuse," Breton rasped.

Schott said, "Liar."

"What's her motivation to lie?" Jacob said.

"Tremsin has connections in the Prime Minister's office. He's been paying people off for years. Everyone knows."

"Does he have any evidence of that?"

Schott frowned at the response. "He says what happened to him is evidence."

"Besides that."

"The timing. As soon as he brought up Tremsin's name, the well ran dry. He's appealing his retirement," Schott said. "He's waiting to hear from the union."

Breton eked out a sarcastic smile.

"Who else is in on this?" Jacob asked. "His boss?"

Schott hesitated, keen to the skepticism in Jacob's tone. "He doesn't think so."

"He's the one who took you off the case."

"Under pressure."

"What's his name?"

"Don't get him involved," Schott translated. "He's a decent human being."

"And Pelletier's not?"

Breton's answer was a dismissive grunt.

The twenty-minute mark had come and gone. "What about the victims?" Jacob asked. "Pelletier said they hadn't been identified."

Breton didn't wait for Schott, instead fetching out his go-to word: *"Bullshit."*

"You know who they are?"

"The woman was a maid," Schott translated. "She worked at the Russian embassy, near the park where the bodies were found."

The nurse appeared through the curtain, frowning at the clock. *"Excusez-moi, messieurs. Le patient a besoin de repos."*

"Un moment," Breton said.

"Désolée, Monsieur Breton, ce n'est pas possible."

"When can we come back?" Jacob asked. "Tonight?"

She shook her head. *"Certainement pas. Demain. Midi. Pas avant."*

"Tomorrow noon at the soonest," Schott said.

"Ma musique," Breton said. *"S'il vous plaît."*

The nurse sighed. On the nightstand, behind the wall of get-well cards, sat a cumbersome CD player. She switched it on and hectic acoustic guitar started up. She adjusted the volume down to a level barely audible, pointed to the door.

"Bonne journée, messieurs."

Back in the hallway, Jacob removed his gloves. He was helping Schott off with his gown when the music coming from inside the room swelled drastically, distorting. He heard the nurse shriek, followed by a pale, crusty laugh.

CHAPTER THIRTY-FIVE

The address of Arkady Tremsin's residence was an open secret. Parisian real estate websites had noted the purchase by an anonymous buyer, in 2008, of a six-story Beaux Arts mansion on Rue Poussin, near the Villa Montmorency. Set well back from the street, the house was largely obscured by a high sandstone wall topped by curlicued ironwork, dense boxwoods plugging the gaps. The place had previously served as a finishing school; bloggers had dubbed its current incarnation Le Petit Kremlin.

"He saw it coming," Jacob said.

They stood catercorner, camera and map conspicuous, peering through midafternoon gloom like ordinary tourists battling jet lag. That was the intent, at least.

"He bought knowing he might have to get out in a hurry."

"Any idea why?" Schott asked.

"I read in a few places that he pissed off the wrong people. But it's all hearsay. Most of the oligarchs who Putin drove out moved to London. A couple to Israel. Tremsin's an oddball. He's second wave, and he chose to come here."

Jacob reoriented the map. "The Russian embassy, where the vic worked? Mile and a half north."

Schott perked up. "Oh yeah?"

More real cop in him than Jacob had thought. "Want to guess what's around the corner? Adjacent to both?"

"The park where they found the bodies."

"If I didn't know any better, Paulie, I'd say you were starting to care."

They crossed over to walk the length of the frontage. Jacob reached up on tiptoes and stuck his hand through the bars, trying to part the branches.

"You're screwing up his landscaping," Schott said.

"I want to know if he has a car back there."

"I'm guessing more than one. Anyway, you won't be able to see crap."

Jacob shook out his wet coat sleeve. "All right, never mind."

But the mansion's central gate was sliding open, a pack of heavy-set men funneling down the driveway.

"Nicely done," Schott muttered.

A towering figure stepped forward, his coat billowing in the wind. *"Propriété privée. Foutez-moi le camp."*

"Come on," Schott said to Jacob. "We're trespassing."

"He doesn't own the sidewalk."

"He might."

"Couple of meatheads frighten you?"

"I count eight."

The leader clapped gloved hands. He was a crude assemblage, long-limbed and asymmetrical, a sizable plug of scar tissue jutting from the left side of his neck.

"Plus vite que ça," he called.

Jacob jerked his thumb at the property. "Nice place," he said. "Yours?"

A pair of men started to advance, but the leader stopped them. He smiled at Jacob and drew back his coat a few inches, showing the butt of a gun.

"Allez," he said.

"Au revoir," Jacob said.

THEIR FINAL STOP was the police commissariat on Avenue Mozart, a ten-minute walk north from Tremsin's house. Clearing the metal detector, they beheld a chic foyer, curvaceous and hopeful in aluminum and frosted glass, as if to declare that good design would save the day.

The smell told the truth. Urine and bleach and defeat.

While the front desk paged Pelletier, Jacob idled by the bulletin board, browsing antidrug and antigang posters whose cute color schemes and popping exclamation points gave them a half-serious aspect. He found himself thinking they should come to L.A., see what a *real* gang was. Then thinking that was an odd thing to boast about.

"Detective Lev."

Odette Pelletier was elegance sprouting through the manure. Slender and blond, with a Modigliani face, she wore tapered jeans and fringed boots that emphasized her calves. A lime-green fitness bracelet bounced on her wrist as she shook Jacob's hand. "I wasn't expecting you so soon."

Not *how'd you find me* or *what are you doing here.* She smiled at Schott. "And you've brought a friend."

Her office was a glass box shared with three other cops. She murmured and they vacated without a word.

"I apologize that it's so cold in here," she said. "Some idiot broke the thermostat months ago and we still can't get it fixed."

"We know how it goes," Jacob said.

She smiled again. "So," she said. "How may I help?"

"Rubbish," she said, when Jacob told her that Breton had zeroed in on Tremsin.

"Complete and total rubbish. *I* was the one who wanted to tap his phones."

"You said his name never came up," Jacob said.

"I know what I said."

"Why hold back?"

"Why on earth would I tell you the truth?" she said.

"You're telling me now," he said.

"Yes, well—if Breton's going to try to steal credit for my work."

"He claims he got yanked for getting too close."

"It's not my intention to smear a fellow police officer," Pelletier said.

"Understood," he said.

"The man is a catastrophe. He has stage-four pancreatic cancer, which he concealed from the department. That alone would be reason to relieve him of duty. But the decision was a long time coming. The fact is that Théo Breton has a terribly high opinion of himself, unjustified by his record."

"I talked to him," Jacob said. "He seemed like a serious guy."

"I don't suppose you have breasts, do you? I have a colleague at the Crim, a very gifted detective. She started out under Breton. She nearly quit because of the harassment, which would have been a tragedy, because at present she's our leading cybercrime investigator. Breton runs a boys' club. He always has."

A blond lock swung loose. She tucked it behind her ear. "To some degree, it's part of the culture. I wish I could pretend he was the only one. He is one of the worst, though. There have been multiple complaints filed. That's why the *parquet* brought me in. They're making an honest effort to reform the ambience."

"I get it. But if he was handling his business—"

"That's the point. He wasn't. If I had time, I'd show you his dossiers. Trust me, you'd have nightmares. Ruined forensics. Loose ends."

She had begun pulling files from a drawer, stacking them up.

"Evidence that goes missing. Evidence that 'reappears' . . . The rules don't matter. But of course they do, and now it's up to me to review all of his arrests resulting in a sentence of more than a year. If an individual is still in prison, I have to check that, too."

She angrily pinched an inch of paperwork, as though catching it by the scruff. "This is not the way we operate. Everything—*everything*—depends on the dossier. The case lives and dies by what we write up. A man like Breton can single-handedly pervert the outcome. Our priorities aren't the same as yours. Above all, we want the truth."

Schott spoke up: "Us, too."

"I'm afraid I have to disagree," she said. "You want convictions. Why do you think your prisons are so crowded?"

Jacob said, "Politics aside—"

"But you can't put politics aside. What Théo Breton represents is a perversion of the system. We cannot abide that. The job—*our* job—is fundamentally one of repression. And because it is repressive, it must be tightly regulated. Breton . . . Four times he's applied for transfer to the Crim. Four times they've turned him down. They kept telling him he was needed here, but the reality is he's never been up to snuff."

She got up, the tassels on her boots whipping as she paced. "I can't believe he had the nerve to claim Tremsin as his. That was my lead. *My* work."

"Where did it take you?"

"Nowhere. There's no case against him."

"Did you do the tap?"

"We didn't need to. By the time the *juge* signed the order, we had already ruled Tremsin out. He was out of the country the week of the murder."

"You're sure about that?"

"A hundred percent. He was on holiday in Cyprus."

A squall of dissent pierced the silence, as two officers dragged a man in tattered clothes down the hall.

"Does Breton know?" Jacob asked.

"Of course. He was still the lead investigator at the time. I reported to him. He wanted to place the tap regardless."

"On what grounds?"

Pelletier smiled. "A grand conspiracy." She threw her hands up. "It was the KGB, it was the CIA, it was the Illuminati. God knows what drugs they have him on. He's not in his right mind. Take him seriously and *you* are not in your right mind."

"The eyelids," Jacob said. "That can't be a coincidence."

"It's a big world, Detective. Coincidences occur."

"Did you look at the photos I e-mailed you?"

She gestured at the cascading stack of files. "I'm a bit busy."

Undeterred, he opened his bag. "That's fine," he said. "I brought them with me."

He began pulling out pictures of Thomas White Jr.

"Detective—"

"Just look," he said. "Look and then tell me it's not the same."

Pelletier ran her eyes over the violent images covering her desk. He waited for her to flinch or gag, for the involuntary beading of sweat at the hairline.

She said, "I'm not saying there isn't a connection between your case and ours. Merely that Arkady Tremsin is not that connection."

"Be that as it may, he's my principal suspect, and I'd still like to talk to him."

"What exactly do you suggest I do?" Pelletier said.

"Stand next to me. Hold up a badge."

"There exist departments whose express function is to meet those needs. Mine is not one of them."

"I'm not asking you to haul him in. All I want is to meet him on his own territory and study his reaction. Before I have to go home, and it ends up with the FBI and the State Department, and everyone on both sides is drowning in paperwork. Including you."

"You're worse than Breton," she said.

"The truth matters to me," he said. "Regardless of what you think."

A beat. She returned her eyes to the photos of Marquessa and TJ.

"It's horrible," she said quietly. "I'm not arguing with you about that. Whether or not we're looking for the same person, he's a demon." She waved at the desk. "Put those away, please."

He complied. "Now tell me what you have."

"And if I refuse?"

Jacob shrugged.

"Paperwork for everyone," she said.

He shrugged again.

She reached in a drawer. Took out a dossier. Opened it. "Listen carefully."

PELLETIER SAID, "Her name was Lidiya Georgieva."

"Russian."

"Bulgarian. You need to brush up on your Slavic, Detective. Born 'ninety-one in Pleven, left school at fifteen, pregnant soon after that. The boy's name was Valko. I tracked down her family. Her mother said Lidiya came to Paris about a year before the murder. She held a variety of jobs, mostly cleaning. A good girl. Sent her money home."

"Breton told me she worked at the Russian embassy."

"Once again: information I brought to him."

"What did the people there have to say about her?"

"She hadn't been there long. A few months."

"Friends here in Paris? Family?"

"No one."

"She had a landlord, at least."

"He was not eager to talk to us. She was in France illegally, which makes him liable for a fine for subletting to her."

"Where was she living?"

"Clichy-sous-Bois. A suburb, quite rough. It's on the other side of the city, and we were looking for someone in the immediate area. An opportunist."

"What about the boy's father?"

"Back in Sofia. They did not have a relationship."

"That's the same situation I'm dealing with," Jacob said. "Single mother."

"It's hardly uncommon," Pelletier said. "Men are men."

"Or you could say the bad guy has his preferences."

"You know, I'm beginning to enjoy this. It's a bit like being on a game show."

"I'm trying to understand how her son got caught up in it."

"I'm getting to that," she said, paging forward. "On the evening of December eleventh, there was a reception at the embassy for a trade mission. The house manager told me they had a last-minute problem. A waitress got sick. They called Lidiya to fill in. She had no one to watch Valko, so she brought him along and stuck him in a back room."

"Was Tremsin invited to the party?" Jacob asked.

"I just told you, he was out of the country." She closed the file. "What's the word in English? I can't think of it. Ah," she said, laughing. "'Monomaniac.' Is that a word?"

"It's a word," he said. "You were saying?"

"The last person to have contact with either of the victims was another waitress, who encountered Lidiya in the stairwell around midnight. Lidiya was in a hurry, running upstairs to fetch Valko. It's a long way back to Clichy, and she was worried about missing her bus. She asked the other waitress to sign out for her. Four days later, the bodies were found in the Bois de Boulogne."

Jacob spread the map on her desk. "Show me where?"

Pelletier let the tip of her pen hover over a blank patch, a triangle of green ink, southeast of Allée de Longchamp. "About here."

"The more specific you can be, the better."

"Bring me a more specific map," she said. "I assure you, there's nothing to see there, now, except mud and trees."

With his fingertip, he traced an invisible line to the embassy on Boulevard Lannes. "What is that, about half a mile?"

"Eight hundred meters." She held up her fitness tracker. "I measured it myself."

"How did Lidiya and her son get from there to here?"

"One can only surmise. It's my belief that they were ambushed after they left the building, convinced or forced into a car. As I said, an opportunist."

"Do we know for certain that they left the embassy by themselves? Did anyone actually see them?"

"If you're wondering whether the murders could have taken place inside the embassy, the answer is no. Even on an ordinary day, it's crawling with security, and that evening there would have been more. There are cameras everywhere."

"Did you review the tapes?"

"Nobody at the party reported hearing shots, or a disturbance of any kind. The idea that someone could smuggle out two dead bodies amid a house full of people in tuxedos . . . It's inconceivable. You must remember: the embassy is technically Russian soil. They were gracious, but they didn't have to be. I had a finite amount of goodwill to spend, and I limited myself to questions worth asking."

"I take it you ran down the guest list."

"To the extent that I could. The foreign nationals who were there—members of various missions—had already departed the country by the time we identified the bodies. Which were found in a park. Which is where we focused our investigation."

Perfectly circular logic. Now that she was talking, though, he decided not to challenge her aggressively. "Were they killed at the dump site?"

"We suspect so. We failed to recover casings."

"Drag marks? Footprints?"

She shook her head. "Prior to their disappearance there was an unusually heavy snowfall, followed by several days of warming and refreezing. It left poor forensics."

"Is there any way you could show me the scene? I'd really appreciate it."

Pelletier chewed her lip. Finally she said, "Let me clear some of the shit off my desk. But you can't show up here without an appointment and expect me to rewrite my schedule. I'll call you."

"Fair enough," he said, taking out his card and jotting down the name of his hostel. "Thanks."

She nodded.

"Last question," he said. "Your contact at the embassy—the house manager? What's his name?"

She frowned. "You're not thinking of going there."

"It crossed my mind."

"As I said, it's a delicate diplomatic matter, so I thank you in advance for not interfering."

He said, "Have you been getting pressure to back off?"

Pelletier's brow tightened. "Pardon me?"

"No offense meant."

Pelletier got up. "I have cases. I have men whose cases I oversee. I have a thermostat that does not work. I'll call you," she said, unlocking the door, "*if* I have time."

She held it ajar. "Don't be too sorry about having come. Paris is best in the winter. Fewer tourists."

CHAPTER THIRTY-SIX

Schott said, "Smooth move back there."

The two of them sat squashed in the window of a kebab shop, cold pressing through the plate glass, heat from the grill brushing their backs. A portable radio taped to the exhaust hood extruded French rap. Jacob had yet to touch his lamb and Orangina.

"Thanks for the moral support," he said.

"She probably wouldn't've called anyway."

Jacob nodded. "What's your take?"

"Turf war. Her and Breton. Plain and simple."

"One of them is right, though. It's linked to Marquessa or it isn't."

"She didn't deny a link."

"As long as it isn't Tremsin."

"He was out of the country," Schott said.

"According to her."

"I'll take her word over Breton's, who, by the way, struck me as a total crackpot."

"She sounded pretty touchy herself," Jacob said.

"Look at it from her perspective. Some stranger shows up out of nowhere, starts poking around, makes the Russians nervous. They complain, crap rolls downhill."

"Don't tell me she's not seeing the similarity. That bit about an opportunist? You want an easy mark, you go for a woman alone, not a woman with a little kid."

"So?"

"So, let's give Breton a chance for rebuttal."

"And if that doesn't pan out?"

Jacob said, "I'm not leaving till I've talked to Tremsin."

"What is it with you and this guy? You're acting like he ran over your dog."

Jacob cut into his lamb. Schott shuddered.

"What?" Jacob said through a mouthful.

"Meat."

"What about it."

"The smell." Another shudder. "It's like death."

The chunk in Jacob's mouth went rubbery and fetid. He managed to swallow, pushed his plate away.

"You asked," Schott said.

Jacob uncapped his drink. "Whatever this smells like, don't tell me."

Schott said, "I never really got the appeal. Take foreign matter and turn it to mush, next day it comes out the other end? Revolting."

"You should be a judge on *Top Chef.*"

"Dress it up all you want. It's just another reminder that you're an animal."

"And you don't like to be reminded."

Schott shrugged. "I prefer to emphasize my finer attributes."

"Vanity," Jacob said. "That's plenty human."

Rain had begun to fall, dreary columns that slicked the street with neon.

"I was in my twenties before I found out about myself," Schott said.

Jacob looked at him. "Come on."

"I consider myself fortunate," Schott said. "Most of us never learn. Someone along the line decides to hide the truth, they go about their business, they marry regular folks, the chain gets weaker and weaker. Within a couple generations, they're lost."

"So what happened with you?"

"I came to L.A.," Schott said. "I was working in the industry—"

Jacob burst out laughing.

"Yuk it up. I got my SAG card and everything."

Jacob conceded that a fellow of Schott's dimensions filled—overfilled—a particular casting niche. "Anything I've seen?" he asked.

"How up are you on your zombie flicks?"

"Not very."

"Then no, nothing you've seen. When we get back, I'll e-mail you my reel."

Jacob smiled.

"Whole culture made my skin crawl," Schott said. "I had a sideline as a limo driver. That's how I met the Commander. I drove him to a charity function. He recognized me—what I was—right off the bat."

He paused. "I think I sort of knew all along. I was different, obviously. And I'd have these memories of people I'd never met, places I'd never been. Me, I came down through my mother's side. When I finally confronted her, she wasn't the least bit apologetic. She said, 'I wanted to protect you.'"

Jacob said, "I hear you loud and clear."

But Schott wasn't paying attention. "It's nuts when I think about us, all those years, gathered around the dinner table, my father and brother going to town on their T-bones while my mom and I sit there, forcing ourselves to cut another bite."

"I thought you couldn't eat."

"It's not a question of can't. To begin with, I'm half my dad, so there's that. But the real issue is wanting to feel normal. If you don't know any better, if people are staring at you, expecting you to eat, you eat. If it makes you feel like you need to barf your guts up every time, you've probably got a condition. You eat."

A stab of self-loathing: Jacob remembered pushing Divya to take a bite of bread.

"It wasn't an easy transition for me," Schott said. "From not knowing, to knowing. Actually, I don't think I could've made it, if not for Mel. He practically saved my life. Not practically. Did save it. I was depressed, and he pulled me out of it."

Jacob said, "You're lucky to have him as a partner."

"You bet I am," Schott said. He paused. "You have a favorite book, Lev?"

"More than one."

"Mine's *The Master and Margarita*, by Bulgakov. Read it?"

"I think I might've, in college."

Schott puffed up his chest in a proprietary way. "Uh-uh. If you read it, you'd remember it. It's that kind of book."

"There's a lot I don't remember about college."

"Yeah, well, then you should take the time to reread it. It's capital-G great."

His enthusiasm made Jacob smile. "What's it about?"

"Good and evil. Human nature. Faith. Everything, basically. Satan shows up in Moscow and starts wreaking havoc. Bulgakov's living and writing under Stalin, and he just gets it when it comes to bureaucracy. Like—Satan, he doesn't come alone. He has a *staff*. Which is perfect, right? A bad guy's a bad guy, but the devil? He delegates."

Jacob laughed.

"There's one scene," Schott said, "early in the book. Two guys get a telegram from a friend of theirs, who they just saw, that morning. All of a sudden the guy's sending them messages from another city, a thousand miles away. The devil picked him up and dropped him there. But of course they don't know that, and they're scratching their heads, trying to work it out, resorting to all kinds of backward logic.

"They're confused, sure. But mostly they're *furious*. They've crashed into the boundaries of their understanding, and that scares the hell out of them. It offends them. The one guy, he feels it's 'necessary, at once, right on the spot, to invent ordinary explanations for extraordinary phenomena.'"

Schott spread his hands on the scuffed tabletop. "It's a throwaway line, unless you think about it. *Necessary*. Why's it necessary? Why can't they shift their minds in another direction? But that's Bulgakov's point. The evidence can be staring you in the face. Most people would still rather come up with a hundred different ways to think around it. Making the leap—it hurts. It drives you nuts. It can kill you, if you're not careful. That's how it was for me, anyway. Why I had to lean on Mel so hard."

"What about him?" Jacob said. "He grew up knowing?"

Schott shook his head. "The Commander recruited him, too. This was back in the nineties, when he first put the unit together."

Jacob was surprised. "I thought you'd been around longer than that."

"That's what I'm saying. For a while, the chain looked like it really was broken."

"And Mallick?" Jacob asked. "Who told him?"

Schott's voice thickened with reverence.

"He's purebred," he said. "One of the last."

Jacob regarded the big man with newfound sympathy. He might have been an attack dog, but he was loyal.

And, from a certain standpoint, necessary.

Having tasted Mai's wrath, Jacob could admit that.

"I know you're not here to do me favors," Jacob said. "But as long as we're working together, I'd like us to come to a temporary agreement."

He'd meant it honestly; he'd glimpsed a heart beating beneath the layers of armor, and his instinct was to respond in kind.

Later he would wonder if his phrasing had somehow landed awry, or his tone.

Regardless, the effect was clear enough.

The screen came slamming down.

"You already made the agreement," Schott said. "I'm ensuring you hold up your end."

A commercial came on the radio. The counter guy fiddled with the dial, selecting limp eurodance that kicked the mood apart, leaving them once again at a smeary table, acting out their indifference for an indifferent audience of foam cups and clawed glass.

"Say you do catch her," Jacob said. "Did you bring the knife?"

Schott drummed his thighs.

"You're going to kill someone with my knife, I have a right to know," Jacob said.

"First off, it's not your knife."

"I beg to differ."

"Nobody's getting killed."

"How do you figure that?"

"Cause she's not alive."

"She sure looked alive to me."

"She does a fine impression," Schott said. "But it ain't real."

"Yeah, well," Jacob said. "I could say the same about you."

He picked up his kebab. "How'd you get it past the metal detector at the station, anyway? Is it up your ass or some other place I can't hope to understand?"

Schott said, "Finish up and let's get out of here."

Drawing his plate near, Jacob took a bite, chewed slowly. Theatrically.

"It may be foreign matter," he said, "but it's freaking delicious."

Schott made a disgusted noise, shoved his chair back. "I'll wait outside."

CHAPTER THIRTY-SEVEN

Asleep by eight p.m., Jacob rolled over at one-thirty a.m., wide awake.

Schott was on his back, snoring, the mattress a hammock beneath his bulk. Jacob lay there awhile, dissecting the noise that filtered up from the street, then got out of bed.

Finding his clothes, he tripped on the nightstand, knocking his phone to the floor.

Schott didn't stir.

Jacob said, "Sweet dreams," loud enough to wake anyone.

Not Schott.

He raised his voice. "Yo, fatso."

Schott continued to saw wood.

They didn't eat, but they slept. Oh, did they sleep.

The slumber of the just? Or the comfort of no conscience?

He got dressed, not even bothering to be quiet.

Down in the lobby, he buttoned up against the cold, grabbed a cheap map off the wire, and stepped out into the Marais.

Once the city's primary Jewish enclave, the neighborhood had largely gone hip. Same phenomenon as the Prague ghetto, New

York's Lower East Side: squalor, polished up; the old soul, decomposing to fertilizer.

Within a block he'd found an Irish pub called Molly Bloom's, a perfectly adequate cliché in orange, white, and green, fiddle music testing the limits of the PA. He ordered three shots of tequila at eleven euros apiece, along with a nine-euro Guinness; drank quickly and got out.

He meant to go straight back to the hostel, but getting lost in the crowd was pleasant after a day with Schott bearing down on him like a slow-moving avalanche. The map showed a ten-square-block area outlined in pink, its watering holes conveniently tagged with martini-glass icons. For several hours he weaved up, down, and around Rue Vielle du Temple, squinting at chalkboard drink specials streaked with drizzle. It became something of a challenge: how many places could he hit?

The answer, it turned out, was most of them. He drank from a plastic flying saucer at a space-themed lounge. He entered a gay bar and in the span of one Manhattan collected three unsolicited numbers. He choked down arak at a place called Medina.

A nightclub bouncer appraised his running shoes and no-brand jeans and waggled a finger. Jacob saluted him and moved on.

The sidewalks coursed with sexual electricity of every variety, the landscape loosely brushstroked. A rainbow flag lifted in the wind to reveal a Star of David carved over a doorway, and he stopped at a boutique window, tracing remnants of gilt lettering.

BOUCHERIE—VIANDE CACHER—בשר כשר

Once upon a time, a place for Jewish housewives to buy their chickens.

Now racks of stiff denim replaced sides of beef.

He'd chosen the hostel for its low rates and centrality, but had to wonder if some subconscious directive had been in play.

He turned to find the next bar and saw a big body, idling in the green light of an apothecary's sign.

Schott?

No. This guy was as tall, but leaner. By no means narrow, but proportional. Hanging back, checking his phone. The only solo act in sight, other than Jacob himself.

Waiting for a friend?

Jacob walked on.

In an effort to get some nutrients into his system, he found a tiki lounge and spent twelve euros on a concoction more fruit juice than booze. Emerging with a pocketful of change, he saw the same man, tucking away the phone.

Jacob doubled back toward Rue des Mauvais Garçons.

Height alone made the guy a lousy tail. He was making no effort to hunch down. Maybe he didn't care about being spotted. Maybe the goal was intimidation.

Good news, if you chose to take it that way. Someone didn't want him here.

As he walked, Jacob fished out his own phone, meaning to call Schott, or text at least. He thought better of it. He didn't need a lecture. Instead he raised the phone as if to take a selfie, fudging the angle over his shoulder.

The flash blew open the darkness, showing an ankle-length coat; knob of flesh on the neck, like a volume dial for the carotid—leader of the pack, outside Tremsin's place.

The photo vanished, replaced by a live image: the man, wearing a pissed-off smile.

Jacob picked up his pace.

He'd achieved his goal: he was hammered. He thought he knew where the hostel was but within a few blocks had begun making random turns, casting about for landmarks as the foot traffic thinned. His shoes seemed to slosh as though full of seawater. He put his head down and pulled his jacket tight, the folded map jabbing him in the ribs. He wanted to get it out but the man was swiftly eating up the distance between, courtesy of his huge stride.

Jacob hooked left, coming up on a small fenced park. Scaffolding covered the street signs. Why didn't they put the damn things on poles, like a normal city?

The romance of getting lost in Paris.

He hopped off the curb, sidling around a pair of Citroëns parked nut to butt.

The guy was fifteen feet behind him, the tread of his boots audible.

Jacob hooked again and found himself passing the same park.

Okay. No. A different park. The city was full of parks. Big parks, like the one Lidiya and her son had died in. Little ones like scattered gems.

A sign. Rue Payenne. He chased a faint glow, arriving at Rue des Rosiers, blessedly semipopulated; turned right, hustled past unlit shop windows. Handbags. Activewear. Sunglasses. Window-box topiary, scooters chained under cover, gas lamps dripping icy wet runoff down his collar and along his spine. He reached the core of the Jewish district, kosher restaurants, kosher bakeries, a chocolatier.

"Mr. Lev."

The hair on the back of his neck stood up.

How the fuck did the guy know his name?

"Mr. Lev." Thick Russian accent. "Conversation, please."

An art gallery opening had spilled into the street. Plastic champagne flutes, lilting chatter, glassy laughter. Jacob wedged through the crowd and dared to glance back. The man was caught up in the morass, his head bobbing like a cork on the ocean.

Jacob broke into a sprint.

He slammed into a T intersection. Rue Vielle du Temple, now deserted. He hooked left, what he thought was south, moving in the shadows, nearly colliding with a trash can set out for collection, dodging the next one. Couple more turns and he'd be back at the hostel. A breach appeared and he took it.

He'd screwed up.

Cul-de-sac, more shuttered shops, less fashionable, foyers barred. Reversing direction would put him face-to-face with his pursuer. He hurried forward, seeking cover, confronting a large limestone building with a moody countenance.

ק׳ק רודפי צדק
SYNAGOGUE RODFEI ZEDEK

It had been assaulted, the stonework gouged. The graffiti that elsewhere animated the Marais and stoked its youthful urgency here took on the laser focus of hatred.

Swastikas. Stars of David on gallows. Multilingual slurs. *La mort aux juifs.*

Stained glass columns ran the height of the façade; the lowest sections sported matching damage, red shards clinging to the twisted leading, scabs begging to be picked.

The man appeared at the far end of the street, began running at him.

Jacob hurdled a sawhorse, bags of cement; he grasped the synagogue doorknob, a big metal fist, greasy with rain. He expected resistance, but it yielded and massive oaken doors yawned inward.

"Mr. Lev."

Jacob scrambled into the vestibule and heaved himself back against the door, securing it with an iron bar, which fell into place with a crash.

He'd screwed up, again.

The guy was huge, and the broken windows sat only seven or eight feet aboveground, easily reachable if he stacked up a couple of bags of concrete. Plastic sheeting flapped in the wind; the leading that remained was bent, fragile, easily kicked in.

Jacob bolted for the sanctuary, a cavernous triple-high room in the traditional layout: central podium, elevated ark on the eastern wall, U-shaped balcony for the women's section. He sprinted up the aisle, through a rear door, and into a courtyard.

Brick walls, razor wire. Dead end.

Back inside, he paused on the threshold. His cuffs dripped on foot-worn marble. What remained of the stained glass dropped colored shafts of moonlight across the pews.

He let his eyes adjust.

Nobody had worshipped here for a long time. Seats dilapidated, books moldering, ragged prayer shawls shingling a slanted wooden rack. A cataract of dust covered the founders' plaque and memorial boards. Cobwebs tangled the chandeliers—two enormous pear-shaped neoclassical fantasies in wrought iron, like suits of armor exploded.

They had to be worth a fortune. Amazing that no one had stolen them.

He crept back to the vestibule. Crouching to avoid the broken windows' sightlines, he made for the staircase that led to the balcony, parting more plastic sheeting (ACCES INTERDIT) and climbing three stories.

The women's pews were more cramped than the men's, the floor steeply pitched and crackling underfoot. A second, shorter run of steps led up the aisle to the back wall, where the stained glass columns topped out.

Jacob teetered, still drunk, fighting vertigo.

He climbed atop a seat and peered out through blue glass.

The man had retreated down the block, shoulders caved in, looking defeated.

Playing dead?

A couple of minutes later, he left.

Wary of coming in alone? Fetching reinforcements?

Either way, time to go. Jacob jumped off the seat, landing in the aisle on the balls of his feet.

The balcony groaned sickeningly.

The floor dropped out.

For an instant he hung in midair, crashing down in a heap as the floor halted a full three feet below its previous level, and there was a hideous structural belch and loud pops cascaded along the length of the building, walls puffing plaster like a controlled demolition *bang bang bang bang.*

The clangor faded to nothing.

He tried to stand.

Another groan of wood, deeper and unhappier.

A host of fresh cracks raced across walls and ceiling.

He lay there, letting the building settle down, stifling his heaving chest so the next breath wouldn't level the whole place, aware of time burning, the guy phoning his posse.

He began worming on his stomach toward the stairwell, distributing his weight as broadly as he could. Sensing every buried defect, every corroded joist. Smelling the mildew digesting the place from the inside out.

Ten feet to his destination. An inch at a time.

He reached the landing.

The stairs were gone.

Thirty feet below, a smoking pile of beams.

He remained flattened, motionless, calculating.

Jump down? Jump into the sanctuary?

At best, two broken ankles.

Then he recalled a second stairwell in the northeastern corner. He'd passed it while looking for a way out.

Getting there meant traversing the left tine of the balcony's U. He sighted along its length. The torque in the floor was pronounced.

A loud scrape, sourceless. Vibrations.

He edged forward, brailling the carpet, hunting for soft spots. Through the walls came a taunting, hungry rumble.

He was a quarter of the way there and it was getting harder to crawl, his body listing to the right in accordance with the steepening floor.

Wind slapped the building, plaster flakes showering his sweat-drenched neck.

He slid along. Halfway.

The balcony had begun to wag. Then bounce. Like a gently activated diving board. Picking up momentum, a deadly rhythm, prologue to collapse.

The worst urge rose: run.

He crawled. The scar on his lip had of course chosen that moment to begin itching ferociously. He didn't dare reach for it; that was extraneous movement, and the balcony was swaying and cackling, a suicidal hag, threatening to give way.

He reached the landing.

Not in the clear yet. There were steps to be conquered. He went backward, treading delicately and briefly. The carpet was loose, the braces torn out. Down, down he went, until he reached the blessed horizontal and giddily broke for the sanctuary aisle. He could see the vestibule doors. He was going to make it. He had to hope the guy had not yet come back. But he was going to make it outside.

A wretched whine from above, and he instinctively froze and looked up and felt an onrush of air and a cobweb tendril kissing his cheek, mild forerunner to the chandelier plummeting toward him.

CHAPTER THIRTY-EIGHT

Bina says, as they bundle her into the car, "I am an American."

She feels ashamed, exploiting her status in front of Ota Wichs, who lacks recourse.

Hrubý tells the driver to go.

"Where are you taking us?" she asks.

Wichs stares through the gap between his knees.

"This is outrageous." She's making a poor show of indignation. Not her forte. Bad service, even in the cruddiest of restaurants, prompted her mother to pitch a grade-A fit. *Don't tell me quiet, this is their job.* The wanton sense of self always embarrassed Bina.

"I de—" Her throat catches. "—*demand* to speak to the American embassy."

"It will rain tomorrow," Hrubý says to the driver, who nods.

"Did you *hear* me?"

Wichs squeezes her wrist to shut her up.

———————

AT THE INTERROGATION CENTER, they are placed in adjacent rooms. Bina's leg is cuffed to a table. She sits there, listening to the screams boring through cinder block. Clamps her ears, brings her elbows together, prays.

A song of ascents: from out of the depths I cry to you, God.

The noise is horrific; the quiet, worse.

Hrubý enters, accompanied by two men carrying black rubber truncheons. They station themselves in the corners, half-faced in ghastly relief.

"I am an American citizen," she says in Czech. "I want to speak to my embassy."

Hrubý opens his briefcase and lays out a series of photographs as though dealing a hand of solitaire. Blurry, taken from a distance, they show her tugging at her head scarf as she enters the Alt-Neu Synagogue. A boy's shape intrudes into the frame: little Peter Wichs.

Hrubý says, "You are an agent of the world Zionist conspiracy."

Bina laughs. She knows she shouldn't, but it's so absurd.

"You deny it?"

"Of course I do."

One of the guards crosses his arms. The other lightly swings his truncheon by its strap. A black drop wells at its tip and breaks free, spreading red on the concrete.

Bina says, "You can't do this."

Hrubý says, "Put her in the bear."

They wrap her head-to-toe in chains, carry her, thrashing, down the corridor.

The cell is morbidly overcrowded. Yet the other women manage to skitter wide. The guards set her, still chained, on the ground. All night long, no one comes near, and eventually she gives up struggling and lays her head down and weeps.

"Good morning."

She has spent the last hour listening to Ota Wichs scream; swallowing snot to balm her bleeding throat, rehearsing four words, shuffling the stresses.

She says, "I have a son."

"What a coincidence," Hrubý says. "So do I."

It appears that he was right about the weather. His jacket sleeve is dark with rain as he lays out the photographs, along with a typed confession for her to sign.

"You are an agent of the world Zionist conspiracy. You have come to Czechoslovakia under the guise of participating in a cultural mission. You have consulted with counterrevolutionary elements in order to obtain classified information and disseminate misinformation."

"Please," she says. "I'm sure we can get this cleared up."

Hrubý presses his middle finger to the photo, obliterating her face. "This is you."

"Yes, but—"

"Then it is perfectly clear."

"No. No."

He frowns, as though it pains him to point out that she has contradicted herself.

"I went into the synagogue. We all went. It was part of our tour."

"You went again. While your group remained at the National Day celebration, you slipped away to engage in counterrevolutionary activities."

"Mr. Hrubý. Please, let me talk to Ota, we can explain—"

"The person you speak of is a traitor to the State."

"He's—no. How can you . . . All he talked about was how lucky he is to live here."

"And you believed him?"

She almost steps right into it.

Yes: a lie.

No: an indictment.

She says, "I swear to you, we didn't discuss politics."

"What did you do?"

"Nothing. We did nothing."

"I understand," Hrubý says. He takes a cigarette from a dented pack and lights up. "You are lonely," he says, exhaling smoke. "Far from home."

He offers her the pack. She doesn't move, so he tucks it away. "He was married to a Jewess, once, but now he comes home to a gentile woman. He longs for a taste of the familiar."

The guards smirk.

"It's not a crime to fall in love," Hrubý says.

She can't begin to imagine what this man thinks he knows about love. "No."

"Then what did you do, in the synagogue?"

"We made pottery," she says.

"Pottery."

"For the synagogue. Ask him. He'll say the same thing."

"There is nothing wrong with art," Hrubý says. "Sneaking off, on the other hand, late at night—it's what a criminal does. You don't look like a criminal."

"I'm not."

"So then tell me what you did. I am the liaison to the Jewish community, I'm acquainted with your customs. For example, perhaps you made a Sabbath candlestick."

"Yes, exactly."

"No. We searched the building. There was no candlestick."

"We left it in the attic."

"We searched the attic," Hrubý says. "We found a pair of jars, not quite dry. Why did you make them?"

He answers for her: "You made them to smuggle out information."

"That's insane."

"Is it?"

"It's—I mean, it's ridiculous. It's clay. It's delicate."

"Wrap it carefully, smile at the customs officers, 'Please, expensive, handle with care,' and they wave you along."

"I just . . . I don't know what to tell you, other than it's nonsense."

"What is the real explanation?" says Hrubý.

". . . spices. Spice jars."

"For the *havdalah* ceremony," he says.

She nods eagerly.

"Ah. But your companion indicated otherwise."

Her stomach drops. "What did he say?"

White wisps curl from Hrubý's nostrils as he gazes at her.

"Whatever he told you, you can believe him," she says.

Hrubý laughs. "He told me an old story," he says. "About a monster. I learned it in school. It's an idiotic myth. Our modern schools don't teach it anymore."

He slides the confession toward her.

"I don't understand," she says. "Can't you just sign it for me and be done with it?"

"That would be dishonest," he says.

After a beat, she picks up the paper.

On 25 October 1982, I, Bina Lev, an agent of the United States and Israel, acting under instructions from the CIA and the Mossad, entered the ČSR under false pretenses

"If I sign," she says. "What will happen?"

He raises his hands, miming freedom.

"And Ota?"

An identical gesture, a secondary meaning: *who knows?*

"Promise me you'll let him go."

Hrubý takes a final drag, stubs his cigarette out on the table, leaving a black smudge on the steel. "The person you speak of," he says, rubbing at the stain with the flat of his thumb, "is a traitor to the State."

Bina puts out her hands to be cuffed.

THE NEXT DAY she waits for the screaming to begin.

There is only a chilling silence.

"Good morning."

The photos, the confession, the pen.

"Where's Ota?" she says.

"You are an agent of the world Zionist—"

"What have you done to him?"

"The world Zionist—"

"Where is he."

Hrubý takes out a cigarette.

With a shriek, she sweeps the table clean, pen clattering, papers slowly drifting.

Hrubý sighs and waves the guards forward.

———

TIME BEGINS TO LOOP.

"You are an agent—"

And she resists, but with waning vigor. Yes, she is an American, yes, they know. So what? They bear her no malice; there is no malice, none whatsoever; there is a nationwide shortage of malice, of any authentic emotion; there is nothing but an erosive apathy, gritty and mucoid and oozing, a net of un-rules that binds them one and all, prisoner and guard alike. You cannot hate a machine for doing its job. The longer they detain her, the longer they must continue to detain her. Her punishment has become its own justification, and hope, once plucked a feather at a time, is torn out in handfuls.

SHE WILL SIGN.

What else can she do? She'll sign. Nothing left to lose. No point worth proving and no way of proving it.

It is the morning of the nth day. The guards arrive to collect her and she rolls over docilely. They pick her up and carry her past the interrogation room, down the hall and outside, to a loading dock, where an ambulance awaits.

The sight of pure sky briefly stuns her. Then she grasps that this is different, that the difference is danger, and she reverts to kicking, screaming, calling for her country, her husband, for Wichs.

They gag her, hood her, strap her in, drive over rutted streets. She is carried and seated, the hood snatched away, the gag removed, and she beholds a faceless room, she might as well have gone nowhere.

Sitting across from her is not Hrubý but a doughy man in a white lab coat, notepad at the ready. On his left index finger, he wears a huge, crude ring made of black metal. He taps it against the table as he scans the file in his lap.

"I have been reviewing your case," he says. "You admit to entering a restricted area, yet deny engaging in counterrevolutionary activity. Rather, you claim that you were participating in an esoteric ritual, seeking contact with an inanimate creature called 'golem.' Am I pronouncing that correctly?"

She curls on the chair, shaking.

"Very well. According to your statement, a member of the local Jewish community requested that you fashion a jar capable of containing this creature. For reasons that are not wholly clear to me, you judge yourself uniquely suited to this task."

He peers over the page at her. "Stop me if you feel I am misrepresenting you."

She can't remember. She's said so many things. Anything to end this nightmare.

"One imagines that one has heard most of what one will hear at this stage of one's career. But this is a delusion I have never encountered. Usually people like to puff themselves up. Apply a bit of historical shine. Jesus, or the Czar. Interesting, as well, that you have displaced the subject of the delusion from your own person onto an imaginary object, as though some part of you recognizes that your beliefs cannot be true. In rejecting the falsehood, you project it outward, thereby 'creating' an independent entity."

He shakes his head. "A golem . . . Fascinating. I'm grateful to Hrubý for bringing it to my attention."

He studies her. "Do you have any idea what I'm saying? I was told you speak Czech. My English is regretfully limited. I'm working on it, though. Nothing to say? No comment whatsoever? All right, let us continue, shall we . . ."

His Czech is perfectly correct, unwieldy in its formality, an over-starched shirt.

"Additionally, you have on multiple occasions expressed opinions critical of the socialist system. For example, you said—this was on the second of November—'You're a liar. You are all liars, your whole world is a lie.'"

"No," she whispers.

He stops reading. "No what?"

"It's not true."

"Which part? That you said it? Or that you meant it? Or perhaps you maintain that *I* am a liar—"

"No."

"—we are all liars, the system is false. Excuse me, though, please: excuse me. I have it here. You said it. Other statements you made convey much the same idea, so let us agree that I am not twisting your words. We must agree that, at one point, at least, you held that position. And this idea is irrefutable proof of madness, for the principles of Marxism-Leninism are grounded in scientific fact. They have been empirically validated. To deny them is by definition a denial of reality."

"You're right."

The man smiles. "Is that what you think?"

"Yes. Yes. Yes."

"But I have pages"—he parades them in front of her—"pages and pages of evidence to the contrary."

"I, I, I've changed my mind."

"Mm." He writes in his pad. "And may I ask how that change came about?"

"Time," she says, "to think it over."

"And are there other things you've changed your mind about?"

". . . everything."

"I see." He puts down the pad, crosses his legs high, hugs his knee. "Can't you see how unhealthy that is, though? To swap your opinions for new ones so easily? It's a sign that your psyche is unstable. It's typical of what we observe in Western patients. You are addicted to choice. You turn this way, that way. You grasp at the shiny ring. The self is never permitted to firm up and thus fails to integrate a sense of purpose or duty."

He reaches under the table to depress a hidden button.

"I understand it's a popular legend around these parts, the golem. Personally, I had never heard of it, although my assistant said his mother told it to him when he was a boy." He resumes writing. "What a concept. Life from nothing. I can appreciate the appeal. What storyteller wouldn't? What scientist? Myths have their place."

The door opens and a young man enters the room.

He is a giant.

Slavic cheekbones dotted with acne, his close-cropped hair colorless in defiance of nature, as though he has gotten a terrible fright and gone white overnight. He wears green rubber gloves. His is the shorter coat of an orderly. On his spindly frame, it hits six inches above the waist.

"*Da*, Doktor Tremsin?"

The doctor puts an emphatic period on his sentence and flips the notepad shut. "Take the patient to room nine to begin immediate treatment."

"MY PRIMARY PASSION," Tremsin says, "is the relationship between brain chemistry and truth. What is the physical mechanism for deception? Can we locate it in space? In time?"

A steel bracket, a quarter sphere like an orange slice sucked to the peel, is latched across her head. A second bracket secures her chin.

"To understand these processes is of the utmost importance."

The gurney has been partially raised, the wheels locked. Leather straps fix her limbs; a wide leather belt across her waist, pliable from countless bucklings and unbucklings, straining and sweating, blood.

"A pill that opens the innermost chambers of the human heart . . . You might call it the Holy Grail."

The tall orderly has left, and now Tremsin stands at the sink, twisting at his ring.

It won't come off. He spits on his finger and it slides loose. He sets it on the counter with a clack, turns on the water, and begins lavishly soaping his hands.

"I'll be honest: at first, I was not terribly thrilled at the notion of coming to Czechoslovakia. The most exciting work is being done back home. Already I had found success far beyond what we had achieved with sodium pentothal, which, frankly, I've never trusted."

Tremsin wrings his hands out, opens a plywood cabinet, finds a needle and a syringe. "Do you have any idea how difficult it is to find a halfway decent bathhouse in Prague? I'll tell you. It's not difficult at all. It's impossible. There are none."

He screws the needle onto the syringe.

"In a certain sense, though, the atmosphere here is more intellectually open than in Moscow. One is freer to take risks, to make mistakes and learn from them."

He cranes back, smiles. "Don't tell anyone I said that."

From the cabinet, he takes a vial containing an amber liquid. "To lie successfully involves many complex and often competing calculations. What do I know? What does my interlocutor know? What does he know I know, and what do each of us not know?"

Tears run from the outside corners of her eyes, collect inside her ears; she is crying backward.

"Don't look so glum. As I said, your case presents a rare opportunity. You're advancing the cause of science. You should feel proud." Tremsin holds up the notebook. "And flattered. I'm dedicating a whole lab book, a fresh one, just to you."

He opens the book, slashes lines. "The third of November. Patient number—ah, but you haven't got one yet, have you? We'll fix that. For the time being, though . . . 'A-me-ri-can.' There. That suits you. Diagnosis: sluggish schizophrenia, distinguished by an exceptionally pronounced systematic delusion. I'll fill in the details later. We don't have a minute to lose. Haloperidol—"

He stops writing and peers at her. "Please try to relax. Can't you see how agitated you are? That's the first obstacle."

He stabs the needle into the vial, draws up a nauseating quantity. He flicks the syringe, holds it to the light, squirts a tiny bit back into the vial. "Let's say thirty milligrams. We'll start there and see how it goes."

He folds her gown over her stomach and crushes a handful of thigh.

The needle bores to the bone.

A freezing cavity blooms.

Her spasms loosen the rags in her mouth. Tenderly he tucks them back in, then begins unbuckling his own trousers, pausing to turn the wheel beneath the gurney, lowering it to a more manageable height.

"I'm sorry about the discomfort," he says. He unbuttons his fly. "It has to deliver deep into the muscle to be effective."

His words are water through a sieve, the holes expanding.

and now

>>> *how*

>>>>> *do*

>>>>>>> *you*

>>>>>>>>> *feel*

"Sister."

She is nothing.

"Sister. Can you hear me?"

Her tongue flopped out, rancid air.

"Here. Over here. Look."

A white flutter at her periphery.

"Take it, please. You've made a little mess."

It's true. Bina can smell it.

"Sister—"

"Shut up, Majka."

"They'll punish her for soiling herself."

"Then they'll punish her."

"All right, sister," Majka says. "I'll leave it here for you. When you can."

"Shut," the second voice says, "your idiot mouth."

Hours pass. Bina finds that she can make the world stand still by bearing down. She lies in something like an outsize chicken coop, a bed with wire walls and a wire roof and a rusty padlock. The room is just big enough to hold four such cages, two on each wall, set end to end. A cuboid window opaque with dirt beats back the light.

"You're awake."

Through two layers of wire, bright blue eyes search her; a sharp, sad smile. "Let's not wake them, eh? Fat Irena is a bitch and she's worse when she's tired. Can you reach the paper?"

A scrap, crumpled and stuffed into the three-inch gap between their cages. Bina tries to pluck at it, but her unhinged fingers dislodge it and it spirals to the floor.

"Don't worry. Let's try again. What I'm going to do is make a baton. Okay? I'm rolling it up, and you take it. Can you take it? Don't fall asleep on me, now."

The paper noses its way into her cage. Bina's hand sways in midair.

"Almost there. A little to the left . . . Now take it."

Bina scissors the paper between her pinkie and her ring finger, and it unfurls, revealing the masthead of *Práce*, the trade union daily.

Majka laughs softly. "All it's good for. Go on, clean yourself up . . . Good. Showers are in three days, that's not so bad. It's on your back. Can you—you can't reach it, that's all right, don't worry about it. It's just a small . . . They won't notice. I'm sorry I mentioned it. I'm glad you're here. I can see you've had a tough time. You've been to see Doktor Tremsin. It won't last forever. It happens with new patients. He might play favorites for a week or two. At some point, he'll get bored of you. What did they bring you in for? Better yet, don't tell me. We'll talk later, when you've had a chance to rest. They'll be coming in to wake us before you know it. Try to gather your strength."

Exhausted, Bina lets the shit-smeared paper drop from her hand. She can hear Majka bedding down a few inches away, a comforting sound soon overtaken.

FOR HER SECOND TREATMENT, Tremsin announces that he is considering reducing the dosage.

"Your file lists you at fifty-eight kilograms. I gather that was true at admission, but it is no longer so, since the file further indicates that you have all but refused to eat. I can count your ribs. Nutrition is essential for rehabilitation."

A single wooden bowl of vegetable stew, brought at dawn by a nurse. No utensils provided—*We might hurt ourselves* Majka whispered, winking—so they sat on the floor, a few feet from the overflowing Turkish toilet, passing the bowl around the circle, scooping up the thin liquid with their unwashed hands. Bina couldn't sit up, let alone feed herself; Majka did it for her. Fat Irena got the final handful. Olga grumbled that she always got the final handful, and Fat Irena said *In your ass* and then they went at each other as the nurse wearily blew her whistle.

"For the moment," Tremsin says, "the important thing is to get a new and accurate measurement. I ask that you please step on the scale."

It wasn't an ordinary fight between women. They were vicious as wolves. Olga's ear disappeared into Fat Irena's mouth, and Bina could feel the crunch in her own teeth.

"The patient," Tremsin says, "will stand on the scale."

What he perceives as defiance is in fact inability: Bina's legs cannot bear weight.

She thinks of her parents, alive in body but not in spirit.

There are many kinds of survival, not all equal.

She raises her head, seizes control of her tongue.

"I have a name."

With satisfaction, she watches the color creep up over Tremsin's collar, into his shapeless face.

He walks abruptly to the door, throws it open, shouting down the hall in Russian until the giant orderly appears.

"The patient will be placed on the scale," Tremsin says.

"My name is Bina."

The orderly dutifully hoists her out of the wheelchair.

"Bina Reich Lev."

"The patient will stop struggling."

"My name is Bina Reich Lev."

"The patient will be silenced."

She shouts once more before the orderly gets the rags into her mouth. He carries her to the scale, draping her across it so that her heels and head brush the ground.

"That's no good. She's half—sit her up, you imbecile."

She flops around.

"The patient will *cease*."

The orderly kneels, applying light pressure to her shoulders.

"Don't make it harder," he murmurs.

"Sit her up," Tremsin says. "Dmitri. What are you waiting for."

Bina stares into the orderly's eyes. He nods.

She relaxes, allowing herself to be balanced and weighed.

"Put her on the table," Tremsin says. "Hurry up."

The orderly moves her to the gurney, his white face orbiting in and out of view as he straps her in. Bending to screw down the chin bracket, he whispers in her ear.

"Blink if it's too tight."

"*Spasiba*, Dmitri Samilovich." Tremsin is scribbling furiously in the lab book. "*Chorosho.*"

She blinks.

The orderly loosens the bracket a bit, bows to Tremsin, and exits.

Tremsin locks the door. "I was right," he says.

He stabs the vial of amber liquid, draws up the syringe.

"You have slimmed down, quite a bit. However."

He taps out air bubbles, squirts off the excess.

"Upon further consideration, given your level of agitation, I cannot help but think that it would be premature to lower your dose."

He throws back her gown. "We'll stay at thirty."

CHAPTER THIRTY-NINE

The last thought Jacob had as the chandelier came down on him wasn't a neat summing-up of his life. No jubilation, no regret; instead, the petty disappointment that he would die drunk, yet not drunk enough.

He thought, breathlessly, that he was still thinking.

The point of the chandelier, a spear finial aimed for his breastbone, ready to butterfly his heart, bounced twice before coming to rest a foot above him, swinging lazily.

It reminded him of something. A Foucault pendulum. He'd last seen one here, in Paris, at the Panthéon. He'd gone alone. Stacy had wanted to sleep in. That one swung from an anchor in the ceiling.

Now he gazed up the chandelier's hollow body and saw the broken chain, stretched taut, tethered to nothingness. He felt a powerful downward wash of air; heard the effortful buzzing of wings. Against the vaulted black, he saw a black speck.

The scar on his lip was on fire.

He scratched at it, hypnotized, as the beetle began to move, towing the chandelier behind. It went up the aisle a safe distance, centered itself between the pews.

Let go.

The chandelier landed with a deafening peal, spraying marble chips, toppling to the left and crushing several seats, its graceful curves deformed, branches bent like drinking straws.

Behind the wreckage stood Mai, naked, glorious, hands on her hips. Her eyes were green tonight, her hair an untamed crown, her skin flushed red. Sweat coursed between her breasts, over her tight belly, which swelled and deflated; sweat collected between her thighs to hang in quivering droplets.

She ruefully contemplated the damage. "Whoops."

Jacob said, "I'm sure they'll understand."

She grinned at him. "You always know how to cheer me up."

He got to his feet, working a finger in his ringing ear.

Mai said, "Are you okay? Are you going to pass out?"

". . . fine."

"Aren't you going to thank me?"

He ought to. She had saved his life. For a second time. The words wouldn't come.

"What?" she said. "What's wrong?"

She could see his aura. He had to remember that. Surely she could tell that he was angry. She might even know the specific reason, his suspicion that the chandelier hadn't fallen on its own, but had required a bit of encouragement.

Was it ungrateful of him to wonder where she'd been thirty minutes ago, when he was being chased?

He put on a smile. "Thank you."

"Be a gentleman," she said. "I'm freezing."

He stumbled over to the rack of prayer shawls, selecting one large enough to cover her to the ankles, holding it out at arm's length as she wrapped herself.

"Just like the first time we met," he said.

"Just as itchy."

"And now we meet again."

"Did you think we wouldn't?"

He said, carefully, "I'm glad you were around."

"Of course I'm around," she said. "That's what 'forever' means, Jacob Lev."

Wind hammered through the broken windows.

She said, "Did you think you could get on a plane and be free of me?"

"I'm here for a case," he said. "And I don't want to be free of you."

"Don't you."

He said, "Look, Mai. What happened, with Divya—"

"'Happened.' That's an interesting way to put it. 'Occurrences occurred.' I like how it sounds, as if you didn't have a choice."

"I said I'm sorry."

"Actually, you didn't."

"Well, I am. I'm sorry."

Her eyes changed, became the color of lead. "Not good enough."

"Really? Cause I was thinking we're even, considering you tried to burn down my apartment."

"*I* didn't do anything. *You* passed out and left the stove on. Not my fault you drink too much."

What was it the couples' counselor had told him, so long ago? Find the hurt behind the anger? "I am attempting to express—"

"What you're attempting to do, Jacob Lev, is turn it around on me."

"I screwed up," he said. "I'm sorry. Okay? I'm sorry. I'm a normal human male."

"The oldest excuse," she said. "Also the most predictable. And the worst."

362

"And that justifies killing me?"

"Frankly, I think I'm being a lot nicer than a lot of women would be in my position."

"What do you expect? I'm going to be celibate for the rest of my life?"

She shrugged. "I wouldn't say no."

"We are not having this conversation," he said.

"And why's that?"

Because you're a beetle.

A monster.

A figment of my fucking imagination.

What he said was, "I barely know you."

"Don't say that," she said. "Ever."

She came closer. Her face was wet and twisted. "I knew you before you knew yourself. I read the pages before they were written."

Fear coursed through Jacob.

"I'm sorry," he said. "I'm not prepared for . . . all I can do is say I'm sorry."

She wiped her cheeks on the prayer shawl.

"I don't want to fight," he said. "It's a nice night. We're in Paris. Let's try to enjoy it. Can we do that?"

". . . all right."

"Thank you."

"What should we do?" she asked.

Another blast of wind; the balcony wailed.

"I'm thinking," he said, "we might want to get out of here."

She gave a wicked smile. "Sounds good," she said, whipping off the shawl and tossing it in his face.

He clawed free. She'd already vanished, though.

"Mai."

And suddenly she was behind him, against him, but she wasn't a woman any longer; he felt a hard breastplate pressed to his spine and legs like iron rods lashed him, strapping him in at the shoulders, waist, thighs. He experienced a brief sensation of weightlessness, dislodged immediately by the stronger, gut-churning sensation of violent acceleration as she flew straight up, hauling him into the air.

"Mai."

She launched forward, their flight path obvious as they leapt over the women's-section balcony and jetted toward a stained glass panel on the left, and he curled chin to chest to avoid the debris and she lowered her horn and punched through glass and lead.

Jacob screamed.

Kept screaming as they climbed through the storm, bursting thunderheads and raging seams of light, higher and higher until the altitude left him gasping for breath.

Mai crested softly, affording him a panorama.

Paris, through patches of black velvet, a coursing circuit board, so splendid that for a moment he forgot to be terrified.

Then she dropped in, streaking toward the earth, dragging him through strata of mist, rain blistering his face, his nervous system sparking, eyelids soldered shut, lungs filling with force-fed wind, the glowing heat of reentry.

"Down." He was yelling so hard he could taste his lungs. *"Down."*

Undoubtedly she was getting a kick out of hearing him squeal: a little payback. He bit down hard, determined not to give her the satisfaction of making him puke.

She flattened her angle of descent and they exploded through the dark cloud underbelly, leveling off over a broad stroke of concrete: the Champs-Élysées, terminating in a luminous bull's-eye, roundabout and spokes, the grinning Arc de Triomphe.

"*No.*"

She dove.

They threaded the monument and the flame of the Unknown Soldier licked his chest and he went eyeball-to-eyeball with granules of concrete before she pitched up to reascend.

"*No. Mai. No.*"

She took him over the rooftops, lustrous zinc tangrams, and vaulted the river.

The crown of the Eiffel Tower flashed by.

She banked hard, circling the observation deck, spiraling inward.

A warm gush of gratitude.

They were going to land.

She didn't land.

She slingshotted out of orbit, the tower's spire shrinking in the distance.

"*Goddamn it.*"

Could beetles laugh?

She zagged along the river, bouncing between the quais, leaping and ducking bridges. Jacob had given up screaming. He was beyond fear, another sensation emerging, a tautness in his groin. He felt her armor, hot as a spent casing, and he surrendered to the present and let beauty flood in: the water, daubed with lamplight, its funk in his nostrils as they dipped to skim its surface; the musical plash of *bateaux* moored till morning, when they'd fill with tourists who'd never know what the city could look like from another perspective.

She went over and back again, showing him a geometry of fantasy.

The Place de la Concorde with its whipping tentacles. The candy box that was the Jardin des Tuileries, the Louvre's pyramids burnished like quartz. He leaned to the right and Mai understood and fulfilled his wish, the two of them rising, soaring.

He heard the sound of snapping fabric and tilted his chin down, laughing to realize he was still clutching the *tallit* in his left hand.

The river forked to accommodate two teardrops of land, the Île de la Cité and the Île Saint-Louis. Below, Notre Dame, a low-waisted stick figure basking in starlight. Mai lined up along the nave of the cathedral, shedding speed, cheating in the direction of the north tower, the air congealing around them, now water, now oil, now thick as honey, until his toes touched stone, and the constriction across his body eased.

He wobbled.

Stood.

He was soaked with sweat and rain.

He felt the *tallit* tugged from his fist.

"Come on," she said. She had wrapped herself in it, her eyes back to green, her amusement plain. She took his hand. "Let's watch the sun rise."

THEY STOOD TOGETHER atop the north tower, fingers laced, facing east, flanked by gargoyles.

She said, "I wake up. Strange place. Strange body. I couldn't tell you how much time has passed. I couldn't tell you when I was last awake. I see a person. Sometimes he—it's always a he—sometimes he's kind. Sometimes he wants me to do horrible things. I can't say no. He says kill and I kill."

She sagged, hiding in her hair. "A day goes by. A year. My mind starts to clear. Fragments come back. I begin putting them together and then it all goes dark." She paused. "It's horrible."

He nodded.

She said, "For the longest time, it went on like that, over and over."

"What changed?"

"There was a woman. She gave me the body I have now."

"Well," he said. "If I ever run into her, I'll thank her."

Mai laughed softly. "It was many years ago. After she remade me, I saw my reflection and recognized myself. Even though I was new. I know it sounds strange. She did that for me."

Jacob said, "It sounds like love."

Mai said, "She looked like you."

Silence.

"She set me free," Mai said. "The tall men were furious. They hunted me, for years and years. A few times, they managed to corner me. They seemed to expect they could snap their fingers and return me to dust. But I wasn't as malleable anymore. The woman knew me. She knew how I was supposed to be. The form she had given me, it was . . . sticky. I always got away.

"In the end, I came back on my own. To see her. I had to. Nothing else mattered."

She could have been describing any addiction.

"She was expecting me. She'd left the garret door open. She said they had ordered her to destroy me. They threatened her. She said, 'I'd never do that to you.'

"She showed me a jar. It looked so delicate, you can't imagine."

He could. He had seen one like it. More than once.

In a garret, shards.

In his apartment, intact. He used it to store sugar.

Mai said, "I did what she asked. I crawled inside. I felt so tired I could hardly move. It was like that, if she touched me, and the jar came from her hands; it had her in it."

He made to release her fingers, but she held on tightly.

"Right now," she said, "this is where I want to be."

She leaned her head on his shoulder. "I broke out. It takes time, but I've done it, more than once. I'll open my eyes and see light everywhere. Not a pleasant light. Sludgy, like a window that's never been cleaned. As long as it's there, I have the strength to kick. When it fades, I fall back asleep. Eventually, though—"

"The jar cracks," he said.

"Usually someone's waiting there to put me back in."

"Not the last time," he said.

"No."

"You saw a man, attacking a woman."

"Yes."

"You acted."

A dreamy smile, as though she was recalling an especially delicious dinner. "Yes."

Reggie Heap, a rapist and murderer. In general, Jacob believed he'd gotten his due. Nonetheless it unsettled him to perceive the pleasure she could take in ripping someone's—anyone's—head off.

"When I touched him, I saw the others he'd hurt, the men who helped him. I went to find them. I found you, too."

Jacob shivered, recalling her, naked in his apartment, a girl he didn't remember picking up, a creation without equal, bathed in early morning sun.

I'm just a nice young lady who came down for some fun.

"They've never stopped watching you," she said. "You do know that."

He shook his head. He hadn't, and while the deception infuriated him, worse was realizing his own naïveté.

"They backed off a bit. They're still in your neighborhood, though. I fly over them most nights. They keep a van at the ready, half a mile from the archive."

The desire to bash Mallick's smug face in gave way to a pinch of anxiety. "Do they follow me in the car?" he asked.

"Of course."

"I try to shake them," he said.

She said, "They know about your mother."

He stared at her. "How do *you* know about her?"

"You visit her every week. It's not hard to see. You have her face."

Silence.

"Why haven't they gone after her?" he said.

Mai bit her lip. "I suppose they think she's in no state to help them."

He said, "Is she?"

Mai considered her answer at length.

"I do love her," she said. "But I love you more."

A queasy smile. "Thanks?"

She laughed softly.

They were quiet together awhile.

"Schott's here," he said. "In Paris."

She nodded.

"You're not worried?"

"Not at the moment. I'm safe. Any house of worship, really. It frightens them."

"I didn't realize they got frightened."

"Everybody's got something they're afraid of. I'm afraid of them. They're afraid of you. You're afraid of me."

"I'm not—"

She shut her eyes. "Please don't lie. I can't stand that."

He wondered what it looked like to her—the texture and hue of his fear.

"He's not the only one," she said. "The man who followed you tonight. He's one of them, too."

"That can't be right," he said. "He works for Tremsin."

"I know what I saw."

"His colors."

She said, "He doesn't have any."

A beat.

"That's why he never entered the synagogue," Jacob said.

"Yes."

"Why you couldn't help me."

She grimaced. "I'm sorry."

He pulled her closer.

"I want to be there for you," she said. "I'll be there, as much as I can."

He said, "So, just to be clear, that's your interpretation of 'forever.'"

She smacked him on the arm. "Stop."

"I'm just pointing it out," he said. "I'm not the only one who picks and chooses."

"You don't understand. I can't go back in the jar."

"I'm not asking you to."

But she was drawn and trembling. "I can't stand it in there. Not one day more."

She was right to be afraid, wrong about the reason.

Subach and Schott had ransacked his apartment. They could've taken the jar. They took the potter's knife.

So that's your strategy for dealing with her. Containment.

Ask yourself what you'd do in my position.

An immense sadness gripped Jacob.

"They're not going to give up," he said.

"You want me to turn myself in?"

"Of course not."

"Convenient for you. Sleep with anyone you want, get your old job back—"

"Cut it out."

She said, "I'm sorry. I don't know how this is supposed to work. You and I."

It can't.

"The woman who set you free," he said. "What was her name?"

"I don't know. I can't remember. I've always had trouble with names."

"Perel," he said. "Perel Loew. Is that right?"

A smile broke open on Mai's face, and she burrowed deep in his chest, and they laughed and cried and rocked together, sheltering each other from the morning chill.

The tower bells began to toll.

She said, "You should go."

"Not yet."

"He's going to wonder where you are."

"Let him," he said.

She raised her mouth to his, and he remembered the taste of her, the way it coated his tongue like earth.

He staggered forward, hungry for more.

But the flesh was gone, and he felt himself embraced, rising, warmth at his back, as she floated him down to the garden behind the cathedral and set him gently on his feet.

Shrunk to a point, she hovered briefly before him, then flew off, a scribble in his visual field, an error corrected by the higher functions of his brain.

CHAPTER FORTY

Back at the hostel, Schott's bed was empty and unmade, his roll-aboard pulled open. Jacob stripped off his wet clothes. His hair was a wind-driven pile, his eyes garish with broken capillaries.

The man who followed you tonight.

He's one of them, too.

Until now he'd thought of Special Projects as Mallick, Schott, Subach, Divya, the rotating cast of characters who manned the surveillance vans. The reality—if you wanted to call it that—now seemed obvious.

Schott had said as much: there were others.

The folks who'd shown up to bully Jan, for instance.

Not all of them knew what they were.

Maybe Tremsin's guy fell into that category.

Maybe Mallick was pulling strings.

Assigning Jacob to the archives in the first place?

Planting the file to snag his interest?

But Marquessa—she was real. TJ was real. They were a mother and a child, tossed away like garbage. In the end, he didn't care if he was playing into the Commander's hands. He could do only this, the only thing that gave him meaning.

IT WAS THE MIDDLE of the night in California. Jacob e-mailed out a picture of Knob Neck to all potential witnesses. He predicted Zinaida Moskvina would be the first to reply. A baker. She'd be up early.

He got cleaned up, texting Schott that he was back before heading down to the lobby for the stale display that passed for a continental breakfast. He sank into a bean bag chair, sipping black coffee, debating how best to act, going forward.

Confront Schott?

Pretend like everything was normal?

Without trust, there's nothing.

He'd have some choice words for Divya when he got back.

He hadn't yet decided on a strategy when the big man came charging in from the street.

Jacob rose. "Hey. We need to ta—"

The slap sent him sprawling, coffee raining down in a lukewarm arc.

A girl standing at the buffet table sputtered crumbs.

Jacob rolled over, his head buzzing.

Schott bent to him. "You're a sack of shit."

The girl hurried out; the desk clerk began reaching for the phone.

Schott turned, snapping his fingers. *"Posez ça. Ne bougez pas."*

The clerk replaced the receiver.

"Vos mains."

The clerk laid his palms passively on the counter.

"Asshole," Jacob said. It came out as *ath-hole*.

"I was right about you," Schott said. "I should have gone with my gut."

"Asshole. Listen. You were sleeping. I got restless. I took a walk. I was followed."

Schott wavered. "What?"

"The guy from Tremsin's house. Knob Neck. See for yourself."

He thumbed to the first image on his phone and handed it over.

"He knew my name," Jacob said.

SAG card notwithstanding, Schott reacted with convincing astonishment. "How's that possible?"

"I don't know," Jacob said. "Theories?"

Schott looked at him.

"He's not one of yours?" Jacob asked.

"One of—are you outta your mind?"

"He's awfully tall," Jacob said.

"Tell me you're kidding. What's gotten into you?"

"*Me?* He chased me for half an hour. I had to duck into a building to get away. He knew my *name*, you prick."

"Don't look at me. I saw him for the first time yesterday, same as you. Call Mallick, you don't believe me."

Jacob laughed. "Okay, right."

"Christ, but you're paranoid."

"Says the pot to the kettle."

Schott lobbed the phone at Jacob, hitting him square in the chest.

"Look me in the eye," he said, "and tell me you didn't see her."

Jacob reached for a napkin and began dabbing at coffee stains. "I didn't."

"Look me in the eye."

"I am."

"You're looking at the floor."

"You fucking hit me. My head is spinning."

"I barely touched you," Schott said. Grumbling: *"Trouvez-moi des glaçons."*

With the possibility of further excitement ruled out, the desk clerk appeared both relieved and disappointed. He ducked through a back door.

Schott paced. "You can't run off like that."

"Next time I'll leave a note."

"I don't want a note. I want you not to run off. Why didn't you call me?"

"I was more focused on not getting shot."

"Were you drunk?"

"I had a drink."

"How many?"

"Leave it alone."

The clerk came back with a baggie of ice. He handed it to Schott, who handed it to Jacob, who pressed it to his face.

Schott lowered his bulk into a plastic chair. He looked haggard. "You should have called," he muttered.

"Duly noted."

"How'd the guy find you, anyway?"

"For all I know, he was following us all day."

"I didn't notice anyone."

"Neither did I."

"What'd he want?"

"You know," Jacob said, "I completely neglected to ask."

"I'm thinking out loud, all right? What's he think he's going to accomplish?"

"He said he wanted to talk. Maybe it's true. I suppose if he really wanted to nail me, he had plenty of time. Or he didn't want to risk shooting in public. Either way, I'm taking it as a good sign. Tremsin blinked."

He held out his coffee cup for a refill.

Schott scoffed. "Yeah, okay."

"You were an actor, weren't you?"

Schott snatched the cup and lumbered over to the buffet.

"I wouldn't say no to a pastry," Jacob called.

"Eat me."

THEY ARRIVED AT THE HOSPITAL minutes after visiting hours began. The hallway outside Breton's room was clogged with bodies, men clumped in protective twos and threes, talking in low tones, a few openly crying.

"Shit," Jacob said.

A waspish Odette Pelletier pushed from the crowd to intercept them. "You shouldn't be here."

"We came to talk to Breton."

"Yes, well, as you can see, it's a bit late for that."

"I'm sorry," he said.

"It's not your place to be sorry," she said. "This is a family matter."

A man crouched against the wall looked up sharply. Jacob recognized the blond goatee, the expression of dislocation.

"My colleague is dead," Pelletier said. "I've been here all night. You're abusing professional courtesy, Detective. I'm going to ask you, one last time, to leave."

Jacob put up peace hands. "Okay. Just so you know: I was followed last night."

A beat. "By whom?"

"One of Tremsin's goons."

He showed her the photo on his phone. She didn't react.

"Did he do anything?" she asked. "Threaten you?"

"Nothing overt. Didn't feel too good, though."

The goateed man was watching them intently.

Pelletier said, "You can file a formal complaint at the station."

"You don't think it's a little strange?" Jacob said. "I'm minding my own business and I get tailed?"

"I think you acted provocatively by going to Mr. Tremsin's house. I will say it again, and I ask that this time you please pay attention. He is a private citizen, entitled to live free of harassment. Now excuse me. I have my men to take care of."

She turned on her heel.

OUT IN THE LOBBY, Jacob punched the elevator button. "We never told her we went to the house."

"You said he was Tremsin's goon. It's a reasonable assumption on her part."

"Or she's in contact with them. That's the easiest way for the guy to know where to find me. I gave her my card with the hostel's address. She tipped them off."

They stepped into the elevator.

"Une seconde, merci."

The man with the blond goatee was running toward them.

Jacob stuck a foot out to block the closing doors.

"Merci." The man tucked himself into a corner and they rode down in silence to the ground floor.

The doors opened.

The man said, *"Suivez-moi."*

CHAPTER FORTY-ONE

He led them down the street to a *bar-tabac* whose interior smelled of radiator steam and shoe leather. Off-duty medical staff warmed hands over coffees.

They took a booth and the blond man introduced himself as Dédé Vallot.

In broken English, he explained that he worked for Théo Breton— or had, until the higher-ups forced Breton out. Ever since then, he'd been passing along progress reports, monitoring Odette Pelletier, logging her calls.

Jacob said, "You were the one who gave Breton my number."

Vallot nodded, accepting his beer from the waiter. It was not yet ten a.m.

"Why did he ask you to keep tabs on Pelletier?" Schott asked.

"She's come from the sky, eh? We thought, who she is, l'IGPN?"

"What is that?" Jacob asked.

"La police des polices."

"Internal affairs," Schott said.

"Ouais. So I make a check. *Pas l'IGPN. Pas la Crim. Les RG."*

Schott sought clarification before translating: "Intelligence."

"How'd you find this out?" Jacob asked.

"My friend," Vallot said.

"And he's reliable."

"The most."

"What's an intelligence officer doing on a murder squad?" Schott asked.

"Her file is . . . Eh. *Expurgé*." Vallot made striking-out motions. "But he told me her university, in Lyon. So I make another check. *Et voilà*: two years, she was study literature in Moscow."

"You're shitting me," Jacob said.

"No shitting."

"Is there a connection to Tremsin?"

"Impossible to say. But . . ." A shrug.

"She told us Tremsin was out of the country the week of the murders," Schott said.

"The plane," Vallot said. "It's belong to him."

Of course it did. "Private jet," Jacob said.

"It goes to Cyprus. Okay. But who is on it?"

"He could have been in Paris after all."

"What about customs records?" Schott said. "A manifest."

"Tremsin pays to the airport. He pays to the pilots. No one cares."

"Pelletier didn't want to follow up?" Jacob asked.

"She sayed it's not important."

"It sounds pretty important to me."

"*Ouais*. Too important."

Jacob sat back. "Did you take this to anyone?"

"Who?"

"Your boss."

"He's listen to Odette. She is above me."

Jacob said, "Have a look at these."

Vallot shuffled through the stack of L.A. crime scene photos, lips curling in revulsion. *"Putain."* He drained his beer, waved on a second.

"You saw the same thing," Jacob said.

Vallot moved the salt shaker to one side of the table. "The mother."

He placed the pepper opposite. "The son."

Jacob said, "I looked for crimes with a similar setup. Other than yours, I couldn't find anything."

"Us not nothing, either."

"There's a ten-year gap. I'm having a hard time believing a guy this fucked up goes on vacation that entire time."

"Théo wants to look in Russia."

"Did he get anywhere?"

"He was lost his job."

"And Pelletier took over."

"Yes."

Jacob said, "I'd like to see the scene. You think you can show me around?"

Vallot hesitated. "It's a bad day."

"I know. I'm sorry about Breton. I take it you two were close."

Vallot nodded. Then he said, "She was in the hospital. Odette. She never visit Théo before. But last night, she's going."

He swirled his glass, looked up at them. "Why?"

"Someone called and told her the news, I assume."

"Who's calling? She's not friends."

Vallot drank a third of his beer, wiped his mouth.

"I sawed him yesterday," he said. "He was look better. Then . . . *Pof.* The doctor sayed he's having a heart attack. I want to know, how? Théo has cancer. His heart, there is no problem."

Schott said, "What're you getting at?"

Vallot tugged listlessly at loose neck skin.

Schott said, "You don't actually think she could've done something to him."

"I sawed him yesterday. He was look better."

Jacob said, "He seemed like a fine guy."

Vallot threw back his beer. "I message you. Today, later, maybe."

He started to uncrumple a twenty-euro bill.

Jacob said, "Let me get it."

Vallot didn't argue, but put his money away.

"I appreciate the help," Jacob said. "One other thing." He showed Vallot the phone image of the man who had tailed him through the Marais.

Vallot shook his head.

Jacob said, "He's one of Tremsin's bodyguards."

Vallot accepted the information with mute resignation and left.

When he'd disappeared from view, Jacob turned to Schott. "The hell are you giving him a hard time for?"

"He resents Pelletier because she upstaged his buddy. So now she's snuffing a fellow cop with end-stage cancer? The guy's talking shit."

"The guy," Jacob said, "is *grieving*."

"Emotions fuck you up," Schott said.

Jacob shook his head, raising a finger to a passing waiter. "*Une bière*."

Schott made a face.

"What?" Jacob said. "You want one, too? *Deux*."

"*Oui, monsieur*."

PORTE DAUPHINE STOOD at the center of a honking roundabout, encircled by an archipelago of brown lawns and concrete. Outside the Métro entrance, Jacob twisted his hands in his pockets, trying not to let on to Schott how antsy he felt. Vallot had texted the location and a meet time of one-thirty, and it was nearing two.

"Maybe he got drunk," Schott said. "Lost track of time."

At five after, Vallot came up from the subway, apologizing for his tardiness.

They entered the park via the Route des Suresnes. The transition from urban to wooded was rapid but incomplete: half a mile in, they were still seeing parked cars, dog walkers, the occasional hard-core jogger in tights. Ranks of trees fanned across lawns peeled to dirt and dotted with frost. Rowboats stacked up for the season crowded the banks of Lac Inférieur. A woman at the mercy of a Saint Bernard hurtled by, and Vallot left the pavement, trotting along a gravel path, away from the lake.

Jacob checked the time. Five-twenty a.m. in Los Angeles. Still no response to his e-mails. He put his phone away and said, "When's the funeral?"

"A week, two."

"He has a family?"

Vallot clucked his tongue. "Girlfriend. Ex. She's arrange."

They crossed a wooden bridge over a slushy stream, which Jacob identified on his map as the Ruisseau de Longchamp. From there he lost track, as Vallot turned down one footpath, then another, the trail steadily degrading until they were tramping in slop. A layer of mist seethed through the tree trunks, damp quiet broken irregularly by chittering or panicked movement in the underbrush.

Vallot paused in front of a gnarled stump sealed with tar. He shifted his backpack to the other shoulder and stepped off the path, motioning for them to follow.

They slogged over dense terrain, the silence folding over itself. They had stopped speaking, Vallot gesturing to indicate a crashed log, a knurl of rock hidden beneath vegetation. Only twigs, explod-ing like buckshot; Schott's chesty panting; the mournful suck of mud, ankle-deep, piling up along the sides of Jacob's shoes, soak-ing into his socks, numbing the skin up to midcalf. His hands had gone numb.

Nothing to see now, except mud and trees.

Fifty paces off the trail and the woods had closed in like a coffin, thatching off sightlines, blunting perspective. The other men were feet away, but Jacob felt the choking solitude that Lidiya and Valko must have felt, even side by side, the devastating awareness that de-spite laws and totems and covenants, you were always, finally, alone.

The place, when they arrived, was self-evident: an oblong patch of earth, a roof of iron sky.

The three of them stood shoulder to shoulder.

Schott said, "I'm amazed they were discovered as quickly as they were."

"The guy who's find, he was hunt for mushrooms. It's for him a big secret place." Vallot paused. "I don't think he's come no more."

He tugged open his backpack and handed Jacob a corresponding bundle of crime scene photos. "For you. Odette was in the office. I waiting for her to leave, so I'm late."

"Thanks."

Vallot rubbed his hands on his corduroys, chinned at the top photo, which showed Lidiya's body at one o'clock, Valko's at seven, a grotesque nativity. "You can see, this the same tree. It has this, eh, a face, yes?"

Jacob saw what he meant: a rough leer in the bark.

He stepped into the clearing, mentally overlaying past atop pres-ent, feeling waves pass through his chest, horror continuing to rever-berate. Left undisturbed, the mushrooms had run riot: evil-looking things, phallic caps grayish yellow and thick with slime, penetrating up through the humus. In the photographs, ice covered the ground.

"She said you had a lot of snow before the discovery of the bodies."

"It was the most cold winter for a long time. This winter, it's much better."

"Feels pretty cold to me," Schott said.

"It's the reason I should go to California," Vallot said.

Jacob knelt before the spot where Lidiya had been left, holding up her photo.

"What's she wearing?"

"It uniform for the embassy. Théo thought maybe the guy's like her for this."

"A fetish."

"*Ouais.*"

"There was no sexual assault, though."

"Maybe someone's coming, he gets scared to run away."

Jacob didn't think so. The scene in the stills didn't look interrupted; if anything, it was more symmetrical and orderly than the one in the Hollywood alley. Certainly Lidiya was better balanced than Marquessa had been. Maybe the killer remembered the problems presented by a disobedient corpse.

Ten years to perfect his craft.

He crossed to Valko's tree. In the photos, the boy had the same submissive expression as TJ White. The same care had been taken to fold his hands.

The physical similarities ended there. Where TJ was round and innocent, Valko had begun to develop the contours of manhood, hard ridges risen below gaping eye sockets. Life had grown him up, fast.

"What's the number on his chest?"

Vallot had a look. "Hugo Lloris. He's a very big football player."

"It was dead of winter," Jacob said. "Where's his jacket?" He cycled back to the picture of Lidiya. "Where's hers?"

Schott said, "Maybe the killer took souvenirs."

Jacob turned to ask Vallot where the embassy was, what was the most direct route. His eye caught on a clump of mushrooms.

"What," Schott said. "What is it?"

Jacob found a twig, poked it between the stalks to extract an object far the worse for wear, its red paint mostly gone, a corroded chain dangling.

A key fob.

The insignia stamped into its center had fared better. It was cast in relief and gold plated.

A tiny image of the Gerhardt Falke S.

CHAPTER FORTY-TWO

Occupying an entire square block, the Russian embassy was a brutalist masterpiece fronting to Boulevard Lannes.

A kind of dry moat, sparsely planted with lindens and broken up by Jersey barriers, surrounded the building. Armed guards in military dress manned every point of entry. Walking the perimeter, Jacob counted thirty-two exterior cameras that he could see.

"Terrorism," Schott said.

It was the two of them again. Vallot had begged off, taking the fob, wrapped in a tissue, back to the station to submit it for prints.

That was his stated reason, anyway. It was clear the guy didn't want to go anywhere near the embassy, and Jacob couldn't blame him: along Avenue Chantemesse, a pair of Police Nationale vans sat parked in contravention of numerous signs.

They completed their circuit and stood beneath the Dufrenoy bus stop.

Jacob said, "Lidiya and Valko leave the building. They exit via one of the staff entrances, along the side. They're running to catch the bus. Two hundred yards. Three, four minutes, max. Five, if he's asleep and she's carrying him."

"What's your point?"

"That's not very much exposure. It doesn't feel like a crime of opportunity."

"You think the bad guy's waiting for them," Schott said.

"Or Pelletier's wrong, and they never made it out alive."

"She said nothing happened in the embassy."

"I know."

"She's making sense. Shooting at a party?"

Jacob studied the picture of the Gerhardt fob on his phone, wondering.

Personal item, carelessly forgotten?

Arrogant monster, leaving his mark?

"How about this," he said. "The driveway around the back goes to an underground lot. Tremsin has them taken there, shoots them or has one of his guys do it. Nobody hears a thing. Upstairs, there's music, there's kitchen noise, it's a silenced weapon. The concrete walls muffle it. The bodies go into the car, the car leaves, goes straight to the dump site. That's why they're not wearing coats: they never got them on."

"Creative," Schott said. "With zero facts to back it up."

"Look at those cameras. The whole place is under surveillance. No way that doesn't include the lot. There's two cameras on the driveway. And even if she's right, and the murders don't happen inside, maybe the exterior angles catch the bad guy hanging around on the street or accosting them. It's negligent as hell of her not to request the tapes from that night."

"A year old?" Schott said. "They're probably gone."

Jacob refreshed his inbox. Still no response to the picture he'd sent out. A kindergarten teacher should have been awake by now. A baker, definitely.

Maybe they didn't check their e-mail first thing in the morning.

He glanced at the embassy's main entrance, over which loomed a gigantic triumphal sculpture, a Soviet remnant. "Can't hurt to ask."

CLEARING THE METAL DETECTOR, they stepped into a lobby whose furnishings drew a drastic contrast with the building's severe exterior: silk drapery, overstuffed furniture, decorative ceramics and gilt clocks and a baby grand.

You could have thrown a great party, right out there.

Jacob and Schott peeked down the halls, trying to get a sense of the layout, succeeding only in drawing suspicious looks. To buy time, they ducked into the visa office. People sat on plastic chairs, wearily filling out forms. Behind the desk stood a Russian flag; beside it, a giant presidential portrait.

The receptionist said, *"Bonjour. Puis-je vous aider?"*

"I'd like to learn more about your country," Jacob said.

The woman's face momentarily scrambled. She spoke into her desk phone, and moments later a man emerged from a rear door. Young, trim, with spiky brown hair, he wore a tailored navy pin-stripe suit, a white shirt, a lavender silk tie ostentatiously knotted.

"Good afternoon, gentlemen." Tepid smile, shallow bow, name tag in Cyrillic and Latin: *A. Rodonov.* "How may I assist you?"

"I was wondering if you conduct tours of the building."

"Tours . . . Unfortunately not. The embassy is not open to the public."

"That's too bad. Such an interesting place. Russia, I mean."

"Indeed. Rich with history and culture."

"We'd love to go, one day." Jacob turned to Schott. "Right?"

Schott gave a tight nod. "Yup."

"I can recommend several local travel agencies," Rodonov said, "capable of putting together a stimulating and appropriate package for you and your, your"—eyeballing Schott—"your companion."

Jacob smiled. "Where do we sign up for a visa?"

"Unfortunately, I cannot accommodate you today, as we are at present closed."

Jacob glanced around at the dozen or so folks scribbling on clipboards.

"You may make an appointment and return at that time," Rodonov said, bending to a computer. "The next available opening is in three weeks."

"What about a job?"

"I beg your pardon?"

"I had a friend who used to work here. She did some cleaning. A little waitressing. Lidiya Georgieva. You happen to know her?"

Rodonov's eyes darted over Jacob's shoulder. "I'm afraid not."

"Kind of a shame," Jacob said. "She was murdered. Her son, too. You really don't remember her?"

"I'm afraid I don't. May I ask—"

"Huh. I don't have my résumé on me, but I mix a mean drink." He thumbed at Schott. "Him, he can sing a little."

Reflected in the glass over the portrait, a pair of guards entered the office.

"Maybe we could speak to the house manager," Jacob said.

For a moment, Rodonov didn't react. Then his fingers twitched, halting the guards.

He said, "This way, please."

RODONOV USHERED THEM to an airless conference room, seated them at one end of a long polished table, and left.

Jacob took out his phone to text Vallot, check his e-mail.

No bars.

He got up and paced. "They could've kicked us out."

"They will, soon as they figure out what we know," Schott said. He brushed dried mud from his cowboy boots. "Crissake, sit down. You're making me nervous."

"You should be." Jacob paused by a carved mahogany credenza to wiggle the spout on a samovar. "I am."

He tried the door. Locked from the outside.

"Fantastic," Schott said.

They waited for twenty-two minutes before a portly man with a gray pompadour entered. As the door swung shut, Jacob glimpsed three guards in the hall.

Whatever diplomatic training Rodonov had received prior to his posting was lost on this fellow. He stuck out his palm.

"Identification."

Jacob gave up his badge. Schott did the same.

"You are policemen."

"We are."

"Why didn't you say so immediately?"

"Are you the house manager?"

"I am the person to whom you are talking," the man said. He placed their badges on the table. "Why are you here?"

"I'm sure Mr. Rodonov told you."

"You tell me."

"Lidiya Georgieva."

"The name is unfamiliar."

Jacob laid out a photo of Lidiya's corpse. "How about the face?"

The man recoiled, gagging.

"No?" Jacob began digging in his bag. "Want to see her son?"

The man put up a hand. He had averted his eyes. "That will not be necessary."

"You sure? It might jog your memory."

"Remove this, please."

Jacob leaned over and retrieved the photo.

The man contemplated the table, reading an invisible chessboard.

He said, "We can agree that what happened to Miss Georgieva was tragic."

"And her son," Jacob said. "Let's not forget him."

"Yes. Her son. Very tragic, we can all agree. However, I cannot see how American police officers should come to be involved."

"The case may be connected to one of ours."

"The correct step would be to broach the matter with the French authorities."

"I have. I wanted to give you the opportunity to provide your perspective."

The man said, "The case you refer to—it must be important, to bring you all the way to France."

"The night Lidiya and Valko were killed," Jacob said. "You had a party here."

"We have frequent parties," the man said. He appeared to have recovered from the shock of seeing the photos; his smile showed smoker's teeth. "Russians are a people full of joy."

"It was a reception for visiting businessmen," Jacob said. "We need to know who was here."

"That is impossible."

"You keep a visitor log. We signed it on the way in. The security tapes from that night, I need to see them, too."

"We've cooperated fully with the French police. Beyond that, I cannot help you."

"I'd like to speak to the ambassador."

The man chuckled. "Out of the question."

"Arkady Tremsin," Jacob said.

Silence.

"You're familiar with him."

"Familiar, no."

"You know him."

"I know who he is, naturally. Everyone does."

"What's your government's relationship to him?"

"There is none to speak of. Mr. Tremsin renounced his citizenship."

"What led him to do that?"

"You would have to ask him."

"I understand he got in some trouble back in Moscow."

"I can provide no further comment."

"What about this guy?" Jacob said, calling up the photo of Knob Neck on his phone and holding it out. "Who is he?"

"I'm afraid I don't know."

"He's Russian."

"I don't know every Russian in Paris, Detective."

"He's hard to forget," Jacob said. "Six foot five. Big ugly scar on his neck."

"I hope you realize," the man said, "that your mere presence here constitutes an affront."

"Against your government or Tremsin?"

The man said nothing.

Jacob said, "I need to see those tapes."

The man smiled faintly. "You have such an amusing way of using that word."

"What word is that."

"'Need.'" He stood up. "Wait here."

Time passed.

Ten minutes.

Schott said, "This is fucked."

"What are you complaining about?" Jacob asked. "You like Russian literature, it should be a special treat."

Twenty minutes.

"You're right," Jacob said. "Super fucked."

Thirty.

He addressed the CCTV camera in the corner of the ceiling.

"Open up, please," he said. "I have to use the bathroom."

He dragged over a chair, climbed up, began waving at the camera.

"Open up or I'm going to piss in your samovar."

A bolt turned; the door opened. The portly man was back, along with a platoon of security guards and, alpha dog in a stylish black pantsuit and unforgiving four-inch heels, Odette Pelletier.

"Get off the chair," she said.

CHAPTER FORTY-THREE

Bina lies on the cell floor, shivering, her head in Majka's lap, soft filthy fingers kneading her locked shoulders.

"I was pretty," Majka says. "That was my problem."

She still is. Bina wishes she could tell her.

"My father was a railway mechanic. When I was seventeen, a hydraulic lift failed and crushed him. His pension wasn't enough to support my mother and me, so I took a job as a typist for the Ministry of Information."

A deep, unexpected laugh. "I thought it'd be a good way to meet a nice man."

From down the hall comes the gruff duet of a scuffle, whistles blown, orderlies responding. The law dictates that patients remain out of their cages from seven a.m. to seven p.m., a requirement scrupulously observed, due to the entertainment it provides: fights are an hourly occurrence on Lunatics' Boulevard.

In some ways, the ward affords greater license than the world outside. Statements that would get an ordinary citizen thrown in jail are here made with impunity. The food is shit, the government a bunch of assholes. Who cares what they say? They're crazy. The result is the highest concentration of rational thought in Czechoslovakia.

Majka massages Bina's forearms. "You feel looser today, sister."

Bina nods her head a fraction of an inch. They wheeled her from room nine less than an hour ago and already she can move her extremities.

A good sign. A bad one? Her body is acclimating, accepting its fate.

From there it's a short distance to surrender.

This morning marked the sixth day of her treatment.

Or the eighth.

The twentieth.

Does it matter?

Yes. Yes. It matters. She has a son, she must see him again, she will see him, she owes it to him to keep count.

When Dmitri, the tall Russian orderly, comes to unlock her cage; when he wheels her down the corridor toward room nine and other patients look away and fall silent; when she is draped like an offering upon the gurney; when Tremsin enters, chatting about the weather; when he screws off the iron ring and clacks it down on the counter and snaps on rubber gloves and draws up the syringe, it is Jacob's face that Bina fixes in her mind.

The image has begun to bleed at the edges.

She can hardly remember what he looks like.

How did it happen so fast?

She is weak.

To keep herself from drifting, she clings to Majka's voice.

"The apparatchik in charge of my bureau—his name was Smolak— he used to keep a bowl of almonds on his desk."

Gently, she bends and straightens Bina's right hand. Bina funnels her entire consciousness there, driving her soul into her fingers.

Majka nods encouragingly. "That's it. Pretty soon you'll be massaging me."

Bina grunts.

"Don't think I won't hold you to it. I could use a massage. I could use a *shower*, eh? It's not hot, but it's water. Keep thinking of that, it'll give you something to live for."

Jacob. I have Jacob to live for.

"This fellow, Smolak, he never ate the almonds. They sat there in the bowl, day after day, driving me mad with their pointlessness. I couldn't stand it any longer. I snuck into his office and stole a few to take home for my mother. You've never seen anyone so excited. The joy a few stale almonds could bring . . . It broke my heart and filled it.

"The next day I braced myself for consequences. Nothing happened, so I did it again. Just a few. Again, nothing happened. I began scooping them out by the handful."

She moves on to Bina's left fingers. Bina shifts her awareness accordingly.

"The bowl . . . It was an elegant little crystal thing. Genuine Moser, I think. It never seemed to empty out. I would come in and find it miraculously refilled. It had to end, of course: Smolak summoned me to his office. He had a strange-looking lamp on the desk. When I held my hands under the light, my skin lit up. He'd put invisible powder on the almonds. It was all over me—under my nails, on my sleeves.

"He was an ugly one, Smolak. He came around the desk and put his hand on my cheek. Then up my dress. He said, 'Show me what you know.'"

Majka shifts out from under her, resting Bina's head on a bunched woolen blanket.

"Can you bend your knees?"

Bina tries.

"Good, sister. Keep at it. 'Show me what you know . . .' I knew nothing. I was a virgin. After he finished, he said, 'You have a lot to learn. But you're pretty, that can't be taught.'

"He sent me to an address in Zličín. It was a plain-looking house. From the outside you'd never guess what went on in there. Our instructors were a pair of StB officers, one male and one female. We knew them as Uncle and Aunt. They would mock up different settings: a fancy restaurant, a bus stop, a hotel room. The two of them would act out scenarios, from a script, which we then had to copy. Bend your leg. You can do it."

Bina fights against the rigidity. Pain flares brightly up and down her spine. Recently, Tremsin has begun adding a dose of purified sulfur to her daily thirty milligrams of haloperidol, interested in how the two drugs interact.

They interact to create a scorching fever; chisels rammed through her joints.

Majka says, "They may have actually been married, Uncle and Aunt. Each would smile when the other one misspoke, filing it away for the future. Their lovemaking was very thorough, too, like they were going down a checklist.

"In addition to me, there were eight girls and three boys. The boys were ravens and we were swallows, so obviously the house was called the Nest. I was the only one from Prague. Aunt said they preferred to recruit from the countryside, because city air destroyed a woman's skin. She never liked me. She always called me by my full name, Marie. No one ever called me that, except her. Uncle, though. He was nice."

Majka reaches for Bina's right thigh, the tenderer of the two. The pressure makes Bina want to weep. She can't. Her system won't respond. So she weeps in her mind. She sees herself doing it and feels some small relief.

She could live the rest of her days like this. An imagined life.

She wonders if she could imagine herself to death. Picture her wrists opening and then actually have it render in the flesh, like stigmata. So easy to yield.

Jacob.

Her innards heave; her knee bends.

"Sister. Well done. You rest a bit, now . . . Those were busy months, in the beginning of my training. We learned how to make conversation with a Westerner, how to flirt; we learned how to drink without losing control. We learned how to please a man, the ravens how to please a woman. We practiced while everyone watched. Aunt and Uncle would take notes or shout out instructions. 'Lift your leg higher.' 'Make more noise! Men like noise.'" She shakes her head. "When the boys ran out of steam—they were young, but we outnumbered them—we practiced on Uncle."

Another laugh. "Perhaps that explains why he was so cheerful. He practiced with the boys, too. Everyone had to be prepared for all types. That was a revelation, that a person could like both men and women. We never questioned or resisted. We were patriots. My mother's pension checks doubled, she could afford cigarettes. The night before there was meat in the shops, someone called to tell her.

"It wasn't all fun and games. We learned anti-interrogation techniques. Not the heavy stuff—they couldn't damage the merchandise—but enough. I already knew some Russian, and they taught me basic English and German. My first assignment was Vienna.

"I don't think they wanted to challenge me excessively, right out of the gate. He was a file clerk in the Ministry for Foreign Affairs. I met him in the lobby of the Hotel Imperial, they used to have a nice café there . . . Can you imagine me, barely nineteen, a seductress? They taught us to step out of ourselves. It's a skill you never forget, it comes in handy throughout life."

Doesn't it. Bina forces up the corners of her mouth.

"How nice to see you smile, sister."

Soft filthy fingers stroke the inside of Bina's wrist.

"They rented me a flat in Alsergrund, and before long the clerk was turning up in the middle of the day, two, three times a week. His breath stank of mustard. He was married—they always were, to give you leverage if things soured—and in his wallet I found a snapshot of his wife. He'd done well for himself. She wasn't at all badlooking. Yet he would lie there, smoking and complaining about her, his boss, his coworkers. He was one of those who believes the world hasn't given him his due.

"I was with him for about a year. I got what I could. Uncle and Aunt were pleased. They reassigned me to Berlin, then back to Vienna. Everywhere I went, I brought my lingerie and my F-21. I carried that stupid camera all over Europe. They even sent me to Oslo, which was considered the most difficult environment for a swallow to operate in, because of the Scandinavians' clinical attitude toward sex. My lover there was very handsome. He thought he was doing *me* a favor. Americans and British were the easiest to turn. I don't mean to be rude, sister; that was what I was taught, and in my experience it held true.

"I was good at my job. My mother had what she needed, right up until the end. When she died, it was in the hospital, like a civilized person, not languishing at the bottom of a waiting list. I traveled. I met people. I served my country and the cause.

"It ended. It always does. I got pregnant. A faulty pill, I guess, or I forgot to take one. The father was a chemist for a Swiss petroleum corporation, working to improve the efficiency of diesel fuel. Odd, what stays with you: I couldn't tell you the color of his eyes, but if you gave me a pencil and paper, I could probably reproduce the formulas.

"I reported back to Uncle and Aunt, assuming they would have me end the pregnancy. That was the usual method. No, they said; it could be used to our advantage. I had recently turned thirty. They wanted to wring every last drop out of me. They had me blackmail the chemist by threatening to tell his wife."

Majka resumes working Bina's calves. "It didn't go to plan. He poisoned himself."

Out in the hall, a bell rings.

"I'd botched the assignment, but they surprised me, saying I could keep the baby. A token, I suppose, for my service. Try moving your ankle, please. Harder. Good.

"My gift . . . His name is Daniel. He'll be seven soon. Almost girlish, he's so pretty."

Sorrow fogs her smile. "You know, sister, I love our conversations, but you should feel free to speak up."

"Jacob," Bina says.

Majka blinks, startled.

"Jacob," Bina says. Her jaw, a wedge. The effort, unthinkable. "Jacob."

"Sister." Majka starts to laugh, tears slicing dirt. "Sister. That's your son? Jacob?"

The bell rings on, insistent.

"Jacob. That's good, sister, a good solid name. Don't let go of it."

The door opens.

Dmitri enters pushing the wheelchair, murmurs in his accented Czech:

"Occupational therapy."

Majka bends over, forehead to the floor, while he slides his rubber gloves beneath Bina's knees and lifts her into the chair.

THEY JOIN THE LINE headed down the Boulevard, a caravan of ghosts in paper slippers. Dmitri flares his elbows to protect Bina from jostling bodies. The blanket slips down her knees and he reaches down to draw it back up.

"Are you warm enough?" he asks.

Does he expect an answer? If anything, she feels hot, because of the sulfur.

Dmitri Samilovich. She's heard Tremsin call him that. A banality she clutches, to keep her memory from atrophying along with her body.

They reach the Group Therapy Room, set with five long tables, twenty seats apiece. He wheels her to her assigned spot.

The law dictates sixty minutes of productive labor per day. For the past week, the women have made boxes out of cardboard scraps. Unable to lift her hands, Bina has received seven demerits, resulting in loss of food, which some might consider a blessing.

Now an excited buzz rises: paper and glue are gone, replaced by lemon-yellow balls of Plasticine.

The head nurse stands on the podium and toots her whistle three times. "Today the patients will be making ashtrays."

The buzz hardens to a discontented edge. Ashtrays? For whom? Each patient receives one cigarette per day, to be hoarded or traded or fought over. Ashtrays? It's a task meant to degrade them.

"The patients will be quiet, please." The whistle shrills. *"Quiet."*

The silence fills with the sound of two hundred diligent thumbs.

Fat Irena leans in. "Did you hear? Brezhnev is dead."

Olga snorts.

"I don't give a damn if you don't believe me. It's true."

"How many times has Brezhnev died before? And yet he's still alive."

Bina stares at the table, distant and swimming, the knob of yellow like a close and unreachable sun.

You can't make anything meaningful from Plasticine. It doesn't last.

Nothing lasts.

"You'll see," Olga says. "You'll be eating your words."

"I'll be eating your liver, you dried-up cunt," Fat Irena says.

A nurse comes storming up the aisle. "No talking."

"She started it," Olga says.

"No. Talking. You," the nurse says to Bina. "Why are you sitting there."

"She can't move," Majka says.

The nurse grabs the ball of Plasticine and shoves it roughly into Bina's hands.

"Work heals," she says, and walks on.

A weak squeeze is all Bina can manage, yet the material yields, as though bowing to a higher authority. The coolness against her burning skin feels delicious and strange.

She is hardly aware of what she's doing while she's doing it. Nobody else notices her. They are busy not talking, busy looking busy.

The bells rings and Majka turns around and her mouth falls open in astonishment.

"Oh, sister."

Bina thinks *The edges could be sharper.*

The women crowd around to gawk.

"Look at that," Fat Irena says. "It lives."

"Hers is better than yours," Olga says.

"Shut your fucking mouth."

Tittering, they clear the aisle to make way for Dmitri and the chair.

He stops short, staring like the rest of them.

The nurse returns. "What's going on here? What is that?"

"You were right," Majka says tremulously. "Work does heal."

"We're not making jars. We're making ashtrays." The nurse snatches the tiny, symmetrical form from Bina's limp fingers and crushes it back into a ball. "Next time pay attention to the assignment."

BREZHNEV IS DEAD. Like the collective soup bowl, the rumor gets passed around so that all may have a taste. After a while even Olga is forced to admit it smacks of truth, and Fat Irena takes to parading up and down Lunatics' Boulevard, crowing that it was *she*, *she* was the one to break the news, until Olga spreads a counter-rumor that Fat Irena got the news from a guard in exchange for sucking him off, leading to a brawl that sends one woman to the infirmary, the other to solitary confinement.

Brezhnev is dead.

They do not allow themselves to hope. Hope is too costly, hope is a mythic beast. Schadenfreude, though, that they have, in spades.

For they have outlived him, the bastard Brezhnev with his pompous eyebrows and his titanic jowls, military medals spilling down his left breast; Brezhnev, architect of their despair, who sent in the tanks in '68 to flatten the green shoots of change.

He is dead.

The next morning, no one comes to fetch Bina for treatment.

"See?" Majka says. "I told you he'd get bored of you, eventually."

That much hope Bina can't afford.

But then a second day passes and no one comes to collect her, and Bina can move her arms and legs. No one has seen Tremsin at all, and more rumors bubble up: the doctor has fled, fearing the retribution that accompanies any change in regime. He has (imagine it!) committed suicide out of solidarity with the General Secretary.

A third day arrives. No one comes to get her. Bina can talk now, a few words at a stretch, and she greedily repurposes the hours spent in Majka's company, scrambling to tell her. Tell her everything, do it while her tongue is working, while she has the chance, before the nightmare resumes, put it all on record: who she is, where she comes from, the names of her loved ones.

She talks until her mouth runs dry, telling Majka the story of her life. A pact: if one of them does not survive, the other will carry her memory out. That night, they sleep with fingertips touching through the wire of their cages, another pact, one beyond words.

THE NEXT DAY, Bina feels even better.

She wouldn't have thought it possible, given her circumstances, but she feels *good*. She decides to tell Majka her story again, start to finish. Only it's different now: she's remembering new things, parts of herself that she forgot to include yesterday.

"It's good to talk, sister. Get it all out."

She will, she will. There's so much more to her than Bina Lev, wife and mother. There's Barbara Reich, the thinker, the seeker, who gave up her name. Both of them.

Why *did* she give up her name?

She almost regrets it now. *Reich* means "rich," she comes from royalty, they hate her because she is better.

By the fifth morning, she has learned not to fear the dawn. No one is coming for her. The worst is over. And she's remembering even more.

She starts talking.

Majka says, "Sister, are you feeling all right?"

Bina's more than all right. She's *fantastic*. She wants to tell Majka, tell the world.

"Lower your voice," Majka says, watching her with worried eyes. "Someone will hear you."

Bina laughs. So someone will hear. So what? She's not afraid of them. She's not afraid of anything.

She walks in circles around their cell, talking about what she's going to do once she leaves. She promises: she's going to get out of this place—fly through the window, if necessary—and once she does, she's going to come back for Majka, for all of them; she will tear down the walls of the asylum and set them free hallelujah!

"Sister, please rest. You're going to exhaust yourself."

Who needs rest? It's the fifth day of her own personal creation, the day of the animals and beasts of the field; she has more energy than ever, certainly the most she's had since Jacob was born, and by the way, did she tell Majka about Jacob, her son, Jacob?

For a moment, her heart swells with pain.

In the next moment, though, the pain is gone, and she resumes walking talking laughing planning. She has so much to do. So much to say.

Fat Irena returns to the cell, eleven thick stitches over her eye.

"What the hell is wrong with her?" she asks. "Why won't she shut up?"

Majka tearfully shakes her head.

Bina doesn't understand. Why is Majka crying? She ought to be happy for her, she feels incredible, the best she has in her whole life.

"She's gone mad," Fat Irena says. "She wasn't before, but the place did it to her."

Bina laughs and goes over to help her. She has healing in her fingertips. She will make those stitches vanish!

Fat Irena swats her hand. "Don't touch me, you crazy cow."

On the sixth day, which is the day of the creation of man, Bina receives visitors.

Her father, her mother, Rav Kalman, her uncles Jakub and Jakub. Her husband. Her son.

Oh how happy she is to see them! She weeps joyously. She missed them. They come to surround her with their love, their thousands of arms.

Dmitri says, "Hold her down."

Bina screams.

The needle goes in.

ON THE SEVENTH DAY, Bina rests.

A CRAG OF FILTERED LIGHT on the ceiling. Weight on her chest.

"Good afternoon."

She sits up, with difficulty. Swivels her aching head.

Beside her sits Dmitri, his spindly frame bent forward. He smiles kindly.

"You had a psychotic episode," he says. "It can happen when medication is withdrawn abruptly. You've been asleep for twenty-two hours. Before that, you were awake for four days. You must be hungry."

She is—painfully thirsty, too.

He nods. "I'll be back in a minute."

Alone, coming to her senses, she takes in her new surroundings: a concrete room, high and narrow, like an elevator shaft. Unlike her previous bed, this one has no cage surrounding it. Otherwise it's just as ugly as her former cell.

She peels back layers of holey, sopping blankets, swings her bare feet to the floor, and stands, leaning on the chair. She lets go of the chair and swoons. Once she's sure her knees aren't going to give out, she hobbles to the window, trying to see out. Bird droppings and soot streak the glass.

Behind her, the door opens.

She spins around, nearly losing her balance.

Dmitri stands on the threshold, looking fairly astonished to find her out of bed. He holds a tray with a mug, a few slices of brown bread.

A syringe.

Bina sees it and her stomach bottoms out; she sinks down against the wall, pressing herself back, trying to make herself small, whimpering and covering her face.

"No," she says. "Please."

"Listen to me," he says.

She hears him set the tray down; the sound echoes strangely.

"Bina. This is not the same as before."

"No."

"He was giving you enormous doses. This is much less. It's not going to hurt you. You need it, or else you could become psychotic again. Please listen to me."

"No, no, no . . ."

He takes a step toward her, and she flinches, bracing herself for the bite of the needle. But it doesn't come, and when she looks again, he is simply standing there, a forlorn look on his face. The syringe still sitting on the tray.

Dmitri picks it up. "I'll be back later," he says. "For now you should eat."

By nightfall, she has started to see and hear things, to rage at the air, attack the walls, every cell in her body in rebellion. She possesses just enough of her faculties to experience it as pure torture.

At some point Dmitri returns with the syringe, and she does not resist as he swabs her arm. He has swapped out his rubber gloves for leather ones, his ill-fitting orderly's jacket for a greatcoat that gives him an unexpected grandeur. He carefully injects her with a small amount of amber liquid. "There."

Almost immediately, calm drapes her. Her head lolls. She starts to lie down.

"No no," he says, propping her up. "I need you to get dressed."

He faces away to give her privacy.

Moving in syrup, she pulls on the clothes he has brought her— underwear, a pair of stiff canvas pants, a woolen sweater, woolen socks. They might have fit her at one point, but her drastic weight loss means they hang on her like damp rags. Rubber-soled shoes are close enough. She wiggles her toes, amazed not to feel the dirty floor. She had forgotten the dignity of real shoes.

He turns, looks her up and down. Nods. "Hurry, please. I left the car running."

CHAPTER FORTY-FOUR

Pelletier's car, a blue Peugeot, sat in the embassy parking lot.

"Get in," she said.

"Where we going?"

"Just get in."

Jacob glanced at the mob of security guards that had escorted them from the elevator. He glanced at Schott.

They got in the back.

"Nice of them to call you," Jacob said.

Pelletier said, "Safety belt, please."

The two police vans had backed up to block the driveway. They parted, staying behind as Pelletier made a right, another, headed toward Boulevard Lannes.

"You can just drop us at the corner," Jacob said, feeling for the door handle. It moved easily but failed to catch. He glanced at Schott, who shook his head: *the same.*

"Are we under arrest?" Jacob said.

She drove south down the boulevard, downshifting as traffic backed up. "You were to wait for my call. You are a tourist, here at the pleasure of the French government."

She stomped the brake to avoid a wayward bicyclist.

Schott said, "You mind telling us where we're headed?"

Jacob could guess: the station on Avenue Mozart.

Instead, Pelletier worked her way over into the right turn lane, shifting into a higher gear and rocketing over the Boulevard Périphérique overpass, bound for the interior of the Bois de Boulogne.

The sun had fallen, leaving bruised spaces between the trees. Jacob became aware of her perfume, light and grassy, saturating the Peugeot's confined space. In the front foot well, a lipstick case strobed bars of streetlight.

"In my view, this is the killer's likeliest route," she said, dodging a man-sized branch felled by wind. "In terms of distance, it would be shorter to have turned at Porte de la Muette. Given the location of the bodies, I consider it more logical that he came from this direction, so that the car was oriented northeast along Allée de Longchamp. It's a busy street. You don't want to be shepherding captives across four lanes of traffic."

She downshifted. "I suppose it's possible he made a U-turn."

Jacob said, "You think Lidiya and Valko were still alive at that point."

"I imagine so. Easier to march them into the woods under their own power."

They wound along for a few minutes. At the next major intersection, Pelletier hung a right, slowing to allow Jacob and Schott a look at the pucker-mouthed women haunting the shadows, dotting the walking paths, shivering in fishnets and boots. A few bold enough to openly solicit passing cars.

"As you can see, it's an active area for the sex trade. I tracked down every prostitute I could find. They all claim to have seen nothing."

A barrier of wooden stumps pounded into the earth prevented vehicles from straying onto the path. Roughly every fifty yards, one had been pried loose, the curb ground down to nonexistence by thousands of tires and front bumpers.

Pelletier said, "You find these turnouts at various places along the *allée*."

Jacob made out the fuzzy mounds of parked cars, the flash of reflective plastic.

A prostitute materialized at the tree line, picking at her sleeve. Stumbling after her came a middle-aged man in a flaccid raincoat.

Pelletier had switched on her hazards and was crawling along, hunting for a particular spot. A quarter mile on, she said, "Voilà."

She eased the Peugeot up onto the path, threading between a pair of oaks. A park bench sat directly in front of them. She steered around it to access a nook of sorts, partially hidden from the road by saplings and hardened vines.

She brought the car to a halt and yanked up the parking brake. "God knows what they imagine the three of us are doing back here."

She killed the motor. The Peugeot fell still.

Jacob could hear distant, fractured laughter, the sonic froth of the road.

Pelletier said, "The important thing, from an investigative standpoint, is that you could leave a car parked here for quite a while without anyone noticing it."

"Long enough for him to get them to the clearing, kill them, come back."

"More than enough." She pointed through the windshield. "It's straight that way, about a hundred twenty meters."

She turned, propped an elbow on the armrest. "I can take you there. As I said, mud and trees. Your shoes will suffer."

He wondered how sincere the offer was, given her heels. "We've already been."

"I see." Not asking how.

She faced front. "I've been thinking about the mechanics of the abduction. My assumption is he held a gun to the child's head to motivate the mother's compliance."

Jacob said, "I need to talk to Tremsin."

"Yes, you've said that. I don't suppose you've come up with a better reason."

"There's this."

He opened the photo of the Gerhardt fob and set his phone on the armrest.

She stared at it impassively. "A key chain."

"I found it at the scene. You know what car it goes with?"

She shook her head.

"A very, very expensive one. That very, very few people own. Eighty in the entire world. I'll bet you can think of someone we know whose name's on that list."

It was a bluff. A decent one. He couldn't tell if it was working.

She picked up the phone to look at the fob. "How did we miss it?"

"It was under ice," he said. "It came up with this year's mushrooms."

She set the phone back down. "I'd like you to hand it over, please."

He said nothing.

"It's evidence," she said. "I am investigating a murder."

"It's in a safe place," he said.

"That's a crime," she said. "Tampering."

"It's safe," he said again.

"Did you give it to Vallot?"

"All I did," he said, "was take a walk in the park."

"What else did he tell you? I saw him making photocopies. Were those for you?"

Jacob didn't want to sell Vallot out. But his hesitation seemed to confirm it for her.

"Give them back, please," she said. "Now."

Jacob said, "He told me about your time in Russia."

Pelletier's mouth opened. She began to laugh. "*Dédé* told you that? Well. Good for him. He's cleverer than I thought."

Jacob said nothing.

"Your little stunt at the embassy," she said. "It was clumsy."

"I was getting the feeling you weren't going to call."

"I would have. I'm busy."

"Investigating a murder."

"Several, in fact."

"Does your boss know what you do on the side?"

She wrenched around. "Do you?"

"I have a couple of ideas," he said. "It was you the embassy decided to call."

"I work *with* them. Not *for* them. That's a critical distinction."

"With them, including Tremsin."

She tapped the steering wheel.

"All that stuff about him falling out with Moscow is bullshit," he said. "He goes to their parties. You protect him."

"It's a bit more complicated than that."

"Then explain it to me."

"I can't, obviously."

"Obviously."

"Don't pout," she said. "What I can tell you is that it's not in anyone's interest to draw attention to Arkady Tremsin. Ours, yours, the Russians, whomever."

"So he gets a pass."

"The greater good needs to be considered."

"That's not my job," he said. "If you really are a cop, it's not yours, either."

"My job, Detective, is to keep him *calm*. In order to preserve various relationships. He trusts very few people. I happen to be one of them. You think it's been easy to cultivate that? He's a paranoid man. He's hardly left his house in four years."

"And when he does? You watch him?"

"Often, yes."

"What about the night of the party?"

She regarded him without malice. "Have you given any thought to your endgame? I know it isn't what you told me, that you just want to look him in the eye."

"That'd be a start."

"What do you expect? He'll wither in the face of your righteousness?"

"I want him to know," he said, taking back his phone, "that it won't be forgotten."

Silence.

"At least two innocent people died," Jacob said. "More will die. That'll be on you. You want to keep him calm? You don't want noise? Let me promise you this: I'm going to make as much noise as humanly possible."

She sighed. "You're not giving me much choice."

"Guess not."

"You really won't shut up, will you."

"Nope."

She nodded. "Wait here."

She got out of the car, taking her keys with her, and walked off, dialing on her phone. Jacob strained to hear to what she was saying but she was too far away, shielding her mouth with her hand.

"We should get out of here," Schott said. "Now."

"And go where?"

"She could deport us."

"Then we've lost nothing."

Pelletier clicked off her call, began dialing again.

"She could bust us," Schott said.

"Go, then," Jacob said. "Feel free."

Outside, Pelletier was returning. *D'accord. D'accord.*

Schott squirmed, gauging the space between the front seats to determine if he could squeeze through and get to the door.

"Forget it," Jacob said. "You'll get stuck."

Pelletier hung up. She got in the car, started the engine, and backed out cautiously, waiting for a break in traffic before lurching onto the road.

She did not speak, heading south and west, out of the park. Recognizing their general direction, Jacob settled in for the brief ride to the police station.

But again, she upended his expectations, reversing a route they had walked the day before.

She said, "I doubt you'll have more than a few minutes, so I suggest you start preparing your questions in advance. Keep them brief."

She pulled into the driveway of Arkady Tremsin's house.

She lowered her window, leaned out, pressed the call box button.

A beep, a clipped *allo.*

She held up her ID to the camera eye. *"C'est moi."*

A moment later, the gates swung open.

CHAPTER FORTY-FIVE

From what Jacob had seen, mansions in L.A.'s high-end neighborhoods were often all show and no go, built wide and high in order to simulate volume, but disappointingly shallow—like the movie sets that had paid for them.

Now he saw the opposite illusion in effect.

As the Peugeot crept toward Le Petit Kremlin, the structure retreated and amplified, revealing an astonishing depth, most of it invisible from the street. A network of path lights gradually disclosed outbuildings, fountains, barbered trees, a gazebo—almost a city in itself. That it fit into the urban puzzle of Paris seemed magical, devilish.

He thought he caught the glint of a sniper scope at the roofline.

Schott cleared his throat uncomfortably.

Fifteen yards ahead, men in cargo pants formed a crescent spanning the driveway. Every one of them was thick in the abdomen— husky by virtue of genetics and bulletproof vests. Two held mirrors on poles; two restrained excited dogs.

The rest clutched submachine guns.

At their center, like an aberrant capstone, stood Knob Neck.

A transparent, three-paneled screen interposed itself between Tremsin's army and the car. Blast-resistant Lexan, ten feet tall, with another several feet of overhang, braced from behind by steel rods and anchored beneath the paving stones. The outer panels angled to contain and redirect a pressure wave away from the house.

He's a paranoid man.

Pelletier was relaxed—used to the process. She pulled up to the screen and parked. She took the keys from the ignition, opened her door, and set them on the ground.

"You want to talk to him," she said, "you'll talk to him. Under my supervision."

Jacob said, "You can show up whenever you feel like it?"

"Of course not. When I told him who you were, he sounded curious. No guarantee, though. He might change his mind. He's a creature of whim. Now hurry up and open your doors. Don't get out, just sit there."

"We can't," Schott said. "Locked in."

Pelletier pressed a button and they shoved both rear doors open. She popped the trunk, then the hood. "Stay where you are. Lace your fingers behind your head. Get comfortable," she said. "This could take a while."

THE MIRROR MEN and the dog handlers came forward, along with three gunmen, one for each passenger.

Up the driveway, Knob Neck was grinning.

Jacob said, "That's the son of a bitch who followed me."

"Dmitri Molchanov," Pelletier said. "Tremsin's chief of security."

The devil—he delegates.

The thick blast shield distorted Molchanov's features, exaggerating his already extreme dimensions. He was broad, like the others. Broader even than Schott. Jacob had failed to appreciate that, hung up on the guy's height. A gust of wind lifted his greatcoat, revealing a V torso, strata of muscle asserting themselves through his shirt.

Crazily, he appeared to have grown since their last encounter.

The bend in the glass.

Or a psychological by-product of knowing who—*what*—the guy was.

His colors.

He doesn't have any.

Jacob looked over at Schott. Tight all over. Vigilant.

The gunmen stood by, weapons trained inside the car, while the mirror men circled the Peugeot, inspecting its undercarriage, probing the trunk. They wore earpieces, touching them and communicating their progress, to Molchanov, presumably.

One of the men stooped to pocket Pelletier's keys.

No exit without permission.

Molchanov kept on grinning. At this distance, impossible to tell what amused him. But Jacob couldn't shake the sense that he was the target.

Was this going to go bad right now, before they got in the building?

He smiled back at Molchanov, and the two of them stayed locked on each other, beaming like a couple of lovesick idiots, until a mirror man went to inspect the engine and the hood was raised and Molchanov disappeared from view.

The handlers approached. The dogs were elegant, subtly vicious animals, with black bullet eyes and golden coats and sharp, feral snouts. One of them poked its head into the car, licked Schott's shin.

"Good puppy," he said. "What's your name?"

"Sobaka nomer odin," the handler said.

"Pretty," Schott said. "What's it mean?"

"Dog number one," Pelletier said.

Jacob's leg buzzed: incoming message.

Roughly ten-thirty a.m. in L.A.

Recess time for Susan Lomax.

Reflexively he started to reach down.

The gunman watching him snapped the barrel into line with Jacob's head.

"My phone," Jacob said. "It's in my pocket."

The guy didn't respond. The gun didn't budge.

"Can I get it, please?"

Pelletier said, "Stop talking."

A MIRROR MAN slammed the hood and rapped it twice.

Pelletier said, "Get out."

Molchanov was already loping down the driveway toward them. He came around the blast screen and air-kissed Pelletier. *"Bonsoir."*

"Bonsoir, Dmitri."

Molchanov smiled at Jacob. "Hello again, Mr. Lev."

Jacob stifled his nerves, showed teeth. "No kiss for me?"

Molchanov laughed. He had a mouth full of huge white veneers. "Okay," he said.

THE SECURITY CHECK wasn't finished. It had barely begun. Jacob and Schott were frisked and wanded; their phones were confiscated, along with their wallets and everything else on them that wasn't clothing. Jacob had left his bag containing Vallot's crime scene photos in the car, but the guards took the worn pair of maps from inside his jacket. Schott lost his sunglasses.

Pelletier stood off to the side, exempt from the ordeal.

"When do we get our stuff back?" Schott said.

"When you leave," Molchanov said.

He touched his earpiece and gestured and guards stepped forward and surrounded them, creating a corral of muscle. A cage that moved. Swept along, Jacob and Schott and Pelletier proceeded to the steps of the mansion, toward the open half of two colossal bronze doors. Figures in relief. Satyrs, fauns, nude maidens—Rodin in a randy mood.

They stepped into a soaring limestone rotunda.

One by one, the guards filed through a full-body scanner, the machine alarming pleasantly.

Bing, bing, bing.

"Jackets and shoes off?" Jacob asked.

"Not necessary," Molchanov said, tapping the monitor. "It will find everything."

With a practiced air, Pelletier removed her wallet, phone, fitness tracker, jewelry, belt. She set them in a plastic bin and stepped through the scanner.

Bing.

Molchanov, reading the screen, murmured something that made the other guards smirk and that caused Pelletier to go red in the face. *"J'ai oublié,"* she said.

She reached into her suit jacket and withdrew a tampon. Tossed it into the bin and stepped through the scanner.

"Okay," Molchanov said.

The guards prodded Pelletier's items and returned them to her.

Jacob patted himself down, turned his pockets inside out.

He stepped through the scanner.

"Okay," Molchanov said.

Schott's turn.

Bing.

Molchanov frowned, studying the screen. He asked Schott to step out, back in.

Bing.

Jacob craned to see the monitor. A guard slid forward to block his view.

"This way, my friend," Molchanov said.

Schott didn't move.

Molchanov waited.

Schott stood there.

Jacob said, "Paul?"

Four exits radiated from the rotunda, a gunman stationed at each. Two additional guards moved into position, isolating Schott, who was blinking now, a line of sweat tracking down his neck.

Molchanov said, "Doktor Tremsin is waiting."

Schott took in a deep breath, bringing his shoulders back, as if readying himself to make a move. But he exhaled and nodded and trudged off, accompanied by two gunmen.

They disappeared through the southwestern door.

Molchanov turned to Jacob and Pelletier and gave a little bow, which on him was a big bow. "Please."

CHAPTER FORTY-SIX

Striding smoothly, ape arms swinging, Molchanov took them down a corridor carpeted in plum-colored plush, veered into a room.

A library, in the sense that it contained books. But no cozy spot for reflection. A rolling hall, cluttered with tables, bookstands, display cases, and tapestry armchairs. The roof was a coffered barrel vault of what looked like ebony, the walls paneled with riotously grained satinwood. Wheeled ladders on brass rails offered access to obscure upper shelves. It reminded Jacob of the Widener reading room at Harvard, if Harvard had been feeling spendy.

A lone gunman stood watch while Molchanov exited via curtained French doors on the far end.

Jacob heard the bolt turn.

"What now?" he asked.

"They're checking up on you," Pelletier said. She had taken a seat on a chaise longue and was idly spinning an enormous globe.

"Again?"

She shrugged.

"I notice you kept your ID."

"They know who I am."

Jacob tapped his foot on the parquetry, watched time tick by on a twelve-foot-tall chinoiserie clock.

"I thought Tremsin was waiting."

"When he's ready for us, we'll know."

Jacob began moving along the bookcases, fingering gilt-edged spines. Most of the titles were in French, English, or German—part of the grand old Russian tradition of looking to Europe for sophistication.

The gunman trailed him loosely.

Would he dare shoot if Jacob provoked him? Shred all that lovely wood and leather?

Where was Schott?

This way, my friend.

A terrible thought seized Jacob.

Schott and Molchanov: two soldiers in the hybrid army.

Schott had known all along.

Jacob looked over at Pelletier. Examining her nails.

"What's happening with Paul?" he asked.

"You were the one who asked to come here, Detective. Relax."

Jacob resumed walking, his pulse high up in his neck.

In a far corner stood a cabinet distinct from the rest, its contents shimmering behind greenish UV glass. Probably the really expensive stuff. First Folios, Gutenbergs.

Decent guess. But wrong.

Inside were drab magazines, dozens of them. Some of the spines were wide enough to accommodate titles in minute print. *Industrial Engineering and Chemistry. International Journal of Minerals, Metallurgy and Materials.* What Jacob presumed were the Russian equivalents.

The issues were organized in chronological order, clustering in the mid-seventies, picking up again in the nineties—the eras when Tremsin had been most active in his lab.

Behold the Doktor's personal hall of fame.

The bottom shelf stood out.

Rather than magazines, it held forty or fifty slim volumes of uniform size, bound in burgundy leather, gilt stamped along the spines, the work of a custom bookbinder.

Jacob squinted to read.

Прага—апрель 1981

Прага—май 1981 (1)

Прага—май 1981 (2)

He reached into his memory, sounded out the Cyrillic characters.

Praga—Aprel 1981

Praga—May 1981 (1)

Praga—May 1981 (2)

He felt the room starting to spin.

She went to Prague.

Steadying himself against the case, he worked his way along, coming to the one he wanted.

Прага—ноябрь 1982

Praga—Nayaber 1982

Jacob reached to open the cabinet.

Locked.

She was never the same after that.

He gave the knob a firm wiggle.

Behind him, the guard said something.

Jacob tugged, harder.

"Stop," the guard said loudly.

Jacob wheeled around. *"What."*

Startled by the outburst, the guy briefly lost the grip on his gun.

Down at the other end of the library, the French doors opened. Molchanov entered.

Alone.

Jacob started toward him, halting with hands up as the guard recovered his aim.

Molchanov said, "Your friend made big mistake."

He displayed a stubby brown object.

Pelletier was off the chaise, on her feet, instantly alert. "What is that?"

"Hidden in boot," Molchanov said. "Wrapped in material."

Mindful of the gun held level with his waist, Jacob came slowly forward until he could identify the object as a wooden-handled potter's knife.

His mother's knife.

"This special material," Molchanov said, jouncing the knife in his palm, "very interesting. I cover knife, put wand, no beep. I take material away, *beep beep beep beep*."

Pelletier gaped at Jacob. "My God. What is wrong with you?"

"I had no idea," Jacob said, which wasn't really true, because he did have some idea; only he hadn't known where exactly Schott had stashed it. "I swear."

"Je suis désolée," Pelletier said to Molchanov. *"Je pensais—"*

But Molchanov had a hand up. "No problem."

He smiled at Jacob. "Remove clothes."

A beat.

Jacob said, "I'd like to leave now."

Molchanov said, "Clothes."

The library temperature was mild enough, calibrated for long-term storage of paper. Jacob shook nonetheless as he stripped off his shirt and pants.

"All clothes."

Jacob stood naked. Pelletier made a show of studying the floor.

Molchanov set the knife down on an end table, removed his leather gloves, and began inspecting Jacob's clothing, feeling along the seams.

On his left index finger was an enormous black ring.

Jacob, shivering, said, "What is that? Iron?"

Molchanov stopped what he was doing to glance at his own hand.

"Where'd you get it?" Jacob said.

"It was reward," Molchanov said.

"Reward for what?"

"Work," Molchanov said.

He tossed the jeans on the floor, picked up Jacob's shirt.

"How about this?" Jacob said, tapping the side of his own neck.

Molchanov's fingers darted to his hunk of scar tissue, as though to conceal it. A habit not quite broken. Quickly, he dropped his hand.

He said, "Also reward."

He started to search the shirt—then, changing his mind, cast it aside.

He took out a new glove, a latex one. Pulled it on.

"Turn," he said.

When Jacob did not, Molchanov said, "I must look for weapon."

Still Jacob stood his ground.

Molchanov advanced like the leading edge of a tsunami. He seized Jacob by the shoulders and spun him around, bending him over the back of a chair and kicking Jacob's feet apart.

Jacob gritted his teeth. "Whatever gets you off, asshole."

"I am not asshole," Molchanov said. "*This* is asshole."

JACOB CROUCHED: shrunken, damp, hurting, nauseous.

His clothes hit him in the back.

"Put on."

Pelletier was still gazing dispassionately at the floor.

Jacob got dressed.

"Okay," Molchanov said. He spoke to the gunman in Russian, and the four of them left the library and began to walk.

THE HOUSE WENT ON and on and on.

Ornate in spots, stark in others, room after room inhabited by domestics of every stripe. At Molchanov's approach, they paused their chatter to give a respectful distance.

An exterminator squatting by the baseboards, a spray tank on his back, stood and doffed his hat.

Molchanov led them through passageways, switchbacks, miles of silk wallpaper. The further they went, the less the place felt like a fortress and the more it felt like a house. A really nice house, but a house. You could even overlook the security cameras, tastefully concealed behind leaded glass shades.

The air moved gently against them, carrying a distinct but agreeable iodine tang.

Jacob felt a dull ache where Molchanov had assaulted him. That had been more than security. It was an announcement—a change of plans.

He wasn't going to talk to Tremsin. He was being *brought* to Tremsin.

Focus. Head up. Back straight.

He glanced over at Pelletier. Serene as cream.

They arrived at an elevator bank. Molchanov punched an ivory button. Pale, lustrous doors parted. "Lady first."

They stepped into the car. Its three interior walls were made of glass, exposing the elevator shaft, which was elaborately mosaicked with an abstract lattice. The elevator panels were made of the same lustrous metal as the doors.

Molchanov pressed another ivory button and the car began to rise—sluggishly.

Jacob saw letters and numbers tiled in among the lattice.

The patterns weren't abstract.

They were chemical diagrams.

A nice slow ride, offering plenty of time for you to admire them.

Jacob said, "His creations."

Pelletier nodded.

Jacob looked around again at the fixtures, wondering what the metal was. Nothing so pedestrian as white gold. Platinum, maybe, or something exotic that would excite a chemist. Palladium. Iridium.

The main panel was engraved with a warning.

EN CAS D'INCENDIE, NE PAS UTILISER L'ASCENSEUR. PRENDRE L'ESCALIER.

In case of fire, do not use the elevator. Take the stairs.

It sounded so much more refined in French.

They reached the top floor.

The doors opened.

Molchanov said, "Lady first."

THE MOSAICS CONTINUED across the floors and walls of a six-sided antechamber. There was only one way to go, through a door incongruously narrow and rustic, roughhewn from light-colored wood.

Molchanov stepped toward it but stopped, his hand going to his earpiece. *"Da."*

Whatever the message was, he didn't like it.

"Nyet. Nyet. Devyanosto sekund."

Molchanov lowered his voice, shot off a command in Russian, hustled back into the elevator. Through the glass, Jacob saw him pry open the panel and turn a knob. The car plunged out of sight.

"What was that about?" Jacob said.

Pelletier shook her head. "He said he'd be back."

She had a brief conversation with the gunman in Russian, which ended with his shrugging agreeably and stepping aside.

"We'll go ahead," Pelletier said to Jacob.

She started across the antechamber, paused. "Have you prepared your questions?"

"A whole list."

"Pick two or three."

He said, "Why's Tremsin curious to meet me?"

"You'll want to address him as Doktor," Pelletier said.

"You said he was curious to meet me," Jacob said. "What did you tell him?"

"That you are an American police officer, in town to talk to him."

"You gave him my name."

"Naturally."

"What else?"

"That was it," she said.

"What exactly did he say?"

She said, "Only that he looked forward to meeting you."

CHAPTER FORTY-SEVEN

She opened the door and they stepped into a cloud.

The room was gigantic, hexagonal, tiled on every surface. There was a six-sided swimming pool, surrounded by frothing whirlpools and five arched alcoves, like the side chapels of a church. They were standing where the sixth alcove would have been. All the recesses were dark except the one in the far right corner. Light spilled through a dense curtain of crystal beads, the angle too oblique for Jacob to see inside.

Through a series of hexagonal skylights, a muffled night slunk by.

Jacob heard a low, methodical whickering coming from the lit alcove, like the sound of a blade drawn through paper, again and again.

Just him and Pelletier. The gunman had hung behind in the antechamber.

Can't see the boss in his birthday suit?

But a cute blonde could?

"Careful not to slip," Pelletier said.

She went around the pool to the right.

Jacob stepped through puddles, his shoes leaving watery black prints.

The slicing got louder. Crisper. Deliberate. Decisive.

Aromatic steam billowed, wet cedar and wet leaves and other scents of the earth. At strategic points sat pyramids of tightly rolled towels, teak chairs, wicker baskets containing dried birch branches for whipping the skin. Footlights set an ambience that under other circumstances Jacob would've described as romantic.

Pelletier stopped a few yards shy of the curtain to announce them. *"Pardon, Doktor. Nous sommes là."*

The slicing droned on.

A gentle voice said, *"Entrez."*

Pelletier waved Jacob forward.

They parted the curtain.

"Odette."

Arkady Tremsin wasn't in his birthday suit. He was wearing a red silk robe and matching velvet slippers, both embroidered with his initials. Never a small man, he'd acquired a paunch, sitting with his legs comfortably splayed, exposing thin ankles suggestive of lost muscularity. His skin was pale. A sharp line halfway up his calves demarcated the start of gray, downy hair. The flesh of his throat was gray and papery and freshly shaven.

"Mr. Lev," Tremsin said.

He was getting his hair cut.

The alcove was a salon, or a private version of one, counters lined with luxe editions of the normal accoutrements: horn combs soaking in antiseptic, etched jars, an array of polished cutting implements, boar's-hair brushes. A single chair, plated in that same white metal.

The silk robe, Jacob saw, was actually a silk smock.

A manicure in progress, as well: Tremsin had his hands resting in tubs of foamy water. Nearby stood a wheeled cart set with nail files and emery boards, and on it, a crude black iron ring, removed so he could soak without the flesh swelling up and causing an uncomfortable constriction.

The woman doing the pampering was petite, with strong features and dark hair. She stood on a low footstool in order to snip around the crown of Tremsin's head. She looked a bit like Lidiya Georgieva.

She made a few finishing cuts, then reached for the blow-dryer.

Tremsin waved to dismiss her, spattering sudsy water.

She exited without a word.

Tremsin put his hand back in the bath. He smiled at Jacob. "Too noisy," he said.

The hairdresser's footsteps faded to nothing.

Tremsin said, "What brings you to Paris?"

His moment. Yet Jacob felt stupefied, entranced by the glint of white metal everywhere, as if he was in the belly of a false god.

Hatred roiling in his own belly.

Tremsin studied him; murmured in Russian to Pelletier.

"You don't look like your father," Pelletier translated.

Jacob, thrown, said, "My mother."

"Ah," Tremsin said. "Better for you."

His *father*?

Pelletier nodded to prompt him. "Please, Detective."

"Marquessa Duvall," Jacob said. "TJ White."

Tremsin's smile arched in confusion. "Pardon?"

"You own a Gerhardt Falke S," Jacob said. "You bought it in 2004 during the L.A. auto show."

Tremsin spoke to Pelletier. It was evident from his tone that he was saying something along the lines of *what the hell is he talking about?*

The anger in Jacob's gut took a nasty detour toward anxiety.

"That's where you met Marquessa," he said. "She was a model. Beautiful girl. Bright future. Did she tell you about her son right then, or did it take some time?"

Silence.

Tremsin was blank. Utterly calm.

He said, "Who are you?"

"What about Lidiya and her son?" Jacob said.

Pelletier said, "Okay, Detective. That's enough, please."

"Lidiya and Valko. Did you ever know their names?"

Pelletier said, "Detective—"

Jacob sidestepped her, toward Tremsin. "Let's talk about Prague."

Now Tremsin sat up erect, jaw grinding.

"You must be proud of your work," Jacob said. "At the hospital. You kept your records. I just saw them, in the library."

Tremsin stood up, flinging a swarm of hair trimmings into the air. "Out."

"I know what you did," Jacob said. "I know everything."

Blood was filling up Tremsin's cheeks as Pelletier took Jacob firmly by the arm and began wrestling him toward the curtain, hissing, "Move. *Now.*"

"I know," Jacob said. *"I know."*

Pelletier shoved him backward through the curtain. His sneakers slid around on the wet tiles. He straightened up as Pelletier came out of the alcove to confront him.

"Wait outside," she said.

Behind her, the beads swung, revealing Tremsin, still on his feet, clenched hands dripping, his chest heaving.

"Wait outside," Pelletier said, "or I will have you arrested."

Jacob walked along the length of the pool toward the exit.

He didn't know what had just happened.

He didn't know what he ought to feel.

What he did feel was rage. Disappointment at the hideous anti-climax.

What do you expect? He'll wither in the face of your righteousness?

He could hear Pelletier trying to placate Tremsin, pleading with him in Russian while he screamed at her, their voices echoing off the spa walls like some petty domestic squabble, idiotically magnified.

Jacob reached the rustic wooden door and paused. He had half a mind to turn around and go back.

Priorities rolled around in a jumble.

He needed to find Paul.

Or: Paul was the last guy he wanted to see.

Get out safely.

Go home. That was enough.

It *wasn't* enough.

It would *have* to be enough.

The argument pouring from the alcove broke off, replaced by a swinish sound.

Tremsin groaning, pleasurably.

Pelletier, doing what she could to keep him calm.

Disgusted, Jacob opened the door to leave.

The antechamber was empty.

The gunman gone.

As Jacob lingered on the threshold, puzzled, another series of sounds reverberated down the length of the room: a different sort of groan; an alarmed shriek; a crash.

Silence. Then frenzied movement, the beads of the curtain swinging.

He treaded back along the pool, came into view of the alcove.

He saw the hand baths knocked over, the manicure cart overturned, the iron ring rolled somewhere out of sight.

Tremsin, flat on his back.

Pelletier, straddling him, her hips hammering back and forth.

The motion was a close facsimile of sex. But Tremsin's smock had fallen aside, his penis semi-erect and visible. Pelletier was fully dressed, using the heel of her hand to vigorously put weight down on his sternum, huffing and struggling and counting.

She was giving Tremsin chest compressions.

Soapy water pooled around them, soaking into her pant legs, his smock.

Jacob stepped through the curtain.

Pelletier looked up and saw him and said, "Go for help."

He didn't move.

"He's having a heart attack," she said.

The heart attack was over. Jacob could see that. Lines of spittle trailed from the corners of Tremsin's mouth; his eyes had fallen open, unnaturally wide. She was pounding on a corpse. "For God's sake," she yelled.

Why did she need him to get help? She had a phone.

"Stop staring and *hurry*," she yelled.

He was staring at her fitness tracker, flung free of her wrist by her frantic pumping. It lay on the tile, six inches behind her left knee.

The green band had come apart and was lying in a C shape. One end appeared normal.

The other terminated in a half-inch-long hypodermic needle, an amber bead quivering at its tip.

Pelletier paused her compressions. Followed his gaze.

Saw the needle and the droplet and said, *"Merde."*

Laughing, she let her hands fall by her sides. *"Merde . . ."*

She reached over and picked up the bracelet.

Sighed, put it back on, carefully inserting the needle into a corresponding hole. The gap snicked together magnetically, leaving the bracelet unassuming. Standing, she smoothed her slacks. Her blouse was undone to the navel. She began closing it.

"It would've come to this, sooner or later. He was always making threats when he couldn't have his way. You can't do that forever. People get tired of it."

She raked her fingers through her hair several times. "Anyway," she said, "it's over now."

Jacob watched the bracelet, wobbling on her wrist.

She said, "I know. Clever, isn't it? Here's an irony to reflect on: the formula's a variation on one he invented, a modified tetrodotoxin. We rode by the formula in the lift. Between the third and fourth floors. His was much slower-acting. Thirty minutes from injection to effect. This one's far better. Sixty seconds, which happens to be the maximum amount of time I can stand to keep his cock in my mouth. He deserves credit for laying the groundwork, though."

Jacob said, "Théo Breton had a heart attack."

Pelletier rolled her eyes. "Please. Don't be boring. The vial is single-use."

She walked to the counter. "You can't blame me for everything."

She kicked off her heels.

She picked up a bone-handled straight razor.

Opened it.

Lunged.

The extra second she had taken to remove her shoes allowed him to perform myriad primal lizard-brain calculations: the distribution of his body weight on a slippery surface, the radius of danger produced by her outstretched arm plus three inches of honed steel, the probable arc of the blade as it aimed for a clean sever of the jugular vein.

By then he'd moved out of the way.

He backpedaled through the curtain, whipping heavy beaded strands at her.

Harmless, but it did the trick, entangling her as he broke for the exit.

He ran, tipping over tables, kicking over chairs. He couldn't move quickly on the tiles. But neither could she. She was barefoot. Fingertips, palms, toes, soles—they were all covered in friction skin. It gave better traction. But not much. Man did not evolve in a spa. She might've been better off keeping her heels on. She was running on instinct, too.

He heaved a basket of birch branches at her, leaves twisting in the steam.

Reaching the door to the antechamber, he realized the mistake in going through. The room was far smaller than the spa. No space to maneuver, no obstacles between them.

The only escape an elevator that ran at a third normal speed. She'd be on him well before the car arrived. And the armed guard might've returned.

He was fucked. He'd been fucked since getting into her Peugeot.

But what choice did he have? He had relinquished all choice the moment he entered the embassy. Before that: when he'd spoken to Vallot. To Breton.

Before all *that*: he'd been fucked since arriving in Paris; since he started to ask questions about a dead woman and a dead child.

Pelletier could cut his throat and nobody would question her. She was the law.

She'd say that Jacob had attacked Tremsin. She'd tried to stop him. Reaching for the nearest weapon, disabling Jacob, but not before the poor bastard's heart gave out.

Alas.

How the hell was he going to make it out of the building alive?

One thing at a time his lizard brain said.

In case of fire, do not use the elevator. Take the stairs.

There had to be stairs. Somewhere.

He hadn't seen any in the antechamber.

In one of the alcoves?

So instead of going through the door, he hooked right, back around the swimming pool, passing alcove one, which housed a vast white marble whirlpool.

No door.

Pelletier came after him, tripping barefoot through the mess of branches, her decision to go shoeless looking more and more imprudent.

Eventually he would run out of furniture to tip and baskets to throw. He'd come full circle and run smack into his own messes.

But for right now he had open floor in front of him and she had junk in her way, and he chucked another basket at her.

She dodged. He was becoming predictable.

He came to the next alcove, a glassed-in sauna. No door.

Alcove three contained a second whirlpool, green onyx. How many fucking bubbles did one person need? No door.

As Jacob continued to run, he realized what distinguished the spa from the rest of the house: no cameras here. It was Tremsin's private oasis. Too foggy, anyway.

Pelletier knew that. She knew this place. She wanted him here.

The next alcove, the fourth, was the barbershop.

Parting the curtain, he looked past Tremsin's body, hoping against hope.

No door.

He stopped then, because Pelletier had stopped too, retreating to the antechamber door. Letting him wear himself out.

She said, "Let's be dignified about this."

"Go fuck yourself."

She laughed.

He laughed, too. He felt woozy and flushed.

The only alcove he hadn't checked was the fifth. Halfway between them.

Forty feet of leaf-strewn tile and fragrant mist and gauzy orange light.

If there was a stairwell, it had to be there.

If he got close enough to find out, she'd be on him in seconds.

Or maybe she wouldn't bother. Maybe she'd bide her time till the cavalry arrived.

A ray of illumination washed over him. He peered up at the skylight.

Peaceful, abundant clouds.

Was Mai behind them?

Schott was in the building. Molchanov, too.

Waiting for her.

She knew. She wasn't coming.

Nobody was coming.

Pelletier said, "Tremsin thought you were someone else."

"Who?"

"We didn't get that far," she said. "You made him upset, though."

"He went to that party, didn't he?"

She said, "I'm not going to answer that."

"Why the hell not?"

"You don't get to learn the truth before you die."

"What makes you think I'm going to die?" he said.

"What makes you think you're not?"

He ducked through the curtain into the barbershop, grabbed a razor with a knurled steel handle from the collection, swung it open, grabbed another blade, and reemerged.

Pelletier had closed the gap between them to ten feet.

She halted.

He opened the second razor, held both weapons out like a teppanyaki chef.

"Do you know how to use those?" she said.

Jacob hated knives. In a way they were worse than guns. Even from close range, ninety percent of shots missed. A knife didn't have to be accurate to do real harm. It could cripple you with a glancing cut.

He said, "I guess we'll find out."

He kicked up a fan of leaves and sticks and slurry and rushed her.

She pivoted sideways to narrow her profile, her razor out, glinting, threatening, and he tried to slide off axis to hack at the inside of her elbow, hoping to disarm her right off the bat. But she was nimble and compact and she folded her limbs against her body and corkscrewed down and away from him.

Momentum carried him past her, and the edge of a blade whispered along the back of his leg, opening the denim several inches below his left rear pocket, close enough that he felt thankful for not buying into the skinny jeans fad.

He jerked around to slow himself, crouched, ready to fight her off.

She hung back, her posture relaxed, quick eyes conducting damage assessment.

They'd switched positions, relative to the antechamber door.

Warmth trickled along the back of his knee, over the swell of his calf.

No pain.

Which was either good or a disaster, the wound either so minor as to be irrelevant or so deep that his nervous system had flooded with override signals, enabling him to do the sensible thing: flee.

He didn't want to look. If he looked, he'd know, and knowing could undo him, mentally. The crucial fact was that he was still standing, his left hamstring strong enough to bear weight.

He went at her again, driving her back over the tiles, swinging the razors in two planes, her belly, her neck. Instinct. Two blades were a bitch to control; he had to slow down to avoid cutting himself, and Pelletier exploited his treadling gait, drawing him away from where he needed to go, which was the alcove behind him, maybe the one with the stairs.

He did the sensible thing.

He stopped attacking her.

Turned and ran.

The next moment swelled monstrously, a blister in the soft tissue of time. He slipped. His injured left leg slewed loose in mud and dead vegetation and his foot lost contact with the ground and he pitched forward, landing on the beak of his elbow, bone on tile, a stunning wave of pain traveling up his humerus and into his shoulder socket. He rolled partway onto his flank, scrabbling with his heels, kicking at the floor, backstroking through debris as Pelletier charged toward him.

He saw her dark brown roots and her neat bared teeth, the diagonal creases of her shirt, her arm spring-loaded across her body, razor held high, front leg planting, torso unwinding to loose the backhand that would spill his innards.

He didn't have time to shout, to shut his eyes, to throw up his arms.

He listened to his heart's closing measures.

A wet socket punched through her forehead, just left of center, and her head snapped back and the live pressure dumped out of her body and she flopped down atop him. Her face mashed his chest, then lolled over so that he was staring into her matte eyes.

The exit wound had taken off the back of her skull. In the airspace above them hung microscopic drops of blood and cerebrospinal fluid, clinging to the perfumed mist, a pink filter through which to view the skylights.

The moon had come out.

A tinny pip, as the razor slipped from her hand and fell to the tiles.

Soft bootsteps approached.

A waxy face drifted into view, a human eclipse.

Dmitri Molchanov said, *"Nu."*

CHAPTER FORTY-EIGHT

He stepped on Jacob's left wrist and kicked the razor out of Jacob's right hand, into the pool. He stepped on Jacob's right wrist and did the same for the razor in Jacob's left hand. He kicked Pelletier's blade in with the other two.

"Up."

Jacob stood. Blood and tissue and splinters of bone smeared his shirtfront.

Molchanov was holding a black-and-brown pistol, surveying the chaos, trying to reconstruct what had happened, his eyes finally fixing on the barbershop alcove.

He waggled the pistol: *move.*

Jacob took half steps, partly because his left leg was starting to throb, partly because he had a notion that he'd be shot as soon as Molchanov saw Tremsin's body.

The bead curtain was still swaying, just perceptibly.

Jacob stepped into the alcove, Molchanov close behind.

Tremsin's smock had soaked up so much water that the fabric had darkened several shades, the true red visible in patches near the collar.

"I'm sure it won't matter," Jacob said, "but I didn't kill him."

Molchanov's gaze shifted toward the main room.

Jacob nodded. "She injected him with something. The needle's in her wristband."

"Hm," Molchanov said. His accent rendered it as *chm*.

He regarded Tremsin dispassionately. "Thirty-six years."

"That's how long you worked for him?" Jacob said.

Molchanov nodded.

"That's a long time," Jacob said.

"Whole life," Molchanov said. "He goes, I go."

Jacob said, "I'm sorry to hear it."

He felt ridiculous. Sullied. Consoling one monster over another monster.

Molchanov touched his earpiece, spoke in Russian. Then he told Jacob to kneel.

"Face down. Arms behind."

Assuming the position limited Jacob to a few inches of peripheral vision, as well as a clear view down the corridor of his shins. Rusty streaks in his left pant leg. He didn't appear to be actively bleeding.

Take what you can get.

Molchanov kicked aside one of the overturned hand baths and stepped toward the counter that held the collection of straight razors. Jacob snuck a glance. The Russian was opening drawers in search of a clean smock, which he draped over Tremsin's body. Then he opened a razor and began sawing the cord off the hairdryer.

He noticed Jacob watching and clucked his tongue. "Face down."

Jacob's head throbbed against the tile. His shoulders screamed from the effort of keeping his arms up and back. He was getting dizzy, bright spots stippling his field of vision. Through the gap in his feet, he noticed a black speck near the junction of the cabinetry and the floor. Tremsin's ring.

A shadow shifted, Molchanov circling around behind him. Jacob flinched. Waiting to be strangled, raped; a blade, a bullet; any combination.

Molchanov tightly bound Jacob's wrists, pulled him up, marched him back through the curtain, made him kneel by the edge of the pool.

Wet warm scummy water seeped into Jacob's jeans.

He said, "What did you want to talk to me about?"

Molchanov raised an eyebrow.

"Last night, when you were chasing me. You wanted to have a conversation," Jacob said. "We could have it now."

Molchanov smiled. "Talking is complete."

The spa door opened. Two new guards appeared.

They held Jacob at gunpoint while Molchanov left the room.

Another silence, longer.

The skylight pinged: the rain returning, tiptoeing at first, then steadily gaining in confidence.

He weighed the pros and cons of trying to run.

He said to the guards, "Your boss is dead."

They didn't reply. A sullen pair, each sporting the beginnings of a beard.

"That makes you unemployed."

No answer.

Molchanov returned carrying a clunky metal cylinder, an attached hose and wand.

The exterminator's spray tank.

He set it down and dismissed the guards. Righted a teak chair and sat down a few feet in front of Jacob, propping the pistol on his knee. He produced Jacob's phone from his greatcoat pocket and began thumbing through it.

Searching for the picture Jacob had taken of him in the Marais?

No: Molchanov turned the screen around, showing the photo of the Gerhardt fob.

"You have it?" he asked.

Jacob shook his head.

"Where is it?"

"I gave it to the French police. They're running it for prints."

Molchanov nodded, unconcerned.

Jacob said, "Tremsin must have paid you well, you can afford a car like that."

"Doktor Tremsin," Molchanov corrected.

Thirty-six years.

He goes, I go.

Jacob said, "Did he have anything to do with Lidiya and Valko?"

Molchanov appeared briefly confused. Then he said, "From embassy."

Jacob nodded.

"No," Molchanov said.

"That was all you."

Molchanov gazed wistfully at the picture of the fob. "After I lost, I called dealership. Three thousand euros to replace."

"What about Marquessa and TJ? All you?"

Molchanov lobbed the phone into the pool.

"How many others?" Jacob said.

Molchanov tucked the gun in his coat pocket, swapping it for the potter's knife.

"Your friend," he said, rolling the handle between his fingers, "did brave thing."

He wiped the blade against his coat sleeve, leaving an iridescent blue trail.

"He tried to fight."

Jacob suppressed a retch of terror and grief.

Oh God. Oh no.

"Very brave," Molchanov said. "Also very stupid."

Jacob said, "He was your kind."

Molchanov said, "I have no kind."

He stood up. He hefted the spray tank, tried to put it on. The straps were too narrow for his huge frame.

To afford himself a little more slack, he shrugged off his greatcoat and draped it over the back of the chair, managing then to get the tank on.

He felt around for the dangling wand, gave a few test sprays.

Jacob said, "You really think that's going to work?"

Molchanov smiled, shrugged. "Bug is bug."

He tugged his scarf up over his face and came behind Jacob.

"What is it with you about mothers and sons?" Jacob said.

Molchanov barked a laugh. "You never knew my mother."

With the sprayer hand, he grabbed a handful of Jacob's hair and pulled back, resting the blade against Jacob's windpipe.

"However," Molchanov said, "I knew yours."

CHAPTER FORTY-NINE

Bina steps out onto the far end of Lunatics' Boulevard, Dmitri close behind.

They pass the other solitary confinement cells. Behind one of those doors, Olga is serving out her punishment. Bina will not get a chance to say good-bye to her.

She won't get a chance to say good-bye to Fat Irena.

To Majka—poor lovely Majka.

They made a pact, yet she's stealing away in the dead of the night like a thief.

No stealth in it: the sedative gives her a shuffling gait and her rubber-soled shoes squeak on the linoleum. The noise draws the interest of other patients. Cages rattle, voices demand to know.

Who is leaving?

Why?

Starbursts of fatigue rock her back on her heels.

Dmitri takes her by the arm and hurries her along.

They pass the snoring staff room; doctor's offices and treatment rooms, Hydrotherapy, Electroshock. She struggles to keep pace with Dmitri's brisk strides. They pass a series of doors marked with numbers. One, two, three. Four, five, six. Seven. Eight.

Her body knows what's coming: it's starting to seize in anticipation.

Dmitri grabs her around the waist before she keels over.

"You must walk," he says.

She hides from room nine, ceaselessly shaking her head: *no, no, no.*

"You are leaving. You are going home."

Sick. A sick joke.

"Look at me," he says.

She won't. He takes her chin in his gloved hand and forces it around and up.

"Look at me," he says. "You have a son."

She gapes at the face strangely handsome, the features continuously reweaving themselves.

"I read it in your file. What is his name?"

She won't tell him. Won't allow him to desecrate it.

She whispers, "Jacob."

"Don't you want to see him again? Jacob?"

More than anything else in the world.

"Then you need to walk." He props her up. "He is not coming to you."

THE GUARD AT THE GATE snaps off a salute. "Sir."

Dmitri hands him paperwork certifying that the patient Bina Reich Lev has been remanded into his custody for discharge.

The guard salutes again and goes to unlock the gate.

Snow throws a shroud over the courtyard. Frigid air needles through her thin sweater. Behind her lies an indictment, rows and rows of cell windows. She will not turn to gaze upon their misery, lest she become a pillar of salt.

Dmitri puts his hand on her elbow, urges her forward.

Bina stumbles through the gate. Cured.

HE DRIVES AGGRESSIVELY, rolling through red lights, taking turns at high speed, muttering to himself about the poor quality of the brakes.

Nauseated, Bina huddles against the rocking of the vehicle, her lubricated mind twisting this way and that, trying to make sense of what is happening.

All questions boil down to two.

Is she safe?

Will she get home?

There's a kind of urgent solicitousness in Dmitri's manner. He keeps glancing over at her, making sure she hasn't evaporated.

"Are you all right?" he asks. He eases off the gas. "Are you going to be sick?"

She says, "Where are we going?"

Without taking his attention from the road, he reaches over her to unlock the glove compartment and withdraws a rubber-banded packet that he drops in her lap.

Her passport, along with a small stack of money.

Dmitri uses his teeth to remove one leather glove. A black ring on his index finger, identical to the ring Tremsin wears. She's never noticed it. On the ward, he kept his hands covered.

"There is a train departing for Berlin in two hours," he says, checking his watch. "Once there you should proceed to your embassy. Beyond that, I cannot help."

Over the river, through a labyrinth of unpeopled streets. She can tell they're in Old Town. When he pulls over, however, the silhouette looming beyond the glass is unmistakably that of the Alt-Neu Synagogue.

He shuts off the engine. "A quick errand, first. The golem—it is no longer safe here. You must go up to the garret and fetch the jar so I can move it elsewhere."

She doesn't reply.

"There is no need to pretend," he says. "I read your file. I know who you are."

Languid wet flakes touch the windshield, dissolve.

She says, "Who are you?"

His smile is stunted. "A friend."

I am your friend.

We all are.

We always will be.

Checking his watch again, he says, "They have recalled us to Moscow, now that Brezhnev is dead. Doktor Tremsin has already left. I am due to depart before the year's out. Hence the rush."

A friend.

She says, "Is he . . . ?"

Dmitri starts to laugh. "Him? No. No. He is the man I work for. He has given me opportunities. I try to be loyal. After he got his marching orders for Prague, I was the only member of the circle who volunteered to come into exile with him. Truthfully, I was glad. It was always the city of my dreams. I studied Czech hoping that I could one day come. I owe him much. But he is a man. No more."

Bina wonders what more a person could be.

She recalls Frayda crushing her hands; an inhuman shadow looming up.

"I won't be with him forever," Dmitri says. "For me, greater things lie ahead."

It must never be allowed to get out.

Under no circumstances can it leave this building.

Bina says, "What are you going to do with it?"

"That is not your concern," he says. He squints ahead, perks up. *"Nu."*

He springs from the car.

A small shape is coming up the sidewalk toward them, a flashlight bobbing.

Little Peter Wichs.

Outside, Dmitri says, "Did you bring it?"

Peter unzips his coat and tugs out his twine necklace with the key to the *shul.*

Dmitri turns to her expectantly.

She looks at Peter.

He raises a mittened hand, smiles shyly.

Aware that she is relying on the assurances of a child, she gets out of the car.

PASSING THE COBBLED TERRACE at the rear of the synagogue, they head up the alleyway, pausing once to allow Bina to vomit.

"You will be fine," Dmitri says. "There is only this to get through, and then you will be on your way home."

At the main entrance, he stands well back as Peter unlocks the door.

"We will wait for you here," Dmitri says.

She says, "I'll need an assistant."

Dmitri says nothing. His eyes dart between her and the boy.

"Either him or you," she says.

Dmitri blinks. The prospect of entering the building clearly unnerves him.

"Do you want me to do this or not?" she asks.

A beat. Dmitri says, "Your passport."

She hands him the packet. He slips it in his coat pocket. "Be quick about it."

Bina places a hand on Peter's shoulder, and together they step down into the darkened synagogue.

IN THE BASEMENT, she prepares for immersion by rinsing off in the camp shower. The freezing water kicks her partly from her stupor. A repulsive second skin covers her from head to toe, filling the plastic tub with a cloudy black liquid, her feet disappearing.

Taking a threadbare towel from the bureau, she scrapes herself down further.

The towel turns black.

She takes another, commences scraping.

It turns black.

She goes through the entire stack, nine in all, and still she is mottled and streaked like a farm animal. Without warning, she breaks into sobs. Her immersion will not be valid. She isn't clean, she will never be clean again, she feels so out of control.

Think about what matters.

Think about Jacob.

She grabs ahold of her bucking mood, wrestles it to the earth.

Walks to the edge of the *mikveh*, encounters her ruined reflection.

Stepping down into the warm water, she wades forward until it covers her breasts.

She dips once, quickly, and resurfaces. Crosses her arms over her heart, dividing the upper and lower bodies, the holy from the profane, an act she has performed countless times. But the distinction has lost all meaning, and she lets her arms drop, weeping once more as she recites the blessing.

Blessed are You, our God, King of the universe, Who has sanctified us with His commandments, and commanded us regarding immersion.

She plunges.

UP ON THE GROUND FLOOR, Peter has unlocked the women's section.

They cross to the curtain that conceals the garret entrance. Peter slides it aside and they crowd into the booth. Bina seals her lips, her eyes, waits for the blast of dust.

Nothing happens.

She looks at Peter.

He has his flashlight pointed at the trapdoor in the ceiling.

He's waiting for her to pull the rope.

He's too short to reach it.

Her whirling sense of déjà vu dissolves, as she perceives the contrast between then and now, what's missing.

Ota Wichs.

She considers what Dmitri appears to know.

The jar. Its location. Its significance. *Her* significance.

She considers that he has saved her, in a way, escorting her out of hell.

To bring her here.

Is there really a train to Berlin?

There are other things he does not know.

Under no circumstances can it leave this building.

Or he knows, and does not care.

For me, greater things lie ahead.

She says, "That man outside. Have you ever met him before?"

Peter shakes his head. "He called on the phone."

"When?"

"Yesterday. He said to come tonight and bring the key to the *shul*. He said don't tell my stepmother."

"Did he tell you what he wants me to do?"

"Move the golem," Peter says. "He said my father asked him to do it."

Silence.

She says, "Have you seen your father recently? Spoken to him?"

"No. But the man said that he would take me to him if I did what he said."

A brick in her throat. She starts to reply, but Peter speaks first:

"He lied, didn't he."

She says nothing.

A businesslike nod. "I thought so. I was excited when he told me. But he lied. My father is dead."

She says, "He might still be alive."

"That's what Pavla thinks," Peter says.

"Well, she's—I'm sure she's right."

"No," the boy says leadenly. "She's wrong."

He appears to be aging before her very eyes.

"He's been arrested before," he says. "We always got a letter. But we didn't get one, this time. So I know. It was the same when they took my mother."

No child of nine ought to wield such arid logic.

Bina says, "I'm so sorry, Peter."

He is tight around the mouth, but dry-eyed, his mind already aligned with hers, toward survival.

"All right," he says. "What should we do?"

She describes a plan, as best she can. It's getting harder and harder to keep her thoughts in order. "Does that sound all right?"

Peter nods. He shuts his eyes against the dust. "Go ahead."

HER SECOND ASCENT is more difficult than the first. The sedative moves through her bloodstream in spurts, and her limbs feel alternately flimsy and sandbagged as she climbs through stinging, choking clouds of dust. She has no strong arms to guide her; no enduring faith; she follows only her instincts and the bead of Peter's flashlight as it ricochets in infinity; flickering, feinting, collapsing to zero.

Jacob.

A heartbeat, a wheel, a contracting womb.

Jacob. Jacob. Jacob.

Up, up, up she goes, toward the new light that spreads like a canopy. She pulls herself onto the attic floor, striving to raise her head, hoping to catch another sweet glimpse of her Jerusalem.

Her chance has passed.

Nothing but broken furniture.

And no time to mourn: Peter has kindled the lantern and stands expectantly.

Bina coughs, pounds her chest. Rises.

They begin to walk.

———

IN HER MEMORY, the journey across the garret took hours. Now space telescopes, and they arrive at the scene, laid as it was on the night of the National Day celebration.

Cabinet, wheel, stool, portable stove.

The lump of clay. The bucket of water, gone scummy.

The tool roll.

She was supposed to come back.

She was supposed to make as many jars as possible.

A hundred more, we'll be fine.

Bina and Peter remove the drop cloth and open the cabinet.

Inside is the completed pair of jars. Despite never having been fired, they've set up well, the surfaces dully polished.

She moves them aside and thrusts her arm deep into the cabinet. Her fingertips skim the old jar that holds the beetle. She senses its warmth, the magnetism. She can't quite reach it. Ota made sure of that.

Peter drags over a crate for her to stand on, hands her the arm from a coatrack.

"Thank you."

She uses the hook to ease the jar out, trying not to knock it over, not to touch it with her bare skin. Once she's gotten it close enough, she lets the boy take over.

He sets the jar on the floor beside one of the newer jars.

"You need to help me," he says. "I only have two hands."

She smiles despite her nerves. "Tell me what to do."

"You lift the lids. I'll tip her out into that one. Then you put the lid down."

She nods. She gets down on her knees. Then she says, "Her?"

"Ready?" Peter says.

She positions her hands over the clay knobs.

"One, two, three."

The operation takes a fraction of a second, Peter's lithe hands darting in, the beetle tumbling through open space and landing at the bottom of the new jar, where it stirs and rolls over, sitting up like a dog, its forelegs working excitedly, waving.

Bina stares, mesmerized.

Peter acts fast, snatching the lid from between her fingers and dropping it into place. There's a moment, before it comes down, when Bina sees the beetle's limbs fly toward her, a gesture of indignation and anguish.

PETER PUTS THE GOLEM in the cabinet, using the coatrack arm to edge the jar far back on the shelf. They cover the cabinet with the drop cloth and tie it down.

Bina wraps the second new jar in a rag. "I'll make copies and send them to you. I'll need the tools."

"Clay, too," he says.

She regards the lump, dried rock hard. "I don't know if I'm going to be able to revive it. I'll try."

They pack the items in a *tallis* bag. When she wraps the old, cracked jar, it no longer feels living, but cold and stiff.

She gives the shuttered cabinet a parting glance.

As they pick their way across the garret, square throbs of dislocation press at the interior of her skull, hideous surges of terror and delight, the urge to laugh, to scream, to speak. Her blurred vision is clearing, but not to normal; instead there is an excruciating sharpness, a hellish bombardment of detail.

They arrive at the peaked door that opens above the rear terrace. Up close, it's hardly larger than it looks from thirty-five feet below.

She anxiously fingers the iron bar that holds it shut, the hinges bloated with rust. "Have you ever gone out this way?"

Peter shakes his head. "It's not supposed to be opened."

"You can come back later and lock it," she says.

He nods.

"You'll go first. When you reach the bottom, what are you going to do?"

"Run as fast as I can."

"Where?"

"Away from you."

"That's right," she says. "It's me he wants, not you. But you must be careful all the same. He's supposed to leave Prague soon. Until he does, you won't be safe. Don't go anywhere without a grown-up."

As if that matters.

She says, "Do you understand, Peter?"

He nods again.

Still she hesitates. She can't abandon him.

"I just thought of something," she says. "You could come with me. I can tell the embassy—we'll tell them that it's not safe for you to stay here. We'll ask for asylum."

"No," he says.

"You'd like America once you got there," she says. "Pavla, too." She is a con woman, crazy promises rushing out of her. "I'm sure we can—"

He cuts her off with a shake of the head. "I can't leave."

"But why not?"

His answer is to indicate the walls around them.

No particular pride. Just resignation to fate.

He's in charge, now.

She says, "I'll send you the jars as I make them. And I'll write to you. You must write back. Tell me you're okay."

He nods.

"And always be careful. Not just for the near future, but always."

"I am," he says, and he nods toward the door. "It's time."

She lifts the bar, grasps the handle.

Pulls.

The door doesn't move.

She tries again, without success.

Digs her heels into the floorboards and throws her weight back.

The door refuses to budge. Peter steps in to help, putting his arms around her waist and leaning, the two of them straining until they get traction, a few inches, a few more, the hinges emitting a piercing shriek.

She whispers for him to go, go.

He flops onto his stomach and disappears over the edge.

Bina leans out to make sure she won't accidentally kick him in the head. The moment her face touches the bare air, the garbage-strewn cobblestones begin flying up toward her, like a lover coming in for a kiss, her thoughts condensing awfully.

Jump.

She won't fall, she'll float.

How lovely.

She pitches forward.

Catches herself on the door frame, shoves back, heart storming.

Quickly she gets down, worming backward, feeling with her foot for the top rung, descending, the *tallis* bag pinched hard between thumb and forefinger.

Jump.

Down, down, down, her eyes fixed on the plaster, rubber-soled shoes treadless on slick rungs, frozen metal burning her bare hands.

Jump, jump.

A high-pitched scream.

She looks back over her shoulder.

Below, Peter Wichs dangles from the bottom rung, still high off the ground, his legs kicking air as he tries to reascend.

Dmitri stands off to the side of the terrace, gun in hand, watching him placidly.

"I have it," she shouts.

Dmitri looks up at her.

She waves the *tallis* bag. "It's in here."

Jump jump jump jump jump jump jump jump

"Do anything to him and I will smash it against the wall."

Peter has stopped kicking and is hanging limply. She grips the bag with one hand, the rung with the other; her own forearm is beginning to quiver. She can imagine that he will not last much longer.

"Help him," she yells.

Dmitri pockets the gun and walks over to the ladder. He's so tall that his outstretched hands nearly reach Peter's hips.

Peter stares up at her, terrified.

"It's okay," she says, nodding. "You can do it."

Peter shuts his eyes and lets go. The Russian catches him easily and carries him to the center of the cobblestones and sets him down, wrapping a fatherly arm across the boy's chest.

"Your turn," he says.

She doesn't move.

Dmitri takes out the gun and presses it to Peter's temple.

"You won't," she says.

And she's right: she still has the bag.

Dmitri smiles. "Doktor Tremsin ordered me to kill you before I left. He doesn't know who you are, what a loss that would be for the world."

"Let him go," Bina says.

"I saved you. Still you chose to deceive me. Why would you do that?"

She raises the bag to smash it.

Dmitri lifts his arm.

Peter stands paralyzed. A dark stain in his trouser leg. He's wet himself.

She yells to get his attention.

"Go," she says. *"Now."*

Peter comes to life, scrambling up the stairs to Pařížská Street, running for the shadows.

Bina waits until she can no longer hear the echo of his footsteps, then turns to grasp the rung with both hands, to catch her breath, which feels insanely lush as it billows out and fogs the plaster, her thoughts gathering in an unstoppable mob.

Behind her, Dmitri is speaking: "You can't stay there forever."

She shakes her head, hard. An instant of focus, instantly decaying.

She cranes back. "Put the gun down. Your car keys, too."

A beat. He sets the pistol and the keys on the ground.

"My passport."

He adds it to the pile.

She orders him into the corner, away from the stairs. He obeys, retreating to the rear wall. The terrace is shallow, he could reach her in one ambitious stride.

Bina descends shakily, pausing every few rungs to ensure that he hasn't moved.

Reaching the bottom rung, she dangles, drops.

Her ankle buckles but she hurries to stand, holding the bag above her head, as if she's going to hurl it to the ground.

He has not come any closer.

She inches forward to collect the gun, the keys, her passport.

"I've done exactly as you asked," he says. "Time for you to uphold your end."

"I'm going to put it down there. Don't move until I say or I will crush it."

He nods.

She kneels where the terrace meets the alleyway. Through the fog clotting her brain she is vaguely aware of pain in her ankle, the joint beginning to swell. She opens the *tallis* bag and sets the old cracked jar on the ground.

The fact that it's wrapped will give her time.

She buries it in trash, to give herself more.

She bolts up the stairs, timing him in her mind.

He is hurrying forth to claim his prize.

She reaches the street.

He is brushing off the garbage, carefully peeling away the cloth.

She reaches the car. So many keys on the ring; and what a moment for her hands, her most faithful servants, to disobey her.

He is lifting the lid.

Discovering nothing inside.

She has not gotten hold of a second key when he comes thundering up the steps. She points the gun and fires and keeps firing till the gun clicks, but still he is coming, and she drops the weapon and flees, skating on the icy pavement until she gains purchase and breaks toward the river, head down, legs pumping.

It is perhaps four in the morning. There is no one else on the street. No taxis. No trams. She should be shouting all the same but her flight is a graceless ballet, her lopsided gait and her pinched breath and behind her the drum of boots on the pavement, his shadow lengthening to overtake her.

Without knowing quite what she intends to do—throw a jar at him? throw the clay?—she fumbles inside the *tallis* bag, grasps a smooth finger of wood, and as a giant hand swallows her shoulder, she swings her arm around and up, jamming the blade of the potter's knife through his scarf and into the side of his neck.

She twists.

Then they are falling, falling together, his body crushing hers, his mouth opening in ungodly silence.

She yanks the knife out and uncorks a cold torrent of blood, blood saturating the woolen scarf and rushing through to drench her, blood in unbelievable quantity, breaking the wine-rimmed cracks between his fingers as he clutches at the gash; blood icy and viscous and numbing like seawater, his eyes smashing around crazily inside their sockets, his expression rictal and incredulous, the immense weight of his torso pinning her until she can wriggle free and crawl away, leaving him writhing on the sidewalk, drowning in a deep mute ocean of blood.

Finding the knife, the bag, she stumbles to her feet and runs.

CHAPTER FIFTY

His neck drawn taut, Jacob felt the edge of the potter's knife kiss his throat, stopping just shy of incision. Overhead the skylights gaped, black pits mercilessly thumped by fists of rain, then slashed to eye-white by lightning. Molchanov released his grip on Jacob's hair, the blade in place to prevent Jacob from moving; the giant raised the sprayer wand and began releasing gas, which mingled with the steam, engulfing them in a noxious white column.

Jacob began to sputter and choke as Molchanov took up a chant.

aa ab ag ad

The insane idea flew into Jacob's mind that the Russian was making a blessing to render the slaughter ritually pure; but the knife remained at his neck and the noises droned on, muffled by the fabric of the scarf, ginning up a rhythm primal and sinister.

af atz ak

He said, "She's not coming."

Molchanov continued to chant.

"She knows about you. She won't come."

Molchanov chanted, pressed the knife closer. Jacob's flesh shrank back.

Moving in agonizing increments, he began to torque his wrists in one direction, then the other, trying to loosen the electrical cord knotted hard as iron. Fighting the urge to hurry, the rubber abrading his skin, running sticky hot from humidity and fear, he kept working until his fingertips began losing sensation.

Success: a quarter inch of give.

Chest thudding, he peeked up at Molchanov. The giant was lost in concentration.

Jacob resumed twisting.

Minutes piled up. The drone continued. Jacob heard new excitement in Molchanov's voice, the blade wanting to have its way.

zu zub

Jacob felt a mild bite, a liquid tickle, as the tip of the knife drew blood.

Molchanov said, *"Zug."*

The air changed.

Jacob felt her before he saw her.

Molchanov felt it, too. A tremor ran down his arms. From high above came a faint glassy tinkle, gale winds fluting across the hole in the skylight, and the winged black diamond that was Mai swooped down at a blistering speed toward Molchanov's face.

Without ceasing to chant, the giant slashed at her with the knife.

He missed. She was a small target, moving quickly; she had pulled up and was now circling back around the room, carving a tunnel through the fog.

Molchanov was trying to do too many things at once, tracking her while maintaining his rhythm while controlling a hostage while preparing for her next sortie. Whatever he was, whatever dark truth reigned within him, he only had one brain and two hands, and in his eagerness to get at Mai he failed to bring the knife back to Jacob's throat quickly enough, and Jacob reacted without need for thought, pitching his head back as hard as he could, the base of his skull slamming into Molchanov's crotch.

Whatever he was, the guy had testicles.

He doubled over, reeling, wheezing.

Jacob heaved himself to his feet and ran for the door, glancing back in search of Mai. She had banked sharply and was hurtling across the pool to join him. Halfway there, she flew through a wafting blanket of poison; her path wavered, a horrible scream tore loose, and she reverted to human form, naked and cartwheeling helplessly through the air.

She plummeted toward the edge of the pool, her head cracking loudly against the tile before she slipped underwater.

Molchanov had gotten up. His scarf had come undone and he was staring at the sloshing pool, disarmed by his own success. He glanced at Jacob, at Mai, his features savagely bunched, conflicted about whom to deal with first.

Beneath the muddled surface, her body sank.

Molchanov rounded on Jacob.

He reached for a gun he didn't have.

The gun was in his greatcoat pocket.

The coat was draped over the chair.

The chair was knocked on its side.

Molchanov took a long step toward it.

The pool erupted in a geyser of foam.

Out of the water rose not a beetle nor a woman, but a tentacle of mud, berserk and swinging, smashing Molchanov backward, tossing him the length of the room.

Jacob crouched in terror as this new thing that was Mai rose completely out of the pool, leaving behind a muddy, dissolving cloud. It was blocky and faceless, melting at the edges as it oozed its way toward him. A tendril developed from where its belly ought to have been, snaked behind him, and snapped the cord binding him, and although it was her, another aspect of her, he couldn't help but cower, repulsed, as it reshaped itself, a slimy, unstable wall reeking of stagnant waters and decay.

A slit opened.

"Go."

Across the room, Molchanov was on his feet and charging, the knife out.

The mud shifted and swept to meet him.

They collided, head-on, rocking the room on its foundations, the air splitting, a storm surge overflowing the edge of the pool and picking up branches and leaves and slabs of dirty water, furniture splintering in reverberating disarray. Jacob landed on his back, hearing a loud wet rip, followed by another scream, low and gurgling.

Go.

She was giving him a chance to save himself.

Like some mechanical embryo, Molchanov expanded, unfolding himself, angle by angle, limb by limb, one powerful arm striving toward the sky, lifting the muddy mass off the ground, clods of earth dropping away to reveal its substructure: Mai's emaciated form.

He was impaling her, the knife hand sunk elbow-deep in her abdomen. Rooting around within her while she wriggled and moaned.

But still her focus was on Jacob.

Go go go

He scrambled toward Molchanov's coat.

The giant saw what he was doing.

Heaved Mai aside.

Ran at him.

Jacob got there first, his fingers closing around the butt of the pistol. He lined up and pulled the trigger, again and again. The first two shots went wide. He kept pulling. The third hit Molchanov square in the chest and produced no effect. The giant kept coming, knife cocked high, the triangular blade brilliantly alit.

Shot four caught Molchanov in the shoulder, spinning him just enough to expose the knob of scar tissue. Jacob aimed the fifth shot there, not because it was a large or useful target but because it was something he hated and wanted to destroy.

The bullet tore through Molchanov's neck, blowing out a cone of flesh.

At once he stopped moving. His knees gave way and he slammed into the tiles, blood flooding out of him with unimaginable force, frigid droplets landing far and wide, making pink eddies in the pool water until the tidal force began to slow, and he began to change.

He retained his great height but his width and depth contracted, the walls of his body rushing inward to fill the vacuum left by the outrush of blood. His arms were gristly twigs, his face a prune. His skin, wherever visible, drained from pink to gray and then deepened to a weird azure, cracks webbing like the surface of old porcelain.

Jacob came forward and knelt down. Molchanov's hands remained at his neck, clutching the potter's knife between two desiccated fingers, as though he meant to operate on himself.

Jacob took it from him.

He placed the gun in the center of Molchanov's forehead and shot him, point-blank. The eruption was white, all white and blue and nothing.

———

Jacob awoke with his cheek adhered to the floor, his torso throbbing as if he'd been run through with a spear, a drilling whine in his right ear. He could taste blood, not fresh but a menacing leak burbling up, the overrich taste tainted by another fluid—bile; stomach acid.

He rolled over and sat up on his elbows.

Molchanov was gone.

His clothes. His boots. His body. His ring.

A mantle of bluish dust lingered overhead. It had begun to sift peacefully down, settling over a wide area, powdering Jacob's skin, stinging his eyes, burning his sinuses.

He got to his feet, dripping, coughing, besmirched. He staggered free of the toxic cloud, toward Mai's inert body, calling her name.

She was a tent of skin, folded against a marble step, gnarled hands bracketing a horrific wound that stretched from hipbone to hipbone, bloodless edges ragged, curling. She appeared to have shed half her body weight.

But her lips moved as Jacob fell to his knees at her side, frantically touching her face, her chest, anything but the injury itself.

She murmured, fading. Leaving him.

The night in the greenhouse came back: mud flooding his throat, entering his veins to heal him. He bent over to put his mouth to hers but she shook her head.

She said, "You."

So quiet. So weak. He'd never thought of her as weak.

"You," she said again, her fingers closing around his.

She went limp.

He looked down.

She was holding his hand.

He was holding the knife.

He slashed open the front of his pant leg. He grabbed a fold of thigh and, grunting, drew an incision six inches long.

Blood sheeted out.

Jacob dipped his fingers in his blood and painted the jagged corner of her wound, watching as the flesh moistened and revived and grew pliable.

He pinched the corner of the wound together.

It sealed like soft clay.

He milked the incision, squeezing out more blood, continuing to balm her, to close her up. At some points the gap between the edges of the gash was so wide that he had to tug, gently, to encourage the two sides to meet. Where the middle of her womb would have been, a sharp tab jutted partway up from within her—an unnatural object, one that did not belong inside her. He thought to remove it, but hesitated, squinting.

Saw it clearly.

A twisted shred of paper, bearing the name of God in black ink.

It was this that Molchanov had been searching for.

Jacob tucked it back inside.

Mai gasped. Her eyes fluttered open.

He wasn't bleeding fast enough to save her, though. He drew several more incisions in his leg, shorter but deeper, kept molding her back together, until at last she was whole again, her face still ashen as she croaked, "Thank you."

He sank back, aching.

He said, "We have to stop meeting like this."

Mai started to laugh. It cracked, turned to retching. He slid over and put his arms around her, feeling the ridge of her spine.

"Can you fly?" he asked.

"I'm not sure," she mumbled.

"Can you try?"

She said, "I don't think I can carry both of us."

"How about just you?"

She looked at him. "What are you going to do?"

"I'll take care of myself."

The wounds on his leg wept, wept.

He said, "You need to get somewhere safe. That means far away from me."

He knew what she was thinking then, because he was thinking it, too: *forever.*

"Don't say it," he said.

She smiled tiredly. "I wasn't going to."

"You were going to say something."

"Only that I'll see you again."

He kissed her on the forehead. Lifted his arms from her.

He turned and crawled through warm bloody water to Pelletier's body. By the time he'd found her phone, found Dédé Vallot's number in the directory, Mai had already disappeared.

Jacob stared at the spot where she'd lain.

He shut his eyes and pressed the button to make the call, breathing in the quiet before the phone began to ring. It lasted a blessedly long time.

CHAPTER FIFTY-ONE

The French name for *intensive care unit* was *service de réanimation,* which Jacob found good for a cheap laugh.

In addition to the lacerations on his legs, he had a grade-three concussion and a perforated right eardrum. His skull was an unholy gob of pain. The doctor declared him ineligible to leave the hospital for at least two weeks, possibly three. Flying was out of the question.

That was fine. He wasn't going anywhere. Vallot, standing at the bedside, sounded sheepish as he asked Jacob to remain in Paris until they'd sorted everything out.

Jacob understood: a crooked dead cop was still a dead cop, and he was last man standing.

The account he provided Vallot was literally true—if inadequate.

Pelletier had killed Tremsin.

Molchanov had intervened and killed Pelletier.

Though hurt, Jacob had managed to escape in the chaos and phone for help.

He stressed certain details—the needle in Pelletier's bracelet—and hoped that the forensic mess would sufficiently plug the gaps.

Listening to himself talk, he wasn't very convinced.

Vallot patted him on the shoulder and said he'd come back later.

"The fob?" Jacob said. "Did you get prints off it?"

Vallot smiled sadly. "I can't discuss."

Jacob smiled back and said he understood. Then he asked to borrow Vallot's phone: Molchanov had thrown Jacob's in the pool.

"I need to get in touch with my boss."

Vallot went outside to give him privacy. Jacob kept the conversation short, relaying a heavily abridged version of the story.

Mike Mallick said, "I'll be there as soon as I can."

THE FOLLOWING DAY, Vallot returned with a detective named Sibony and a laptop. They'd pulled the mansion's security system footage and had been going through it for hours. The movements of people within and without squared with Jacob's account.

There were, however, no cameras inside the spa, making it impossible to verify the final, crucial minutes. One thing in particular they couldn't puzzle out.

They showed Jacob a time-stamped clip, soundless but in sharp, glorious color.

Molchanov, accompanied by two guards, riding up in the elevator.

A few minutes later, the guards rode back down.

Molchanov hadn't left via the elevator.

He hadn't left via the stairs.

The detectives had recovered his greatcoat, sopping wet.

But where was he?

Jacob said, "I don't know."

An uncomfortable silence.

Sibony commandeered the laptop and opened up a second clip.

An agitated Paul Schott paced in a cramped room, held at bay by a horde of guards.

"Fuck," Jacob said.

He now knew what had drawn Molchanov in such a hurry; what had called the lone remaining guard off the floor. It was all hands to contain Schott, who snarled and stomped like an enraged steer, flushed, shaking, heedless of the forest of machine guns waving at him. Nude except for a pair of socks because they had strip-searched him.

Very brave.

Also very stupid.

Schott ran at them.

For a man of his size, he moved incredibly quickly—so fast, in fact, that none of the guards got a shot off. They piled on him instead, bodies merging to become a single frenzied ball of aggression, all fists and feet and errant muzzle flashes. Knowing the ending, Jacob found it hard to watch. At one point, Schott appeared to get the upper hand. He grabbed a weapon and took one of the guards as a human shield. He was yelling, attempting to muscle his way forward. He appeared to be making progress. The other men began to back off.

Jacob wanted to look away.

Dmitri Molchanov launched into the frame, firing without hesitation, emptying a clip through the guard and into Schott.

A bright flare bleached the screen, wrecking the camera's focus before everything went black.

Vallot paused the video and opened a new window, showing a photo of the room, evidently taken later.

A bluish haze dusted on the walls.

Jacob sagged, sick with pride and loss.

The French detectives waited for his response.

What could he say?

Test the dust? Run it for DNA? Compare it to the stuff upstairs?

He let the silence drag.

Sibony sounded disturbed to admit that they'd been unable to locate his friend.

They weren't finished searching the house, Vallot added.

MALLICK ARRIVED THAT AFTERNOON. The bags under his eyes were larger than ever. He shut the door, dragged over a chair, fell into it, and said, "Talk."

Jacob complied, editing out his night over Paris with Mai, reducing her role in the spa to a cameo.

The Commander didn't react until Jacob described the video of Schott's final moments. Then his cheek twitched. "They have it on tape?"

"It's inconclusive," Jacob said. "They're operating under the assumption that his body was moved somewhere."

Mallick stared at him.

"I'm sorry, sir."

"For what part, precisely?"

"For what happened to Paul, sir. Truly sorry."

If Jacob had ever expected a show of emotion, it was then. But Mallick just gave a curt nod. "Well," he said. "This is a lot to unfuck. Even for us."

Jacob said nothing.

Mallick said, "How close did you get to her?"

"Not close."

"I'm not sure I believe you."

"I don't know what to tell you, sir."

"The truth would be my preference."

Jacob said, "Does Moscow have its own branch of Special Projects?"

"What's that supposed to mean?"

"Molchanov was trying to get to Mai. Same as you."

"Not the same," Mallick said. "Not at all."

"Then who was he?"

Mallick shook his head. "He isn't the main problem."

"Not to argue, sir, but he was a hell of a problem for me."

"You're missing the big picture," Mallick said. "He's one individual. What matters to me, Detective—and it should matter to you, too—is that there are others like him out there, waiting for their chance. Looking for her. Hunting her."

Pale fingers clutched the bedrail. "Do you understand now, why it's so urgent that we get her under control? If we don't, someone else will. Believe me when I say you don't want that."

Jacob said, "How many others?"

The Commander's brief look of bewilderment turned to dismay. "I don't know. Frankly, I don't even want to think about it. However many there were before, you can bet there's going to be a lot more now, given how this went down. There's no possible way I can stop the flow of information. With Pernath, we had corpses. But this . . . How many people were in that house? Fifty? A hundred?"

"They didn't see anything," Jacob said.

"At least a few of them did," Mallick said. "They saw what happened to Paul. Forget them. A *video*? I don't want to *begin* to think about it."

His long legs shifted restlessly. "I'm not designed to operate in today's world. None of us are. Media. YouTube . . . We're forever scrambling to play catch-up."

Jacob said, "Adapt or die."

A hollow laugh. "The Internet is full of noise," Mallick said. "Nobody believes anything anymore. That's what I tell myself. But who can say?"

He looked at Jacob. "Now you know what keeps me up at night."

"If it does get out," Jacob said, "they'll be hunting for me, too."

Mallick said, "I think that's a fair assumption."

Silence.

"This is why we need to trust each other," Mallick said.

The policeman's promise: *help me help you.*

"I appreciate the offer, sir."

"That doesn't sound like yes."

"I need to think about it."

"What's there to think about?"

"It's a limited sample size," Jacob said. "But when it comes to keeping me safe, sir, your track record sucks balls."

A beat.

"Well, Lev," Mallick said. "I appreciate the candor."

The two of them sat for a while, a mutually respectful stalemate. A nurse came in to take Jacob's vitals. When she'd gone, Mallick stood up.

"I'll need the knife back," he said.

"What knife, sir?"

Mallick smiled faintly. "Have it your way."

"Can I ask a favor, sir?"

"I don't need to define 'chutzpah' for you, do I, Lev?"

"Call my father. Tell him I'm all right."

Mallick nodded. "I'm at the Bristol for a couple of days. Room six thirteen if you need me. Otherwise someone will be in touch as soon as feasible."

"I appreciate it, sir."

Mallick said, "See you on the other side, Detective."

JACOB PAGED THE NURSE, asking her to check if his tall friend was still on the floor.

She came back reporting that he'd signed out.

Jacob thanked her, and she smiled and left, shutting the door quietly.

He counted to thirty, peeled back the blanket, and hobbled to the bureau.

In the bottom drawer was a plastic hospital bag containing his crusty, bloody socks and soiled shoes—the only clothing salvageable after the ER staff cut his shirt and pants to ribbons.

He pulled the sock out of the left shoe and fished out the two items he had taken from Tremsin's house, smuggled out in one of those crusty, bloody socks.

Tremsin's ring. The potter's knife.

Jacob set the ring on the bureau.

Taking care not to tangle or yank his lines, knelt down, bending the blade of the knife against the linoleum.

The metal was thin but surprisingly tough. He grunted, his blood pressure monitor letting out a concerned bleep.

Jacob waited for it to level off, then resumed bending, bringing the blade to a ninety-degree angle before it snapped free of the handle and shot off like shrapnel, skittering under the bed.

He retrieved it and deposited it in the biohazard bin. The wooden knife handle he placed in the trash. He dropped the ring in the sock, rolled the sock up, stuffed it in the shoe. He rolled the shoes in the bag and put the bag back in the bottom drawer.

His heart rate monitor was alarming again.

He got into bed and groped around for the morphine button. He pushed it and earned an instant frisson of *don't care*. Rough edges smoothed and he thought about Divya Das, back in L.A., wondering if he would get to sleep with her again.

He pushed the button again. Now he really didn't care. He was the happiest, most carefree motherfucker in Paris.

He thought about Mai, frail and reduced, but sheltering, growing strong again.

He thought about his father. He wasn't ready to forgive, but he wanted to be ready, he wanted to get there, and to encourage himself, he pushed the button a third time.

The machine beeped. It wouldn't give him any more. He didn't mind. He didn't feel let down. The machine cared about him, and how nice to be cared about. He pushed the button anyway, and listened to the machine beep its refusal, and he thought about his mother, and he kept pushing the button, because it felt so satisfying to make a simple request, a simple chemical request. Even if the answer was no, there was reward in the asking. In some sense the asking was the reward, and so he kept pushing the button, long after the curtain had come down on consciousness and his head ran amok with images strung along the line that separated dreams from nightmares, long after the nurse had returned to find out what the racket was about.

CHAPTER FIFTY-TWO

Five days later, a deputy U.S. ambassador of reassuringly medium stature showed up to deliver Jacob a fresh passport and inform him that the embassy had succeeded in getting him cleared to leave France.

"Whether you're healthy enough to travel is another question."

The doctor didn't think so. He refused to discharge Jacob, saying he could permanently damage his hearing if he got on a plane too soon.

As it turned out, a physician's order carried a lot more weight in France than in the United States. Jacob spent the next several days stalking the halls.

He had to get away from the dry croissants, the stale coffee.

He had to escape the morphine machine.

There was a computer on the floor available for patient use. Jacob hacked chronologically backward through his e-mail. It was mostly junk, but there was a message from Divya, wishing him well.

And another from Susan Lomax.

She'd sent it on the afternoon of the visit to Tremsin's house, at ten thirty-four a.m. California time, in response to the picture of Dmitri Molchanov Jacob had earlier mailed out.

Her reply was brief.

That's him.

Jacob leaned on the keyboard tray, feeling short of breath.

If he'd contacted her sooner, maybe she'd have replied sooner.

Maybe he wouldn't have gone inside the house.

Maybe Schott would be alive.

Jacob considered deleting the e-mail.

He kept it as a reminder to himself. Of what, he wasn't sure.

BORED SHITLESS, his head annoyingly clear, he found himself thinking about Arkady Tremsin, who had mistaken him for someone else. He spent a long afternoon combing through open-access academic databases, reviewing all of Tremsin's coauthors.

He found his answer in the February 1995 issue of *Chemical Research*.

A NEW METHOD FOR THE PURIFICATION OF TELLURIUM ALKYLS
A. L. Tremsin, J. M. Saint-Seurin, K. Viswanthan, F. L. Lev

One quick search revealed F. L. Lev to be François Louis Lev, emeritus professor of chemistry at the University of Lyon, at present teaching at the University of Calgary. The guy had an active Web page with a link to an e-mail address. Jacob thought about writing to him but decided there was no point.

EARLY ON A FRIDAY MORNING, Dédé Vallot came by with Jacob's suitcase, retrieved from the hostel, as well as his badge, his wallet, and the Marquessa Duvall file, released from evidence.

The two of them got into Vallot's white Citroën.

Within the confines of the car, he reverted to the guy Jacob had met in the bar—expansive, animated by a mixture of camaraderie, wonderment, and contempt for authority.

The investigation had started out promising. The fob had been printed and linked to Molchanov. Lacking proof of death, the higher-ups elected to consider him missing. He was wanted for questioning in the deaths of Lidiya and Valko Georgieva. Paul Schott was also listed as missing. The *juge* looking into Pelletier had requested a review of her records: phone, financial, and so forth.

That ended before it began. Vallot had it on authority from his buddy in intelligence that the General Directorate for Internal Security had intervened. The case was now classified. Vallot had been reassigned to the stabbing of a drug dealer.

He apologized for putting Jacob through the wringer. His exact words were: "I'm sorry for being this asshole."

"If you'd like to make it up to me," Jacob said, "I have a suggestion."

AT THE AIRPORT, Vallot pulled into the parking structure, cut the engine, and handed Jacob his phone.

Jacob typed in *Prague November 1982*. "Toward the back of Tremsin's library, in a locked case. The titles are in Cyrillic. There are a bunch of them. I only need the one."

Vallot put the phone away without looking at it. "I think it's too difficult."

"Consider it, okay? That's all I ask."

Vallot nodded and popped the trunk.

In it were Schott's suitcase and a plastic bag containing Schott's clothes and cowboy boots, recovered from the mansion.

"I'm sorry for your friend," Vallot said.

"Yours, too," Jacob said.

A COP ON ONE END to see him off, a cop on the other to greet him.

Mel Subach waited behind LAX customs, leaning against a carpeted structural piling. He was noticeably thinner, but not in a healthy way, his nose filigreed with thin red lines, his blondish hair a crown of cowlicks.

He shook Jacob's hand but avoided his eye. No banter as they got in the Crown Vic and headed for the 405.

Before signing the discharge order, the doctor had again cautioned Jacob against flying, and now Jacob felt a burning pain in his ear and heard an ominous fizzle, like a swarm of insects just over the horizon. He breathed through the discomfort and stared out at his city, its palette of beige and gray and chaparral brown, so different from Paris. The sour quality of the light. The corroded taste of the air.

It felt honest.

"Must be nice to be home," Subach said finally.

Jacob sensed the rebuke. He was home; Schott wasn't. As it was, he was wracked with guilt. He didn't need more. But he glanced at Subach in the rearview and read the devastation written there; he remembered the *shivah* for his mother, the consolations that served primarily to bang the gong of absence.

What you wanted was a quick fix. A patch on your heart, strong enough to get you to the next station.

Quietly, he began to recount Schott's last days, including the mundane and the unpleasant, the strange and the heroic. He talked about Schott getting sick over the smell of lamb kebab; he repeated, to the best of his ability, Schott's mini-sermon from that night.

Mel said, "I must have fifteen copies of that dumb book lying around. He kept buying it for me, like if he just did that enough, he could get me to read it."

Jacob told him what else Schott had said: that Mel had saved his life.

Subach kept driving, watching the road, the hollow of his cheek glistening.

Jacob told him about getting slapped silly by Schott in the hostel lobby.

Mel burst into phlegmy laughter. "Yeah, he did have a temper on him."

Jacob said that Schott had promised to show him his acting reel.

"That? It's god-awful," Subach said. "That's why he was driving a limo. He told you he didn't like Hollywood, right? Bullshit. He was just a lousy actor."

Jacob told him about getting locked in a room at the Russian embassy. About the look on Schott's face when Molchanov separated them.

He told him about the video and said, "He fought like hell."

Subach dragged his sleeve across his nose. "Thanks for that."

Jacob nodded.

"So," Subach said. "What's your first order of business?"

"Call my victims' family."

"And then?"

"Haven't thought that far. See an ENT, probably."

"The Commander's asked me to advise you that your work at the archive is temporarily suspended."

"Fine by me," Jacob said. "Where do I report?"

"He hasn't decided yet." Subach paused. "He said don't expect a bonus."

As they pulled up to the apartment, Jacob leaned forward and handed over the bag containing Schott's boots and clothes.

Subach stared inside it for a few moments. "Don't think these'll fit me anymore."

"The boots might," Jacob said.

Mel nodded uncertainly.

"Anyhow," Jacob said, "don't be too hasty. You'll probably gain the weight right back."

Subach laughed. "Get bent."

Jacob smiled and climbed out of the car.

He phoned Dolly Duvall.

She said, "You're sure it was this man."

"A hundred percent sure, ma'am."

"And he's dead."

"He is."

Silence filled the line.

"I feel something," she said. "I just can't say what it is yet."

She exhaled. "Well. You told me you'd do your best, and I believe you have."

"It's good of you to say so, ma'am."

"Now I need your address."

Jacob said, "Ma'am?"

"Do you want a cake or not?"

HE HAD MESSAGES on his answering machine, one from his father, one from Divya, and two in the last twenty-four hours from Detective Jan Chrpa in Prague.

Please call, it's important.

Jacob, it's again Jan. I called your mobile. Where are you, please?

It was after midnight in Prague. Jacob dialed anyway.

"Ahoj."

"I hope I didn't wake you up," Jacob said.

"No, it's okay, it's quiet."

The feuding kids seemed to have gone to bed. Jacob could hear Jan shifting the phone, opening a squeaky drawer. "I did not want to e-mail. I thought maybe they check."

They probably would. But it no longer mattered; it wasn't Special Projects that posed the greatest danger to his mother.

"Thanks," he said. "I was away on a case. What's up?"

"You remember about this division, ÚDV."

"For crimes committed under Communism."

"Yes. They have a big building, it's like a library. I made searches for the things you said. Arkady Tremsin, in the computer there is nothing. But many files are missing."

"Purged."

"Yes, or someone put in the wrong place. Or there is a file, but the names are black. Bohnice hospital, the material is large, many boxes. It will take me too long, so I started to read the murders from these years." Jan paused. "Jacob, I was surprised."

Marie Lasková, thirty-seven.

Her six-year-old son, Daniel.

Shot to death.

Their eyelids removed. Their bodies propped.

Marie had recently been discharged from Bohnice.

"They are behind the synagogue," Jan said. "In the same place with the head from last time."

Jacob said, "Unsolved."

"Yes. But wait, it's getting more weird. Any Czech person can request to look at the files. This is so people can know the truth. When you ask, you must put an application with name and birth number. This file, there is only one person who wanted it," Jan said, "Peter Wichs, this Jewish guy works at the synagogue. I thought, ah, okay, he's in charge of security, it's important to him. But the murder, it's in 1982. This guy now, I remember him, he is the middle of forties, so then he was a boy."

"Do you know when he requested the file?"

"First time is nine March, two thousand. Then again, twenty June."

"Same year."

"Yes, two thousand."

The date a branding iron.

June 20, 2000.

Three weeks before Bina's second suicide attempt.

He said, "Are there photos in the file? Of the victims?"

"Yes, some. I can send copies."

"Please. Thank you."

"Okay," Jan said. "Something's wrong?"

". . . no." A beat. "What are the nicknames for someone named Marie?"

"Nickname?"

"What you call someone for short. For my name, it's Jake, or Jack."

"Ah. Okay. Marie could also be Marča, Mařenka, Máňa, Manka—"

"Micah?" Jacob asked.

"Yes, this too."

"Can you spell it?"

"M-a-j-k-a. It's important?"

She screamed that name. She was screaming it in her sleep.

Jacob told him about Dmitri Molchanov.

Jan said, "It's him? Not Tremsin?"

"For the murders, yes."

Jan said, "Where is Molchanov?"

"Dead."

"Ah," Jan said. "Good."

Before they hung up, Jacob thanked him again and promised him a third beer.

His injured ear was throbbing. He walked to the kitchen to get ice, wondering how early was too early to call Peter Wichs.

CHAPTER FIFTY-THREE

1. červenec 2000

Milá Bino,

It is with apprehension that I enclose the photographs you requested. For the last week I have wrestled with whether to send them or not. They are extremely disturbing, and I hoped that reading the report would satisfy you that the past is better left buried.

However I am also aware that there is no straight path through grief, and the destination lies beyond a shroud. We proceed forward never knowing if we will arrive in a garden or a ruin, or indeed if we will arrive anywhere at all.

But I beg your forgiveness: you never asked my permission.

Permit me to remark that your Czech remains impressively fluent, which is fortunate, because I could not hope to capture my thoughts in English. I suppose I presume to write to you in this manner because I still see myself as a nine-year-old boy in your presence, slightly insolent. I believe too that part of me wants to shield you, as a form of repayment, however poor.

I must clarify that I was delighted to hear from you, whatever the reason. I realize that may not have come across over the telephone.

Inevitably there is pain attached to revisiting that period, and a distorting film hangs over my memories. Some details of what took place appear to me firmer than this chair I sit in. Others are lost completely. And we must acknowledge that time is indiscriminate, flattering good and evil alike.

You asked about my father. I still do not know the exact circumstances of his death. I believe the article you read mentioned that the criminal archive has only recently been opened to the public. Thus the demand for information has been great, while the majority of the files remain to be organized. Eventually my father's name will make the register. I accept that this day may not come soon. I suspect work will slow when somebody decides that the energy is better spent inhabiting the present, or building the future.

Sometimes I feel compelled to agree. As a nation we seem eager to throw off the yoke of history, or at least to capitalize on it. Did you know there are plans to open a museum of Communism? It will be at Na Příkopě. The curator consulted me, in my capacity at the Jewish Museum, for information about our community. In the end it was decided to keep the two subjects distinct, both parties preferring to retain ownership of their piece of the story.

While visiting the archive for a second time, I took the opportunity to look up the men whose names you mentioned. I think it will not come as news to you to learn that I could find nothing relating to either of the Russians.

However there is a substantial dossier on Antonín Hrubý, who at the age of sixty-eight is retired and living in the suburbs. The government has been slow to prosecute those who thrived under the former regime. Many remain in positions of power, for they alone understand the system well enough to keep it running. A select few have been held accountable, in what feels like symbolic justice.

Yet, as before, I think we must strive for acceptance. Half a century was taken from us. We may choose to spend what time remains to us seeking vengeance, or celebrating existence; this choice becomes our monument.

A confession: just the other day, I decided I wanted to see Hrubý for myself. I took the bus to his neighborhood. He lives in a small house with a drab brown roof, one of several identical houses in a row. As I approached the door, I became frightened, not that a monster would emerge, but that he would be no such thing.

A neighbor was in her yard, tending her roses. Fortunately she turned out to be a gossip. She told me Hrubý lives alone. He has no wife, and his son moved to Brno. She said that he spends his days volunteering at the animal shelter. She mentioned, specifically, and with some measure of disdain, that he is a vegetarian. Eventually she realized I was a complete stranger and grew suspicious, so I left.

Someday, perhaps, I will work up the courage to knock.

What else can I tell you?

Pavla passed away last year, of ovarian cancer. We remained close, and for this reason, it shocked me to learn that she had recently undertaken conversion to Judaism. I never knew her as a spiritual woman. I'm quite sure she was an atheist, the crucifix she wore being an inheritance from her grandmother. According to the rabbi, Pavla had expressed a wish to end up with my father, on the slim chance that there was an afterlife. Unfortunately she became too ill to complete the process.

The rabbi too is a convert, an interesting fellow. He used to be a playwright. Lately we have as a community faced internal friction, the typical arguments between those who would keep things the way they are and those who would make changes. I'm ashamed to say that the debate has at times gotten ugly. I suppose you could regard it as a sign of recovery, we are now healthy enough to indulge in hurting each other.

As for me, my work at the synagogue continues. I believe I mentioned I have not married, so if you happen to know any eligible young women who love a challenge, please send them airmail to Prague.

I wish I had more to say. In truth, I do, but I don't know how to say it. I suppose that I am stalling, because I don't want you to look at the pictures.

However there is one more very important question, namely, that of the jars.

The situation here sits on the knife's edge, with just the one jar that you left behind. I understand that you found unusable the clay you brought back from Prague, but I do not think it feasible, as you suggested, for me to send you a fresh package. We could try, but my belief is that it would be far preferable if you were to return in person to complete the work here. Given the untimeliness of my father's death, I am somewhat uncertain as to the absolute necessity of this. As you can imagine, we began many conversations that were never completed. It may in fact be that I am wrong and that it is not necessary.

Regardless, I humbly ask again that you consider sending me the second jar as a stopgap. I confess that I found your reluctance to do so difficult to understand. Perhaps we could discuss it further once you have had a chance to look at the materials, which I hope will not prove too upsetting.

S úctou váš,
Petr Wichs

CHAPTER FIFTY-FOUR

Sam opened the door and drew a sharp breath. "Thank God."

"I asked Mallick to send you a message," Jacob said.

"He said you'd been held up but that you were all right."

Sam's dark glasses shifted in the direction of Jacob's bandaged ear.

"It's nothing," Jacob said. "I went to the doctor yesterday. I'll be fine."

"But you're back," Sam said, as though to cement it.

Jacob nodded. "Can I steal a little time?"

"What am I doing." Sam stood aside. "Yes. Of course. Come in."

"I was hoping you'd come with me, actually. I'm going to see Ima."

Sam swallowed drily. "Let me get my coat."

JACOB TOOK a roundabout route.

They'll be hunting for me, too.

I think that's a fair assumption.

And Bina: was she a target now, too?

Could he visit her after today?

He would need to talk about it with Sam. They would need to

talk about Jacob's conversation with Peter Wichs; they would need to talk about Prague, and about Paris.

If Vallot sent the notebook, they might need to talk about that, too. Although Jacob wasn't sure he'd do anything but burn it.

So much to talk about. They were scions of a tradition of words, and they hadn't spoken, really spoken, in more than two years.

"I was thinking," Jacob said, "that we could start studying together again. Not the usual stuff. Golem literature. Maharal. Family history. What do you think?"

He glanced over.

Sam said, "I think that fortune favors the prepared."

"It's a deal, then."

"It's a deal."

THEY ARRIVED at the care facility. Before getting out of the car, Jacob said, "Do you have a cousin in Calgary? François Louis?"

"I don't think so," Sam said. "Why do you ask?"

Jacob grabbed the door handle. "Never mind."

BINA SAT under her fig tree. Her fidgeting hitched as she saw Jacob and Sam step from the dayroom and walk across the patio.

"Hi, Ima."

Sam tucked the blanket around her waist. "Hello, Bean."

They each kissed her on the cheek and sat flanking her.

It was midafternoon, the light desultory, the day ready to be over. Through a window Jacob could see residents wheeled into a semicircle around the TV. Rosario was making the rounds, dispensing medication. She looked up and noticed Jacob, reacting with surprise, and pleasure, when she saw it was three of them on the bench, not two.

She gave a little wave.

Jacob waved back.

She smiled and returned to her duties.

Wind rattled the branches, throwing a flourish of dry leaves.

Jacob said, "I have something I want to show you, Ima."

He reached in his pocket and took out a plastic baggie from which he removed the iron ring. Placing the ring in the center of his palm, he held it out to her.

"I got them," he said. "Both of them."

Bina's head moved slowly. She stared at the ring. Her expression remained inscrutable, and for a moment, Jacob feared he'd assumed too much. Or worse, that he would cause her to fly apart, irreparably.

Her hands stopped moving.

She said, *"Majka."*

Sam began to breathe rapidly. He said, "Jacob?"

Bina tilted her head back.

She was smiling.

Jacob followed her gaze to a large jointed branch of the fig tree. It was bobbing gently, as though something had been sitting there, just a moment ago.

ACKNOWLEDGMENTS

David Wichs, Zach Shrier, Rena and Mordecai Rosen, Julie Sibony, Emily at Paris Paysanne, Rabbi Yehuda Ferris, Lev Polinsky.

35674055861901